"How to write a blurb foɪ flesh? With a manifesto-like introduction which crashes in with guns blazing against the hallowed literary establishment, the stories in this collection are translated with such riveting, bawdy, hilarious, smelly, violent, Pinoy force that we are almost led to believe, once again, in the glorious possibility of translation, at the same time as we are gladly confirmed in our conviction regarding the futile impossibility of blurbs."

—Ramon Guillermo (University of the Philippines),
author of *Ang Makina ni Mang Turing* and *Translation &
Revolution: A Study of Jose Rizal's Guillermo Tell*

"*Ulirát: Best Contemporary Stories in Translation from the Philippines* is a dazzling collection of new stories originally written in Filipino, Cebuano, Hiligaynon, Waray, Ilocano, Kinaray-a, and Akeanon, and competently translated into English. This landmark anthology presents an alternative canon that is wide-ranging in its imaginative peregrination, distinctly Filipino in its temperament and consciousness, but happily accessible to the rest of the world."

—Jaime An Lim, author of
The Axolotl Colony: Stories, Hedonicus: Stories,
and *Literature and Politics: The Colonial
Experience in Nine Philippine Novels*

"These stories are populated with non-humans—animals, insects, shapeshifting aswangs—and the no-longer human—dismembered bodies, spirits, saints, voices on tapes—and through them we are brought to a Filipino ulirát of what humans mostly suffer: memories of those that were lost and left behind in our long history of subjugation, and visions of futures where true love and freedom are finally possible only because we no longer desire them. When the anthology tells us that these are stories in translation *from* the Philippines, it also reminds us that the nation is within us, and that while we dream in more than a hundred languages that are not fully comprehensible to one another, our stories share that view from outside the spaces of power that makes them closer to each other, closer to narratives of truth."

—Edgar Calabia Samar, author of the Janus Silang series of books and *Walong Diwata ng Pagkahulog*

"By turns lyrical and gritty, myth-infused and naturalistic, horrific and tender, the stories showcased in *Ulirát* afford English-language readers a rich sampling of the literary output of some of the finest writers working in and across the sensorium of Philippine languages. A must-read for anyone interested in the quotidian travails and wondrous metamorphoses undergone by denizens of a haunted republic in a haunted world."

—Caroline S. Hau (Center for Southeast Asian Studies, Kyoto University), author of *Demigods and Monsters: Stories*, *Tiempo Muerto*, and *Necessary Fictions*

ULIRÁT

ULIRÁT

BEST CONTEMPORARY STORIES IN TRANSLATION FROM THE PHILIPPINES

Edited by
TILDE ACUÑA
JOHN BENGAN
DARYLL DELGADO
AMADO ANTHONY G. MENDOZA III
KRISTINE ONG MUSLIM

Foreword by GINA APOSTOL

Stories by

Corazon Almerino, Merlie M. Alunan, Roy Vadil Aragon, Genevieve L. Asenjo, John E. Barrios, Rogelio Braga, Kristian Sendon Cordero, Allan N. Derain, Early Sol A. Gadong, Omar Khalid, Perry C. Mangilaya, Timothy Montes, Carlo Paulo Pacolor, Doms Pagliawan, Zosimo Quibilan, Jr., Jay Jomar F. Quintos, Firie Jill T. Ramos, Isabel D. Sebullen, Elizabeth Joy Serrano-Quijano, Ariel Sotelo Tabág, John Iremil Teodoro, and Januar E. Yap

With translations (from seven Philippine languages) by

Tilde Acuña, Merlie M. Alunan, Roy Vadil Aragon, John Bengan, Erika M. Carreon, Shane Carreon, Bernard Capinpin, Soleil Davíd, Daryll Delgado, Eliodora L. Dimzon, Sunantha Mendoza-Quibilan, Amado Anthony G. Mendoza III, Kristine Ong Muslim, Eric Gerard H. Nebran, and Ariel Sotelo Tabág

Gaudy Boy Translates,
published by Gaudy Boy LLC,
an imprint of Singapore Unbound
www.singaporeunbound.org/gaudy-boy
New York

For more information on ordering books, contact jkoh@singaporeunbound.org.

ISBN 978-0-9994514-2-7

Cover design by Flora Chan
Interior design by Jennifer Houle

CONTENTS

ULIRÁT

Contents

THE SPEECH OF ONE'S OWN

There's no joy like your own tongue—the tongue of your mother, your tongue-ina, as Filipino poet, novelist, and dramatist Eric Gamalinda has ingeniously punned. This anthology leaps out to me with that joy—and it is no conundrum that it does so even in translation, in English.

Because one condition of the Filipino, with our one hundred and fifty tongues on our seven thousand or so islands, is to know that the languages we call our own have shadow-tongues, sister-speeches, alter-egoists on some other island who have equal joy and possessiveness about their words.

We're used to the way alter-tongues, such as English, mediate our encounters with those sister-speeches.

As a Waray child on vacation in Cebu, clutching my Christmas money, I'd calculate from the mood of the salesgirl at Gaisano which other language to use since she wouldn't know my own—my funny Cebuano? my stilted Tagalog? my annoying English? I knew if I chose the wrong mediating language she'd hand me the Hello Kitty barrette with the disgust of a sophisticate whose tongue ruled at Colón Street in Cebu.

And if you were in my city Tacloban, and you don't get the pun in the answer to the Tagalog question, *paano nahubog ang Pilipinas?*, how was the Philippines shaped (answer: by drinking San Miguel Beer!), you are clearly not Waray. But perhaps you know Tagalog enough to get the explanation—*nahubog* means *shaped* in Tagalog but *got drunk* in Waray.

What I hear in these pages is the fun, high jinks, audacity, ease of mind, voluptuousness, dexterity, confidence, and genius of artists in command of their world.

To be brief, this collection is a classic.

The stories have this sense of powerful license, their worlds embodied in hilarious, outrageous, fantastical, and sobering ways. This is partly because the writers have chosen to make art in their tongue-ina—their mother-tongue.

(The other part is that the editors selected with a great eye for the strangely quotidian so that the familiarity of the stories slaps you in the face.)

And when I say *their worlds are embodied*, I mean it—these writers speak the *body*—in all its bawdiness, its frank flesh, its smells, sweat, and saliva.

This is no slight matter because the world of their art is, in many ways, indescribable—it's hard to summarize the many ways the Philippines is complex.

Linguistically attached to Indonesia and Malaysia, the country, except for indigenous lands and provinces in the Muslim south, remains Catholicism's irredeemable outpost in Asia. Its abiding love for the Virgin Mary has both medieval and animist tones; its homophobia is gay-loving. Culturally matriarchal, at the same time the country holds the horrific honor of being the only state in the world (apart from the Vatican) that still outlaws divorce. Proud of its history of resistance, it is often blind to the endurance of its most resistant people—the tribal lumad and Islamic south. Site of the first anticolonial revolutions in Asia, the Philippines waged war against empire twice but remains cursed by its multifarious colonial demons—occupied in 1521 first by Spain, in 1898 by the United States (not to mention for twenty months in the 1760s by England and three years during the Second World War by Japan), the Philippines, a republic since 1946, is heir to outrages and angsts and traumas and wounds, both self-inflicted and imperial, as well as two dictatorships and, through the years, the usual fairly basic regimes run merely by oligarchic goons, not to mention the shadow cast by a global corporate order that eats countries like the Philippines alive, and the climate apocalypse that as we speak sits right smack against its flooding, monsoon shores.

The past and present of the Philippines would break a less resistant, less inventive, less stubbornly life-entranced (though as these stories witness, also quite joyfully morbid, and beast-loving, and violently hungry) people.

The evidence of Philippine vitality lies precisely in the endurance of its tongues.

After centuries of occupation and violence and rebellion and grievous memory, what we have to show for our survival is our words.

We have long had English and later also Tagalog (Filipino, as this collection calls it) as official languages in schools and government. But despite the sway of colonization, capitalist despotism, multinational encroachment, nationalist projects—we have kept our tongues.

Language, for me, has always been the country's wonder.

The Philippine languages, of which seven are represented in this anthology, are of the Malayo-Polynesian Austronesian family, but like all vibrant languages, our words have mongrel etymologies— infusions of Sanskrit, flecks of the Arabic, occult and inextricable veins of Chinese (so embedded in the culture we have no other names for certain favorite things except for its word in Fujianese), smatterings of indigenous Mexican from the old Acapulco galleon trade, and, of course, our vocabulary of idiosyncratic, playful, unabashedly appropriated Spanish, which we have owned in our gloriously indifferent way, our English a garnish on top.

And yes, English, too, we appropriate.

There is a Waray word we used to say with great fun as kids, *pachis*, that's long puzzled me, for instance. The *–ch* sound is not really in our alphabet. It often indicates a foreign origin. It was only as I researched the Philippine–American War that I understood. *Pachis* in Waray is a humorous, childish word for enemy, or betrayer. It comes from America: *Apache*.

Our words also reproduce our historical state.

Like Samson with his hair, our strength lies in the languages we have kept for ourselves: our secret weapon against the colonizer, our amulet that grounds us. I argue it's not regionalism that makes us adamant about being Waray or Ilonggo or Ilocano, regionalism as pathology being a colonizer diagnosis and a tool for division (but yes, our intramural spite can be intense). It's not that our tongues define us, create our "being." In fact our languages, so prone to borrowing and puns and play, explode the fallacy of such essentialism.

What attaches us to our group's speech is that the world seems simply more accurately told, *im-mediate*, unmediated, when we speak in the tongue we call ours.

Which is a fallacy in itself, but a fantasy useful to contemplate.

Thus, this anthology fills a void that even Filipinos don't quite know is there: when I read these stories, though yes, they are in translation, I hear a pungent, unmediated world that, even if it exists only in illusion, I miss.

A dialectical imagining occurs in these stories—there's the imagining of the writer creating her world in Kinaray-a or Ilocano or Hiligaynon and there's the imagining of the Kinaray-a or Ilocano or Hiligaynon when we read the English.

And both of those imaginings are entwined, providing a mirror of a reality hard to explicate.

Because of the hegemony of English—the language of learning—on the islands, this twin imagining *in print* is a relatively new experience for the Filipino (though IRL it is our daily experience of the world).

That is, this book is not only novel for the rest of the world that this anthology invites.

Of course, this is not to say the artists in this anthology do not speak other tongues, acknowledge their solidarity, enlacement, or mutuality with other tongues, or see other tongues as also theirs, part of their education and linguistic and national patrimony—many of the writers probably speak several of the other languages: Tagalog, English, the various forms of Binisaya.

But the editors of this anthology are entirely correct to say that no other anthology of Philippine literature has similar ambition and scope.

I would add, no other anthology has given me this pleasure: the existential jolt of recognizing ways of seeing my world that I have, in fact, experienced but, despite all my years of reading, have not encountered on the page.

This is an experience hard to explain, but I'll try.

Because the vitality of our languages is simply a matter of fact to most of us, it is almost invisible as an aspect of our cultural strength and psychological sustenance. We speak our languages, but in general we don't read them. I grew up reading in English. In addition, our speech's vitality is hermetic, for the most part: that is, a Waray joke may not translate in Cebuano, and vice versa. So Hiligaynon, which I will decipher through my Waray, would be as hard to read for me as French, which I still decipher through Spanish. And yet what we all share is that Filipinos revel daily in wordplay, and our everyday language is joke-filled, scathing, unfixed, rebellious, and creative, if only to match the predations of our world. For me, this is evident even in the plots and twists of these stories although in some I am only guessing at their linguistic games.

Beset by the Filipino reality of our multiple languages, growing up I've had a clear-eyed understanding of our contingent, precarious selves, or even our likely bodily translation into other selves (such as into cats, or mushrooms, or Kafka).

This, too, these stories convey.

Above all, these stories lay bare blunt historical, political, and economic realities that remain, on many levels, unspeakably surreal.

The island I grew up in, Leyte, speaks two different languages—the north is Waray, the south Cebuano. As a child, I instinctively understood my desires' mutability and strangeness because my neighbor, a fellow Leyteña, but from Maasin, spoke the same desires differently.

It's likely this is true of many other multilingual cultures—or maybe just the unconscious state of the human that it's best to keep under a lid.

In any case, this richness of our everyday existential understanding begotten by speech was only ordinary—nothing to write home about.

And certainly in school, learning and writing in English, we did not.

The country's pragmatic arrangement with English—the way we've worn the colonizer's cape, but keeping our own speech-clothes underneath, tight on our skin—serves many purposes, among them power, convenience, money, nostalgia, idiotic class supremacy, economic rationality, and of course art. I will say, we have a long history of art in English. Philippine Anglophone literature is a solid canon. It is indelibly part of the Filipino self.

Unfortunately, it need not have been a hegemonic one.

As a Filipino who writes in English, I do so without compunction, with no angst or grief; it is my historical condition.

But as a Filipino who dreams in Waray, I have waited too long for *Ulirát*.

Of course, I have a vested interested in a collection like this. But in my view, so should the world. This anthology of people speaking in their own languages yet claiming a consciousness as a nation is instructive. *Ulirát* expands the imaginative and geographic boundaries of our narrow art world here in America, but it also gives a glimpse into the possibilities of mutuality, a shared recognition that we all have stakes in each other's survival, no matter if we cling fiercely to our own tongues.

GINA APOSTOL
NEW YORK, NEW YORK

INTRODUCTION

*U**lirát: Best Contemporary Stories in Translation from the Philippines* intends, at the very least, to change the way anthologies of Philippine writing are produced and presented to the rest of the world. This book seeks to offer up stories that embody the depth and range of contemporary Philippine fiction. To do this and still be able to claim representation of Philippine literature, we figure that it is imperative to represent, by way of translation, as many languages as possible from the over 150 languages in the Philippines. Previous efforts, though laudable, focus only on Anglophone literature, leaving out vigorous writing in local languages.

Ulirát is Tagalog for consciousness, and it speaks to one of our aims when we were making selections for the book. The anthology intends to forward a "consciousness" predicated on a more nuanced representation of English-language Filipino literature, a niche dominated internationally by the works of Filipinos who write in English. Our goal is to introduce Filipino writing to a wider audience without the shortsightedness of electing Philippine writing in English as wholly representative of the nation's literature.

Another of our aims is to have *Ulirát* serve as a tribute to story forms that have been historically left out in most national anthologies by major Philippine publishers. We want to use it to disrupt the homogenizing impulse of "national" literary anthologies coming out of the Philippines. Philippine languages for which short fiction is not an urgent form, however, need not be forced to conform to the literary conventions endorsed by this anthology.

HISTORICAL BACKGROUND

The first year of the twenty-first century saw the release of the Isagani R. Cruz–edited *The Best Philippine Short Stories of the Twentieth Century: An Anthology of Fiction in English* (2000). The groundbreaking anthology contained fifty short stories, all originally written in English, the language first brought to the Philippines by the British when they invaded Manila from 1762 to 1764 [1, 2]. The English language, however, only gained widespread adoption in the Philippines during the forty-eight-year American colonial occupation—along with approximately three hundred thousand dead Filipino revolutionaries and civilians, including the fatalities during the 1880s to the early 1900s when American colonizers introduced epidemics to the indigenous population, the people of the Philippine archipelago also learned English [3, 4]. Among the selections in Isagani R. Cruz's anthology were Paz Márquez-Benítez's "Dead Stars"—the first successful (successful in the sense that it was the earliest known story to have met American short story conventions) piece of English-language short fiction written by a Filipino—and Manuel E. Arguilla's "How My Brother Leon Brought Home a Wife," which was reputed to be the most famous Filipino short story in English.

The Filipino scholar and historian Resil B. Mojares, in his *The Origins and Rise of the Filipino Novel: A Generic Study of the Novel*

Until 1940 (1983), was able to locate the roots of the modern Filipino novel in traditional storytelling forms [5]. No similar attempt exists for contemporary writing practices across the country with respect to the short story form. Leopoldo Yabes's *Philippine Short Stories: 1925–1940* (1975) covered only short stories originally written in English [6]. Half a century later in 2010, Gémino H. Abad edited a series of short story anthologies: *Upon Our Own Ground* (Volume 1 [1956–1964], Volume 2 [1965–1972]), *Underground Spirit* (Volume 1 [1973–1982], Volume 2 [1983–1989]), and *Hoard of Thunder* (Volume 1 [1990–2000], Volume 2 [2001–2008]) [7]. Augmenting Yabes's efforts, Abad's anthologies continue to include only—despite institutional support from the country's premier state university—the easiest to survey: Philippine short stories originally written in English.

The modern short story form [8] may have been formally introduced into the Filipino classroom by American colonialists in the early twentieth century, but the genre developed early on from religious texts such as sermons, novenas, and brief accounts of the lives of saints. A century before the Americans came, the short form found life not only in Spanish, but also in Bikol, Ilocano, Hiligaynon, Cebuano, Tagalog, and other Philippine languages during the rise of the printing industry. The Tagalog had "maikling kuwento," Ilocano "sarita," Kapampangan "salita," Hiligaynon "sugilanon," Cebuano "mubong sugilanon," and Waray "susumaton." Anecdotes and tales, such as the Tagalog "dagli" and the Visayan "binirisbiris," were also precursors of the literary genre known today as the "maikling kuwento," or the short story. These forms may be traced back to oral narratives that include ballads, folktales, and epic cycles that have long been widely practiced in the islands.

Since English was the medium of instruction in universities, Americans and American-trained instructors turned to the short story form as handy material for teaching. Short stories comprised many of Filipino university students' earliest attempts at literary writing in English. The University of the Philippines's *College Folio* published imitations of Anglo-American adventure stories. Most of the first short stories published in local magazines were also riffs of the O. Henry story that usually ended with a surprise or twist. The formula also entailed the teaching of a lesson, melodrama, and sentimentality. In 1925, critics hailed Paz Márquez-Benítez's "Dead Stars" as an exemplar of the short story form in English.

By the 1930s, the short story became a popular genre in magazines such as *Liwayway*, *Sampaguita*, *Bannawag*, *Kasanag*, *Kapawa*, *Bag-ong Suga*, and *Bisaya*. The Tagalog maikling kuwento found sophisticated expression in the works of Rosalia Aguinaldo, Deogracias Rosario, and Amado V. Hernandez. Vicente Sotto, Amado Osorio, and Vicente Rama were among the early practitioners of the Cebuano mubong sugilanon. The Hiligaynon sugilanon had no less than Magdalena Jalandoni as a leading practitioner, and later Ramon Muzones; both writers also wrote novels in serialized forms. Isabelo de los Reyes is considered to have written the first short story in Ilocano with "Ti Langit Ti Inanamatayo" ("Heaven Is Our Hope"). Writers such as David D. Campañano, Constante Casabar, and Benjamin Pascual followed de los Reyes's lead. The short story in Bikol was likewise honed by Salvador Perfecto, Juan Nicolas, and Nany Calderon, Jr., among others.

Though still influenced by their predecessors' Romanticism, the next generation began to turn to Realism, since writers, particularly those writing in local languages, wanted to depict social reality in fiction. This turn can be attributed to two developments in the tumultuous 1930s that led to the weakening of the Commonwealth government: the emergence and steady rise of the Communist Party of the Philippines earlier in the decade and the establishment of the Philippine Writers League in 1939. By the 1940s, the preoccupations of Filipino writers in English and in the vernacular had evolved: the former grappled with the "social relevance" of their literary production (read: content), while the latter struggled with utilizing "modern techniques" and establishing "literary standards" (read: form) [9].

After Márquez-Benítez came Paz Latorena, Manuel Arguilla, Arturo B. Rotor, Loreto Paras-Sulit, Francisco Arcellana, N. V. M. González, and Bienvenido Santos, all of whom wrote early forays into the realist short story in English. Written by Serafin Guinigundo and Brigido Batumbakal, the best Tagalog stories in the realist mode depicted alienation and the harshness of urban living. Liwayway Arceo, Genoveva Edroza-Matute, Norma Miraflor, and Rogelio Sicat would carry on this illustrious tradition. Macario Pineda's early innovations would anticipate the formal playfulness of short stories in Tagalog in the 1980s and 1990s. The localized short story form would also develop in Bikol, Ilocano, Hiligaynon, and Cebuano.

The arrival of New Criticism in the 1950s would change the course of the short story's evolution. English-language writers grappled with the theme of Filipino identity while being attentive to universal concepts and sense of craft. Trends such as existentialism and modernism, including the stream-of-consciousness style, would also leave a mark even in writers of the sugilanon. Similarly, Ilocano writers such as Jose Bragado and Constante Casabar developed a heightened sense of craftsmanship.

In the late 1960s until the 1970s, many writers synthesized polit-
ical commitment with modernist storytelling in the face of Ferdinand
Marcos's dictatorship. Ricky Lee's "Si Tatang, Si Freddie, Si Tandang
Senyong, at iba pang mga tauhan sa aking Kuwento" ("Tatang,
Freddie, Old Man Senyong, and the Other Characters of My
Story"), Wilfredo Virtusio's "Maria, Ang Iyong Anak" ("Maria, Your
Child") [10], and Edel Garcellano's oft-forgotten novel *Ficcion*
(1972) [11] exemplified the said attempt to fashion a fictional form
that negotiates both political commitment and aesthetic innovation.
Soon, metafiction and postmodernism found their local iterations in
Tagalog and Cebuano fiction. At present, short stories in various
Philippine languages cover a gamut of contemporary themes, from
trenchant histories, protracted people's war, state-sanctioned violence, migration and the diaspora to sexual politics and gender
identities.

Substance and appearance are two sides of the same literary coin,
hence the convergences, divergences, negotiations, and polemics
among writers of this historical epoch—and of the periods to come.
It should be noted, too, that most documented events in the emerg-
ing "national" literary scene occurred in urban centers such as Manila,
Cebu, and Iloilo, since folk literature of the hinterlands was not considered literary due to its oral and communal characteristics.

Stories most certainly exist prior to the interruption of colonialism. They thrive outside the twentieth century's gatekeeping mech-
anisms of corporate and academic publishing that favors "realism"
with "local color" or, by the twenty-first century, the "speculative"
mode—either as spectacular embellishment (still "local color" but
fantastic) to be interesting or as an indispensable component to con-
front pressing societal issues while exploring genre storytelling.

Of course, outside the political imagination of residents of the Philippine Republic are stories of the countryside engaged in the protracted people's war—fictions of utmost relevance, wakefulness, and timeliness that problematize Philippine reality. Unfortunately, these stories are beyond the anthology's scope, although we will discuss them briefly in another section.

Until *Ulirát: Best Contemporary Stories in Translation from the Philippines*, there has never been an anthology as ambitious and sweeping in its scale. *Ulirát* represents the first broad-stroke attempt to anthologize contemporary short story specimens translated from seven of the over 150 languages in the Philippines and to present the results of such an effort to English readers. The book's relevance is also partly contingent on how and why it subverts present-day conditions and trends of literary productions in the Philippines.

Most anthologies and journals published by commercial and university presses in the Philippines feature literary works in English and Filipino. Recent exceptions include *Sa Atong Dila: Introduction to Visayan Literature* (2013), *Susumaton: Oral Narratives of Leyte* (2016), and *Tinalunay: Hinugpong nga Panurat nga Winaray* (2017), all edited by Merlie M. Alunan [12]. These anthologies feature works originally written in various Visayan languages alongside English translations. Peñafrancia Raniela Barbaza's *Orosipon kan Bikolnon: Interrupting the Philippine Nation* (2017) and *Mga Osipon ni Ana T. Calixto: Paggigiit sa Sadiring Sanwa sa Osipon: Maikling Kathang Bikol, 1950–1956* (2018) translated selected Bikolnon prose: the former into both English and Filipino, the latter into Filipino; both books are also critical studies that conceptualize the old Bikol word for "story," *orosipon*, and its intervention in nation-building [13].

"National" writing workshops, especially the oldest and most prestigious ones, Silliman University National Writers Workshop (SUNWW) and University of the Philippines National Writers Workshop (UPNWW), have both been singularly instrumental in shaping the country's existing literary landscape to value English and Filipino—in this order—over other languages. Unsurprisingly, both the SUNWW and UPNWW have unabashedly colonial roots. SUNWW was established by Edilberto and Edith Tiempo, after being mentored by literary arbiters of taste at the Iowa Writers' Workshop, an appendage of the CIA in influencing the creative writing scene in America as well as the rest of the world [14, 15, 16, 17]. UPNWW, on the other hand, was established after the American colonial period and has since been influential in affecting national policies, shaping public opinion, and enacting societal change—to and from regressive neocolonial sustenance and progressive anticolonial resistance.

Still under the clutches of imperialism, like Latin America [18] and other poorer nations of the "Global South" [19], the Philippines suffers not only from the widening gap between the rich and the poor but also between hegemonic languages and marginal ones—a crisis that can be traced as far back as the early twentieth century, when the country endured "benevolent assimilation" and seemingly prospered under American colonial rule. At that crucial period, Filipino nationality and symbols that represent our national identity were "invented" and established, including the national language and its Tagalog foundations [20] by bureaucrat capitalists in where else but the capital—which was once Quezon City but has most of the time been Manila.

It should be noted, however, that as shown in the classic Filipino novel *Sa mga Kuko ng Liwanag* by Edgardo Reyes [21], the working class of Manila and other cities bear the brunt of the oppressive structures of Philippine society. This underrepresentation is eclipsed to some extent by what is considered the most prestigious of awards in Philippine letters: the Don Carlos Palanca Memorial Awards, whose namesake was once president of La Tondeña Inc. distillery, where the first labor strike after Marcos's declaration of martial law took place—and was later repressed. Ironically, the strike served as an enduring beacon of resistance, the literary award as a glossy artifice of conformity.

The selection of authors in this anthology also shows symptoms of disparity and signs of exclusion—most contributors are from the so-called middling middle classes, educated ones who are aspiring to be or are already professionals in their respective fields. The concluding story of this anthology, by Allan Derain, a standalone excerpt from a much longer work, zeroes in on the "literary scene," regulated to a great extent by institutions, which include UP, where the main characters studied. Here, international readers will be made aware of the fact that beyond toxic Filipino pride, an anthology exhibiting the "best" Philippine literature can be self-reflexive at the same time.

Before World War II, the then–Philippine President Manuel Quezon urged Filipino writers to preserve the Spanish literary heritage, welcome the "modern" offering of Americans (which included the short story form), and develop a literature based on the national language [9]. After failing to teach Nihonggo during its occupation, Imperial Japan's Asia for Asians campaign encouraged writing in

Tagalog—not to foster anti-imperialist nationalism but to play the game of identity politics and exorcise American influence. Language policies—which affect literary production—aimed to reinforce colonial, imperial, and neocolonial interests pre-WWII, during WWII, and post-WWII, respectively.

To describe the national language situation in the Philippines as one of a yawning disparity between the languages of the "center" and of the "periphery" may sound rather simplistic. After all, Filipino politicians make extensive and effective use of vernacular languages to canvass for support during elections. However, we also remember that, more often than not, once installed in office, these politicians switch to using "official" languages, such as English. A hierarchy between the languages is thus maintained. It is also wise to bear in mind that although stories, whether written in "official" or "marginal" languages, have the power to raise the class consciousness of the reader, they may also be weaponized by the comprador and landlord classes to limit the reader's vision.

In *Isabelo's Archive* (2013), Resil B. Mojares discusses national literature in relation to the ideas of Jose Rizal, the national hero of the Philippines, and argues that inventing and developing a national literature requires three moves: 1) asserting difference (the distinction of one's literary output) and contiguity (all literary output that claims to be part of the Philippine literary tradition is adjacent to each other); 2) internationalizing, which necessitates translation as a way to introduce extant national literatures to the "world republic of letters" [22, 23]; and 3) creating a strategic discursive community from within and outside national literary borders [24]. This anthology therefore is an attempt to demonstrate how unique the "major" Philippine languages are, how they represent Philippine literature despite their differences, and how from within the Philippines, we could create or develop a community, if not a network, of readers and writers.

In assessing the "quality" of the entries in this anthology, the discursive literary community must come to terms with uncomfortable truths. Such judgments are determined by conflicting structures of power and negotiated through different stages of the production, which temporarily culminate in anthologizing acts. Rather than assembling a "best of" anthology to end all "best of" anthologies as infallible dispensers of literary value [25], we share our work for scrutiny, which will lead, we hope, to developing better methods and conversations on inclusion, exclusion, and representation.

THE STORIES

To us, the editors, the best stories are the kind that burn in one's memory long after the first reading. We are taken by stories that have a strong sense of place, a distinct viewpoint, and an unshakeable way with voice—an orality that persists in the written form. Stories we find memorable neither take themselves too seriously nor take for granted tradition and possibilities in the art of fiction writing. It is unfortunate that we are proficient in certain languages only; hence, like most readers throughout the archipelago, we can only access particular vernacular languages in translation. Considering our limitations as readers and translators, we asked ourselves what stories could best show the range of styles and concerns, as well as a sense of our storytelling traditions. The stories in this anthology were sequenced in an order that best shows the scope of topics and themes the writers pursued; we also considered the overall tonality and narrative flow when deciding the ordering.

Ulirát: Best Contemporary Stories in Translation from the Philippines opens with an arthouse-horror nod to a monumental twentieth-century work of fiction. Through a setup eerily reminiscent of the nuclear family in Kafka's novella *The Metamorphosis*, Soleil Davíd's crisp translation of Carlo Paulo Pacolor's "Ang Batang Gustong Maging Ipis" ("The Boy Who Wanted to Be a Cockroach") expands not only the notion of body horror literature but also raises important ideas about human beings' treatment of nonhuman animals. Is the titular boy changing in response to his material conditions, or is it the people around him who are changing? Can an individual ever truly be free if the trigger and extent of his transformation—no matter how consensual he sees his transformation to be—are still influenced by societal codes? Pacolor is the sole writer from whom we selected two very short works for this anthology, representing both flash fiction and children's stories.

On the surface, Kristian Sendon Cordero's "Kulto ni Santiago" ("Santiago's Cult"), translated from Filipino by Bernard Capinpin, is quintessential urban fantasy. There is the telltale first-person viewpoint to narrate the transplanting of colonial-era supernatural elements into modern times. Its compatibility with the familiar mainstream mold stops there, though. Cordero's short story is a layered, multigenerational narrative steeped in themes of religious mania and violence enacted in various forms—physical, emotional, and sexual.

Isabel Sebullen's "Aswang" reads at first like a story about the flesh-eating shape-shifters that populate the folk imagination. However, the "aswang" in the story represents horror that can happen anywhere. Sebullen's narrator, in avenging his family on a monster, cannot evade doing something monstrous himself. "Aswang" updates the grisly horror genre and offers an indictment of a macho-feudal Hiligaynon society.

Corazon Almerino's "Sugmat" ("Relapse"), about a Filipino migrant couple who go through so much in their effort to build a life in California, is harrowing and, in its own way, stubbornly hopeful. The story stands out for its compelling narration of a family assailed by misfortune. It is also a story about immigration to the US that powerfully asserts a Visayan perspective, as the female narrator swings between fear, grief, rage, and belief.

"Ang Tulo Ka Mayor sa Hinablayan" ("The Three Mayors of Hinablayan"), written by Omar Khalid and translated from Cebuano, is studded with remarkable details as it retells infamous and very real power struggles in a certain town in the Visayas. Apart from the story's humor, the translation reconstructs the allegory of a town pulled apart by politicians. With a first-person-plural narrator who seems to be spinning fact into absurdity, Khalid demonstrates a propulsive rendering of oral storytelling in the written form.

Ariel Sotelo Tabág's "Voice Tape," while on the surface is an "Araby"-esque coming-of-age story, presents a subtle critique of Marcosian economics, which focused on labor export and foreign remittances in order to sustain an already ailing Philippine economy saddled with debt and gross mismanagement. Narrated in an overwhelmingly nostalgic tone, the story is a paean to the fiction-writing tradition that preceded Tabág's while also confronting exigent problems of his generation.

Roy Vadil Aragon's "Siak ni Kafka, Pusa" ("I am Kafka, a Cat"), on the other hand, while an obvious nod to Franz Kafka, Haruki Murakami, Neil Gaiman, Samuel Beckett, and all the other purveyors of the absurd, is a deliriously and fiendishly entertaining

ULIRÁT

exploration of the frontiers that separate humanity and animality. Although a bit indulgent at times, Aragon's prose is reminiscent of Thomas Bernhard's rambling and sometimes odious style.

While both stories are situated in Ilocano-speaking provinces, it is not a stretch to say that the issues, experiences, and realities they bring forward are also present in works from the other regions. This just shows the contingent and contiguous nature of "regional literature"—what with its ceaseless attempt to assert difference, to carve out a space of its own, while on the other hand finding itself simultaneously belonging to a larger collection of works that imagine and narrate the nation.

Genevieve L. Asenjo's "Turagsoy" ("Mudfish Lady"), translated from Hiligaynon by Eric Gerard H. Nebran and Eliodora L. Dimzon, exemplifies the quintessential Eastern and Western Visayan narrative shift where the notions of movement and leaving—being elsewhere, closer to, or farther from the center—hover over the story as either a prospect or a threat. There is always that tension between keeping things as they are and giving in to change, between extolling tradition and simple living and candidly acknowledging the poverty and want, even the violent histories and gender inequalities.

Merlie M. Alunan's "Pamato," translated from Cebuano by Shane Carreon, is a lush and tactile fever-dream, where the implements and mechanics of a game played by Filipino children are used as launching points for rehearsing the narrator's past mentally. Both painful and reaffirming memories are brought to the fore, unfolding in a sequence of vignettes and nostalgic episodes.

Meanwhile, Doms Pagliawan's "Tipa-Manila" ("Manila-bound") is a seemingly simple story of an elderly couple setting off for the first time from a quiet town in Samar to Metro Manila. It exploits all the conventions of a classic journey story (as not so much about the destination as the journey itself), but takes it so much further, as it becomes a narrative of survival and return.

"Pagkagising, Natuklasan Niyang May Tumutubong Kabute sa Butas ng Kanyang Ilong" ("When He Wakes Up, Mushrooms Are Sprouting from His Nose") is another Carlo Paulo Pacolor story, this time a rambunctious piece of flash fiction translated from Filipino by Erika M. Carreon. It pursues a similarly fraught, at some points dangerous, line of inquiry on physical transformations as the other translated Pacolor story that kicks off this anthology.

Zosimo Quibilan, Jr.'s "Gel" offers a tender look into the fragile, sometimes unsettling, ever-changing dynamic of romantic relationships. Sunantha Mendoza-Quibilan's translation from Filipino captures the fitful silences of interrupted intimacies, genuine or mimed.

Early Sol Gadong's "Sa Lum-ok Sang Imo Suso" ("In the Softness of Your Breasts"), about two women who see each other for the first time after ending their relationship, represents the penchant for eroticism in short stories written in local languages. However, more than titillation, Gadong immerses these women in contemporary concerns, such as rapid urbanization and the war on drugs, without losing the story's sensuousness.

Elizabeth Joy Serrano-Quijano's "Dili Pwede Mogawas" ("Can't Go Out") combines the young narrator's innocence and urgency of circumstance to take hold of the reader from the opening lines, inviting them to assess their own role in the reality the story represents. Serrano-Quijano never glosses over the locality she is describing: a Blaan village in Southern Mindanao, whose people are involved in the war between the Armed Forces of the Philippines and the New People's Army.

John E. Barrios's triptych "Relationship," translated from Akeanon by Merlie M. Alunan, offers an ironic view of lack, a bubbling resistance to, but never wide-eyed acceptance of, the situation. Its sensitive and poignant handling of sexual tensions, given the strong temptation to romanticize life in the countryside and life outside the National Capital Region (NCR), is one of the reasons we chose it for this anthology.

Jay Jomar F. Quintos's "Ilang Tala at Talababa Hinggil sa Pangungulila" ("Some Notes and Footnotes on Loneliness") gives shape to what many Filipinos experience: the contact of two or more languages. In telling the story of two colleagues coming from different linguistic backgrounds, the work calls attention to the rubbing together of Tagalog and Cebuano, like bodies generating heat.

Currently in exile in London, where he sought and received refuge from the harassment and death threats of the Duterte regime, Rogelio Braga wrote "Fungi" as part of his short story collection *Is There Rush Hour in a Third World Country*. The story's main characters—two kids who we are made to believe have found a "magical" object in a dumpsite where they scavenge for fabric scraps and other discarded items for a living—follow Joseph Campbell's archetypal "hero's journey" monomyth down to the finale. We chose "Fungi" for its empathy and its staunch refusal to go for cheap shots and poverty porn in its harrowing depiction of the lives of the Filipino urban poor. A "best of" short story anthology using the Philippines as a thematic pivot is not complete without a narrative that aims to capture and question Filipino consumerism, the absence of national industries, and the lives of people in the slums of Manila.

We like Perry C. Mangilaya's "Ahas" ("Snake") mainly for its unique charm and ambition. The story encourages the reader to empathize with a man, a construction worker rushing home from Manila to his rural hometown, in denial about his wife's cheating. Even in the face of mounting circumstantial evidence, the man is unwavering in his belief that an engkanto, a supernatural being, has impregnated his wife. It would be interesting to read feminist interpretations of "Snake" vis-à-vis Philippine society's patriarchal and feudal culture.

Timothy Montes's laugh-out-loud but moving love story "Kanan Lab-asero Gugma" (The Fishmonger's Love Story") is translated from Waray by Merlie M. Alunan. With its theme of a beloved's return that turned bitter, the story reflects popular concerns in poor rural communities where characters look forward to reuniting with former friends and acquaintances at a town dance.

Januar E. Yap's seamless interspersing of the spectacular and the historic make "Ang Suhito" ("The Savant") a heady read. Part of the task in translating this story into English is conveying the narrative games and the folk and pop references from Yap's colloquial Cebuano. The story is proof that although a translator writes for a reader who only reads English, the reader must also somehow grasp the Cebuano in the translation.

"The Breakup" by Firie Jill T. Ramos, translated from Waray by Merlie M. Alunan, unfolds with the similar Eastern and Western Visayan narrative drive as Genevieve L. Asenjo's story. It charts the inescapable Filipino filial entanglements whose burdens women are forced to carry.

Translated from Kinaray-a by Merlie M. Alunan, John Iremil Teodoro's buoyant and hearty "Why Berting Agî Never Smiles"

shares the Timothy Montes story's seemingly typical rural community setting, but where characters have a refreshingly candid attitude
toward sexual relations, and this time the meeting place is at a wake
instead of a town dance.

Throughout this introduction, we have highlighted the serious
imbalance in the distribution of literary, cultural, political, and economic influences, capacities, and resources in the Philippines. This
anthology is a humble intervention in this disproportionate order of
things. As centers of neocolonial commerce and un/witting benefi-
ciaries of semi-feudal oppression, the cities of the Philippines con-
centrate in themselves literal and figurative traffic, especially the
Filipino- and English-speaking National Capital Region (NCR), or
Metropolitan Manila, where the last story of this anthology, an
excerpt from Allan Derain's *The Next Great Tagalog Novel*, takes
place. The story, evocative of neo-futurism in its piquant imaginings,
gives much-needed context to the state of Philippine literature in
general and Filipino fictionists in particular.

CHALLENGES AND FUTURE WORK

There are more than 150 languages in the Philippines, and yet,
despite our bold claims and aims, we have only managed to translate
(or find translations for) and anthologize stories from seven languages.
Although our attempt to gather translated stories in one volume
remains unprecedented in history, there have been setbacks, a rundown
of which you will find below. These setbacks have limited *Ulirát*'s linguistic diversity, geographical representation, and, ultimately, claims of
improving existing anthologizing practices in the Philippines.

One, when we were gathering short stories for *Ulirát*, we were
guided by the working subtitle "The Best of Twenty-First Century

Filipino Short Fiction in Translation"; hence, the exclusion of excellent works published before the year 2000. We also wanted to include writers who have only started to publish in the last two decades. The latter gatekeeping ruled out works by several "titans of letters" associated with the various regions in the Philippines, with one exception. We included Merlie M. Alunan, a writer of an imposing stature, to represent writers who began their literary practices in English and then later contributed significantly to the manifold growth of writing in other Philippine languages. Alunan is an accomplished anthologist herself, translating and compiling stories across the Visayan islands through *Sa Atong Dila: Introduction to Visayan Literature* (University of the Philippines Press, 2015) [13].

Two, copyright issues hounded us, as expected. We managed, for example, to make an arrangement with an author who writes in Ibaloi, a dying language of the indigenous peoples in the mountainous Benguet Province of northern Philippines, a story that would have greatly enriched the depth of selections in *Ulirát*, but our efforts to obtain permission from the publisher of the author's short story collection have been unsuccessful. A similar problem cropped up involving a Kapampangan short story, whose English translation we had commissioned for the anthology. We regret not being able to include this major language of the Philippines.

Three, we decided against the convenience of publicizing a call for open submissions, a move we knew would be viewed by some as a deterrent to impartiality and inclusivity, although that was far from our intention. We read books, magazines, and journals that published fiction, and then drew up shortlists from our reading. The stories we read numbered in excess of one thousand pieces, some of which were included in our other Philippine fiction anthologies assembled concurrently with *Ulirát* but with none of *Ulirát*'s bare-faced ambition and best-of aspiration. Our readings yielded many strong contenders, including two Carlo Paulo Pacolor stories whose English translations were readily available. We also relied on our personal contacts and their networks in soliciting prospective materials. We figured that by finding the materials ourselves, instead of passively waiting for them to come to us via an open-submission system, we could arrive at the best possible and most organic formulation. The mere posting of an open-submission call would have tipped off potential submitters to write the kind of stories they *believe* would appeal to us or would "survive" translation. We could then end up with a crop of stories that do not accurately represent the kind of writing being done at the moment but writing that is crafted in a tempting translation-friendly form or in an appeal to what is perceived as our aesthetic sensibilities.

Four, the nature of the form and genre is in itself restrictive. The staggering linguistic diversity in the Philippines does not immediately correspond to extant literary practices in these languages producing short fiction. Many ethnolinguistic groups in the Philippines, for instance, have relied since prehistoric times on oral narratives for storytelling and propagating their culture. Short fiction, both its form and conventions, remains a staunchly American invention; we simply imported it. Naturally, the practitioners of the written form tend to be those who have been formally educated in the Western literary tradition or who at least have had a brush with it.

Five, it is not surprising that Filipino-Tagalog, Cebuano, and Hiligaynon have more entries compared to other languages among the selections. These languages have either had strong institutional support or a long-established publishing industry since the early twentieth century, especially Filipino, which is largely based on Tagalog, as the legislated national language. Prestigious universities in the Philippines publish journals that accept prose submissions in Filipino. In the past decades, popular magazines, such as *Liwayway*, have also served as reliable venues for short-story writers and novelists in Filipino. Furthermore, short stories in Filipino-Tagalog are required reading in high school and elementary language classes. Though not as widely read as its Tagalog counterpart, the Cebuano short story has a vibrant tradition, and it has been in circulation through periodicals and magazines such as *Ang Suga* (1901–1911), *Alimyon* (1952–1963), and *Bisaya* (1930–present), among others. Hiligaynon has had *Almanake Panayanhon*, as well as *Yuhum* and *Hiligaynon* magazines, that continue to publish short stories to this day. It would be much, much harder to find venues that publish Akeanon, Karay-a, Waray, Surigaonon, Chavacano, Meranaw, Maguindanao, Tausug, and many other languages. Academia's renewed interest in what is called "regional literature" in the 1990s led state-funded writing workshops to accept works in languages other than Filipino-Tagalog, and these workshops subsequently encouraged university and independent presses to publish writing in "regional" languages.

And six, we started with the assumption that we could do all the translations ourselves and would authoritatively insert "edited and translated by" next to our names on the book cover. In the end, we had to ask for help from other translators. Our material circumstances were critical determining factors that sorely limited the breadth of selections in this volume. Literary translation is laborious and time-consuming; securing the necessary skill sets to produce high-quality literary translations for an international audience is prohibitively expensive, too.

Thus, we welcome the recognition of our sustained push for *Ulirát*, despite said material limitations that tempered our ragtag idealism, as a rejoinder against what we lament and, most importantly, criticize: the Philippine government—through the Komisyon sa Wikang Filipino (Commission on the Filipino Language) as well as the six agencies attached to the National Commission for Culture and the Arts—cannot seem to come up with enough funding to support literary translators, who are responsible for much of our understanding of world literature, and to sustain the production of high-quality translations. While the Bicol region has enjoyed a spate of well-funded translation projects in the past few years, it is only because of foreign support for the Ateneo de Naga University Press by the embassies of the Czech Republic and Hungary. As for the book you are now holding, it is only possible because of Gaudy Boy, an international publishing imprint.

The same material conditions stated above were also behind our inability to translate and anthologize in *Ulirát* numerous complex works of art written in recent years. Such innovative works included Chuckberry J. Pascual's linked stories in *Ang Nawawala* (*The Missing*) (Visprint, 2017), U. Z. Eliserio's politically incorrect irreverences in *Apat na Putok* (*Four Bangs*) (Polytechnic University of the Philippines Press, 2018), Mayette Bayuga's dizzyingly inventive "Ang Heredero ng Tribo Hubad sa Isla Real" ("The Heir to Isla Real's Tribe of the Naked"), Luna Sicat-Cleto's "Ang Lohika ng mga Bula ng Sabon" ("The Logic of Soap Bubbles") told through Sandali's (literally, "Moment") stream-of-consciousness, and Roland Tolentino's *Fastfood, Megamall at iba pang kuwento sa pagsasara ng ikalawang milenyum* (De La Salle University Publishing House, 1999), stories that use various storytelling modes. For instance,

Tolentino's "Palabok," "Sa Kanto ng Annapolis at Aurora" ("In the Corner of Annapolis and Aurora"), and "Fastfood" respectively appropriate the titular recipe, multiple points of view, and annotated vocabulary and grammar books.

Regretfully, we were also unable to cover in *Ulirát* other notable collections of short fiction in Filipino published by the University of the Philippines Press, including the new edition of *Utos ng Hari at Iba Pang Kuwento* (*King's Decree and Other Stories*) (2002) by Jun Cruz Reyes, who has a cameo as a character in Allan N. Derain's story in *Ulirát*; *Pamilya: Mga Katha* (*Family: Stories*) (2003) by Eli Rueda Guieb III; and *Barriotic Punk: Mga Kuwento sa Baryo at Kanto* (*Barriotic Punk: Stories in the Barrio and Street Corners*) (2002) by Mes De Guzman.

In the nineties, a group of Filipino short-fiction writers, which included Luna Sicat-Cleto, Roland Tolentino, Eli Rueda Guieb III, and Mes De Guzman, released five anthologies: *Engkwentro* (1990), *Impetu* (1991), *Habilin* (1991), *Alagwa* (1997), and *Relasyon* (1999). Then in 2014, Jun Cruz Reyes anthologized in *Labintatlong Pasaway* (*Thirteen Deviants*) Filipino-language stories he characterized as "transgressive" and "postmodern." These efforts are part of the long tradition of short fiction in Filipino, from Marcos's martial law–era *Mga Agos sa Disyerto* (*Counterflows in the Desert*) (1964), which features stalwarts of short-form fiction (Efren Abueg, Dominador Mirasol, Rogelio Ordoñez, Edgardo Reyes, and Rogelio Sicat), to contemporary successors of de facto martial law period that *Mga Gago sa Disyerto* (*Assholes in the Desert*) and similar zine collectives dissect and problematize. *Agos* may approximately be transliterated as "counterflow" in the *disyerto* ("desert"), referring to unproductive land, whereas *gago* ("assholes") may be associated with the aforementioned "transgression." Unfortunately, *Ulirát* cannot cover this historically important period.

Also out of our reach are short stories written in so-called "red areas," where communist "organs of political power" practice an alternative way of life, because beyond textual transgressions are actual revolutionary short fictions. Among the most noteworthy of these works are Gelacio Guillermo's collection *Kabanbanuagan: Mga Kuwento ng Sonang Gerilya* (*Kabanbanuagan: Stories in the Guerilla Zone*) (1987) and *Muog: Mga Naratibo ng Kanayunan sa Matagalang Digmang Bayan sa Pilipinas*, 1972–1997 (*Fortress: Narratives of the Countryside in the Protracted People's War in the Philippines*) (1998), an anthology of literary works that includes short stories.

Meanwhile, Bikol-language fiction, one of the most advanced and developed in the country, is unjustly underrepresented in *Ulirát*. Save for Kristian Sendon Cordero's story, originally written in Filipino and not in Bikol, we were not able to include fiction written in Bikol. Aside from the abovementioned reasons, this is because of the period we initially selected and the choice of some writers from the region who write in English or Filipino. Had our scope included twentieth-century fiction, one of scholar Peñafrancia Raniela Barbaza's English translations of a Bikolnon story would have been a valuable addition to our selection. The region's veteran writers such as Niles Jordan Breis, Romulo Baquiran Jr., and Merlinda Bobis are known more for their works in Filipino and English. The same can be said for writers from other regions, such as Leoncio P. Deriada, who had a prodigious output. Additionally, Rosario Cruz-Lucero, with her wide range of scholarly interests in the broad discipline of Philippine studies, has written short fiction in English that integrates folk beliefs with modern sensibilities.

Given the long litany of challenges detailed above, the perception of *Ulirát* as a self-flagellating mechanism of what-could-have-beens disguised as trailblazing in its protestations would have been understandable, even expected. It is in this spirit of self-critique that we hope to influence and refine future work.

CONCLUSION

All in all, as a representative sample of the diversity of languages and the rich ethnolinguistic heritage of the Philippines, *Ulirát* quivers on shaky footing with its relatively paltry scope. But, as a selection of Philippine short fiction in any language, few recent books—or perhaps none at all—can match the incredible breadth of the stories collected here.

We are grateful to every reader who will give this book a chance, most especially because the challenges we have detailed here, among them language barriers and geographical boundaries, can be overcome by establishing a literary network, if not a discursive community. Rather than a singular monolithic effort at gatekeeping or representing the Philippine islands, may our work be a call to let a hundred stories bloom and let a hundred anthologies contend.

TILDE ACUÑA
JOHN BENGAN
DARYLL DELGADO
AMADO ANTHONY G. MENDOZA III
KRISTINE ONG MUSLIM

AUGUST 11–OCTOBER 2, 2020
PHILIPPINES

ENDNOTES

[1] Cruz, Isagani R., ed. 2000. *The Best Philippine Short Stories of the Twentieth Century.* Makati City: Tahanan Books.

[2] Malacañan Palace. n.d. "The British Conquest of Manila," Presidential Museum and Library. Republic of the Philippines, http://malacanang.gov.ph/the-british-conquest-of-manila/. Accessed October 2, 2020.

[3] United States House of Representatives, History, Art & Archives. n.d. "The Philippines, 1898–1946," https://history.house.gov/Exhibitions-and-Publications/APA/Historical-Essays/Exclusion-and-Empire/The-Philippines/. Accessed October 2, 2020.

[4] De Bevoise, Ken. 1995. *Agents of Apocalypse: Epidemic Disease in the Colonial Philippines.* New Jersey: Princeton University Press, ix.

[5] Mojares, Resil B. 1983. *The Origins and Rise of the Filipino Novel: A Generic Study of the Novel Until 1940.* Quezon City: University of the Philippines Press.

[6] Yabes, Leopoldo, ed. 1975. *Philippine Short Stories: 1925–1940.* Quezon City, University of the Philippines Press.

[7] Abad, Gemino H., ed. 2010. *Upon Our Own Ground* (Volume 1 [1956–1964], Volume 2 [1965–1972]) & *Underground Spirit* (Volume 1 [1973–1982], Volume 2 [1983–1989]) & *Hoard of Thunder* (Volume 1 [1990–2000], Volume 2 [2001–2008]). Quezon City: University of the Philippines Press.

[8] Most data from this point until the end of the section are from Cruz-Lucero, Rosario, ed. 2018. "The Short Story." *Encyclopedia of Philippine Arts* Literature Volume, 2nd edition ed., vol. XI, Pasay City: Cultural Center of the Philippines.

[9] Arguilla, Manuel & Eduardo Nedruda & Teodoro Agoncillo, eds. 1940. *Literature under the Commonwealth*. Manila: Philippine Writers' League.

[10] Lee's and Virtusio's stories were later anthologized in *Sigwa: Isang Antolohiya ng Maiikling Kwento* (1992/2007, Quezon City: University of the Philippines Press).

[11] Garcellano, Edel. 1972. *Ficcion*. Quezon City: Kalikasan Press.

[12] Alunan, Merlie M., ed. 2013. *Sa Atong Dila: Introduction to Visayan Literature*. Quezon City: University of the Philippines Press.

____ed. 2016. *Susumaton: Oral Narratives of Leyte*. Quezon City: Ateneo de Manila University Press

____ed. 2017. *Tinalunay: Hinugpong nga Panurat nga Winaray*. Quezon City: University of the Philippines Press.

[13] Barbaza, Peñafrancia Raniela. 2017. *Orosipon kan Bikolnon: Interrupting the Philippine Nation*. Quezon City: University of the Philippines Press.

____. 2018. *Mga Osipon ni Ana T. Calixto: Paggigiit sa Sadiring Sanwa sa Osipon: Maikling Kathang Bikol, 1950-1956*. Quezon City: Ateneo de Manila University Press.

[14] Cruz, Conchitina. 2017. "The (Mis)Education of the Filipino Writer: The Tiempo Age and Institutionalized Creative Writing in the Philippines," *Kritika Kultura* No. 28, February 2017, https://journals.ateneo.edu/ojs/index.php/kk/article/view/KK2017.02802/2406. Accessed October 2, 2020.

[15] Jones, Josh, "How the CIA Helped Shape the Creative Writing Scene in America," *Open Culture*, December 14, 2018, https://www.openculture.com/2018/12/cia-helped-shaped-american

-creative-writing-famous-iowa-writers-workshop.html. Accessed October 2, 2020.

[16] Nguyen, Viet Thanh. 2017. "How Writers' Workshops Can Be Hostile." *The New York Times.* https://www.nytimes.com/2017/04 /26/books/review/viet-thanh-nguyen-writers-workshops.html. Accessed October 2, 2020.

[17] Bennett, Eric. 2015. *Workshops of Empire: Stegner, Engle, and American Creative Writing during the Cold War.* Iowa City: University of Iowa Press.

___. 2014. "How Iowa Flattened Literature." *The Chronicle.* https:// www.chronicle.com/article/how-iowa-flattened-literature/. Accessed October 2, 2020.

___. 2020. "How America Taught the World to Write Small." *The Chronicle.* https://www.chronicle.com/article/how-america-taught -the-world-to-write-small. Accessed October 2, 2020.

[18] Galeano, Eduardo. 1973. *Open Veins of Latin America: Five Centuries or the Pillage of a Continent.* Translated by Cedric Belfrage, New York: Monthly Review Press.

[19] Prashad, Vijay. 2013. *The Poorer Nations: A Possible History of the Global South.* London: Verso.

[20] Mojares, Resil. 2006. "The Formation of Philippine National Identity under U.S. Colonial Rule." *Philippine Quarterly of Culture and Society*, 11–32.

[21] Reyes, Edgardo. 1986. *Sa Mga Kuko ng Liwanag.* Manila: De La Salle University Press.

[22] Beecroft, Alexander. 2015. *An Ecology of World Literature From Antiquity to the Present Day.* London: Verso.

[23] Casanova, Pascale. 2000. *The World Republic of Letters.* Translated by M. B. Debevoise, Harvard University Press.

[24] Mojares, Resil B. 2013. *Isabelo's Archive*. Mandaluyong City: Anvil Publishing, Inc.

[25] Cf. Braga, Rogelio "Philippine Literary Mafia." https://rogeliobraga.com/2020/02/24/philippine-literary-mafia/ (2020) and De La Cerna, Julian "What Is an Editor?: Ricardo de Ungria as Producer of Knowledge" in *Philippine Humanities Review* https://www.journals.upd.edu.ph/index.php/phr/article/view/7226/6293 (2019); both, accessed October 2, 2020.

ULIRÁT

BEST CONTEMPORARY STORIES IN
TRANSLATION FROM THE PHILIPPINES

THE BOY WHO WANTED TO BE A COCKROACH

by Carlo Paulo Pacolor

Translated from Filipino by Soleil David

He was a good kid, so he always asked for permission before doing anything.

One time he wanted to be a freshwater crab, so he first called his mother at the hospital where she worked. He asked, "Please, 'Nay, can I be a freshwater crab?"

"Yes, son, yes," his mother answered, quickly putting the phone down.

"Why a crab?" his amused older sister asked.

He explained that last Saturday, a fishmonger came past their house bearing freshwater crabs, and when their father bought some, the boy saw how strong they were, how their pincers made people cry out. His older sister snickered.

When his mother came home from work, she hurried to the room where his father was, ignoring the boy who had tucked his hands into his thighs, scuttling crablike. His parents also ignored him when the boy came into their room and tried to climb onto the bed still imitating what he had seen: the crabs trying to climb but slipping in their scrambling attempts.

His mother said to his father, "So at dawn they brought a teenager to us. The mother had no idea what to do—his intestines were hanging out from him. The mother was saying, sew them back in, please, sew them back in. But I couldn't tell her that I couldn't sew his intestines back. Well, someone had broken into their house and the teenager fought back. As if he was any match for them. After all that, they still took everything."

The boy hit his head falling on the floor but he didn't cry. His mother told him to be careful, his father told him he could no longer be a crab. They called for his sister, who told him how painfully crabs die, how their soft innards boil in their hard shells. "Do you want your intestines boiled?"

The boy was never a freshwater crab again.

The next week, he called his mother at the hospital again and asked, "Can I be a catfish? I want to be a catfish!"

"Whatever you want," his mother answered with a yawn.

"Why a catfish?" asked his older sister, amused.

He explained that the other Saturday, he and his father had gone to the fish market where he saw catfish thrashing in their nets, flopping about even when they were taken out of the water, looking very much alive. He said it was amazing that there were fish that could breathe on land, and they were funny, too; they even had mustaches! His older sister smiled.

After dinner, they were surprised when the boy went into the bathroom without being told, shouting, "I'll go, I'll go!"

While tidying up the dinner table, his mother told his father, "His flesh was all burnt. If I were him, I wouldn't have gone back to rescue anybody. They weren't even related or anything. There were reporters all over, you'll see it on the news later: Hero Ends Up in Hospital."

The bathroom faucet kept running. It was while watching the evening news that his parents finally noticed the sound of water pouring into the drain. No wonder the boy hadn't come out of the bathroom.

This is what they saw when they opened the door: the boy lying on the bathroom floor, body thrashing about, two lines of toothpaste drawn on his upper lip.

"You're wasting water," his mother said, pulling him to his feet.

"You can't be a catfish anymore," said his father, wiping off his toothpaste mustache.

They called for his older sister to get him dressed, and as she powdered his back, she asked, "Have you seen how mischievous catfish are killed?"

"No," the boy answered.

"They grab them by the tail and smash their heads on a rock. Do you want your head to explode?"

The boy was never a catfish again.

But a good kid always asks for permission.

The next week, he wanted to be a frog. He called his mother and when he heard her voice, he asked, "Frog, 'Nay, can I please? Please?"

"Of course, son, of course." And her voice disappeared at the other end of the line as a patient came in.

"Why a frog?" asked his older sister, bemused.

They're hard to catch, the boy answered, making leaping motions with his hands. Last Saturday, he'd gone to the fields with his father and his father's friends to catch frogs. When he caught one, it slipped out of his hands, and no matter how many times he tried, he couldn't catch it again in its agile leaping. "Like this, Até, like this." His older sister laughed.

That night, when his parents went to bed, his mother embraced his father and said, "If I were the wife, I wouldn't want to live. She couldn't stop crying—who wouldn't cry if their husband was paralyzed? I think he's an alcoholic, he fell asleep at the wheel and his car almost ended up under a truck."

Suddenly, a crash was heard from the boy's room, followed by another. The parents jumped up, as did the older sister. When they turned the lights on, they saw that the boy had jumped off a low shelf, which had fallen along with him. The shelf had not hit the boy. But his mother slapped him because she was frightened, his father shouted that he couldn't be a frog anymore, his sister was upset because she was the one who had to clean up his mess.

"Frogs die painful deaths," his sister told him. "They're run over and flattened by cars. Do you want to be squished?"

And the boy was never a frog again.

A few weeks passed without the boy calling his mother to ask for permission to do things. His father had stopped taking the boy out with him the last few Saturdays. His sister didn't ask him any questions, like "Why?" which he loved answering. When he came home from school, his older sister would just tell him to do his homework, and when his mother and father came home, he would mostly sit still, answering their questions about his day respectfully and politely, asking if he could brush his teeth, wash his face, go to bed. He lay down even though he wasn't tired at all, and most of the time he could hear his mother's accounts of work echoing through the walls until he fell asleep.

At the dinner table, he listened quietly as his mother told them about an infant: "This one-year-old kid, can you believe it, he fell down an entire flight of stairs. All the way down! But he survived! I asked if anyone caught him, but no one did. I asked, was there a plant or something soft to land on? But there wasn't. A miracle!"

The next night when, again, the boy found that he couldn't sleep, he turned the light on and observed the stillness in his room. Nothing was moving except for the curtains, no sound could be heard except for his quiet heartbeat. He was starting to get drowsy when he saw a cockroach cross the floor. He had seen his mother do this: take a slipper to crush the cockroach. He had seen his father do this: roll up a newspaper to whack the cockroach. He had seen his sister do this: chase the cockroach with a soft broom to beat it. But the cockroach would never die.

The boy slept soundly that night.

The next morning, he called his mother at the hospital. "'Nay, I want to be a cockroach, please let me."

"Ask your sister." She put the phone down as a patient was dying beside her.

"Até, may I be a cockroach?"

"Why a cockroach?"

"Because they don't die. They don't get hurt."

His sister did not smirk, smile, or laugh. She only shrugged. "Ask Tatay."

The moment his father came home, he greeted him with, "'Tay, will you let me be a cockroach?"

"Yes, you're a cockroach now."

The boy jumped for joy.

And so, while his older sister was cooking, he crawled near her feet and she started screaming. She chased him with a soft broom. He grew antennae, his eyes got bigger. His father was reading the paper, and the boy crawled across his neck, making him stamp his feet in angry surprise. The father rolled up his newspaper and tried to whack the boy but the boy escaped quickly. He grew wings, he grew four more limbs. When his mother came home, he swooped at her from the corner of the ceiling, and she ducked and ran, wanting to cry for help. She hastily looked for a slipper and swung it about but she couldn't hit him. He was small now and he moved fast. His family didn't have to worry anymore. He would never get hurt, he would never die.

All through dinner he hovered over his family, who were unable to eat in peace. His mother couldn't talk about work as she kept looking up at the ceiling; his father and sister, likewise. Until sleep overtook them, their eyes were wide open, anticipating the boy's every move. No one slept well for fear, and everyone was still yawning as they left the house the next morning.

The boy's mother didn't notice that he'd climbed into her purse. Before he had become a cockroach, he was never, ever permitted to go with her to the hospital. She said it wasn't a place for children. But what about cockroaches? When he emerged from the purse, no one noticed him as their gazes were at human-eye level. Everyone had business to attend to. Some were crying, some were close to dying, some were breathing their last. The boy suddenly felt an extreme sadness, and he wanted to go home and play, become a different animal, answer the question why.

But what was this? Shiny shoes almost crushed him, stretchers and wheelchairs almost wheeled over him, a broom almost swept him up, and something he'd never expected to fear, disinfectant almost jetted him! He hid in a corner, went into a hole, and when he looked into the darkness, he saw a lot more of his kind.

He was a good cockroach, so he wanted to ask for permission. "Can I please be a boy again?"

But not one of them answered. They only grazed silently. He then remembered that he hadn't eaten yet. The cockroach found his footing in the dark where he didn't need eyes to see, until he exited through another hole where the light blinded him. His feet quickly took him to the base of a dumpster where tens of thousands of cockroaches scuttled. And not only that: there were even rats, ants, flies, and other animals he had never become. Animals that he thought also wouldn't die. He carefully climbed up the dumpster and went through a crack.

He had happened upon a feast. He walked on top of a piece of tissue paper filled with phlegm, some mango peel, bubble gum, a half-eaten piece of bread, a Styrofoam cup still containing coffee, a toothpick with a bit of food on it, until he arrived at a chicken bone from which bits of flesh still clung. Three cockroaches were already nibbling at it.

"May I please eat with you?" he asked them.

But none of them answered. He realized he no longer needed permission—and more than that, he no longer needed to be good. He took his first bite.

And he never was a boy again. ♦

SANTIAGO'S CULT

by Kristian Sendon Cordero

Translated from Filipino by Bernard Capinpin

As soon as the lamp was lit at six every evening and the chickens would flutter down from the cacao and jackfruit trees, Father would leave. He wore a shabby military fatigue, boots as large as my legs, and an antique amulet on which was inscribed an angelus that only Father could read and understand: *Que cecop, deus meus, deus noter.* I had once attempted to say it aloud, but I almost swallowed up my tongue. He said that the prayer was sacred, that words had their own power, and that these should not be taken lightly. When, one time, he had caught me in the act of stashing it in my pocket, Father had warned me that if I would continue to utter the angelus, all my hair would fall off and my tongue fully contort. I had wanted to use the triangular amulet with an open eye in the middle as a slammer. That was said to be the Lord's eye. The vision of the open eye, which seemed to have been carved off the sky by lightning, was said to have been seen by Father's grandfather. The amulet weighed as much as a dozen marbles and twenty flattened bottle caps which we used for tatsi. Whenever Father wore the amulet, no metal or bronze could wound him, except lightning, snake bite, or any bite from a wild animal. Instead of scolding and welting me with his belt after catching me, Father would calmly ask for his amulet and would merely exchange it for a peso he took out from his ear.

These past few months, Father's departures had become more successive. He came home in the early hours of the morning as did the bats living in the old bell tower in the church of Santiago, who was Father's favorite saint. So when I was born on the day of the saint's feast day, he did not hesitate to make me a namesake of the mounted saint.

Santiago was the patron saint of cavalries and soldiers. He was one of the Lord's twelve disciples, a brother of San Juan. Prominently seen strewn underneath the figure of Santiago were decapitated heads and dismembered men. They wore flashy turbans and had beards which seemed to be hair-curled by Mother's friend (like that of Plaridel's or Antonio Luna's seen above blackboards). The men scattered below the patron saint's feet were apparently called Moros—enemies of the Christians. Even before the arrival of the Spaniards, they were said to often raid towns and abduct young women to take as child-bearers and slaves. Moros were said to have been weaned on pigs' hearts when they were in the womb. These people were the same ones that San Miguel trampled upon in the gin bottle.

If one should examine it closely, Santiago's eyes were said to overflow with anger. His eyeballs, said an old sacristan, were cast from gold that came from a mountain of ice in South America while the head and arms were fashioned from pure ivory in Africa. Many have tried to steal the santo but no one has ever succeeded. The Moros, who still continue to wreck havoc, had also attempted to steal it during the first years of the Spanish era, but due to the miraculous statue, they could not sack our town because of beginning rumors that Santiago's horse would come alive and would sprout flaming horns as that of a bull if ever an enemy should come near it. It was believed that its eyes were more powerful than the amulet Father wore and anyone wielding it would attain unbelievable strength. There had also been some rumors in town that each time the santo went missing from its altar, it accompanied Father's group whenever they raided the towns of Topas, Malawag, and Tapayas, which were reportedly breeding with rebels that Apo had ordered to be pursued. These rebels were the new Moros.

I often saw Mother and other women in our town before the same icon of Santiago. During the feast day of the patron saint, they contributed to have a new dress sewn for the santo. It usually wore red embroidered with golden thread that was said to have come from Manila. This thread was the same one used in the First Lady's dresses according to the old women whose scapulars were like skin on the bodies.

One Sunday, after attending church, I saw Mother rubbing her hands on the statues, her eyes closed as if they had been soaped, and groping the santo in the same way as a person, whose eyes were suddenly splashed with soap, would feel for the dipper to rinse them off. Like the saint's other devotees, Mother believed that the saint had the power to heal. So there was always a line before the holy statue to be able to rub it with their handkerchiefs, which they would dab to their aching parts, mostly at the back, the nape, the temples, the lips, the chest, their trembling hands and feet, and there were those who coyly wiped their blessed hands even on their breasts and penises. Some would sneakily rub with coconut oil to make candles for the altar. It was used for hilot and Santigwar. Because of the old women's rubbing of the statue, the balls of the saint's mounted horse shone. It was like an incredibly softened and ripened duhat.

Mother was a teacher in our town. There were only four of them teaching the six grades, each with twenty students. Mother had been my teacher when I was in grade one and grade three. She was also assigned to be my teacher when I would enter grade five the next year. Once we arrived home from school, Father would have left by then. Only steamed rice would be waiting for us. At the beginning, Mother frequently went to church and was an active member of the Confradia of Santiago. But these past few months when the mass on her throat grew bigger, which was perhaps brought about by more than a decade's worth of teaching and inhaling chalk, her churchgoing became less frequent. I remember that when Mother noticed that her mouth dried up easily and it was as if she felt a live frog inside her throat, she offered a novena to the saint and gave tithe to the mass within the month. However, no improvement was seen in her illness which became a huge mass on her throat. It grew larger than the balls of Santiago's horse.

As the mass grew, Mother became more irritable at home or in school. One day, I heard that she threw a coconut floor scrub at one of her students because of a mistake in spelling out her name. Instead of writing "e," the student replaced it with "i" in our surname De la Fuente. They almost resorted to the kapitan of the barrio when the child's parents complained. It was a good thing that Father had gifted the kapitan three bottles of lambanog. While Mother's mass was continually growing, like a rat constricted by a snake, her faith to the saint dwindled further and further. She tried petitioning from other santos or santas. She went to Ombao Polpog and promised San Vicente to have a bronze throat made to hang on the saint's costume when she was cured. She also went to Hinulid in Calabanga and walked ten kilometers one Good Friday just to remove the impinging mass. But it seemed that the heavens were conspiring against her. So after a few months of trying to get well, Mother seemed to accept that the mass was like a part of her body. It was like a strand of hair or nail which sprung and grew. Mother looked pitiful because I knew that she had difficulty swallowing food, even her saliva. Her wincing and spitting almost together with her loud cursing, which became her new angelus, was proof of this.

After her last and futile covenant lighting lady-shaped candles in the cathedral of the Virgin of Salvacion in Tiwi, even her shadow had not stepped foot inside a church anymore. She diverted her attention to playing cards during Saturdays and Sundays. She consulted an albularyo but she was only advised to go back to Santiago, a thing Mother had not done because her mass had the size of a nearly unripe pomelo, while Father more frequently stayed in the camp.

Mother would not trust any doctor. She had sometimes said the doctor might only excise the frog inside her throat and use it to teach new medical students. Mother was probably only joking then, but Father and I did not bat an eye.

"Your father's an aswang!"

Shouted my playmate Intoy when I lost at teks and grew tired of playing it. It was as if Mother's spirit had possessed me and had wanted me to force-feed my playmate with sand when I heard Intoy saying it.

"Is there an aswang that prays to the saints, aber?" I retorted back at Intoy, clutching his remaining three teks cards of Panday and Pedro Penduko.

"Ay, whatever, our neighbors say that your father is an aswang! That's why your mother has a mass on her throat and why you don't grow because you have blood of asbo!"

Not contented, he continued to shout until he went home: "Tiago, midget, supot!"

He acted like a ravenous crow hurling insults at me until he was swallowed up by the dark which gradually enveloped the town. The last thing I heard was the sudden crack of his voice.

I went home carrying the teks I acquired as thick as my books. I hid it in a small cabinet so that Mother would not find it. That night, I could not take my mind off Intoy's claim that my puniness and Mother's mass were because my father was an aswang.

To be an aswang was even more terrifying. There were stories around town that, long before the missionaries arrived, our town had been a nest of malignant and evil spirits. Only Santiago could be able to vanquish their camp. The aswang were evil beings and those devils were often seen wandering during a new moon to devour new victims. An aswang must take a coconut shell with two eyes and smother it with guano before it could levitate in the darkness and kill. There were two types of aswang: an aswang who could fly or a manananggal, and an aswang who walked, which is called asbo. They were both acolytes from Hell and on days when God was dead, they gathered in the Mayon volcano to reaffirm their allegiance to the dark powers. Aswang were afraid of water, especially holy water, and once, when a woman was thought to be an aswang in our town during the Japanese occupation, she was dragged to the river, her hips tied to a large stone, and was thrown to the water. If the woman was an aswang, she would not sink as she would use her powers to walk on water and to escape. But when she sank and died, the woman was innocent. That woman died from bleeding, her blood admixed in the river. The woman had been two months pregnant and her husband had just been found dead while gathering coconut. The two were rumored to be spies for the Japanese.

Most believed that there were more female aswang and that they were more powerful than the male aswang. Female aswang were more ferocious when angered, like giant hens. When the moon was full, the aswang appeared, some strolling in the air or if not, at the basement, feasting on the spit of the ill. *Fuera dios, fuera hulog*, this was the angelus the aswang chanted which meant, There is no God, I will not stumble. There was another angelus uttered repeatedly by aswang until their spreading wings sprouted: *Siri, siri, daing Diyos kun banggi, labaw sa kakahoyan, lagbas sa kasirongan.* (Do not fear, do not worry, there is no God in the night, above the forest, outside the basements).

Sometimes, they took the form of a boar, a cat, or even a dog. Phlegm acted as a vitamin to them, and blood was water to quench their thirst. Aswang could not be killed, they only hibernated, so before they went off to hibernate, the aswang must first pass on a black orb to whomever relative or person they chose to propagate the line. An aswang could not rest until it could pass the orb on to others. I heard these stories retold by elders of the town who little by little had died and perhaps had been victims of aswang themselves. But still their tales remained, cautioning not to tell stories about aswang during Tuesdays and Fridays because the aswang's hearing was more acute on those two days.

The moon had almost sunk beneath our window and the stars, which I had caught a glimpse of through the small hole in our roof, had already passed when I sensed Father's arrival. Even before Mother had grown a mass, they slept separately. Mother slept restlessly; hence she needed to be surrounded by pillows to prevent her from falling off. The pillows surrounding her bed looked like dead men. Father slept on the floor, beside me. Father's snoring sounded like horses in a chase. I felt the throbbing of his heart like a beating drum. Father perspired. He smelt of burnt slippers. When Father hugged me tightly, I felt like a small pillow embraced by a huge giant. I pretended to sleep. Father's muscles on his arm were large, like small pan de sal, like rats. I felt Father's breath blazing, grazing my nape. It was like a strong gust dancing the tiny grass of my head. Before I was visited by sleep, I saw Mother's large shadow inside the mosquito net and the pillows which seemed to be bursting, its blackened cotton protruding.

At daybreak, we were horrified by the bodies by the river. Six men had been found being nibbled on by crabs and shrimp. Bullet holes were found in their heads and abdomens. One of the bodies had been burnt because his head looked like it was poured over by asphalt, and another one had his penis cut off and swallowed. They were like frogs mangled by cars. The dead men were presumed to be rebels. From Tigaon and Sorsogon, said a teacher. The aswang have attacked, said an albularyo, one of the elders in town who before had been suspected of being an aswang. The slain rebels were young except for the old one poured over by asphalt, added another teacher. The rebels were already skin and bones as though they had been starved for months. One of the dead men still had his eyes wide open, and they almost protruded out of the skull covered with wounds which were being lapped up by tilapia and carp.

Because of what had happened, classes were suspended the whole day. Everyone talked about the dead men, from the church to the market, saying fish sales had slackened because of the news of the corpses found in the river. Those who sold fish were most disturbed because their catch that day had putrefied.

The bodies were placed in a cart pulled by a white carabao and brought to the municipal to be photographed and to be claimed by the relatives of the dead. As was expected, no one came and introduced themselves as relatives of the rebels. After the priest had blessed them, they were immediately buried in a vacant lot nearby the cemetery that night. According to the albularyo whom Mother had once consulted, the woman who had drowned in the river was now taking her revenge. Many more bodies would surface from the river. He said the aswang had killed off the rebels.

That day, I went back home early after my ears seemed to be swollen from the stories I had heard about the dead bodies and aswang. I found Father still asleep. I noticed his small wound on his right arm infected because of flies. His face and feet had abrasions. The pants he took off last night were covered with amorseco.

As he had always done, Father left that night before the lamp was lit and before the one kilo of beef he bought had been cooked to tender. He said that there would be drinking at the camp which was one creek and three hills away from our town. Father had not once brought us to the camp. Children were not allowed to be near such places. A party was being held in the camp because the new chief of their battalion had arrived from Albay. He was absolutely delighted that the soldiers had won in their encounter with the rebels.

Before heading to camp, some soldiers had offered a mass as gratitude to the patron saint. That was most likely why they were deemed Santiago's cult by some of our townsfolk, most especially Ka Pedring who owned a large plot of farmland in a town said to be a nesting ground of the enemies of Apo, who was Father's and other soldiers' overall chief. I had not seen Apo aside from the picture that hung in our classroom where he is alongside his family. They were like kings and queens, and my teacher said that Apo's family owned much gold which came from a Japanese general's loot and old churches in the Visayas and the North which Apo's wife had let him demolish. What was said to be lacking from the family's possessions was the eye of the Matamoros (Santiago's beatific endowment by some sisters of the parish). But news had reached us that the First Lady had written to the curate, requesting that the statue be sent to the Palace in Manila to be shown to a cardinal from Rome. The whole town could refuse. The patron saint might be incensed at having to be separate from its throne for a long time. The saint had never been away from its retablo. The curate could do nothing even though the First Lady had already sent money for renovations in the convent. There was talk about how the priest had sent an antique relic instead to add to the collection assembled by the First Lady who was somehow satisfied.

Whenever a high-ranking official came to the camp, it flooded with drink and food. A pig was slaughtered, and cash was handed out to the soldiers. Some girls, those from the Red House, were permitted to enter. Many of these girls claimed to be from Polangui because they were told to say that they were from Polangui if they were asked even though some of them were from Masbate or Samar. I had only seen them once in town when they joined the procession and followed the float of the Santo Sepulro. They were the girls covered with black veils and who walked barefoot carrying straw brooms.

The meat Father had left was still tough even though I already had forked it and had added jackfruit leaves. The beef still had a rubbery texture although the coal I put in the fire was almost dwindling, boiling our viand.

Our viand looked better when Mother mixed sweet potato and kangkong sprouts to the braised dish. The yellowish-white marrow slowly seeped out from inside the bones. Mother asked me to pluck some calamansi from our yard. The sour fruit was used to remove the oil and counteract the fat. The calamansi can be used against aswangs, said the elders. The calamansi's fragrance was more potent than that of garlic, although elders say that garlic was all the more effective against the aswang.

Mother had finished cooking our dish at eight o'clock. It had not yet tenderized but it was more satisfying than eating our own tongues. I dumped my rice into the soup though the image of the bodies found in the river still occasionally came back to mind. This was all right because our meal was beef rather than that of Intoy's, who I saw was washing shrimp and crablets a while back when I passed by their street to buy kerosene.

It was easy to sleep when one was full. After I finished washing the dishes, I went up to spread the mat and hang the mosquito net. Mother remained at the table, playing solitaire. She neither studied nor prepared for her lectures. She said she already knew the lesson. She had already in her head the entire textbook, which, she said, was older than me.

Father came home smelling of chico. Not like other drunks, Father was not rowdy or disposed to making a scene. He quietly felt the heat of the alcohol emanating from his body. He needed to muster up his courage to speak or do whatever he intended, and he would go by it with drink. That father of Intoy's, whenever he would come back from Saudi and have a drink—Jesus, he would chase his mother, wielding a machete and taking off his clothes in the road.

Intoy's mother was said to have another man in the rebels' mountain. That was why it was not a stretch, for Intoy, that whether rebel, Moro, or soldier, they were all aswang. His mother was cast under an aswang's spell by the rebels' leader, known by the name Ka Don. He was once a pastor of a sect before joining the rebels. The women in town swooned at the thought of Ka Don. He was like a movie star. You would not make him out to be a rebel. It was rumored that it was not only Intoy's mother who had been swayed by Ka Don. Almost all the other towns beside ours had someone captivated by the said leader. There were also some of us who sympathized with the principles of Ka Don, who seemed to possess a natural charisma to people, especially farmers and tenants. According to Ka Pedring, the rebels were good people and could be considered heroes by those like Ka Don. But aside from Ka Don's handsome looks, he was also known to be an executioner. Days after the six bodies of the men had been found along the river, Apo's adversaries retaliated. Two of Father's fellow soldiers were gunned down inside the Red House. Their skulls were smashed, and they were hauled outside. The two corpses were dragged around the village by a motorcycle. The two soldiers looked liked bopis when they were found in the middle of the plaza the next morning. You would first have to puke before weeping or shuddering at the sight of their corpses.

Father entered the mosquito net and woke me up. He kissed me on the forehead and the faint smell of gin lingered. His beard brushed me like a makahiya's thorns. I seemed to have felt a shiver when Father did it. Most especially when Father held my skinny arm, and then he seized my crotch, and he laughed as if he was tickled.

"How my son has grown. I'll feel for your birdie to see if you've become a true man." My father spoke teasingly, but I was taken aback and cowered. I shamefully covered my penis. I saw how it was smaller than Intoy's. But Father insisted on groping it like inspecting jocote to buy in the market. Father uncovered my hand and touched my penis. I tried to stomach it while he fondled it like a rooster to be played in a cockfight.

"You should be circumcised during the school break, so they'll say that you've become a man. You need to carry on my line, the De la Fuente family . . ." Because of his drunkenness, Father appeared to mumble his words. The only thing I knew of circumcision was that it was done by the river. In the river, the tip of the penis was made to soften like the beef we had eaten. As to why the river, which was the source of livelihood for some of us, was always associated with blood, with death, it was the river through which the rituals of birth, baptism, and death flowed.

It was also by the river that the priests had brought Santiago's statue. Before the missionaries came, the river had been a breeding ground for crocodiles, and one priest had also died after being attacked by a crocodile while he was bathing. Only the priest's rosary and crucifix was left. This was the town's first miracle because once the crocodiles had started consuming priests, the crocodiles died one after another until the entire population had gone. I was a man now,

21

but I would only truly become one after being circumcised. The old albularyo performed it in the town. You couldn't refuse or else it would bring a great shame to our family. A child fathered by an uncircumcised male had crusty eyes and was sickly.

Again, Father embraced me tightly. I felt his eyes scanning my whole body. I was like a mirror Father looked to. I was scared to be circumcised, but that was better than having to give birth or having to menstruate. Women perhaps had been more cursed than men.

I slowly turned away from Father. I did not see how he looked. The fear I felt was perhaps thicker than the blanket I used. That moment when he grabbed hold of my penis, I was afraid that I might see that he was an aswang, and at the time when he embraced me, it was then that he turned back to a man.

He still held my penis until he slept. He gave off snores successively which could have turned to kisses to Mother. But Mother was engulfed by the dark when evening came. She was like a large mass inside the mosquito net.

While Father held my penis, I felt my legs stiffening as if my thighs up to the tip of the prepuce in my sheathed penis were pierced by wire. It was like a plucked flower breaking off to brandish its petals. I was by then at the verge of dozing off among other sensations when a liquid slowly oozed from my penis. The liquid was like sap exuding out the banana's heart at twelve midnight during Good Friday, which according to stories was a source of power to fight off the aswang.

———

From that day on, I waited for Father's arrival each night. During the times I waited, I was visited by new dreams of large and generous hands to which I was like a bushel of rice hulls being pounded until the grain came out. The more days I waited, finding bodies by the river had become more regular. Some corpses were also found in the thicket, the bodies dismembered and wrapped in sacks of cement. They were like the men seen in Santiago's statue. Dismembered arms and decapitated heads, according to one drunk, haunted the river. No one dared to pass by that part of the river when the geckos started clucking among the bamboo, unless one used kalampunay. Doing the laundry by the river became less frequent while the crabs, shrimp, and fish caught here became larger. But only a few people bought them. The most expensive was one piso for a kilo of shrimp while crabs could be obtained for free. It was also reported that a catfish was seen in the river and swallowed an entire carabao while it was wading there. The catfish that had been seen was said to be as large as Mang Andoy's dinghy. Have the crocodiles come back?

"Your father and his fellow soldiers are the ones killing the bodies in the river!" Intoy said as a taunting comeback when we went home together from the market. "Both your father and those in the mountains are monsters!" Intoy added in reproach while pulling down an eyelid as though he were taking out dust stinging his eye and stuck out his tongue.

"If your father is an aswang, then you'll become an aswang too!" my friend shouted and scurried away when he saw me picking up a stone I was about to throw at him.

I had no idea why Intoy called my father an aswang since my father had been appointed his godfather during his baptism. Father would often give him presents for Christmas. Last December, he was given a toy gun, the same gift as mine. But Intoy easily broke it because there was not a day he did not bring it to school, gloating that it had been given to him by his father in Saudi.

I watched Father many times just to prove that he was not an aswang. He was not scared that I had calamansi leaves in my pocket. He looked directly at people's eyes. He entered the church to pray in Santiago's altar. I suspected Mother more, who was more spiteful these past few days. Some children had started calling her a witch because of her sternness which was known throughout the town. Some had even complained about Mother's grating demeanor. She had also often screamed at me whenever she noticed that some of her cards were missing. I sometimes saw her talking with the king of cards, kissing and singing the jack a lullaby, while stepping on the queens.

Sometimes I stole some pieces of Mother's playing cards. The two cards seldom used, which had pictures of clowns, and I betted them in teks. My classmates were all impressed because my teks were unique. They were new and smelled imported. "From what movie is that?" asked my playmate. I said, "From Dolphy and Panchito's," which made them more amazed. They have not yet heard of that movie in the Betamax rental store.

When Mother found out, she chased me with a long stingray whip which was feared amongst aswang. I fled from the house and went to a hill and washed the wound Mother inflicted on me with tender guava leaves and Pay Isong's nganga spit. Being hit by a stingray's tail was like being bitten by an eel. Probably a circumcision was more painful. The tail was covered with spikes. An aswang hit by its lash would die. The tail was always underneath Mother's sleeping mat. That was most likely why Father did not sleep with her?

To determine that Father was not an aswang, I waited for him to fall asleep when he arrived early. He was obviously tired, and if

Father had not snored, he would be mistaken as someone dead. I slowly groped for his penis. Carefully. I wanted to prove that he had what I had. That was proof that he was not an aswang like what Intoy had claimed. I pretended to toss and turn and then slightly lifted my shirt. I felt nervous like a rat being chased by a cat when I slowly placed and directed my knee toward Father's crotch. A single piece of flesh seemed to be attached to it. I quickly shook my thigh and felt Father's penis harden. It was like a mass. I noticed that it grew while something was placed on top of it. I became more worried and so I gradually took off my thigh placed on it and carefully loosened my embrace on Father. Father still slept soundly while I opened and closed my palms because I felt that I wanted to grab hold of Father's penis more. I wanted to make sure that we were both the same. But I feared that Father or his penis would get mad. I just prostrated myself on our hard floor. The floor was just as hard as Father's warm body. The soil's aroma wafted from the basement of our house and from my father's body. Petrichor. Mother had said that that vapor was bad, that kind that comes when the brief rain suddenly waters a dry land. The vapor was bad for the stomach. That was the smell that exuded out of Father's skin. But for me, that night, it was as though the ilang-ilang in our yard had bloomed. I hugged my pillow and again groped my penis which had also hardened like a banana ready to be plucked. When I felt that sleep was already knocking on my eyelids, at once, I let in the racing dreams. In my first dream, it had rained sampaguita.

After I had ascertained that he was not an aswang, on some nights, Father did not come home. Other nights, I thought of his penis. It grew when he was touched, when it was pressed upon, when it was held. Like mine. This was similar to what was believed of Santiago's statue, that both the saint and his horse grew. It was said that before it had been brought here by the missionaries, its feet had not yet touched the ground from where he was mounted on his horse. Now, the saint's boots almost touched the shelf. The horse's balls also grew, said a woman I had often seen rubbing the statue.

Meanwhile, gunshots had been heard more frequently from the other town and it seemed that it was moving closer and closer to our town. The sound of a gunshot was different from that of fireworks during the New Year. These past few nights, the sound from the successive blasts was sharp. It was like a thunder's roar. Stones seemed to pour down onto steel roofs.

The flow of the river became boggy because of the blood mixed with it. Before six in the evening, people would have already packed away and retired to their homes. There were aswang roaming around at night, announced the albularyo. Raidings also became more frequent. The other day, Ka Pedring's house had been broken into and all the rice stored in it was taken. Ka Pedring was accused of helping Apo's enemies. Even Intoy had ceased his taunting and his bad-mouthing when, on one afternoon, my friend witnessed his uncle gunned down by soldiers because his uncle had smitten a soldier who had brashly slaughtered and made a meal of his goat. Ka Pedring's daughter had also disappeared after the soldiers had intruded their home. Only a bloodied sanitary napkin was seen being fought over by stray dogs after the said abduction. After some nights searching for the girl, the whole town presumed that Ka Pedring had gone mad. The old man mimicked the gecko's clucking by the river while holding that one sanitary napkin.

It was almost a month before I next saw Father. We were awakened by the loud knocking at the door and by the dog's barking. Mother, who slept beside her scattered cards, and I were wakened at the same time. There were five soldiers waiting outside. They talked with Mother who seemed to have accepted a letter without writing. She told me to get up. We had not yet even changed clothes or gargled. We immediately rode the soldiers' jeep. The first rays of the sun had the color of blood. It appeared to be dusk, as though red flowers smeared the sky's light bulb. We passed by the river. Some were fishing for fish and crabs to be sold in the market. They seemed to be wearing black veils. The folded acacia leaves were fanned out.

It had not yet been half an hour when we arrived at the municipal. We entered a small room which smelled of pig shit. There was a body covered by a blanket which had the color of moss stuck on the stones I used to see on the river. The soldier swiftly took off the covering blanket and immediately went out and lit a crumpled cigarette stick from his pocket.

Father was the dead body. We recognized him instantly because of his amulet. Father looked like a butchered cow. The left side of his face was shattered, and fresh blood dripped from his nose, ears, and a crack on his skull—fragments of a broken bottle. I saw his penis sticking out of his mouth, the piece of flesh that proved to me he was not an aswang. It was as though in that part of him Father had stored his humanity, strength, anger, even his reasons to embrace, to keep quiet and to avoid sleeping with Mother, to convince me to be circumcised, and to his devotion to Santiago. It was like I felt Father's entire hardship when I saw his nearly shredded penis. And even though Father looked that way, Father's whole body seemed to become a magnet and I felt him drawing me closer.

27

I hugged Father as when he hugged me the night he held my penis. I did not mind the dripping blood which was dried up right away by the August breeze and which became a huge birthmark, a map on the skin. There was a bullet that had pierced through his amulet. It hit the open eye. Father's body was still warm when I embraced it until it cooled to that of the river's water. I looked around and when I made sure that those five soldiers who did not seem to mind were still outside, I slowly took out with much care and delicateness Father's dismembered penis from his mouth. It still bled and it seemed to have shrunk like the meat we had used as bait in the river when the fish were still just as large as my palms and not as large as carabaos. I looked at Father's penis and I remembered the dark orb which the aswang had to pass on before dying. I slowly put it in my mouth and swallowed Father's penis as soon as the rooster's crowing which I heard right after the gecko's clucking.

The first beams of the sun were blinding, melting. ◆

ASWANG

by Isabel D. Sebullen
Translated from Hiligaynon by John Bengan

Since I got here, P're, no one has dared to come near me. They're scared because they think I roast humans. Maybe, you've read the news about how I beheaded my grandfather and fed his chopped-up parts to a pig. That's why as long as I live, I'll stay locked up in this place. They say what I did isn't the deed of someone in his right mind.

Maybe you'll be surprised because I'm no ordinary person. I am the grandchild of an aswang. You're in luck because I'll tell my story only to you. P're, this is a story about the aswang. Not just any story at all. This is about the aswang but it's a better tale than Peque Gallaga's *In the Company of an Aswang*. You know, I watched that film because, after all, we're from Iloilo. Pure Ilonggo here, P're, from Dueñas. Yes, Teniente Gimo's hometown. You know, the notorious aswang? Many people from Iloilo became angry over why we should let Tagalog folks think that we here in Panay are all aswangs. You know the Tagalog, ignorant as always. They believe anything they hear.

Whether or not you believe, it's true that there is such a thing as an aswang. In fact, I'm the grandchild of one. Back then, I thought an aswang had long sharp teeth and could transform into a dog. But P're, it turned out the aswang doesn't partake of its own flesh and blood or prey on its neighbors. They said it's better to have an aswang for a neighbor than a thief. Because a thief doesn't choose who they steal from.

Perhaps you're ready to hear my story, no? Be patient, my man. I hope you have a strong stomach. You might lose what you had for dinner, P're, just like I threw up when I saw how Lolo Oka preyed on my younger sister. My body trembled. It's so hard to begin the story because I'll remember how I ended up here.

P're, my grandmother was one of the loveliest maidens in Dueñas. She was always the queen in our town. Not only was Lola Salome beautiful, she was smart. She was also the only daughter in her family. Lola Salome looked like Gloria Romero. If you see Lolo Oka, you'd think that they were not a match. Lolo Oka had large bulging eyes and dark skin. It's not like he was ugly, but he was out of her league. Back then they'd say Lolo used some kind of love potion with Lola. And also, my Lolo was rumored to be an aswang. As they used to say back in our place, perhaps there were a lot of men jealous of Lolo for being Lola's husband. They made up stories about Lolo's aswang lineage.

Lola Salome was about to finish her degree in education when Lolo eloped with her. And so, her parents had nothing left to do but marry them off. Lola had told me before that she didn't believe Lolo came from a family of aswangs. He was kind, she said, and very loving to his children, especially the women. Tatay Nilo, my father, was Lola's eldest son. I was their first grandchild.

Tiyay Soledad came after Tatay. They had a seven-year age gap. After Tiyay Soledad, there was Tiyay Regina. Afterward, Tiyay Milagros, and then Tiyay Carlota, the fifth child; the youngest was Tiyay Consuelo. My aunts had a three-year age gap between each of them.

My father was young when he got married. Only eighteen. You know how young they got married back then. Tiyay Soledad was only eleven when Tatay got himself a wife. Tatay then built a house next to Lolo Oka's.

Lolo Oka was a doting father to his children. He diligently bathed and washed his daughters since they were little. If you were a teacher, you'd have to bring work to your home. And so, Lola would let Lolo take care of the children because she didn't have the time.

Not to brag, P're, but my aunts were all beautiful. Especially Tiyay Consuelo. I was even older than her. Like Tatay, I'd reached a certain age when my younger sister Hermie was born. I was about nine years old. Many bachelors back then wanted to pursue Tiyay Soledad. But Lolo Oka always carried his talibong blade with him. And so, no man would go near Tiyay Soledad.

Tiyay Soledad was in her second year of high school when she got pregnant. What was troubling, P're, was that she wouldn't say who the father was. No matter how hard Lola beat her, she wouldn't say. Lolo had to intervene because Lola was almost about to kill our aunt. But there was nothing to be done about it anymore because Tiyay Soledad kept the father's identity a secret. Even Tatay Nilo couldn't believe that her boyfriend was able to sneak in on her under Lolo's constant watch. More stringent than the civil guards during the Spanish period.

Wait, P're, maybe you're wondering why the story seems not to be about the aswang anymore. Like in most stories, you have to know the main character better so you'd fully grasp my account. And so, how sad it was to have your daughter pregnant without a man to claim responsibility. Lola wept and wept because she never dreamed it would happen to Tiyay Soledad. Most of the folks in our place, they felt really sorry for Tiyay. She was a quiet and kind young woman.

Lolo's house was really big because Lola was an only daughter, and so she inherited the "big-house." Every single one of Lola's children had a room of their own. Maybe Tiyay Soledad's boyfriend had climbed into her window.

What was baffling was that she never told anyone who it was. Lolo acted as if nothing had happened. The child must be raised, he said, no problem with that. When Tiyay Soledad was pregnant, Lolo watched over her every night. He slept outside of Tiyay Soledad's room. He said that she might do something if no one would watch her. Sometimes, he slept inside the room.

Tiyay Soledad died while giving birth. She lost a lot of blood. She gave birth on her own, that was why. She didn't even call anyone to help her. It happened that Lolo was at the rice fields and Lola was at school. They were wondering why there wasn't any movement inside her room until the evening. It turns out she was dead. Her child, who would have been a boy, also died. Our house was just next to theirs since my younger siblings were still little. But many were confused why nobody made a sound. They said that maybe Tiyay Soledad intentionally didn't cry for help. It was like she'd committed suicide. The child looked like Lolo Oka. He too had bulging eyes.

Everyone was sad when Tiyay Soledad died carrying to her grave the secret of her son's father.

Everything changed after Tiyay Soledad passed away. Even Lola Salome was miserable all the time. She went on teaching to distract herself. She loved Tiyay Soledad dearly. There were rumors that an aswang had attacked Tiyay Soledad, that was why she died after giving birth. They spun so many tales.

We hadn't forgotten yet what happened to Tiyay Soledad when we found out that Tiyay Regina and Tiyay Milagros also got pregnant. Almost a two-month gap between them. Lola was furious over why her daughters just wouldn't tell them that they already wanted to get married. Lola Salome was angry at Lolo Oka for being too stringent a father that his daughters ended up pregnant. Like Tiyay Soledad, the two other daughters behaved as if they had shut their mouths and thrown the key away. Lola suddenly looked old. It was as though she couldn't handle what had happened. Tatay became angry with his sisters; he claimed that they hadn't been thinking at all before getting themselves pregnant. But the two would only cry, and everyone who saw their situation felt sorry. When asked who the fathers were, they could only express so much pain. Only Lolo was stopping Tatay from laying a hand on his sisters.

Since the two younger siblings became pregnant, I would often see Tatay walking around Lolo's house. Sometimes, Nanay got upset because he wasn't getting sleep anymore. Tatay was losing weight because, as they said, his two younger sisters had been shamed.

Tiyay Milagros decided to move to Manila. She wanted to give birth there and asked Lola to send her money. She would look for a job after giving birth. Tiyay Regina stayed behind. One day, Lola found her dead—she'd killed herself. She'd been pregnant for five months then. Tiyay Regina had drunk poison. Lola even found an unfinished letter that she wrote. She wanted to confess something but decided it would be better to just take her own life. Afterward, Lola Salome nearly went mad because her two daughters either died young or killed herself.

Tiyay Milagros didn't come home for Tiyay Regina's funeral. She didn't send a letter, even a short one. Tatay couldn't believe it because of all her younger siblings, Tiyay Regina doted on Tiyay Milagros the most. She was different among them. She had the courage to face the truth.

Lola stopped working as a school teacher. She did nothing but raise her two remaining daughters who were now growing into adolescence. Tiyay Carlota was about to turn thirteen because I'd already grown into a young man back then. My younger sibling Hermie, she was nine years old. She was older than Tatay's youngest sibling Tiyay Consuelo by three years. I, who was their nephew, was much older than my other aunts.

Tiyay Milagros returned home to take Tiyay Carlota so she could send her to school. Without telling her parents, Tiyay Milagros had married a well-to-do man. She gave away her child for adoption. She didn't want to remember. Lolo was so against the idea, P're, believing that something bad might happen to Tiyay Carlota in Manila. But Tiyay Milagros told him to leave them alone or else his monstrousness would be exposed. Tatay was surprised after hearing what his sister had said, so he came and talked to Tiyay Milagros before she left. I was also puzzled why after the siblings talked, Tatay and Lolo Oka frequently had spats. It was as though Tatay's respect for his father had disappeared. Tatay didn't want Lolo to go near my sister. He might just prey on her too. Tatay said he didn't want to inherit Lolo Oka's monstrousness.

Of all of Lola's children, Tiyay Consuelo was the most beautiful. That was why Lola Salome guarded her closely like Jawo. She would accompany Tiyay Consuelo in her room. That was why Tiyay Consuelo reached the age of eighteen without suffering the same fate that befell her older sisters.

One night, P're, Tiyay Consuelo's scream woke us up. Tatay jumped up and ran to help. I followed after him. Nanay and I were startled. We ran to the big house. There we saw Tiyay Consuelo crying. She then embraced Tatay. Lola was still asleep, as though she had taken something that knocked her out. In a corner, Lolo Oka stared out at us. He was sweaty and panting like a dog cornered. It dawned on me why Tiyay Milagros called Lolo an aswang. He'd tried to eat Tiyay Consuelo.

Tiyay Consuelo might have been traumatized because she stopped speaking altogether. Sometimes Tatay and I saw her murmuring and laughing to herself. She was terrified of Lolo Oka. Whenever she saw him, she would scream. I would often hear Nanay and Tatay talking. Many felt sorry when they found out that Tiyay Consuelo had gone mad. What a pity for Lola Salome's daughters. Virtuous and lovely, but ended up either pregnant or insane. Who wouldn't be ashamed?

If back then Lola's family had only our neighbors' admiration, now they were disdained. Many had long suspected that Lolo was an aswang. But those were hearsays and nobody could prove that he was indeed a monster. Even Tatay couldn't make Lolo confess to being an aswang. I had many unanswered questions, P're. What kind of aswang was Lolo? Why didn't Lola find out that he was an aswang? What was sad, P're, even my siblings were scared that Lolo would prey on them.

Tatay sent Hermie to Manila to study. She was admitted to the University of the Philippines and so I was happy for her. My sister was smart and she wanted to earn a degree. We wrote letters to each other and she told me that Tiyay Consuelo wasn't really a madwoman. She only pretended so she could be sent to Manila. Tiyay Carlota already had a job. She took a degree in psychology. Tiyay Consuelo took up medicine. I thought everything was normal again, P're, and the worst had already gone as far as our family was concerned.

We forgot about the tragedy because years passed before the most terrifying thing happened. Buday, our youngest, suddenly went missing. She was only five years old and often played near Lola's house. We were certain that the worst was behind us. But we ran about in panic when Buday went missing. Tatay carried his talibong blade and went looking in every corner. I remembered that maybe Lolo brought Buday with him to his hut and so I went there with my talibong.

P're, I had not vomited like that before. I nearly emptied my guts out. Because, P're, I never expected that Lolo was an aswang after all until I saw it with my own eyes. I saw blood slipping down Buday's little legs. My eyes blazed seeing what Lolo was doing to Buday. P're, he was making Buday suck on his penis. I didn't say anything, P're, and just struck Lolo with the blade.

That night, Nanay was surprised when I brought home some carved meat. I fed it to the pigs. They seemed to relish the meal. After dinner, I told my parents about what happened to Buday. I led Tatay to the hut where Buday's body lay. I wasn't able to help her,

P're. She was dying when I found her. What could a child do against an aswang with huge eyes. But I didn't hide Lolo's head. I wanted to show everyone that even if he was my grandfather, I didn't spare him because he was an aswang and a demon.

I am a good man, P're. I don't drink or smoke cigarettes. Tatay and I are the same in that we don't have vices. We took after Lola's ways and those of her family. And until I was brought here in Muntinlupa, I made Tatay swear he will never take after Lolo Oka the aswang.

My family had left Dueñas. They moved to Iloilo City. I have been here a long time in Munti, P're. I have accepted in my heart the court's decision. They said what I'd done to Lolo was far worse! Hermie would visit me, and also my aunts and their families. Perhaps, they haven't forgotten yet that they had been victims of the aswang.

Like I told you, P're, Lolo the aswang didn't have fangs. He didn't feast on human liver or drink blood. He didn't change into a pig or a dog. In truth, his eyes were large. Lolo was not the same as the aswangs in Peque Gallaga's movies. Lolo was an aswang of the flesh. ♦

RELAPSE

by Corazon Almerino
Translated from Cebuano by John Bengan

It returned while I was reading the documents. As before, I swallowed two aspirins.

It had been a year, exactly a year since it happened, the pain came back, again and again. Like fire snaking into the nerves of my head. Sometimes, it went away quickly. Other times, like the night before, the enemy was elusive. Whooshing. Ablaze.

Dodong was picking at his dinner of chicken adobo, mashed potatoes, and spinach salad. Then he sat beside me on the sofa; he wanted to sit on my lap. Soon he got away from my arms. He groped for the table, into the kitchen, and on the walls while tracing a path to our room. I arranged our home this way so that he would find it easy to navigate the deepest corner of his world.

Apart from using a crutch, he'd become skillful with his hands. To reach. To examine an object. To heed the expanse drifting before him. And whenever he lost patience, he'd hurl whatever he got his hands on. (Sometimes, he'd accidentally hit me in the face!) His ears, bless them, would prickle even just to the leaves rustling along the sidewalk of our apartment building. Because dodong was only two years old, he'd be terrified whenever his early-intervention teacher taught him how to feel the corners of our home, the different parts of his body, and even his toys. He'd burst into tears when we let him walk on sand and grass. He'd puke whenever others went near or held him. He'd hit his head on the wall when he couldn't hear my voice.

He walked into the room. I followed him. Lay beside him. Tucked him under the sheet.

"Goodnight, baby Jesus. Good night, Daddy. Goodnight, Mom," he rattled off lazily his goodnights.

He couldn't almost pronounce the words. Then he'd grope for my face and kiss me. "Goodnight, son. Daddy says goodnight, too. Sleep tight," I breathed. And I kissed him.

Dodong fell asleep immediately. I didn't have to hum a lullaby. He'd taken after his father even when asleep: he'd lean his right hand on his forehead. When he laughed his dimple would show like the lost twin of Boyet's dimple. Both of them hunched when they stood. Like the idlers sharing coconut wine by the street on our island in Santa Rosa. Both knock-kneed.

I tiptoed back to the living room. On the sofa. I curled up. It had been some time since I took my meds, the pain an obstruction. Had it been days? I had not seen the doctor in a long time. It had been a long time.

"Chona, por favor, ver a su doctor," my Mexican friend Consuelo had said to me. She had a similar condition. She often had head-aches, and her doctor told her it was migraine. But, as Consuelo said, migraines were like a riddle of rice and mango: arroz con mango. Mango and rice entwined. One couldn't settle where they began and ended. Consuelo told me there were many reasons why migraines recurred. Lack of sleep. Stress. A restless mind. Or perhaps grief that hardened.

The papers were a mess on the table in front of me. A heap. I picked up the letter from HUD, which said:

Section 8 assistance is available only to U.S. citizens, non-citizens with legal immigration status, and "mixed families" (families in which at least one, but not all members are U.S. citizens). Assistance to mixed families will be prorated. The same program rules and regulations for determining eligibility status for Section 8 rental assistance apply to everyone. To be eligible, the household must be either a family or a single person whose income does not exceed the area limits as set by HUD.

HUD establishes annual income limits by family size as:
Extremely Low Income = 30% of area median income
Very Low Income = 50% of area median income
Low Income = 80% of area median income

The rental subsidy that my social worker prepared had been approved, but our apartment wasn't included in the list for government subsidy.

Boyet's salary from last year was enough for the three of us. Sometimes we could barely make ends meet. I stopped teaching when I got pregnant. "This is sink or swim. We shouldn't get washed away," Boyet had said. We made the promise to endure after hearing the different stories of Filipinos who had been washed out by the currents of this land choking on fortune and wastefulness. A land in a rush, owned by only those in a hurry. Sometimes, a land of nightmares.

Boyet and I had settled in California for some time. We were the only married couple accepted among special education teachers that the American principal had interviewed in Cebu. A few had been hired: some were flung to New York, Maryland, Kansas, Texas, and here in California. We owed the agency that had flown us here a lot of money. We settled our debt—most of us—after three years.

When we arrived in Los Angeles, the agency put us in a large apartment in the cornermost part of the city, but we were placed in separate schools—some taught in Compton, in Inglewood, and then others in east Los Angeles. We were all crammed in one place, as though we lived at the back of Cogon, Ramos, but our neighbors were from Lorega. A tangled bunch. Quiet—then suddenly, gunshots. Houses and cars were pried open. The wailing of ambulance and patrol cars never ended. We crouched whenever there was a commotion, but I'd also slowly crawl to the window to peep outside. When the police had gone, the roads clear, we'd smirk.

Nothing could faze us: even if our neighbors would kill each other the whole week or our students would misbehave, there wasn't a Sunday when we didn't reek of barbecue smoke and stewed fish. Our laughter leaped from the windows, the cold breeze carried our karaoke songs and plunged them into the seas: washed and drowned under the waves.

Before long, we were separated. Most of us had been able to set out on our own. Boyet and I found another school downtown. It was also time to move out since we wanted to have a child. Every Wednesday morning, we visited the church to pray to the Virgin of Guadalupe. To ask for the fulfillment of our dream.

True enough, in April that year, I stopped getting my period. My mind was delirious. My body was like cracked earth where branches grew and stretched out. Boyet brought me to the hospital. After the blood and urine tests, the doctor made me lie down, and with his frightening technology, he peered into my womb, and said: There's a little being there. Four weeks old.

My tongue couldn't taste anything. My belly shrank in raw pain. I vomited. Turn off the lights! Turn off the TV! Throw away the beef steak! I had screamed at Boyet while I caught my face on the sink. In a few minutes, he stood behind me, stroking my back while I was wrapped in my own sweat. He guided me to the sofa. He made me drink water. He washed me. He tried to appease me, "It's only at the beginning, Day. The doctor said you won't feel much after the first trimester."

True enough, I felt much better during the second trimester. But, it came back. There were times like the other nights, after what had happened to Boyet, that I felt like I was having morning sickness again. All the noise around me was piercing. The lights on the ceiling could blind. I took out the ice from the fridge and put them all in the ice bag, which I rubbed hard against my temples and the tip of my skull. My thighs were numb. If only I could slice open my body to look for what was aching. And weed it out.

The letter from HUD said that there was a vacancy near Cesar Chavez that had been reserved for us. Maybe we could move there the next month. I didn't know what to bring, what to leave behind, what to keep, what to throw away. The old sofa, which was as old as the things that we'd bought when we first moved in at this apartment. The bed. The wind chime. Bonsai. TV. Table. Dodong's walker. Crib. Boyet's books. This home of ours had three rooms: the restroom, the bedroom, and the living room whose function often changed—living room now, a lawn during rainy season, dodong's playground, but when we had the specialists come over, it became a space only for him to live. The double-hung windows faced downtown Los Angeles; at night these became our telescope into the dance of lights against this city's sky.

Our apartment was a bit crammed. In a 1920 Art Deco building. Expensive because it stood between downtown and Beverly Hills. Our landlord was so hardworking. Every year he sent maintenance staff who would clean and repaint walls. White paint—maybe to mask the gloom, and to bury the remembrances of those who departed. We needed it for his school. I was the last one to sign.

Dodong was turning five in December. A little chubby one. As Boyet and I had been accustomed to, I prepared something for dodong's birthday. Enough for a few close friends.

Born at twenty-six weeks gestation, the report began. Dodong was only six months in my belly when the water that ensconced him ripped and streamed out. Christmas was approaching then. Happy Holidays: words painted in vibrant colors. Those words greeted the people who came in and out of the hospital. Boyet held my hand tight while we waited at the lobby. It had been two weeks since I gave birth to dodong. We had come from the Neonatal Intensive Care Unit, or NICU. We wanted to visit dodong; hoping that it was a peaceful night for him. But the monitor suddenly screamed. Boyet and I stared at each other. Then the doctors and nurses surrounded his Isolette. One of the nurses came to us. We were asked to leave. Intubation—was what I last heard that the doctor ordered.

The front yard of the hospital glittered with Christmas lights. The lobby was adorned with poinsettia, wreaths, and a giant Santa Claus. The nurse asked us to wait there because the waiting room next to the NICU was too crowded. The doctors would just come to us after they'd attended to dodong. I leaned on Boyet. I buried my face in his chest, and my mind slowly settled:

It had been at 1:19 a.m. on a Wednesday. The time I gave birth to dodong. Baby is out! I heard my child's shrill cry. In a minute, a satisfying feeling latched on to me. The nurse showed dodong to me nestled in his Isolette, I wasn't allowed even to caress his little finger. "Too frail even for a touch," Dr. Bates explained. They sent dodong straight to NICU, where they tended and treated premature babies.

Me—I was made to stay in a room I shared with another woman who had just given birth. Her child's cry bounced on the wall. I watched them both every early morning: her holding her baby, nursing, and the baby suckling. I only felt the heat of envy by then. I turned sideways. Hugged my pillow, recovered. I conditioned my mind like this: I was also holding dodong, breastfeeding, humming a song. I swayed him in my arms, danced as fast as I could until he cracked up for the first time.

However, out of nowhere the nursed walked into the room and interrupted my thoughts. She told me that a tube had just been inserted into dodong's mouth. Needles had just been inserted into his arms. Blood had just been transmitted.

The NICU was the place of battle. According to the doctors, a premature baby needs a strong heart. The infant has a lot of adversaries—sleep apnea, bradycardia, respiratory distress syndrome, hypotension, anemia, intracranial hemorrhage, retinopathy of prematurity. In the midst of this battle, a baby may survive. Some go home scarred for life. While others grow weak and just sleep for eternity. The Isolette replaces the womb that could no longer bear. But compared to the real womb, the Isolette has many limbs. Rubber tubes inserted into the baby's mouth, a substitute for the umbilical cord that tied the child to the mother's body. Tangled monitor cords. And other grotesque parts.

"I'm the only one to blame for what happened to dodong," I had stammered to Boyet. "My womb is thin and fragile." Boyet hugged me. "Don't blame yourself. Only God knows why all this is happening."

We prayed the rosary for an hour while waiting. True enough, the doctors came and took us to the conference room. In that room, they explained to us every single thing that was happening to dodong. "Bleeding in the head," began Dr. Bates, the head of the medical team. "Grade one. Typical of a severely premature baby. It will resolve by itself. Staph infection, too. Also typical. He's on a heavy load of antibiotics. That will take care of it." They reminded us of protential medical issues that dodong would have to cope with and that we need to keep our hearts strong. Boyet and I got up. "There's one more thing we would like to discuss with you." Dr. Bates gestured that we sit down again. "We checked his eyes, and the results didn't look good. The disease has severely affected the retina. We need to save whatever vision is left." At that moment, Boyet slumped. He bawled. My body numbed. My eyes had dried up. "Please, don't fall apart. You need to be strong for your son," the doctor said in closing.

Before we returned to the NICU, we dropped by the hospital chapel. We knelt before the image of the woman crowned with stars and rays of light while her feet stood on the moon. The Virgin of Guadalupe. Boyet couldn't stop crying. He prayed. At that moment, he was like a child who had been informed on to his mother. A child looking for a protector after being bullied by a playmate. For my part, I didn't pray. I faced the image with utmost indignation and regret. Whoever heaven listened to, Boyet's prayer or my anger, our goal of seeing dodong overcome after two months at NICU was accomplished. He came home with us with a healthy body, save for his eyes. He lost his vison completely.

Dodong was more than a year old when he started going to this school. There were four of them in the class. One of his classmates was Javier, Consuelo's son. This is where Consuelo and I met. Became friends. I was startled when I first met Consuelo. She looked like my mother reincarnated and younger. Her hair was black as crow. Her eyes were brown and sharp like Mama's. Her nose, pointed. Also, Consuelo was short. Compared to Mama, Consuelo had five children. Mama only had one.

The school used a different approach. There was a group of mothers. While the teacher taught the children, we the mothers would gather and express each of our thoughts and feelings. We just took turns sobbing. We wept from resentment—and the usual and investable question: Why my child?

Sometimes, when we were not overcome with anguish, our sharing was a mess of stories about food and illnesses, and immigration. Three crossed the Mexico–US border. Uncommon women. With strong knees. Crisp laughter even though their hearts were soaked in worry. Consuelo was the organizer of activities. Like the immigration protest the police dispersed.

This year—after a long time—our group didn't talk about husbands. I couldn't resist. I grasped for Boyet's name. Successively. Every time I mentioned Boyet, the group fell into an awkward silence, and suddenly one of them would talk about someone else's husband. "Este fuerte," Consuelo clutched my hands tightly the other day after telling me that I needed to sign the authorization letter for a psychological service the school was offering. Two other women from the group also urged me. Consuelo went out of her way to call my doctor's clinic about my headaches.

I might have taken after my mother. Scared of doctors. I remembered when I was still in college, Mama's nose bled while we were having dinner. She was coughing, too. She spat into the sink. She spat and spat. I brought her a glass of water. I saw the clumps of blood she'd spat out. I ran outside and asked help from neighbors. Noy Pitu looked for a tricycle. Nang Upeng and Basing boiled some herb for my mother to drink. The tricycle that would have taken her to the hospital arrived, but Mama refused. She said she preferred Ingko Teryo the healer over doctors. She told the neighbors to go back home and made a joke about the spirits of my father and our grandparents messing with her because she hadn't been visiting the cemetery.

The following day, as I got home from school, I walked in on Ingko Teryo going around our house, carrying a dead chicken, and he was twisting the bird's neck. Blood flowed and streaked on the soil where our house stood. My mother said it was Ingko Teryo's caution to the spirits and encantos who'd been offended. Mama even added to the ritual. She joined the Baliw-Baliw, a festivity that warded off disasters. Mocking death until death itself cowered away. Mama towed a piece of wood she'd dressed up in black. She lashed the wood with fronds. And then she tossed it into the sea. Get out of my body, you beast! Damn you! After you swallowed my husband, now you come for me! Mama's cursing of her enemies reached the sky. Death that snatched the life of my father, and which now wanted to grab hold of my mother at that time. I believed Death was frightened. I felt that my mother's exorcism of her enemies pierced to the bone. But a week after the festivity, my mother threw up blood. I brought her to the hospital. The next day, she never woke up.

———————

The authorization letter had been on the table for some time. Waiting for my signature. I felt a pang in my core while reading. My sweat wouldn't let up. The veins in my head seemed swollen. I need to see a clinical psychologist? Maybe he'd find in me what he was looking for right away. Maybe he'd needle me with questions about Boyet, invasive questions that would push me to the depths. Maybe I'd shrivel in front of him. Maybe in his assessment he'd say that I'd only imagined this pain in my head. Other people like clinical psychologists could easily pick up on grief that had congealed. They could easily spot a mind in disarray.

I got up to play a CD. What Boyet had recorded for dodong. These were stories he would read at night. He recorded his voice reading: dodong, this is the story of Dominic deer and Daddy deer, "Noises in the Night." One evening, Dominic deer was running home. It was getting late, and the woods were growing very dark. Dominic had never been alone in the dark before. All around him, Dominic heard scary noises. "Daddy!" yelled Dominic. "Daddy, where are you?"

Boyet had prepared everything: photos, songs, stories, his encouragements for dodong—all in his voice. He left behind only two songs for me. First was his footsteps inside the house—from the bedroom, the bathroom, to the living room. Second was his heartbeats.

It had been a year since it happened. It was February when he had successive fevers and chills. He kept vomiting. There was blood in his stool. His fever reached 103°F. I brought him to the emergency room. I placed dodong in a stroller, while Boyet hung on my shoulder. Boyet was in the hospital for three days. The laboratory tests piled on. He had a CT scan. He had a colonoscopy. He had an MRI. Ways to examine if the enemy that had taken the lives of my parents had also moved into his body.

I left dodong with Consuelo each day I visited Boyet. The day he was going to be released from the hospital, the doctor spoke to us. Everything looks good except the sigmoid colon. Boyet had a large tumor in that area, and in lower parts there were nodules. He had a biopsy. The doctor went on arranging treatment methods they prepared for him. Medication. Surgery. Radiation. Chemotherapy. Boyet leaned on me. Not a movement, not a sound.

I listened to the doctor, word for word. I held Boyet's hand, and let my mind drift to our hut where, for the first time, Boyet had stepped on our yard. Carrying a guitar. Singing. His voice accompanied by cicadas, the breeze, and furious waves. Mama lit the small lamp by the window, and said in jest, "Did you bring some coconut wine?" That was how our life together began. But, at that time in the hospital, the darkness had begun to come for us.

I told Boyet that we look for another doctor. Second opinion. Perhaps, we'd return to Cebu to seek treatment from Ingko Teryo's grandchild. Or ask for a miracle from the Virgin.

"We'll get a second opinion," I told the doctor openly. But Boyet disagreed, and nodded in consent that he'd start the treatment immediately. I stared at Boyet. I was hoping that he was listening to me. But he went on negotiating with the doctor. So, I shouted, "I want a second opinion!"

The enemy was impatient. He could bend even time, cut it into pieces, and slam it down. Boyet went in and out of the intensive care unit. Shriveled—his body eaten away by the enemy. His thick hair fell away from chemotherapy. According to the doctor, the chemotherapy "will harm even the healthy cells—those cells that normally divide quickly." His mouth was like soil taken over by drought. That sweet smile of my husband was still there, but his eyes drowned in fatigue, in worry.

One day, after taking dodong to school, Boyet called out to me from the bedroom. He wanted his diapers replaced. He'd soiled himself again. As I was wiping after my husband, he asked me for something.

"Help me," he said.

"What?"

"I don't want to leave like this. Help me," he pleaded. In the next month—while he could still talk, while he could still read dodong stories, while his whole body had not yet turned to rot—I'd help him go before the three months he had left to live.

My husband who, back on our island, had climbed to the top of our house to replace the roof Typhoon Ruping had blown away, had grown weak. My husband who was a devoted believer in God had had his faith stolen from him by the enemy. He'd counted the pills: 110. Pain reliever mixed with sleeping pills. Was it narcotic? High dosage, and should be taken only for bouts of so much pain. Help me, Chona. He repeated his appeal. I gathered my thoughts and my heart. But, I couldn't stop what had come out of my mouth: You will turn me into a criminal? Is that what you want? Boyet wept. He shrank. Screamed. Bled from his nose. I took him in my arms. Pulled him up to sit. I appeased him. And my voice turned soft.

"How can we do that?" I asked him. What he wanted was next month, October 20, in the evening, after I put dodong to sleep, I'd feed him the pills until there were none left. A hundred and ten pills, he said. As if these were food. A gulp of water would do the job. Not too much water in his stomach so he wouldn't throw up. I'd wait for him to shudder, shut my eyes until it was over. Then I'd sleep beside dodong. I'd pretend I only found him by then not breathing any-more. And I'd call the hospital, his doctor, tell them my husband wasn't breathing. He'd prepare everything including the codicil that would prevent authorities from doing an autopsy. I nodded. Then and there Boyet began to prepare what he'd leave behind for us. He'd arranged everything.

Weeks went by. Every day that passed, I searched for my husband in his ruined body. He was shitting blood again. Unceasing fever. In and out of the hospital. He was skin and bone. Pale. His eyes had sunk and deepened. More laboratory tests done, and the results showed that the disease had affected his liver, lungs, and kidneys. The air of death and life spun in my head. I wanted to stand by my husband in whatever way that was easy for him. There was no dig-nity, Boyet said, if this was how he was going to die. I too grew weak. But what came to my mind was my mother and others who were dying like her who fought with the enemy to the last day. Death does not belong to sickness, but instead it is life's, and only life, even in its cruelty, has the grace to offer each and every end. And beginning.

The day came. I had returned from taking dodong to school. Instead of going home, I went to the hospital. I met with Boyet's doctor. I told him about what Boyet had requested from me. I was shaking telling the story. My tears didn't dry up. I had promised to Boyet that I would keep it to the grave. But I thought of dodong the whole time. I would teach dodong to hold on to life even if there are times when life shoves him away.

The doctor helped me prepare the documents needed so that I could immediately receive respite caregivers who would monitor Boyet. Patient is high risk for suicide: the reason for asking the government for respite care. The caregivers arrived that afternoon. They had twelve-hour shifts.

We hid Boyet's pills, away from him. Everything that he could use for his purpose, including dodong. In that moment, Boyet had stopped talking to me no matter how much I tried to make him understand, how much I tried to appease him. He stared at me with his sunken eyes. Like I'd gravely offended him. Like he was rebuking me.

It took more than two months before Boyet passed away. A priest speared him with blessed water. Allowed him a confession. Offered him a holy mass.

At night, when the stars are out, we can't just rely on our eyes. We have to use our ears and noses to guide us, too. Boyet's voice echoed in the living room. Dodong came out of our room. Awakened.

"Mom, I'm thirsty," cried dodong. He hugged me. I put him on the sofa to wait, and I got a glass of water. He drank it, but still cried.

I rubbed his chest and his back. "It's all right, anak. We'll be all right."

I turned off the stereo. I carried dodong. I danced him around. Sang him a lullaby. Just like when he was a baby. He cried over anything he didn't understand, and I would respond to all of this with an embrace, a dance, a song.

We'd move in the next month. New place. I'd begin choosing what I should bring, what to leave, what to keep, and what to set free. ◆

THE THREE MAYORS OF HINABLAYAN

by Omar Khalid

Translated from Cebuano by John Bengan

Even if you open the documents at the National Library, the Library of Congress in America, the US Military Library, or if you search on Google, Multiply, Facebook, Wikipedia, the "trending" topics on Twitter at the time, or if you look at the familiar and traditional manner of a resident of Hinablayan now (still so offbeat and jocular in spite of what happened), there is no doubt, no arguing, that this story is true. At one point in time, we had three mayors—one lying down, one sitting, and one standing.

Every person who hears this story would swear and say *damn, maybe the screws in these people's heads have turned loose, is it even possible to have three mayors in one term? That's against the laws we abide by, so possibly this is hearsay; you won't read in Republic Acts, Executive Orders, or Presidential Decrees that a town can have three mayors lest you earn the wrath of Senator Miriam Santiago who's an authority when speaking about the law, as though she was just supping mung bean broth when citing the Constitution as she'd say: "da lo eskpresli probayds"* and others would then imitate the singsong Ilonggo accent of the brilliant senator.

Someone from College of Political Science at the University of San Carlos even wanted to study the phenomenon that took place in the city of Hinablayan but didn't push through because they'd been so stressed after finding out the research sponsor, a former president of the republic, had passed away (according to the story, said president and her chubby husband had been poisoned after they saw a healer on a hill in Kampawog, which was the headline that came out in *Banat* and *Superbalita*; they ate boiled lizard, the story goes, to treat their illness that the doctors in San Lukas Medical Center and Veteranarian's Memorial Medical Center couldn't cure despite the expertise in medicine of resident doctors in these hospitals) and this president was known for her "cuteness" after having done breast augmentation at Vivian's Beauty Salon.

There was talk that a senator wanted an investigation on the blunder, considering the Constitution's faultlessness after it had gone through several edits, refinements, amendments, since the time of Aguinaldo, Marcos, Tita Cory, and until her daughter Kris had gotten an STD and her son Noynoy and Shalani broke up . . . a small city still managed to elect three mayors at once. However, it was clear that the senator's concern didn't lie in our city's well-being but in his ambition to run for president in the coming year. He was so mad when the investigation didn't materialize because, sus, it would have been time for his star to rise *this was a time to show that the Senate was not to be taken lightly; it is an honorable and august body, there has to be an investigation on what happened in Hinablayan, in aid of legislation . . .*

Folks at the Guinness Book of World Records were even considering having an entry on our city in their latest edition, but they were too afraid to cause an uproar should they open a new category because other cities might follow suit just to break our record, and then all the cities in the Philippines would also have three mayors, heaven forbid, across the seven seas!

Our city became so famous because of what happened. All of its ugliness (like the notorious killings in the barrios of Butason, Manlawaan, and Ban-aw) had been momentarily eclipsed by our city's rare political situation.

The story goes like this:

After the election, the also-ran Poncing Sungsong filed a complaint against the mayor-elect Peping Ruto. Poncing wanted a recount of all the ballots. He couldn't believe he lost because he had given huge amounts to leaders of twenty-nine barrios. He even applied for a loan at the bank with his property as collateral, which included a coconut plantation, a cornfield that should have been harvested at the time, and his house, so long as he won the election because *aah, if we won, we would have recovered all expenses, how could we not recoup after spending on coffee, rum, noodles, and NFA rice just so people would attend our assemblies and miting de abanse; the people would have to understand; if running for president of the chapel organization or the PTA cost a lot, what more running for office in the city which is a big position; let's not be hypocritical, my friend ... let's see, let's see if there's anybody out there with a wide forehead who's prepared to say that he never gave anything?*

But Peping was unmoved by Poncing. He used all the influence he had. His son, who was famous for his large testicles and clout in Manila at that time (and rumored to have been the lover of a gay undersecretary owing to his nine-inch weapon, but they broke up eventually because the undersecretary had ringworm on his butt), had worked under the table with officials who could easily be bribed. The teachers who worked during the election were paid to testify that Peping's votes were legitimate and weren't the handiwork of certain assiduous individuals. That the mandate given to him was the voice of the people of Hinablayan, and therefore, the voice of God.

This was why the recount lasted for two years because every ballot was contested by each side, attended by their respective supporters. They rehearsed each syllable to make it sound like the name of their candidate. They lifted every ballot to the sun just as bettors of the numbers game "last two" looked for tips in the egg of a huntsman spider. Even Peping's nickname "squid" and Poncing's "rice pot" had been included in the acrimony. Both their lawyers kept showing off expertise in their skills in election law along with rowdy supporters *fight, Attorney, show them the law school where you graduated is the best of them all* where the core of their arguments were very pointed words but only ended in murmurs *that's what happens when you join fraternities, Attorney, you were not able to study well the SCRA and the jurisprudence about electoral protests.*

Someone from the Commission on Elections said that pet names, nicknames, and middle names could be counted so long as these were declared in the certificate of candidacy. Chaos ensued whenever they read a ballot that bore similar sounding names or types of squid (such as pusit, tamala, tabugok, kumubutan, buko-buko) since they would have to count whether those were votes for Peping. Then there was one ballot that was so difficult to read since evidently the hand which wrote it had been spasmodic, but to the delight of Peping's loyalists, if you squinted, you'd read the word "bukya"—jellyfish. Peping's people roared in excitement since jelly-fish, they claimed, was akin to squid, therefore it was a vote for Peping. But Poncing's group disputed the claim, stating that jellyfish didn't belong to the squid family. Immediately, they called the Bureau of Fisheries and Aquatic Resources and Mr. Zac Sarian, editor of the *Agriculture Magazine*, to provide their opinions on whether squid and jellyfish come from the same evolutionary origin. They also inquired whether various pots and jars such as tadyaw, anglit, and banga belonged in the same family as rice pots to prove that such entries in the ballot could be counted as votes for Poncing. But they said it depended on the kind of rice pot—some were made from metal, others were made from clay.

The backers of each side were likewise emboldened and so pleased because each time there was something to follow up at the Commission on Elections in Intramuros regarding the recount, they also showed up because they wanted to express that *our candidate isn't alone in this fight to end corruption and injustice in our beloved town of Hinablayan; we are ready to risk our lives because we don't want frauds to prevail in our city.* Of course, they would receive hundreds of pesos for their families and so they were happy about what was hap-pening. The managements of Philtranco and Eaglestar were happy because supporters filled their buses going to Manila, many of them even booking in advance.

When the recount was nearly done, a big twist came about. Peping's blood pressure rose when the Commission on Elections was about to announce the results. Since it was becoming obvious that his chances were getting slimmer, he suddenly fell over. According to his personal nurse (also known as his girlfriend since they'd been seen feeding each other buy-one-take-one burgers), the blood pressure apparatus nearly broke because of Peping's 230/190 BP reading. It was a shame since he'd been comfortably hanging around his seat at the Office of the Mayor in the city hall and then suddenly he'd be forced to pack his things up. And so, he was really dead.

Poncing was overcome with joy since nothing stood between him and the Mayor's Office anymore. Oh, he said, even if the recount need not be concluded, he would still be declared mayor since his number-one opponent was dead. All the animals being sold at the night market in Baginbin—chicken, goat, cow, carabao, duck, guinea, turkey—he purchased; grilled, butchered, stewed, made into bas-oy, pakdol, paklay, and kaldereta dishes. And the biggest party took place in our city, which hadn't seen such a celebration before.

The people panted from having been stuffed and the others dipped themselves in puddles and rolled bottles over their stomachs so they'd be able to digest, since the fuckers couldn't anymore breathe, you could crush a louse on their bellies; if you snapped your finger on them, you'd know how tightly wound those guts were!

Poncing invited foreign media companies such as CNN, Fox News, the BBC, *The New Yorker*, *The Atlantic Monthly*, even political bloggers, not to mention the attendees from ABS-CBN, GMA, TV5, NBN, IBC, the *Manila Bulletin*, the *Philippine Daily Inquirer*, and the *Philippine Star*, so that his first day in office was indeed a grand one.

Early in the morning the following day, twenty beauticians led by Dr. Vicky Belo and Dr. Manny Calayan surrounded Poncing. Before they began with the "total makeover," they softened the grime around Poncing's neck with chlorinated water. Then, they scraped Poncing's aged face riddled with blackheads and pockmarks, made him drink a lot of glutathione so his dark skin would glow a little since, they said, he took after Vice President Binay; they put a wig over his sparse hair, which at closer view looked like large strands of a boar's hair. Poncing looked so dashing after, since he'd prepared for the event, and wore a Pitoy Moreno suit—the very suit believed to have secured for Pitoy Moreno, without additional patrons, his induction into the Order of National Artists.

The road going to and from Poncing's large house was lined with streamers made from sackcloth, cement sack, rice sack, pollard sack, copra sack ... emblazoned with congratulatory messages and compliments from Lalok's Ukay-Ukay, BLAMCI Cooperative, Fuso Funeral Homes, Inday Taratitat's Seven-Seven Herbal Tea, Jun & Judy's Furniture, Olong's Original Tandok, along with many balloons that stuck out and unfurled Poncing's victory.

Poncing's convoy (comprised of all the trucks he owned for loading copra, tractors spattered in mud after having gone from his vast cornfield in Samrak, habal-habal motorcycles and sikad-sikad that he hired for his grand first day of work) came out into the dewy air and the early morning, accompanied by the roar of his rejoicing supporters.

However, when the convey was near the city hall, the cheers subsided. Vice-Mayor Litoy Duhaylungsod's men blocked them from entering *the new mayor didn't want to be disturbed, he won't accept guests because he has a lot of documents to sign since these have been neglected by the late Mayor Peping.* Litoy had discreetly made his move at midnight of the previous day, filing a report to the Office of the Mayor by virtue of succession, he claimed, and even if you open the laws and manuals of the Department of Interior and Local Government, the Supreme Court Annotated, Presidential Decrees, or perhaps Executive Orders, being Peping's vice-mayor he would be next in line for the mayoral seat *why won't I report, after all I'm the vice-mayor, and there is a vacancy in the mayor's office.*

Poncing's dandruff flared up in his anger, he stepped down from the tractor, planted both hands on his waist like an average hoodlum who'd just sniffed solvent, faced Litoy's men, and as though he'd forgotten he'd spruced himself up that day and spent so much money on his stylists and it would end up that he'd only start a fistfight with men who hadn't even taken a wash yet *are you for real? Has Litoy lost his bearings this time? I was the one who filed a petition to the Commission on Elections and now that Peping is lying in state, I am definitely the mayor now! So tell your boss that the real mayor has come to claim the office! He must vacate the mayor's seat at once so as not to further affect the function of the Office of the Mayor!* But Litoy's loyalists didn't allow the convoy to pass lest they get fired for going against the mayor's orders, especially since now a job was so damn hard to find!

So the convoy had to stop at Nang Baray's dried fish store. And even before seven in the morning, the howling of his loyalists was deafening when Poncing declared that Nang Baray's store would be the official but temporary Office of the Mayor of Hinablayan, and also that Litoy was a fake mayor.

Since that day, a great confusion spread over our city. We didn't know where to entrust our fate and direction of our future since the Department of Interior and Local Government also washed their hands of responsibility, citing that they were also awaiting the opinion of the Supreme Court about the leadership crisis in our city. It happened that the judiciary itself also had the befuddling dilemma of which Chief Justice to recognize (most of the members of the Integrated Bar of the Philippines opposed the President's appointee since their convention did not recommend said person since he was allegedly a "midnight appointee" of the previous administration), thereby delaying their capacity to tender a legal comment on the rare case of interpreting the provision in Local Government Code of 1991. The police also absolved themselves, claiming that they served the national government, and so they didn't intervene in the matter.

Peping's relatives also groused because the mayor had not even been buried and yet people were already fighting over his seat *such crassness! The entire city is still mourning, and the flag should be at half-mast in respect for the departed mayor but the fools, already wrestling over the position? Can't they wait for higher authority to designate the next mayor? Ahh, we won't bury Mayor Peping anymore until we arrive at a resolution to this mess because before he died, he dreamed of order and stability in Hinablayan.*

And because Litoy stood firm on his principles, he didn't vacate his seat as mayor at the city hall even if he heard many threats coming from Poncing's camp. An insider said that Poncing hired the remaining members of the Kuratong Baleleng gang, the ones who hadn't been rubbed out, to liquidate Litoy. But Litoy wasn't afraid at all. He supposedly employed guns-for-hire notorious for high-profile crimes in Cebu and Manila, and was believed to have ties with criminals in Afghanistan and Pakistan.

However, these rumors remained so. It seemed that these were merely black propaganda coming from both parties. Jesus, how could they afford these first-rate criminals when their supporters had gone white-eyed from hunger after subsisting on gruel down their respective queues. All they got from the politician they favored were promises *go ahead, just keep supporting me because when the day comes when all this is resolved, I will give you jobs: as street sweeper, miner, marketplace collector, parking boy, messenger, the mayor's massage therapist, the mayor's bodyguard . . .*

Someone also said that Litoy had sent for a urinal pan to his office so that he could take a dump and piss in there because he was afraid of getting distracted and that someone would steal his seat.

Those applying for a mayor's permit didn't know which office to enter. When someone from Hinablayan won the Miss Universe Beauty Pageant, she made a "courtesy call" at Peping's wake because the dead man had helped her a lot when she was still doing modeling gigs to work in Japan. But when Julio "Dinamita" Montane clinched the flyweight division (trained by no less than Freddie Roach and divined as the one who shall follow in Manny Pacquiao's footsteps), he made his "courtesy call" to Poncing. Meanwhile, when the Hinablayan dragon boat team were about to leave for Tajikistan to compete in the qualifying round for the next Olympics, they went to Litoy to ask for fare subsidy.

Months passed, Poncing's people slowly retreated when they noticed that he'd rarely been giving them money. The bank also asked Poncing to settle his loan, and if he didn't, they'd seize his properties. When he was unable to pay rent for Nang Baray's space, the old woman asked him to leave since *your unpaid lease has gotten bigger, Cing, it would be better if you leave; I'll just go back to selling dried fish, dammitz . . . just gradually pay what you owe me because I let your people get dried fish on credit since you promised you'd pay when you return to city hall; I don't know, it looks like there's no more chance, Cing, that you'll get the position, uy!*

Not long after, the bank confiscated Poncing's house and land and he had nowhere to go so he was often seen standing in front of the city hall, sighing and tsk-tsking at the luck he'd drawn with the supporters he still had: his wife and children. As for Litoy, he never left the city hall fearing that someone would steal his position, gone pale after staying away from the sun for so long, and said to have been afflicted with beriberi after not exercising. Meanwhile, his family had yet to bury Peping, frozen stiff inside a refrigerated casket.

The stalemate in our city lasted for several years. We had three mayors—one lying down, one sitting, and one standing.

Until the people's ire rose. We couldn't bear anymore the city's lack of direction. We couldn't endure the ridicule coming from other places. One day, and I don't know whatever insect we'd eaten, everybody gathered at the plaza because we remembered the history of EDSA where the people's voice was heeded.

The flurry of the crowd was like a super typhoon suddenly romping into city hall. We ransacked the different offices like escapees in a mental hospital. Litoy lurched when we ganged upon him for his seat, and he tumbled and landed face-first on his urinal.

And in front of the city hall, we set fire to the mayor's seat—the seat that caused our problems—the seat that caused the division of people into three factions—the seat only made from wood that had caused such disquiet and chaos ...

When the fire died down, leaving behind some ash, a nurturing stillness engulfed the city—a kind of stillness and calm that we hadn't seen for a long time—a gentle calm that our souls had been longing for. And we saw the mound of ash on the ground slowly being lifted away by the wind into the end of dusk. ♦

VOICE TAPE

by Ariel Sotelo Tabág

Translated from Ilocano
by Amado Anthony G. Mendoza III and Ariel Sotelo Tabág

I felt eighteen years younger the last time I took a vacation in my hometown in Santa Teresita, Cagayan—back to the years when something "happened" to Uncle Ato; when Nanang and I were searching for my Best in Math certificate in elementary and high school in order to bump up my rank and salary as a public school teacher in Cubao. And of course, as in all frenetic searches, we found "something different."

Nanang told me that she put the certificates in a slim messenger bag with "LA"—Tatang's favorite cigarette brand when he was still a chain-smoker—neatly engraved on its lower right side. She had had no choice. The attic in our small house was already full of certificates I got from the writing competitions I had joined and won. We unzipped the bag, the bag we got while exchanging the many cigarette packs Tatang had smoked, but we didn't find the certificates.

It turns out that Nanang had rolled them into a bamboo tube flask where our birth certificates—us three siblings—were also stored. (There were actually four tubes because Tatang and Nanang thought that there would be four of us. But because raising four kids would be difficult, Tatang asked Nanang to have herself ligated when they were in Aparri.)

But what Nanang and I first found was the worn-down bag located under the dresser. It was so worn down that Tatang and Nanang put it away in a room downstairs, in the kitchen, where Tatang stores most of his stuff like bolos, sickles, an assortment of seeds (corn), and his tikbalang sculpture made out of the wood of the santol tree (I always believed that he got his penchant for artistry from his readings of *Bannawag* magazine). And yes, the height of Tatang's magazine collection far exceeded that of a human.

There was an assortment of things in the dresser: old photos of, mostly, Nanang's dead relatives, old clothes, a silverware and china collection that was only used whenever a vote-buying politician paid a visit to our house, and some of our old test papers in elementary with full marks.

But what was this "other thing"?

It was a voice tape, with a dedication "4 my one & onli lab ATO," which Nanang found under the pillow of Uncle Ato, her younger brother. The voice tape was dated February 16, 1992, the day he got ran over by a bus and died.

I was already on my way to school at that time. In fact, I was at the sidewalk, in front of Pook Tactac where our house and the twenty-hectare yard of St. Francis Academy, the high school I went to, are located. I was already in my second year in high school, that's why I had the guts to go in late often. Just like that time I decided to hide myself behind a mango tree since the flag ceremony hadn't begun.

That's when something seemed to have screeched and crashed out west. It sounded like two bulls locking horns but ten times louder. Shortly after, students and other bystanders started screaming—some of them were probably on their way to the public market since it was a Tuesday—rushing toward the front of a vacant and swampy lot where we used to gather watercress leaves. They all formed a huddle in front of a Manny Trans bus.

"My goodness! He's been run over!" screamed an old woman who sounded like Ms. Usita, my former teacher, who used to live beside the vacant lot. She had this knack of noticing everything that was happening in our neighborhood, and because of that, people regarded her with contempt.

"He's dead! He's already dead!"

I had a hunch. I was a bit surprised because it was the first time I had had that kind of hunch. It was really strange. I didn't have or feel this hunch when Nanang often cried because Uncle Ceferino, second to the youngest among her six siblings, was allegedly taken away by the NPA; or when Tatang wept for the death of our one and only carabao who drowned during a storm in 1989.

My goodness! Could it be my friend Boying? My heart wept for a bit, wept for Boying who often went to school late like me and who really liked to loiter at our school's other gate, a stone's throw away from the place where the accident had taken place. Could it be that in his rush to escape our school principal Sister Caridad's gaze, he ran off without noticing the speeding Manny Trans bus? Perhaps. But thank goodness it wasn't Boying.

ULIRÁT

I immediately ran back to our house, instead of joining the huddle, and saw Nanang cleaning the floors.

Despite my panting caused by both fear and exhaustion, I told her, "Nanang, someone got ran over by a bus! It seems to be ... seems to be ... "

Mother didn't ask me for more details. My palpable fear was enough for her. Without hesitating one bit and even forgetting to wear slippers and tie her hair, Nanang ran outside.

I immediately followed suit despite the nagging feeling of unease and restlessness.

I wished it had been the bastard Kalbo, the CAFGU officer who beat up and almost shot Uncle Mulong (Nanang's youngest sibling). Uncle Mulong was a good man. After his fishing trips, he used to give us shrimps—big as the thumb on my foot—that I really loved, luno and samaral the size of Tatang's palms.

Nanang immediately let out a loud shriek and started weeping when she reached the huddle. When I reached the huddle, people were already trying to placate and pacify her. She was screaming so loudly that the only words I could make out were, "Oh Lord! Oh Lord!"

I was terrified with what I saw.

Now I was sure that it wasn't Boying who got ran over. Nanang would not react the way she did if it were only him.

But who was it? Was it Tatang? But I was quite sure it wasn't him. He was sure to be busy bathing and letting his carabao drink in the river, and he wouldn't pass the national highway since he had already sold his bicycle in order to pay for Nanang's medical expenses when she had accidentally stepped on a shard of glass while chasing the hen that was supposed to be butchered for Tatang's birthday.

My siblings were also out of the equation since they were already at school when the accident happened.

It was Uncle Ato. And as if I had accidentally bumped into an elemental being, I was able to clearly hear Nanang's guttural cries, "My brother! Ato! My brother! Ato!"

Even now when Uncle Ato has long been buried, I'm still terrified by the memory of my Nanang's incessant cries.

It was almost two in the afternoon when the funeral car parked in front of the lot of Nanang's relatives in Palor. The surname of Nanang's father is Sotelo. He came from Santo Domingo, Ilocos Sur, and was able to marry someone from the Palor clan.

Uncle Ato's shiny coffin was ushered into the living room by a chorus of weeping. But Nanang's was the loudest among them. Tatang even had to pull her away from the casket as she was already causing a scene.

Uncle Mulong also asked the visitors who were playing cards to clear the table. The nerve! They even got there before Uncle Ato's coffin. (To this day, our village still serves as the stomping grounds for gamblers.)

"Save the gambling for later. We have yet to set things up." That was Uncle Mulong, in an unusually deep tone, telling off our shameless visitors who had come from God knows where.

Now, what happened next still baffles to this day. After we placed Uncle Ato's coffin in the living room, people started talking to Nanang. It turns out, the shiny coffin (which cost ten thousand pesos) was the wrong coffin. We had to return the coffin. The people from the funeral parlor inspected Uncle Ato's body once more, covered it with a white blanket, and carried it out of the coffin.

"You didn't even look after him!" It was Tatang, reprimanding his nephews for something they weren't able to account for. We had no choice. We had to lay Uncle Ato's body on a sofa and drape it with an Inabel blanket (a gift from Nanang for his wedding).

———————

Because Uncle Alfredo, the eldest among the siblings, drives a 6x6 truck (for logging) to Aurora (at that time, I didn't know where in the world it was), while their youngest sister was with her husband in Ilocos, and Uncle Ceferino was taken by NPA insurgents while Uncle Mulong can't read and write, it was Nanang who took charge and pressed charges against Manny Trans. She was also the one who informed Uncle Ato's wife (who was in Aparri during the accident) of her husband's death.

The relatives of Uncle Ato's wife also came. They even wept with us at the beck and call of our aunts and uncles.

Since I was the eldest among us cousins, I was the one tasked to look after Uncle Ato in the living room. For company, I had with me four lighted candles and a platoon of insects trying to smuggle themselves inside through the windowsill.

It was cold that day. Nightfall was slowly approaching. I remember how my jaws and thighs started to stiffen because I was shaking ceaselessly. I couldn't even stand to look at or watch the comings and goings of my relatives and visitors, the noisy chattering of gamblers, the bonfire, the old mango tree outside near Nanang's almost run-down house, and the setting of the sun. I was scared of Uncle Ato's ghost appearing from behind, of not knowing how to escape if it did, indeed, happen.

That's why I forced myself to face Uncle Ato's body which was covered by a blanket. I couldn't stare at his head for long because I recalled Lilong Martin's story about how he scooped up Uncle Ato's crushed brains from the pavement and put it in a small dipper. And now that I was recalling things like these, I couldn't avoid but feel my stomach turning.

I apologized to Uncle Ato for choosing to fix my gaze at his lower body. What he had between his thighs was way more plump than the small upo vegetable of my grandmother (Tatang's mother) that I used as a toy to stroke and caress my uncircumcised penis. It was Lilong Martin, who also happened to double as our village doctor, who told me that I have to play with my penis if I want it to get bigger. Though I doubted his advice, I nevertheless tried it when I was alone in the house. I should've known better. It didn't work, and it's probably the reason why my penis didn't grow past five inches.

Why was I thinking of such things in the dead and cold of the night? Maybe it was in order for my shivering to stop. Or perhaps I was just as shameless as the gamblers outside.

After recalling my lascivious encounter with the upo vegetable, I started to recall similar and related memories. I, for instance, recalled seeing Uncle Ato and his wife having sex in our house, which was under construction at the time. I was five years old at the time, and Nanang asked me to get a hammer. That's when I saw them doing the deed.

I saw them totally naked on the second floor of our house. They were in a position similar to those one sees in the pages of *Playboy*— the magazine often passed around by Uncle Mulong and his friends.

Now I, who grew up with *Bannawag*, also tried to flip its pages. And since then, the position of Uncle Ato and his wife and *Playboy* magazine has remained etched in my memory.

Nanang arrived by nightfall. She went straight to the living room and started to sing-chant a dung-aw:

My goodness, Ato, my brother so good and kindhearted
Why did you leave us without bidding farewell
Who will look after your children?
Your wife can't go home because she's working in Abu Dhabi

"Can't go home?" I heard someone from downstairs.

"She just got there," answered one of the visitors, which was immediately followed and drowned out by a chorus of laughter and screams from the table of gamblers.

I was close to tearing up. I went down and asked my Uncle Mulong to buy me soft drinks because I felt like vomiting.

Unlike my Uncle Alfredo and Uncle Mulong, I can't recall my Uncle Ato ever giving me money. In fact, he was the one asking me for favors. If I'm not mistaken, two weeks after his wife went to work abroad, he approached me while I was reviewing for my second periodical examinations and gently asked, "Dante, let's write your aunt a letter."

"Us," he said, which meant he'd be dictating what I was to write. Nanang saw her brother approach me. She just nodded at me as if to say that I relent to her brother's request. And while I was a bit bummed since I was reviewing for Filipino and English, two subjects I consider my Waterloo, but I had no other recourse. And to make me feel more guilty, I also noticed that Uncle Ato had just come from the farm: he reeked of sweat, wore a sleeved shirt, had his bolo on his waist, and his rattan knapsack on his back.

"Okay, Uncle," I answered begrudgingly.

I was about to tear a page from my Aspen notebook which had Robin Padilla as its cover, but he stopped me. He smiled at me and shyly brought out a new ream of paper from his knapsack.

If only I was able to keep a copy of Uncle Ato's letters. If he wrote in the present, I would've been able to save them in a computer. But during that time, we immediately sent what we were able to compose. If I remembered it right, Uncle Ato's first letter was more or less like this:

Dear Love,

How are you doing? Didn't you feel dizzy when you rode the bus and plane? How's your boss? Is he any good? He better be good or he'll get what he deserves.

How's the food there? Are you eating well? If you can't take it anymore, just go home. I won't mind. We can still make it here.

Take care of yourself. Don't worry about the kids, your boys. They can already cook rice, look over our farm animals, and clean the house. Inang (Uncle Ato's mother-in-law) wants Princess to live with them. But we have talked about this, right? That I'd be both their father and mother while you're away. It is only Princess who makes me miss you less. At each passing day, I see a bit of you in her face and in her ways.

*Don't you worry too much about sending us money immedi-
ately. Ate's helping us with our everyday needs.*

Your love that always longs for you,
Ato

P.S.
*Dante wrote this letter for me so you'd be able to read and under-
stand it better.*

I was the one who suggested we write a postscript, thinking that in
doing so, Uncle Ato's wife would buy me something as a form of
reward.

If I'm not mistaken, we were able to compose and send three
letters. All of them were brief, just like the way he talked—full of
brevity. And high-pitched as well. It didn't suit his body that was as
burly and muscular as that of Roland Dantes. They really resembled
each other, with the only difference being that Uncle Ato didn't
sport a moustache.

That voice of his was able to soften (for a moment) his sporadic
bursts of violent threats. One particular instance was when his carabao was stolen by cattle rustlers.

"I could kill someone right now," bellowed Uncle Ato in his
high-pitched voice. He didn't say anything more after that. Tatang
and Nanang were taken aback. It was rare for them to see Uncle Ato
speaking like he did. Good thing Uncle Mulong was there to break
the rising tension.

But after a few moments of silence, Uncle Ato once again spoke:
"Lend me some money. I'm going to drop by Ilocos for a day or two."

One day, Uncle Ato surprised us when he came rushing to our house after he arrived from Santo Domingo, Ilocos, where the relatives of his wife's father lived. He quickly ordered us to close all the windows and doors even though it was only three in the afternoon. He didn't answer when Nanang asked him why. After acceding to his request, as if digging for gold or hauling out vegetables or fruits that he stole from the neighbor's backyard, Uncle Ato brought out a gun from his knapsack. I immediately noticed the gun's pale yellowish color, similar to those that I've seen in Betamax movies.

"You're out of your mind, Ato. Think about your children," said Nanang who was already in tears.

"I'm going to pay for this with rice grains from our cousin," Uncle Ato curtly replied while holstering the gun on his waist. Without a word to anyone, he quickly went outside again.

It was great news for us when we heard that he did not use the gun to start fights. It was only to intimidate and scare off potential enemies. A few months after he was buried, Uncle Mulong told us that the gun was already jammed and rusty when Uncle Ato got it.

The bad news for him and for us though was his alleged beef against a CHDF officer. According to rumors, Uncle Ato did the officer in because the latter would often start fights or punch someone when the former got drunk.

One of the frequent victims of the said CHDF officer was Uncle Mulong who, at the time, was also turning out to be a miserable drunk.

One night, the said CHDF officer got so drunk. On his way back to their headquarters, he encountered Uncle Ato in a very narrow passage. No one knows what and how it happened. Rumors just started to spread that someone from the CHDF had died. He was reported missing in action by his colleagues. Uncle Ato would later admit to his crime to Uncle Mulong. Later on, some years after his death, Uncle Mulong told Nanang and the rest of the family the whole story.

———————

Uncle Ato married young. He was only eighteen years old when he asked for Nanang's blessing.

"I'm going to get married."

"Do you have anything saved up?" asked Nanang.

"Even ants can survive these times."

According to Nanang, Uncle Ato only got married because he was already fed up playing the peacemaker whenever Uncle Alfredo and Uncle Mulong got into nasty fights. Most of their rows were caused by Uncle Mulong trying to challenge and/or usurp Uncle Alfredo's authority as the eldest son. Or, if we're going with Nanang's analysis, it's because Uncle Mulong already started to drink and smoke heavily like Uncle Alfredo.

All the siblings and some relatives helped make Uncle Ato's wedding possible. One can say that the wedding was a bit lavish: a sound system was rented for the eve and the day of the wedding, a number of local town officials also served as principal sponsors, they were also showered with presents, and as is the custom in provinces, there were pigeons to represent the newlyweds' (Renato and Magdalena) pure and everlasting love. Rice grains and coins were also thrown at them as they were entering the family house of Nanang.

After a few months living in the family house, Uncle Ato asked permission to build a house in the lot nearby, a few blocks to the east.

"We won't stay for long. We'll move to our own place soon," said Uncle Ato.

"Among your brothers, he's the most decent," Tatang jokingly told Nanang during the night.

The following morning, Nanang and I went to the site where Uncle Ato's house was to be constructed. Lilong Illo the carpenter arrived with my uncles shortly after. After discussing specifics, they started digging up a pit where they could install the house's foundations. They threw coins at the hole. Afterward, they also put a drop of gin and white-feathered chicken's blood on its foundations.

"So that they lead a good and comfortable life," answered Nanang when I asked her about the ritual. They had also done the same when they built their own house.

It was also morning when Uncle Ato and his wife moved to their new house. The house wasn't that big. It was the size of the stone houses you see in grade one textbooks. All the windows were installed facing the east in order to attract good luck and blessings. They also made sure that the door at the entrance did not face the door going to the kitchen.

"It will last long," said Tatang, commenting on the materials used to build the house.

———

Uncle Ato first bought a large jar for rice, one huge earthenware for water, one jar each of shrimp paste and salt, and the photo of Sagrada Familia which Nanang tore from our old calendar. Nanang made me hold a huge pot of coins. After putting it down, I filched one golden coin from the pot, which I had to return immediately since I saw my Uncle Ato watching me from behind.

They made their offerings in the living room. They also asked Aling Baling to offer prayers for them. After the housewarming ceremonies, we had our fill of rice cakes and rice coffee.

But what would you expect from someone who only managed to graduate from primary school? We were at the tail end of the 1980s, a period when getting a job required a numerous amount of qualifications and certificates.

They led a very poor life or, as the elders were wont to say, a hand-to-mouth existence. Uncle Ato inherited a small patch of land which yielded just enough to feed him and his wife.

Uncle Ato's wife, on the other hand, was another story. She was, to say the least, a handful. While it's true the she came from the village, her finnicky and pompous ways reached the city. I heard she got it when she worked as househelp in Manila. The problem with that, of course, was that her means (and their house) couldn't keep up with her whims.

That was also a time when going abroad for work became a craze in our village because a husband-and-wife tandem who used to work in Abu Dhabi became recruiters. From what I recall, it became really easy for people to go to Abu Dhabi because of them. People from our village went to Abu Dhabi in waves. The placement fee was relatively cheap. An interested family would only have to sell one or two carabaos in order to pay for the said fee.

One day, coming home from school, I heard Uncle Ato asking Nanang where he could pawn his small farmland—in addition to the female carabao he already sold—in order to pay for his wife's placement fee. After having sorted out everything, Uncle Ato's wife was finally able to go abroad.

Up to this day, I'm still grateful that I have yet to again experience something similar to what I went through during Uncle Ato's death.

When my grandfather (Tatang's father) died, it was my grandmother who looked after his body during the wake. When Uncle Alfredo died, I was already studying at the National Teacher's College. I only managed to attend his burial. However, Uncle Ato's burial was different. There are simply a lot of things that baffle me up to this day. Take, for instance, the old ladies who were prohibiting everyone from sweeping the floors until the end of the wake. According to them, anyone who doesn't follow suit will be riddled with lice.

But as is with hot-blooded young men, curiosity got the best of me. I secretly swept the kitchen because I was disgusted by the fish bones and leftover rice grains under the table.

Two nights after, I was scratching my head nonstop. "Stop scratching your head. It won't do you any good," Nanang told me off. I really suffered from the itch in my head. After Uncle Ato's burial, Nanang removed the lice from my scalp using a suyod. "They brought something with them," Nanang added, just like a saying in their town. "This kid's really a handful," said Nanang repeatedly.

Uncle Ato's death marked my first and only experience with ghosts. This was also the time that I had proven the remarkable eyesight and sense of smell of dogs. Our dog Samson, during the time I was gathering our clothes (including that of Uncle Ato's), barked. According to Nanang, Samson smelled Uncle Ato's presence, his ghost. And every time Uncle Ato's death anniversary came around, Nanang almost always smelled the scent of candles, reminding us, according to her, that Uncle Ato's soul is just nearby.

Nanang told me to bring the voice tape we found in Tatang's messenger bag to the cemetery. I relented because I felt that listening to it would answer most of my questions about Uncle Ato.

Uncle Ato's wife wasn't able to come back to the country for the burial. This really irked me. It made me loathe people who chose (and choose) to work abroad, away from their families. Is money really that important that one can forego the burial of a loved one? Of her own husband? Of course, back then, I didn't fully understand the difficulty of her situation in Abu Dhabi.

The night before Uncle Ato's burial, our relatives decided that our two cousins, the children of Uncle Ato, would live with us. The other two, since there were four of them, would live with Uncle Ato's mother-in-law. Uncle Mulong, on the other hand, would be the one who lived and watched over Uncle Ato's house while the latter's wife was away.

The people from the funeral parlor had a hard time carrying Uncle Ato's coffin out of the house. While they were having a hard time smuggling the coffin past the window, someone blurted out a joke about Uncle Ato not wanting to leave this world.

"He's waiting for something!" shouted someone from the back.

"Behead the chicken!" another one screamed.

They had to do it so that there would be no consecutive deaths in the family. In my mind, I was asking the Lord to make the ritual work. I didn't want anyone from my family to bid us farewell without us being ready.

The rooster was then completely beheaded. Its blood spurted onto the coffin and the clothes of the pallbearers. The head of the rooster fell to the ground, lifeless, writhing for a few seconds until it became one with the earth.

A few weeks after Uncle Ato's death, his house also started deteriorating. The first to see signs of decline were the windows. Because Uncle Mulong didn't exert any effort to maintain the house when he lived there, he did not once try to repair the windows. Meanwhile, when Uncle Ato's wife came back to the Philippines for a visit, she stayed in her mother's home. The die had been cast. All that was needed was to wait for Uncle Ato's house to completely fall into shambles.

After offering a mass for Uncle Ato, I saw his mother-in-law talking to the priest, Fr. Ed. Uncle Ato's mother-in-law was a member of an association of devoted Catholic women. I once served as an altar boy and it isn't my personality to listen in to other people's conversation, but from where I sat, I heard the last few words of Fr. Ed's advice for her: "I only wish that authorities take into consideration the children's welfare and interests. It would be really difficult for them to live in separate households, especially now that they rely on each other for strength to carry on."

To cut the long story short, the children lived with their mother's relatives.

———

The month of March was about to end and from what I remember, Nanang had been going to and from the court to build a case against the bus company. It was also at that time when rumors about Uncle Ato started to circulate our village. A friend filled me in with the rest of the "story."

"People say that your uncle did it on purpose."

"What do you mean?"

"That he deliberately got himself ran over. That it was his intention to die."

I was at a loss for words. But not because of shock or disbelief. I contemplated if it was wise to hazard a response. I racked my brains for my memories of him and the accident: he went to our house, sat at a makeshift wooden stool under the shade of a camachile tree, and fixed his gaze on the small patch of land he used to farm. Nanang spoke to him, but he barely responded to her. She eventually left him to his own devices.

I also remember watching him from a small hole in the walls of our kitchen. He was like a statue, deep in thought, unperturbed by the scorching heat, the chattering of our neighbors, and the squealing of pigs.

Everything was still and tranquil since Nanang had already fed the pigs. Even my siblings and I made sure that our movements in the kitchen did not make too much noise. While we were silently fooling around, pinching each other, and letting out laughter without sound, Nanang eventually broke the silence.

"You son of a bitch! It's already dark!"

Uncle Ato probably thought that Nanang's words were for him. Again, as is the case with him, without a word to anyone, he left the house and went south.

"What do you think?" my friend asked, breaking the ebb and flow of my memories.

I did not respond.

He continued his story. "People saw your uncle sitting at the waiting shed very early in the morning. Some students say that they saw him jump right in front of the speeding bus."

A few months after he was buried, I stood in front of the place where he died. I noticed the bloodstain starting to fade from the cemented road. While I was counting the steps—I counted fifty—from the road to the mango tree where I hid during the accident, I couldn't help but find it strange that Uncle Ato went to the northern part of our village the night before the accident. He usually takes the path north, passing through a narrow and muddy embankment that spell the distance of his house from ours. He never took the highway when going to our house. But during that day, coming from the north, he did.

I told Nanang the rumors spreading about Uncle Ato's death.

"I see that people don't have anything much better to do but spread lies about others," said Nanang, almost in tears, while chopping vegetables.

"Don't let it bother you if what they say isn't true," Tatang replied while pouring himself a glass of water. I did not wait for Nanang's answer. I went straight to our backyard and cried until my eyes hurt.

Uncle Ato's wife arrived by the end of the March the following year, a week after Nanang got the settlement money (amounting to twenty thousand pesos) from the bus company. It happened that I was at the church that time, performing my duties diligently as an altar boy. Nanang and Uncle Ato's wife agreed to make a trip to Aparri.

I was awoken by Nanang's arrival from Aparri. While I was shaking off my sleepiness and rubbing my eyes, I saw Uncle Ato's wife seated on the sofa in the living room. She was wearing a yellow dress which perfectly matched her fair skin.

For some reason, the first thing that came to my mind was my upcoming circumcision. My eyes lit up a bit as I was walking toward the living room.

"Look who's already awake! What a fine lad you are," she said, immediately standing herself up from the sofa. She approached me and planted a kiss on my cheek. The smell of her perfume (probably from Abu Dhabi) was strange yet beguiling.

But what really woke me up was the sight of a tall red dresser standing near the front door.

"We bought it from Aparri," she said. "I think it suits your house well." She laughed.

I replied with a shy smile. A few moments later, Nanang came out from the kitchen with soft drinks in her hand. "Where are your siblings?" she asked.

"Excuse me. I have to pee," I said, excusing myself from their presence.

Before I went back to Manila during my last visit to our town, instead of relenting to Nanang's request that I bring the tape we found to Uncle Ato's grave, I opted to visit first the lot where the latter's small patch of farmland was. I stood there for quite some time and started to imagine myself seated in front of Uncle Ato's body, his body covered with an Inabel blanket. But when I opened my eyes, all that was left for me to see were the remnants of wood and planks salvaged by Uncle Mulong from the past typhoon.

But I still couldn't help but feel a shiver on my spine. If not for the ghost, it was probably caused by a mixed feeling of longing and regret.

Voice Tape

When Nanang gave me the tape, I suddenly recalled the state of Uncle Ato's house upon our arrival days after his burial. The living room was a mess and the sheets were all over the place. Nanang broke into tears while cleaning up, while I was busy tending to my younger cousins. To stow away my cousins from the tense situation, I took them to a nearby store and bought them candies and snacks.

Nanang told me that she found the tape under a stack of pillows in Uncle Ato's room. On the other hand, the radio casette Uncle Ato had borrowed from us was in the kitchen.

While we were out, Nanang and Tatang listened to the tape. For years, it was Nanang, Tatang, Uncle Ato, and his wife who knew the contents of the tape. But just recently, I became the fifth one. Nanang told me that I was old enough to know the truth.

It was great that the tape had a case, and that the voice of Uncle Ato's wife in the recording was clear despite her muffled sobs: "Forgive me, Dear. I did not want this. They'll kill me if I resist. Just think of the bright future ahead of us and our children.... My contract will be over soon." ♦

I AM KAFKA, A CAT

by Roy Vadil Aragon

Translated from Ilocano
by Amado Anthony G. Mendoza III and Roy Vadil Aragon

I just woke up one day as a cat. No explanations. It wasn't any different from Franz Kafka's novel—a man who suddenly transformed into a cockroach or a beetle—that I wrote a term paper about. I was awoken from the sudden tugging of my blanket. It was pulled away from me and brandished in the air several times. As a result, I slid and fell from the bed. I was a bit startled. But it was just Mother. Didn't she see me? I am fully aware that our cats snuggling their way to our beds, especially in the dead of the night, gets to her nerves. According to her, cat fur, when inhaled, can cause asthma. The meowing and growling of cats whenever they try to smuggle themselves between our warm bodies also annoy her. But she isn't as bad as she used to be. In fact, she did want to raise cats in our house.

I forced myself to sit up, stretched like most cats are wont to do, arched my nimble back, and let out a yawn. I jumped onto the floor and ran to the kitchen. And just like most of my sleepy mornings: I rinsed my mouth, washed my face, and quickly dashed to the table to make myself a cup of coffee. But just as I was about to take a seat, someone, who was cooking fried rice from last night's leftovers, shooed me away. I tried to speak but I was curtly reprimanded: "Stop your annoying meowing." It was my older sister, Ate Mating, who works as a call center agent. She then followed her initial scolding with an endearing assurance: "You can feast on the fish heads later. Just wait." My Ate Mating loves cats. She patiently and lovingly bathes our cats, even using her own Dove soap on them. She doesn't believe that bathing cats will cause storms or heavy rainfall. Even with the availability of various medications, she diligently removes fleas and lice from our cats. I also remember her bathing our dog, Sister Joc-Joc (named after my sister's favorite nun during her days as a college student and a former government official who allegedly plundered millions and then ran off to the US), with Safeguard. But she's not with us anymore. She was probably caught and butchered by our drunk neighbors.

I approached my sister and started curling and whipping my newly acquired tail between her legs. I pointed at my wet nose using my tongue. I started to feel hungry. This does not come as a surprise, I guess. Cats are always known to be hungry, always pestering their owners for a morsel of food. In my case, it was all the more true when I started to get a waft of the fish that my sister was frying. Fried dried fish is my favorite, especially when served with unripe tomatoes and dipped in Ilocos vinegar. It's a pity that I only get to feast on the head, scales, and bones of the fish, just like most cats are accustomed to.

Oh, and here comes Garfield and Exodus, our two un-neutered cats. I am sure they already smell what's cooking. They also snaked and bunted their way between Ate Mating's legs while letting out a chorus of meows. I just find it strange that they're not surprised or threatened by my presence in their territory, the kitchen. Exodus even approached me and licked my behind, probably sniffing the faint scent of last night's dinner, catfish stew in tamarind leaves. I even recalled giving them one catfish head each last night.

I'm a bit scared of the possibility of them ganging up on me, similar to what they normally do against other male cats, especially their rivals who seek the affection of flirtatious female cats. But I guess I am safe for now. Exodus just licked me. Not just because of the leftover scent of last night's catfish stew. Licking and grooming are ways for cats to show their affection to their fellow cats. With their own tongues they will clean you with care and affection. How is this different from Jesus washing the feet of his own disciples?

Could it be that they recognized me as their master, Ranilio? And that it is only natural for their master to loiter and saunter around their domicile? Or maybe I am yet to truly become a cat and they still see me as human? And just like that, I sank further into my thoughts: Why didn't mother notice that a cat was curled up in bed when she entered my room? Why didn't she look for me, I, Ranilio Callautit, Jr., her son who just finished his AB English degree two years ago; I, son of a former civil servant who died during my second year in college. Why wasn't she surprised by the presence of a new cat in the house? Why didn't she notice the presence of a black-and-white cat, far different from Garfield's solid orange shade and Exodus's ashen fur? Why didn't Ate Mating say anything when we spoke earlier?

My mind is in shambles. Why did I become a cat? Could it be that *I* transformed as a cat? Am I still human now that I'm a cat? Am I cat now even though I'm still human? Perhaps. Thoughts and questions like these won't ever cross the minds of cats. Is there a cat who knows Franz Kafka? Is there a cat who loves to read? In any case, how will I regard myself? Am I now a human cat? Or a cat human? But there's no question about it: I am as feline as any cat could and should be. That is, if someone would say that I still resemble my mother or Ate Mating. Where I'm from, there is a belief that cats, given time, (even dogs sometimes) will eventually start to resemble or take the appearance of their owners (but even back then, my Ate Mating and I resemble our mother, who won in a beauty contest in her town back in the day, both in face and in complexion; our father is not too shabby as well, even though he had darker skin and a shorter stature). Or maybe it is only my mind that remained human, my ability to think and to reason. But aren't cats the same? Even in their cat-ness something human exists in their consciousness.

It has been a week since I became a cat. Apart from my transformation, nothing of note or amazing occurred. Everything remained normal in our house. And I am yet to be regarded by my mother, sister, and even by Garfield and Exodus as someone (or something) different or strange. There's nothing to fret about. Mother's not looking for her son, Ranilio. Ate Mating is not looking for Ranilio who used to drive her to and from work in the city center. Perhaps Ranilio was never really lost in their eyes. Probably because I'm always out and being a pain in the ass during mealtime. Probably because I can still enter my room through the window in the morning. Mother will still wake me up even when I am tucked in my Inabel blanket. I am a sleepyhead and I'm rarely never asleep. The only thing that's different is Mother's habit of staring deeply and longingly at my graduation photo at the bedside table. She would even caress and hug it sometimes. On the other hand, not even my acquaintances, colleagues, and closest friends asked where I went or looked for me. I also missed the opportunity to follow up my job application in a newspaper company where a close friend works as a layout artist. He didn't even give me a call. Not that I mind. I just find it unusual.

Everything seems normal even after I became a cat. It even got to a point where I don't see it as a problem, with the only exception being moments where I question whether I've completely become a cat or if some part of me remained human. Not that I wish to return to my old self. I don't even miss or seek the things I was accustomed to when I was still human: reading books and magazines, fiddling with my computer and surfing the internet, listening to music, watching movies, and riding the motorcycle. I can still read. I can still recognize the words and letters in my midst. I still know how to use a computer (I might find it difficult to use a computer because my hands are now paws, even if there is this "mouse" to be chased, nay, used). And of course, I can still listen to music and watch movies because my Ate Mating often listens to music on the stereo and watches DVD movies. Even with my hands turning into paws, I can still use my beloved iPod. But I don't know about my Nokia N95. With my small claws, I'm pretty sure that I'd have a hard time pressing its keypad. Au revoir to my textmates. I'd also probably miss riding my Honda XRM. The only thing that comes as a surprise is its current state: it's already in shambles, a bump or two away from being scrap metal. Someone must have borrowed and crashed it while I was busy being a cat. Again, not that I mind. I am not even remotely interested in reading, fiddling with computers, and riding motorcycles anymore. I can barely appreciate a good song or film. I would much prefer to play with Garfield and Exodus. Or perhaps sleep all day. Or just like any cat, continue to pester our masters for food.

Be that as it may, there are still things that make me doubt my complete transformation as a cat. For example, even if they don't understand a single word I say whenever I talk to them, I can still understand my mother and sister's words—I can still understand their fluent Ilocano. I am also surprised that I understand Garfield and Exodus. It is not meows that I hear from them but fluent Ilocano as well. And when I talk to them in Ilocano, they can perfectly understand me. Am I now speaking the language of cats? This is, of course, not new. There are people who have been known to understand and speak the language of cats. Take, for instance, Nakata, the wandering old man in Haruki Murakami's (my favorite Japanese writer) *Kafka on the Shore*. Or the talking cat in Neil Gaiman's (another favorite writer of mine) novel *Coraline*. Yes, I'm fully aware that both are stories of fantasy. But how do I distinguish what's real and what's not if I've indeed become a cat?

This is probably what I get from reading too much fiction, especially those of the magical realist and fantastical subgenre; the works of Kakfa, Murakami, and Gaiman; and of stories about cats. Perhaps I am now in a situation that most people would describe as Kafkaesque. But why be so literal about it? Is there really anything magical about my situation? In the term paper I wrote about Kafka's work, apart from the allegorical, psychological, and social interpretation of his work, I suggested that the events in the novel can be read as a sign of reincarnation or karma. Not that I believe in reincarnation and all the New Age shenanigans that were the craze during my college days. It's just all fluff, something to impress my professor. And impress him I did. I got full marks for my term paper.

But what really bothers me, what really makes me nervous and sends chills to my spine, is the fact that my mother and sister call me by my name Ranilio. At first, they don't call me that name whenever they talk, call, feed, or reprimand me. But one day, my mother suddenly started reprimanding me like this: "Wake up, Ranilio. You were even snoring while asleep in the hammock." This incident happened again in the kitchen. My sister started reprimanding me like a cat: "Ranilio, get off the table! Go to your feeding bowl in the corner! Ranilio, don't be such a bother!" That's when I realized that they were really talking to me as a cat. But why did they use my human name to address me? If I have indeed become a cat and they're aware of it, why would they use the name of a person who just happens to be their own son and sibling? They still see and know me as Ranilio, right? But why don't they seem surprised or disturbed by the fact that I've become a cat? Could they have known about my situation from the onset? Am I the only one who doesn't know?

But if I am really to be a cat, I need to change my name—a name that would separate my being a cat from my being human (or my humanity from my cat-ness?). Just like how Garfield and Exodus get to have their own names.

I was the one who gave Garfield his name. It was right around the time we adopted him from our neighbor. It was my Ate Mating, on the other hand, who gave Exodus his name. I don't know where she got "exodus," but she said that it wasn't from the Bible. Maybe it was from famous Bong Revilla films during that time. For her, "exodus" had this cool and mystical ring to it. On the other hand, I obviously got "Garfield" from the popular cartoon series featuring a fat orange-shaded striped tabby cat. Our Garfield also has the same orange-shaded fur.

Ate Mating and I realized that we were the only ones who knew the names of our cats. We discovered one day that Exodus and Garfield didn't know their own names, let alone have a penchant for names and naming. They ignore me whenever I call them using their names. It is only humans who possess names, who like to name things. I thought this to be only true in fiction, a flight of fancy, just like how Coraline's cat friend explained to her why cats don't need names. According to Wuss-Puss, cats don't need names because they already know themselves. From what I know, just being called "cats" already suffices for them. I also noticed that they recognize themselves and others through scent. You know me when you smell me. But I will also tell them that they still need names to set them apart from each other. And that is why I insist on calling them the names that we gave them.

As for myself, I need a new name—a cat name—so that I can respond when Garfield or Exodus ask for my name. A name will also help when the time comes for me to introduce myself to cats outside the house. I will also give them names, especially the females.

And just to be safe, I'm just going to be the one to name myself. How does Haruki sound? No go? Yes, its final syllable does not sound good in Ilocano. It might raise some eyebrows. What about Murakami? Nah. Doesn't sound good. Sounds like the word for cheap in Tagalog. The cat names in Murakami's novel—Mimi, Kawamura, Goma, Okawa—also just aren't cutting it. Even the names of cats from popular films, TV shows, books, and comics like Tom, Felix, Puss 'n' Boots, Cheshire Cat, or Cat in the Hat sound flat to me.

I know! I'll just call myself Kafka, a fitting tribute to the writer who presaged this mystical feline phenomenon I'm going through.

Naming someone Kafka, albeit uncommon, isn't something new. Murakami named *Kafka on the Shore*'s protagonist, Kafka Tamura, after his favorite author.

———

I am Kafka, a cat, now a cat, bow! Prettier than Franz, because naming someone Franz is akin to naming someone who is human. Kafka, like Exodus, has a cool, mystical, and exotic ring to it. A very fitting name for cats.

———

Kafka, a cat, that's me. Kafka is more suitable than Ranilio—the name I was baptized with, my dad's name—and my surname Callautit.

———

I have yet to roam the streets outside. I only go out at night to dig up a hole in a sandy patch near our house in Block 34 in order to cover my poop. I'm still scared of the outside. Rabid dogs might chase me. Or I might encounter someone who butchers cats on a whim. That bastard Romy who lives in Block 36, an old, unmarried man who works as a medicine salesman—he shot both Garfield and Exodus twice with an air gun just because he felt like it. Fortunately, both of them survived. Maybe cats do have nine lives. As for Garfield, the bullet only grazed his thighs. Exodus, on the other hand, was hit on the back, between the cartilaginous part separating the flesh and the skin. Both Garfield and Exodus suffered dearly from the wounds. The two could barely walk, mustering only enough strength just to crawl. They lost their appetites, refusing to eat even when fed their favorite catfish stew or fried fish. At that time they were almost skin and bones. To treat their wounds, I used betadine, sulfathiazole powder, and amoxicillin diluted in Nido. They eventually got well. I didn't need to bring them to a vet. There weren't any in our town during that time anyway. The bullets from the air gun remained in their bodies. I was livid and bursting at the seams during that time. I confronted Romy and I almost came to blows with that skinny and balding motherfucker. I really want to beat him up bad. According to him, and he was adamant about it, both Garfield and Exodus tried to steal food from his table, that they were stray cats. But that's impossible. Garfield and Exodus had plenty to feast on in our home. There was no need for them to sneak into other people's homes for food. Romy was clearly mistaken. He probably thought that they belonged to the gang of strays who were terrorizing the subdivision. But that's also impossible! Both Garfield and Exodus regard those strays as enemies. I even remember Garfield getting into a nasty scuffle with a dirty big black cat who tried to enter our house (because we forgot to close our windows) a few times. There was also this cat with a color pattern similar to that of Exodus. Most of them, especially the males, were their rivals for the affection of females. But even if both Garfield and Exodus were strays, it still does not give Romy the right to have a go at them, to shoot them. In fact, most of the cats he shot were house pets. As a result, a lot of residents filed or reported their pet cats missing. They also probably thought, like we did in the case of Sister Joc-Joc, that they were caught and butchered by the drunks in our subdivision. It turns out it was Romy all along. He is the only person in the subdivision who owns an air gun. Aside from that, somebody witnessed him just before nightfall shooting cats who were mating and fooling around in a vacant lot near his unit. He didn't admit to anything, of course. According to him, he only shot birds, stray cats, and civet cats.

But I have to go outside. Damn that old Romy! I'm gonna shit all over his backyard. I'm going out with Garfield and Exodus to look for mating partners. Why bother myself with plans and details? The only important thing is that I'm going out. And I'm really stoked about it. And even if I'm still inside, I can already smell in the wind a waft of an in-heat female's pheromones. Cats truly have a strong sense of smell. They can smell any scent from afar. This is my chance. I had a girlfriend before (when I was human), but because I was too timid and inexperienced, I wasn't able to do anything with her. The only thing I could muster was a kiss (that was more like a gentle boop with my lips) and nervous caresses and touching. Even when I was at the peak of my lust, I was still scared to go for it. I was scared of being rejected, of her breaking things off with me. I was also scared at the prospect of being embarrassed, of being laughed at because I didn't know what to do. If only I had started to think about these things when I was a bit younger. And now that I've become a cat, I'm starting to feel this great urge to mate. Cats are indeed lustful beings. And I don't even feel an ounce of shame. Cats don't feel an ounce of shame when it comes to expressing their desires and feelings. Or maybe this is what animal instinct is? I suddenly recalled the time when I tried to observe what Garfield and Exodus were up to when they go out at night. There was this one time when I was able to secretly watch Exodus have a go at a female cat in front of my room. I saw how Exodus tried to make the female cat submit to his will, skillfully (and forcefully) grabbing her neck and getting on top of her. This went on for a few minutes, with the female wriggling and spinning around the floor while Exodus was trying to woo her. Their groans and cries got louder, sometimes even leading them to break off from their embrace and chase each other anew. Yes, they do mean business. This is feline foreplay in the flesh. After the long-winded wooing by Exodus, he was finally able to get on top of her once again and mate to their hearts' content. I wanted to take video footage of them doing their business, but it was just too dark outside. I was supposed to upload it on YouTube with the title "Tuguegarao Scandal." I'm sure shameless fools will come rushing to watch it, thinking that it's another video of an unfortunate couple caught doing the act. But let's leave the prurient interests of humans behind. Now that I've become a cat, I can finally experience it! I can finally mate with other cats! The only thing that worries me is that Garfield and Exodus will beat me to the punch. That they won't let me score with female cats. But I don't care. If they dare cross me, I'll fight them tooth and nail. It's funny that even in the world of cats, women are still the root and cause of all discord. While this is true for humans who think with their balls, I hope this isn't the case with cats.

And then it finally happened! I never knew it was that good! That's probably the reason why cats let out a loud meow after they climax. Her name is Lolita. And that night, everything was ours. It was the first for both of us. Ha! I was able to best both Garfield and Exodus. From outside the subdivision, I was able to smell Lolita's scent, and oh boy was I in for a treat. Her scent is like a drug, like the traveling scent of dried squid being fried, or dinengdeng saluyot leaves and bamboo shoots for dinner. I named her Lolita because if she were human, she probably would be around twelve to thirteen years old. Young, so young, like the character in Vladimir Nabokov's popular and controversial novel. She spread her wings (and legs) too early. If I was still human, considering everything we did together, I would already be facing corruption of minor and statutory rape charges. It's a relief that stuff of that sort are a wash in the world of cats. With that said, I promised to visit Lolita every night. I just hope that I'll be able to give her more kittens than any potential rivals in my midst. That's just how female cats are. No one male cat can ever own them. Everyone gets to have a go in order to multiply their progeny. I have to retract my previous statement. Cats are different from humans. Female cats are not the root or source of discord in the feline world. In fact, it is the females who encourage solidarity among all cats.

But I'm worried that mother and Ate Mating will get mad and fed up with our nightly rendezvous. Back then, there were times when Garfield and Exodus would be out for weeks. This is normal for most male cats. There are even cases where male cats would completely be without homes and become strays. Mother and Ate Mating might think that it's best to neuter Garfield and Exodus—to keep their sexual urges at bay. Of course, as I've also become a male cat, it's not outside the realm of possibility that I get neutered. But you see . . . just imagining my testicles being crushed makes me feel very queasy. What scares me the most is the way they neuter cats in my place. They would tightly tie the testicles with a rubber band until they slowly and gradually separate from the body. They would get swollen, eventually dry up, and finally fall off the cat's body. Goodbye, testicles. No more midnight rendezvous for you, Casanova! No more chest-puffing for you, tomcat! You've got nothing to brag about anymore. Nada. Zilch. What a tragedy for a young male cat at the peak of his virility. To be neutered when you're just about to hit your stride. While it is true that neutered male cats become fat, fluffy, and timid house pets, they are also sure to lose their urge to mate, become vulnerable, and grow old to be listless and useless.

———————

Nothing beats mouse flesh, especially those that come from the little ones! When I was still human, I once tasted a stew made out of rodents in the farm. It wasn't so bad. A bit gamey, but it was tolerable. But now that I've become a cat, I like them better raw, marinated in vinegar like ceviche. Garfield and I saw a small one last night after having feasted on fish head, bones, and scales mixed with rice. We were just lounging around the doormat placed beneath a sofa made out of narra wood, rubbing our bellies full with food. Both Exodus and Garfield were busy grooming themselves, while I was preparing to doze off, when something moved from the other side of the room where Mother's old wooden chest containing her *Bannawag* magazine collection is stored. We were sure that it was a mouse. It had been long since a mouse got lost in our house. Poking holes and gnawing at mother's magazine collection had been a long source of joy for these rodents. I don't know. Perhaps they find the taste of Ilocano poems and stories printed in old paper so good that they risk becoming the snack of resident cats. Ever since we adopted Garfield and Exodus, rodent invasions into our house became very rare. But this time, Garfield, Exodus, and I weren't mistaken. It was definitely a mouse, a small one at that. Not even the sound of the smallest of movements can escape our ears. In addition to that, a rat's sweet smell wafting through the air is a treat for us cats—a clear proof that a mouse has entered the house. For a cat, a rat's stench is the most aromatic scent, far better than the scent of grilled catfish, dried squid, dried fish, or smoked fish. If you're a cat, a rat's stench means heaven. This is all the more true when you are able to grab, claw, and coil your limbs at its soft flesh. That's when you'll start to slowly and gently tear and gnaw at its mouthwatering flesh—you'll finish off everything until no trace of that rat remains in this world. You'll gobble up everything: flesh, bones, intestines, skin, tail, head, and even its fur.

And after just a few seconds of discerning its movement, we finally pounced onto our unsuspecting prey. The rodent let out a scream before scampering away and hiding in the recesses of the chest where our claws couldn't reach him. Garfield and Exodus were waiting for him at both sides of the chest, while I kept watch from above. The rodent's fear was palpable, clueless as to where to hide or escape. Finally, the rodent tried to escape by going between Exodus's legs. Exodus tried to grab the rodent but it was able to go past Garfield's legs as well. With all the speed and accuracy in the world and his claws unsheathed, Garfield struck the rodent and was able to bloody it before it escaped his jaws. With the blood gushing out from its body and the feverish scent it gave off, my desire to catch the rodent became more pronounced. As it moved away from Garfield, I quickly pounced on it and dug my claws on his wounded body. Better luck next time, Garfield and Exodus. I won tonight's derby. What's the use of sharpening one's claws if they can't catch a prey?

I hissed and growled at Garfield and Exodus when they tried to get a piece of my bounty. There's no sharing in the feline world, especially when it comes to hunted prey. If you're unlucky, then jealousy and regret are sure to be your dinner. And if you even try to snatch or filch the hunted prey of a fellow cat, rest assured that all hell will break loose. If a fellow cat is feeling charitable, he might leave you a morsel of skin and fur. That is if he's already full or already had enough. In my case, since it was my first catch, I didn't share any of it with Garfield and Exodus. It wasn't even enough to fully satiate me. If what I caught was as big as those sewer rats, I would've definitely shared the bounty with them.

I saw a kitten's flea-ridden carcass at the road near our house. He was so small, probably a week old. We shared the same fur pattern: black and white. He was just like me. Yes, *just like me.* I suddenly felt nervous. Could it be that he was one of my offspring with Lolita? Or with the other females I had ties with? I wouldn't be able to tell. It's been months since I last saw Lolita and the others (cats don't really pay heed to these things). Garfield and I are in the dark when it comes to the pregnancies of our "girlfriends." It's not like they give us monthly updates after we've planted in them the seeds of our new progeny. And of course, they're not obliged to inform us if and when they're impregnated by others. But one thing's for sure: Garfield and I indeed got our partners pregnant. All the signs are there: after the deed, they started giving us the cold shoulder, scampering away when we tried to approach them. I can't get the dead kitten off my mind. A mama cat won't ever abandon her children. She would definitely protect and love her children. She would not let them out of her sight, she would hide them when she goes out to look for food, and carry them from time to time.

People won't really understand the importance of cats in households. Cats are normally viewed as indolent, voracious, and useless creatures. Asleep for most of the day, their movements, or their willingness to move, are primarily motivated by food. They can also be bothersome as they counter-surf and snatch food from the table. They also snack on the neighbor's fowl—just one of the many reasons to get into a fight with them. The worst would be their "zooming" behavior, or their penchant to unleash their pent-up energy fighting, mating, or just plain wrecking anything in their path during the dead of the night, when everybody's already asleep.

But there are far more good cats than bad ones. As long as the master's patient, kind, and loving, like Ate Mating and I to Garfield and Exodus, a cat will surely repay his/her master with affection and loyalty. If you have a cat, no mouse will dare to enter or establish a territory in your house. Your beloved books, papers, documents, and clothes are safe from the gnawing of rats. The same goes for the rice grains that they love to munch on.

And besides, people won't get anything much from cats since they can't be butchered and sold to the market like, say, chicken, pork, or goat meat. Only drunks, who view cat meat as barchow, would try to butcher cats.

And besides, it's rare for people to buy and have cats as pets. That is, unless you're an imported cat with a certain pedigree like, say, a Siamese or a Persian. If you're just a lowly domestic or stray cat, especially if you're a kitten, you'll just be given up for adoption. Most of the time, you're seen as another mouth to feed, a child that needs potty training. In some cases, you'll be abandoned or drowned in streams, or placed in a sack with your siblings and thrown into the river so you won't be able to find your way back home. To hell with your lives! To hell with you starving or being vulnerable to dog and human violence! Just hope you get lucky to come across a person with a golden heart who would pick you up and give you a home.

Yes, of course, there is also racial discrimination among cats. If you're a native cat who is ugly and scrawny, you have no right to live. No one will buy or pay for you. Only people as wretched—people who can't afford imported cat breeds with majestic fur (that require a score of imported cat food, shampoo, and soap to maintain and protect from lice and fleas) and puffy cheeks—as you are will give you affection. If only you were a native chicken. People would surely pay top dollar just to have a sip of your delicious and piping hot soup (when stewed).

The Philippine cat truly arouses pity—it has no worth in this world. Just take, for instance, the everyday image of a cat being run over by a car. When its crushed body is for all the world to see, not a single soul will dare approach or pick it up. People will just ignore it until a hundred more cars and trucks run over it and flatten it to the ground, until it becomes as flat and thin as paper, until it disintegrates, until it completely vanishes from the road, like dust becoming one with the wind. No one's interested in a dead cat. No one will pick up its carcass like, say, a dog, chicken, goat, or pig. If one of the aforementioned got run over, people will surely be on each other's throats, with the aggrieved party asking the assailant for some kind of reparation or settlement.

I'm saddened by these thoughts. But what can I do? Do I just accept my being a cat? My cat-ness? Even if I'm not so sure that I want to be one. Do I treat everything as a dream? Will I wake up one day and find myself back to my human self? So many questions. But none of them really matter. What's important is I'm here. Existing. Alive. I enjoy my life as a cat. Why would I wish to return to my human form when I'm satisfied now and in what lies ahead for me in the future as a cat?

There's one more thing that worries me: that people will take notice if I continue to act and think like a human. This is what normally happens when animals display some sort of human in them. A lot of people become intrigued or interested in that sort of stuff, but not when a human displays his/her animalistic side. I'm scared for my life. They might try to catch me, sell me, and pass me off as some sort of carnival attraction. Or perhaps be brought to a laboratory and be studied by scientists. I will surely be subjected to many forms of abuse. What's worst would be them performing some sort of lobotomy in order to properly scrutinize my brain, my body, and the source of my intellect. A cat's nine lives won't be enough to survive such a procedure. That's why I really need to be a cat—a normal and ordinary cat. I will never think about my humanity again. I will abandon my human self from back then. I will teach myself to forget that I ever existed as a human. I am a cat. I am Kafka, a cat. I am not Ranilio Callauitit, Jr., human. I am a cat. It is only proper that I act as a cat and not as a human. Meow. Meow, meow. Meow! Meow, meow, meow. Meooowww! ♦

MUDFISH LADY

by Genevieve L. Asenjo

*Translated from Hiligaynon
by Eric Gerard H. Nebran and Eliodora L. Dimzon*

I

*I tried to drain the pond
There in the rice paddies
The turagsoy I caught
I cooked into linagpang*

That morning, the delicious smell of fried pinakas woke Inday Lupog from her sleep. Her saliva welled up like spring water as she imagined dipping the fish into spiced vinegar and eating it with still steaming rice. Gloria rice, that's what they'd been cooking lately. She found it really tasty. That's why she was becoming plumper. Boy Eks, a visiting salesman of herbal medicine, had teased her about it. He called her Inday Kayutingan, round like batwan. A few more gulps of food and she would no longer be needing her crutch made of madre de cacao. In truth, she had gone far with Boy Eks. She remembered when they'd walked upstream where the bananas grew. Ah, such pleasure! Fanned by the flames of desire and lust, even the hiss of the slithering lizards and the itch brought by the grass had no power at all, drowned by their sticky, sweaty lovemaking.

She lay curled up in her mat until the sound of a siren made her sit upright. This was an unusual sound in the barrio, reminding her of the revving sound of the Kawasaki motorcycle of Boy Eks as he navigated the hilly path leading to the village upon his arrival and of the same explosive sound upon his departure for the city of Iloilo so early in the morning even before the roosters had the chance to wake up and crow. She checked herself in the mirror before opening the window, parted the blossoms of the kalachuchi which grew beside their house, and peered outside.

Something had happened while she was lost in her reverie. She could see that the entire barrio had gathered under the acacia tree beside their wooden fence. It was like that time in December when they had watched the tsunami reports on TV, but this time, their attention was on the parked Bombo Radyo vehicle. She could see her mother with the crowd, an unusual sight for someone who believed that gossip is a malevolent spirit that hampers the progress of civilization.

She was tempted to get down from their hut to catch the flowing conversations which seemed to gush forth from the people, but she decided to stay where she was. Her position offered a vantage point and she could see the people—a sea of moving heads, eyes, and mouths in the morning sunshine. Theirs was a small village nestled in a forest that had gradually thinned out as time went by. She noticed that most of her neighbors had rebuilt their homes with cement and roofs of CGI sheets. In a few years, decrepit huts like theirs would eventually vanish—replaced by more modern structures.

"Oh, so that's Bombo Roel!" exclaimed her Tiya Era, who had just come out next door. "No wonder his voice sounds pleasant on the radio—it's to make up for his ugly face!" she cackled at herself, pleased with her discovery.

Apparently, news of what had happened at around 2:30 early that morning had already spread as far as Hong Kong, Saudi Arabia, and Canada. There was sudden pandemonium: people with cellphones raced to the cliffside, where the signal was supposedly the strongest, while some even climbed coconut trees. It wouldn't take long, maybe this afternoon or tomorrow, before GMA 7 and ABS-CBN would also visit the village. Enteng, driver of the tricycle owned by the Juarez family, together with their Barangay captain and a few peacekeeping tanods, had already fetched Father Boyet.

What was the fuss about? Just two days since he died, Ontoy Pakit rose from his coffin! He had come home, nauseated and vomiting, after cockfighting in another village. He went on to have high fever by nighttime, was given homemade remedies, including a drink of hot water and lagundi leaves, but didn't live to see the morning. Well, would you believe it? During his wake, he got up and proceeded to casually ask for coffee and pandesal from those keeping vigil while playing a game of cards. All hell broke loose as people scampered to get away from the house, upturning tables and chairs, leaving scattered cards and bets and a broken door behind. "Who wouldn't be scared? He still reeked of formalin when he asked me for a stick of cigarette!" said Nonoy Butod, a pot-bellied man, when he recounted Ontoy's pagmaranhig.

If you were to ask Oray Loleng, the oldest in the village, who, at ninety-two, still drank tuba like a fish, Ontoy Pakit was clearly a pinalakad. If he wasn't embalmed, they still could've saved him.

Inday Lupog was a bit ignorant about these things. She had still been a snot-faced girl when people talked of the story of Tiniente Gimo and Felicidad. The former was an infamous clan leader of aswangs, and the latter was a woman who peddled really delicious ginamos. Everybody praised Felicidad's tasty concoctions, only to realize later, after she faced arrest as an aswang, what made the paste delicious: blood and the minced body parts of her victims.

This morbid thought persisted when Inday's mother returned to continue her talk of the supernatural while preparing the table for breakfast. Her nose did not fail her, they were indeed going to eat fried pinakas, and her mother was serving it with sliced tomatoes, all the while talking about Ontoy Pakit's case. If, indeed, he is a pinalakad, she said, then the corpse inside the coffin is but a dummy, and his soul is still held ransom by the responsible creature, such as an aswang. She went on to claim how Ontoy deserved such a cruel fate—he's a huge braggart especially with his gamecocks.

It amused her to think about this belief since it contrasted with what she had just read last Saturday. On this day, her mother would usually leave the hut to sell the buri hats that Inday wove. The trek was a bit long. From their house, it would take five bends in a forest pathway, eight acacia trees, and three bridges before reaching the marketplace. Upon her return, the money from the hats would be used to buy dried filleted fish wrapped in newspapers. From these, Inday would read about the world beyond their village. She read how people had already explored the planet Mars, and how in Japan, a person could be away from home and still have the power to control his appliances, like turning his lights and television on and off, all thanks to modern technology.

She thought about how far humankind has come, and was suddenly enveloped by a bout of sadness. She had lost her appetite and pushed aside her plate of fish and Gloria rice. Her downcast eyes studied her weak legs.

She had been walking to school, Baranasan Barangay High School, in another village, when she felt the fever creep over her entire body. She couldn't get out of bed for a week. Afterward, she felt alternating numbness and stabbing pain on her legs that prevented her from walking. *Santisima de Hesus! Why does it have to be me?* she thought as her world fell apart.

She had accidentally incurred the interest of a tamawo, said Baylan Roming. To appease the malevolent spirits that caused her to be incapacitated, they offered a lot of sacrifices: a large black boar, a dozen white chickens, abundant platters of native delicacies: ibos and suman—but to no avail, she still couldn't regain her ability to walk. A lot of people felt sorry for her. They thought she had promise—she had participated in History and Science Quiz Bees in the neighboring cities and provinces, including Negros, Kalibo, and Antique. All she could do then was to rely on her late father, who had carried her to school until she graduated. For a long time, she resisted the urge to hurl curses at the tamawos. If they had been kinder, she would be working at Manila now, or maybe overseas. She could have been a teacher—or even a lawyer, which had been her dream. Two years after the tragedy, a nun on a catechetical mission visited their barrio. It was during one of the lectures that she had learned the truth.

Again, she felt her world turn upside-down upon learning the cause. It was polio that had struck her and not the tamawo in the balete tree! The free immunization offered by the government did not reach their barrio, and of all people, the odds of contracting the disease fell unluckily against her favor. What could someone as poor as her do but swallow the indignity and accept that this was to be her fate?

Just my luck, Inday thought as she ran a hand over her hips, past her belly, onto her breasts—her ripe budding breasts. She felt a quiver of excitement. She felt like a flower in bloom, ripe for the taking. These past few days, she had lain on her mat, imagining the sound of a revving motorcycle—of Boy Eks stopping at their doorstep. He'd be back, she was sure of it. The man still had debts to collect from the people in the barrio.

He owed her something too. He had a big debt to pay. Her enthusiasm got fueled by the words she heard from a friend: Maring, who was two years older than her, and whose husband, Gering, worked in Saudi Arabia. The conversation had happened sometime back, but it left an impression. Maring visited to get her to weave a new mat. Out of the blue, her friend had exclaimed, "I want to get fucked." Inday Lupog felt goosebumps all over. She felt her throat dry up like a pond parched by the summer sun. Meanwhile, Maring continued to talk about how her husband had brought with him her unwashed underwear to sniff through nights of loneliness while he was abroad. "Why should women like us be ashamed to admit that we also want sex?" Maring seemed rebellious, but later told Inday Lupog that her exclamations were just brought about by her yearning for her husband. God forbid, she'll get caught with another man. It would truly be shameful, now that their eldest daughter, Gingging, was growing up to be a young lady.

Recently, Inday Lupog found the inspiration to continue weaving mats and try new designs for her hats, which she planned to sell for a higher price: she was saving up to buy *Almanake Panayanon* and

Hiligaynon magazines. She had enjoyed reading them when her father was still alive. Back then, Doroy, who had worked overseas, was the only one who could afford a TV set. She had forgotten her love for reading when she discovered the enjoyment to be had from listening to radio dramas of Bombo Radyo, and later still, when she began to limp and hobble her way next door to get a glimpse of the news on their neighbor's TV.

They had finished breakfast. Hours later, at noon, Bombo Radyo patrol's vehicle could be heard leaving the village. The excitement had died down. Ontoy Pakit's corpse had gone back to rest in its coffin after Father Boyet had sprinkled it with holy water. The cheerful Inday Lupog started singing "Igso-on sa Tabuk Nayon":

> *Dear friend from another village*
> *Come visit our house for a moment*
> *Although we don't have rice left*
> *There's buyo you can chew on*
> *What will I do with your buyo leaves*
> *I have plenty of them at home*
> *What I really want*
> *Is the ring on your finger.*

But she had forgotten the rest of the song, so she quickly shifted to another:

> *Here's Kantilay, son of Venencio*
> *With a bow and a big lizard slung upon his shoulders*
> *He also carries*
> *A poor turtle, with a bald head*

"Inday! What are you singing? You sound like a crazy person!" said her mother, chastising her for her antics. It was not only Inday Lupog's singing that sounded like thunder, but also her loud laughter. It was like the sound of sinigwelas seeds falling on a GI sheet roof, like coconut leaf-stalks crashing on the ground. She felt derision for what happened that morning, but now, the sadness and pity that she felt for herself shifted toward the people in the village.

II

The turagsoy in my linagpang
Is floating in the soup
I seasoned it with ginamos
How we sweated while we devoured it!
Those who had partaken it, say
It truly tastes delightful!
The turagsoy in my linagpang
I couldn't get enough of it!

In the succeeding days, Ontoy Pakit's pagmaranhig inspired a lot of other stories and opinions. Some pointed out that they should've fetched Baylan Roming right away. Others believed that it was a new case of SARS and that the hapless Ontoy would have been cured if he had been brought to the hospital. Some said it's just like the case of the children in Bohol, who died after eating cassava. He probably ate something rotten or poisonous. Whatever the case was, one thing was certain: it was clear that Ontoy's family hesitated to bring him to the hospital because the head nurse is the mayor's child, and in the past election, the family supported the other political party. They were certain that they would just be ignored at the hospital because of their affiliation. It was better then for Ontoy to die with dignity.

The people were initially happy about the fame brought by the incident to their barrio, but they erupted like volcanoes in rage when they saw the Kapuso TV network reporting on TV that Panay, their province—was the lair of aswangs! A flood of text messages from younger family members and relatives who were working in Manila told them about the discrimination and ridicule they suffered at work. Some who had only been applying got rejected because of the news.

But Ontoy Pakit had his funeral, and the story of his pagmaranhig got buried along with him before the rival network (Kapamilya) got wind of it. Life went on in the barrio, and the people had no time to sulk at the Kapuso network because they were too busy organizing and attending bayles, arriving from and leaving for Manila (and some, overseas). Even the cockfighting pits and the gambling tables were always filled with people.

During these times, Inday Lupog had already used up two Mongol pencils, and filled up the notebook she asked her mother to buy. She had also finished writing down the lyrics of "Igso-on sa Tabok Nayon," and had also added the novelty song "Tamilok":

One night, the moon was shining brightly,
there was a person, who went to the market,
drank tuba, got drunk, got lost,
went to the rice paddies, fell, and splashed into the mud,
where the carabaos wallow.

She also sang while writing down: "En evri aftirnun, tri oklak/Ay red ur liter/Ahay" and other loas:

There by the hill
There's a coin rolling
Jes Lapid shot it
The side got hit!

While her notebook got thicker, her waist got wider, her stomach rounder, and her breasts fuller. Her mother did not notice it at first, since Inday Lupog was naturally plump—why would she even entertain any devilish notion about her daughter, whom she hadn't seen leaving the house with her crutches for quite some time now? If there was anything amiss, it was her regression to childish pastimes. If she wasn't weaving anything, she was busy writing and singing songs, reading things, and sewing tiny clothes—it was like she was playing house like a child again!

"It's useless," said Inday Lupog when she was asked why she no longer watched TV next door. One day, however, the calm in their home was broken by Inday Lupog's retching. Tiya Era was sweeping the backyard when she heard her vomiting in their outdoor kitchen. By noon, everyone in the barrio had heard the news—it was like Ontoy Pakit's pagmaranhig all over again. And it also started with vomiting—the first symptom. That meant the aswang still roamed freely in their barrio. Oray Loleng once again shared her belief regarding the matter: the aswang has heard of Inday Lupog's singing, and has fancied her voice. They then called Saning, the manughilot, and their suspicion was confirmed: there is something in her belly. Would they then allow someone to follow in the footsteps of Ontoy Pakit?

Hiwit. This was the new word that sailed around the whole barrio. While she wanted to run away from the talk of maranhig, she now wanted to run after this hiwit to keep it from escaping the lips of the people. She tried to keep the word out of her mind, and so her eyes, as in hunger, devoured every page of the *Almanake*, the *Hiligaynon* magazines, and her notebook. She wanted to swallow them all and transmit them to the new life that grew in her womb.

She shuddered at the thought. Was it a right and proper thing for a child to inherit? Were the facts and stories from what she had been reading actually free from talk of the superstitious and supernatural? Where would she get the words and images to nourish the child that was soon to be born into this world? But what of the world outside? What was taking Boy Eks so long? The rainy season was coming, and with it, the opening of classes. Wasn't it that sex is delightful and the stories and escapades witnessed by the river, hills, and the bamboo grove are sweet? Why did the elders hide them on the pretext of the hideous hiwit?

Inday Lupog's sigh cut through the air like a flash of lightning in the sky. Despair gnawed at her heart and she moaned loudly. There was nothing that her mother and the gathered women could do except to make the sign of the cross and light a kamangyan. Inday Lupog perspired profusely and wet her panties. The group of men composed of the barangay captain, and the tanods had all made up their minds to keep watch that night. The order had been circulated all over: nobody will inform Bombo Radyo as well as the Kapamilya and Kapuso networks. They should wait until they have caught and killed the aswang, like Felicidad, before they consent to be interviewed.

For several nights, the tanods surrounded their house. Others were stationed under the house, avoiding the light from the oil lamps so that they could see the aswang the moment it entered through the window or the roof. Others stationed themselves above the acacia and calachuchi trees because an aswang can transform itself into a bird. Aside from rope, bolo, and sharpened bagakay, they also brought with them a manunggal. It is believed that the aswang is afraid of manunggal. But aside from some movement sounds and the occasional falling of small branches caused by the blustering wind, there was no sound of tiktik or kakak. The barangay captain and the tanods seemed more dignified in their watch.

Some young women and men, especially those who had been to college, would usually gather after a mass or a basketball game and engage themselves in a sort of gossip. Unlike their elders, they believed that it was an aswang nga itum ulo (figuratively, an ordinary human) that was to be blamed for Inday Lupog's vomiting.

This talk continued during basketball league events and the preparations for another bayle to coincide with the end of the Flores de Mayo celebrations. By that time, the tanods had stopped their nightly rounds and vigil at Inday Lupog's house. "It's to her advantage, at least she'll have someone with her when her mother dies," said the youth. They even secretly wished that Boy Eks would not return to collect the debts of their parents. They cursed his name each time they would talk about what one of them witnessed where the bananas grew.

III

Others shed tears
Though they are not sad
It is because my linagpang with turagsoy
Is so spicy.

The drizzles became more frequent until they became rains which healed the cracks of summer and enlivened the whole barrio to prepare the paddies for planting. Standing by the window, Inday Lupog looked at her mother planting roses in their front yard, as well as kamote and tagabang in the side areas. Her mother's hair was gray now and her varicose veins were visible all over her arms and legs. Though she wanted to help, she was now heavy with child.

A small cardboard box was now filled with baby clothes that she made herself and those given by the people in the barrio. Some of these came from Hong Kong, America, Canada, and Manila. Her collection of *Hiligaynon* magazines had doubled and she had filled three more notebooks with songs including those from Flores de Mayo and Christmas carols.

Suddenly, Inday Lupog, her mother, and the whole barrio heard the revving of a motorcycle going uphill. In a moment, the sound became peculiarly deafening, indicating that the motorcycle was caught in the mud. She saw the people of the barrio coming out of their houses; the men running in the direction of the sound. Among them, she saw her mother carrying an iron bar.

There was something inviting about the floating clouds and flying birds in the sky. From where she was, in her imagination, Inday Lupog was transformed into a beautiful aswang flying happily. She gazed down upon Boy Eks and his Kawasaki motorcycle. He was naked and his erect penis was inviting her to come. But the familiar sensation that used to creep between her thighs was gone. Her child was on her wings. Though Boy Eks was pleading for her to come down, she ignored him.

That noon, Bombo Radyo listeners who were having lunch heard of the whole barrio's beating of a man who was believed to be an aswang. ♦

PAMATO

by Merlie M. Alunan
Translated from Cebuano by Shane Carreon

BIKO-BIKO

This is how biko-biko is played. Get a stick and draw lines on the ground. The lines forming a house with rooms. Then, an agreement on the ways and pathways in entering and leaving the house. So you'd know where to go up or down, toss a stone, your pamato, inside the lines of the house. Where your pamato touches down, that's where your room is.

Your pamato must be smooth. Must be a size right on your palm, must weigh just so, so when you cast it, it won't hurtle off anywhere, it'd land exactly where you'd want it to be. It's not easy to find this kind of stone.

When you do find it, take special care of it. Before slipping it into your pocket, give it a whisper, so it'd get hold of luck and follow whatever it is you want it to do. When it's already right in your pocket, touch it once in a while so it won't get lonely. This stone would then become your pamato.

THE SEAFARER

A seafarer keeps a piece of steel, sometimes a large piece of rock, in the boat. Doesn't matter what shape it is, the rock, as long as it is of the right size and weight. Docking, the seafarer drops the rock into the water, anchoring the boat from being carried away by the current and the waves. To speed up the boat, the seafarer pulls up the rock right before setting out to sea. But these, of course, has got nothing to do at all with the game biko-biko or with traveling by boat. You see, a story can always begin on land and end up, before you know it, in heaven.

THE MAL-AM IN DUEÑAS

The town called Dueñas is known in Iloilo as the hometown of Tenyente Gimo, the famous ungo in all ka-Illonggohan. I was born in Dueñas and I also grew up there. Now, don't you start thinking I'm an ungo, all right, not everyone is ungo in Parian or Naga, those places where the powerful live here in Sugbo.

In Dueñas, the old people are called mal-am. When I was grow-ing up, there was Mal-am Tikyo, also Mal-am Tonyang. Now that I'm about sixty, in Dueñas I would be called Mal-am Milay. "Masakit ya akon tuhod. Mal-am dun," is what one would say in Kinaray-a. "Sakit akong tuhod. Lagas na gyud," is how we'd say it in Binisaya in Dueñas. In other words, "My knees hurt. Really old now."

Mal-am Silay was our neighbor. We called her Ma-am Silay as though we had a lisp. She was not an ungo, uy, but we children always thought she looked like one. Her skin was so wrinkled, like the tobacco leaves after they've been dried out under the sun. She had no teeth, her cheeks were hollow, the bones in her elbows and knees poked out. She was also very thin, very bent, barely able to stand, and hardly able to walk. On top of that, she was also blind. The mere sight of her sometimes would give Idik and Butsoy the creeps, they'd run away just seeing her coming.

LOVE

Every day, Mal-am Silay would come down her bamboo steps and ever so very slowly make her way to the well by the spring to bathe. Her adolescent granddaughters would walk with her. Daday would be a step ahead, carrying the hungot, the coconut shell bowl holding the soap, pumice, and grated coconut for the mal-am's long gray hair. Behind her, Talya would be bracing the poor old blind walking. The three of them would slog one step at a time through the rocky footpath to the spring.

Along the way, they often passed by us playing biko-biko. We'd be sweating. Smelling rancid, bahong adlaw, after a day in the hot sun. Unbathed. The noontime earth searing the soles of our bare feet. We didn't have any footwear. There weren't any of those rubber slippers back then. Mal-am Silay was also barefoot. The callus on the soles of our feet were so thick the heat didn't bother us at all while we played, springing and skipping about. Daday and Talya's wooden slippers clunked along the rocky path. Caring, Melinda, and I would then stop playing to stand aside and gape at the slowest procession we've ever known. Sometimes, I would follow the three of them to the well to watch the mal-am bathe.

At the open well, Talya would draw up a bucketful of water and gently pour it over her grandmother. Daday would rub the pumice on her back, soap her arms and legs, her wilted breasts. Both of them carefully washing the old woman's gray hair with milk from the grated coconut pounded with lemon leaves. Water would cascade down and shimmer on her shriveled skin. Then, from the encircling trees, a cool wind would breathe on the mal-am's naked body. Ay, it made my hair stand on end. Talya would then knot the mal-am's wraparound. Daday, too. After washing her hair with milk, they would comb down the dried shredded coconut from her hair. Her hair would shine and smell of lemon, and would be let down for the sun and wind.

The three of them would walk again, ever so slowly, heading home. All I could do was sniff my snot and excitedly run ahead of them, understanding nothing. My eyes full of what I had just seen, I'd burst out laughing a laughter reaching the tips of all the fronds of all the coconut trees. But I had no idea what it was that made me happy. I couldn't say anything because I knew nothing. In those days, no one could have guessed how many sacks of rice I would have yet to eat, and what pains, fears, hunger, losses I would have yet to come through before I could know what love is, and finally learn how to say the word.

DEPARTURE

One day, we left Dueñas. We packed away all our things—mat, pillows, cauldron and clay pot, plates and ladle, some of our clothes—Nanay, Tatay, my three siblings, and I. We got on a bus, taking with us everything we packed. We boarded a ship, and for days were on the sea.

Nanay cried, and my siblings. Our relatives, too, cried when we left. But I didn't cry, see. Even if I wouldn't get to play biko-biko anymore with Caring and Melinda. Botsoy and Idik who were champions in siyatom and tatsi. Even if I wouldn't get to go to the well by the spring anymore, with Mal-am Silay, Daday, and Talya in their daily procession to the bathing place.

Really, I didn't cry. I told myself, Ah, I'd come back soon. And when I did, they would still be there.

Por vida, that was so long ago, uy. And I wasn't able to return after all.

PAMATO

Across Siquijor, in the islands of the Kabisay-an, and farther still, at the smoky peak of Kanlaon, then close to Parian, and even past Naga. I reached Iligan, land of the Muslim. For years I took shelter under the Talinis, beside the waves of sugarcane at the foot of Cuernos. There were many houses I walked up into and walked down away. Even though I was born and raised there, Dueñas, after some time, became one of the many that I turned my back on. Reminiscing those I have loved, left, and never seen again, I finally understood love.

In my memory, the clunking of Talya and Daday's wooden slippers are still audibly clear. And the soles of the old blind lagging and dragging on the bare ground in her daily pilgrimage to the well. I can still hear in my memory the very sound of flowing water drawn up from the deep well, the rustling wind from the groves, our loud and hearty laughing as children playing by the wayside—perduring and ageless in my memory.

Ay, one shouldn't keep returning to the days past. Mal-am Silay has long turned into ash. The old language, now scraped away by the years from my tongue.

But whichever shore I may have found myself, whatever I may have crossed over, climbed on, or went down through, even though those I have left behind are long gone, would I ever find—the pam-ato I have been safekeeping in my mind, smooth, with its right weight, good enough as needed, landing where I wanted it to be, following its purpose, fighting off the waves and the currents, unfail-ing in its meaning. ◆

MANILA-BOUND

by Doms Pagliawan
Translated from Waray by Daryll Delgado

As soon as Man Caloy received the letter from Amado, his son who worked in Manila, he went straight to his good friend's house near the plains, even when the day was getting late. He needed to know what was in this letter that his son had sent him. The messenger who handed him the letter, who came all the way from the town, was in too much of a hurry to leave, so he wasn't able to ask the young man to read the letter to him.

Like his wife, Man Caloy could not read, not only because he needed to wear eyeglasses but also because he had not had any formal education whatsoever, not even grade one level. He grew up, got married, spent all his life farming, but never learned to read. Luckily, all of his five children got some education. No one made it to college though, they all got married early, and had to start earning a living as soon as they could. Or maybe they were frustrated because they wouldn't have afforded college education anyway.

The light was already dimming when he reached his friend's

house. With the letter in his hands, he couldn't help the smile on his face as he was met by his friend right outside the house.

"Oy, what's up, Padi, are we drinking today?" his friend asked, surprised at his visit.

He told his friend about his purpose for the visit. Inside the house, they faced each other across the table, a bright lamp between the two of them. "What does it say, Padi?" he earnestly asked.

His good friend brought the lamp closer to the letter, reading it with some difficulty. His eyes glimmering and slightly teary against the lamplight.

"You're being asked by Amado to go to Manila, Padi, you and Madi. December 11, he says, and he'll be at the pier when your boat arrives in Manila," his good friend told him.

"That means next week already," Man Caloy said, thinking deeply, while stroking his graying and tobacco-smelling beard.

In the days that followed, the elderly couple, Man Caloy and Mana Bising, were kept busy preparing for their journey. They spent some time pondering on a good welcome gift to bring to their son, Amado, who had settled in Manila with a wife, and lived presumably in his own house in a place called Tondo.

They were both deeply elated. Who would have thought, both of them making it to Manila for the very first time. For sure, their son would take them around Manila. Who wouldn't be exhilarated by that thought? They couldn't help but tell anyone who happened to pass by their house, which stood alone on a hillside, on their way to the farm, the good news, the wonderful stroke of luck the couple had.

"That's really good for you both, as you've just been here on your own," said one passerby.

After several nights spent preparing for the trip with hardly any sleep, they finally agreed that they would bring the white young pig on their journey, to give to their son. This would be their offering to Amado, the best thing they could ever give. Amado would surely love this pig which was so healthy and smooth-skinned, alert, and bouncy like a ball, especially when it was being playful or when it was just showing off.

A part of Mano Caloy wanted to hold on to the pig. They loved this pig: they always fed it their leftover food; always bathed it inside its pen; sometimes they would carry it and caress it; or comb through its hair to make sure there were no lice. This pig was like one of their own children, or a beloved grandchild who gave them so much joy.

"Oh, just give it to Amado. What can we do, there's nothing else we can bring for him," exclaimed Mana Bising, trying her best to appease Man Caloy who was finding it difficult to let go of the young pig.

———————

The day they had been waiting for came at last—the day of their departure. At dawn, the sun not even out yet, the couple was already up to cook, eat, and take a bath. They could finally leave. Good thing the owner of the land they were farming as tenants agreed to lend them some money for the trip to Manila, on the condition that if they failed to pay him back, all their farms and their produce would go to him.

They looked as though they were going to attend a wedding. Man Caloy, in his white long-sleeved shirt, black trousers, and his white hair and wide forehead shiny with Three Flowers pomade. Mana Bising, for her part, pulled her hair back in a bun, and also wore a white dress that sometimes stuck to bulging parts of her body. Because of the tightness of the skirt, she had a hard time moving her skinny and varicosed calves. Of course, she was also exuding a strong fragrance from the perfume that she splashed on herself.

They had with them a sackful of clothes. They also had a batulang that was filled with vegetables and crops. But the most important parcel was the pig whose feet Mano Caloy tied, otherwise if it was fully bound up, it might just injure and hurt itself from struggling so much. Poor animal, he thought, if that ever happened.

When the sun rose, they were already walking the six-kilometer distance to the main road where they could take a jeep that would take them to Catbalogan. Mano Caloy had the sack of clothes on his back, and the pig secured against his side. Mana Bising was like a little girl trailing behind, dragging the batulang filled with vegetables.

They reached the town center close to eleven in the morning, and went straight to Pier 1 in a tricycle so they could purchase boat tickets. They almost didn't make it. The tickets nearly ran out as there were extraordinarily many people bound for Manila. Good thing, Man Caloy said, good thing they came early. Or else, they wouldn't be able to get on the boat. Amado would have shriveled dry in the sun waiting for no one at the pier in Manila, said Mana Bising.

The passengers had to wait a little for the boat which was coming from Tacloban. They were told that it would reach them only at one in the afternoon. The couple sat by the roadside, they could barely suppress their eagerness to get on the boat for the very first time in both their lives. As soon as the boat appeared, they immediately made their way to the front of the queue of passengers, squeezed themselves through the crowd in order to be the first ones to board the boat.

The young pig whimpered in discomfort throughout the scuffle and fray. It twisted and bent its body in an effort to free itself from the ropes that bound its feet. He probably thought that the world was going mad, or that his life was about to end.

It didn't take long for Man Caloy and his wife to board the vessel even amid the large number of people behaving in a seemingly disorganized way, but when they reached the sleeping quarters all the cots were occupied by other passengers already. Apart from the fact that the whole section was filled with people, there was also too much baggage and cargo on the ship so that there was almost no space for people to step on. Of course they also had nowhere on which to settle their own haul. It was sweltering, and all kinds of smells had blended and were trapped together in their section: cigarette smoke, all sorts of unpleasant body odors, sweat, urine, and so many others.

Blame it on the fierce heat of the sun outside; intensifying the heat. Though Man Caloy heard some faint thunderclaps and noticed the dark clouds forming in the distance. Good if it rains, he thought, to lessen the heat somewhat.

While they went round and round the passenger section looking for a place to settle in, Man Caloy continued to bear the heavy sack and carry the young pig in one arm, while Mana Bising behind him had her hand on his back. Man Caloy felt a stab of hunger. They had not had any lunch because they didn't want to leave the spot where they had waited for fear of being left behind while they were getting food. They had satiated their hunger with tobacco in the meantime while they were crouched by the roadside.

Truth was, when they stepped on the boat, Man Caloy was already trembling like how he usually got when he was hungry. They did bring some food with them, wrapped in anahaw leaves, but Man

Caloy had stuck it somewhere in the middle of the sack he was carrying so that it wasn't easy to access.

Just like what the other passengers who just boarded the vessel did, Man Caloy and his wife just put down their cargo and perched near one of the walkways even if the location was inconvenient and they had to contend with people passing and overstepping them frequently. There was nowhere else to settle on. What's important, said Mano Caloy, was that they made it to Manila, otherwise Amado would be kept waiting there at the pier.

"And we'll right away hand him this young pig, so he'll be happy," Mana Bising responded, smiling brightly, her yellow teeth showing, her breath slightly sour.

"But, of course. He'd be very pleased indeed," Man Caloy said. "I think it won't be long before this pig is good for roasting as lechon." He adjusted his hold on the swine and caressed its belly. He couldn't put the animal on the floor in front of him because of too many people passing who might step on it.

While the pig was pressed against his chest, it suddenly twisted itself, exerted effort, and emitted a loud sound from its anus. The pig expelled feces, which caused Man Caloy to swing the pig away from his body and let go of it, so that it fell on the floor, and as soon as it was able to stand it ran as fast as it could, seemingly in fear.

Man Caloy's long-sleeved shirt was full of the pig's shit. But he immediately went after the animal. The chase took him to different parts of the boat. The pig was fast; it quickly went under the labyrinth of cots. The old man bumped and hit corners in his effort to chase after the pig, he stumbled over cargo and people who yelled angrily at him because of the pig shit that he scattered around in the process.

In a short while, Mana Bising was on her feet ready to help in capturing the animal. She thought it was important that they catch it immediately or else it might jump into the sea. They both looked like children in a game of chase and catch. The problem was that the boat was too crowded and there were too many nooks and crannies that the pig could go into. They were both drenched in sweat. Man Caloy, his clothes sticking to his entire body, was also starting to smell really bad because of the feces still all over his front, splattered across the whiteness of his shirt. People he passed scrunched up their faces, the others actually covered their noses.

Fortunately, some of the spectators felt sympathy for the couple. They helped in trying to catch the young pig even if they knew they were in danger of also being splattered with feces. They formed a trap around the area where the pig was until it had nowhere else to go.

Outside, a heavy rain started, coupled with loud thunderstorms and lightning. From the loudspeakers, an announcement echoed: "Pwera bisita, pwera bisita." Man Caloy wondered what that meant. And why it was repeatedly announced.

As for the young pig, when it realized it had nowhere else to go, it stopped in front of Man Caloy and then suddenly bolted toward the walkway all the way to the ramp, and did not stop until it left the boat and reached the port.

They went after it all the way outside the boat, Mana Bising panting behind him in difficulty. It was not in her to let anything go to waste. Even a single grain of rice that fell from her plate during their mealtimes, she picked up; how much more for a pig they had raised and were going to offer to their beloved son?

The other people did not join them anymore in the chase. Outside, they were immediately soaked to their skins by the heavy rain and the violent storm winds that came with it. The pig's pace increased under the rain since there were no longer any barriers, save for the few people with their umbrellas standing on the sidelines. Man Caloy, for his part, was now free to spurt out curses. He was feeling murderous, he would have murdered someone if it were a person causing them this much anguish. They were exhausted from running, especially Man Caloy who was older.

When the swine reached the edge of the port area, it turned right, toward the informal settlers' residential area. There under the maze of shanties it continued to run. Man Caloy and his wife continued their pursuit of the pig but he stumbled when he reached the undersides of the houses and hit the posts and his feet sunk into the dark murky ground. There was so much trash and waste buried in the muddy ground, including animal and human waste since the houses did not have proper toilets.

Man Caloy decided to take off his muck-covered shoes and threw these to Mana Bising who was taking shelter under the roof of another house, also soaked to the skin.

Finally, the swine ended up against the corner of two walls and had nowhere to run. Man Caloy immediately jumped on it, caught its feet and lifted it. The young pig struggled against him, still trying to break free, adding more filth to the white shirt.

The couple ran as fast as they could back to the boat, carrying the pig with them. They didn't know that the boat was already some distance from the port. It was already making a turn for the open sea and preparing to move faster. They only learned of this when they reached the place where the ramp and anchor had been.

"Hooyy, wait, we're still here!" Man Caloy yelled, waving his hands frantically, jumping up and down like a lumatod. Mana Bising joined in the screaming, they took turns, their voices loud. Man Caloy attempted to jump into the sea to swim after the boat, but Man Bising held him back and reminded him that he didn't know how to swim. Despite their loud wailing, the boat kept going until this was swallowed by the dark wall of rain.

Mana Bising howled, her tears melding into the streaks of rain on her cheeks. She sat on the ground and started kicking her feet. Man Caloy, meanwhile, quietly tied the animal to the metal hook on the portside, then lifted it while it was tied and overwhelmed the animal with punches, slaps, scratches, pinches, squeezes, and flicks. When he was done, he slammed the animal against the concrete, it could barely emit any sound anymore after its loud cries.

The swine sprawled on the ground, barely breathing, body trembling. From its mouth, fresh blood spurted, which the rainwater swiftly carried away.

Man Caloy was trembling as well, his breathing short and heavy, his fists clenched, his eyes sharp. The animal looked to him like a devil with horns. With every thunder and lightning, it was as though his ears were struck. He thought of his sharp sundang. If only he had his bladed weapon with him, he would have chopped this beast down, no matter if it had seven or nine years. He would have finely sliced this animal, as it might just be pretending to be a pig when it was in reality a demon.

Immeasurable misfortune is what this animal brought to us, Man Caloy thought. He wished the swine was never born, or that it died young, or was swallowed by a python to rot in the snake's belly. So much regret and bitterness filled his heart. Not only did the boat leave them behind, it brought with it all their precious belongings which they had had with them since they were both young. Nothing,

Man Caloy thought, this pig is worth nothing. It deserves to be thrown into a sea of trash so it will rot and die in the middle of so much filth.

"Hala, we better head home," Man Caloy told his wife who was still wiping away tears from her face like a little girl left behind by her parents. "There's nothing we can do because we've been left behind." He turned and started walking away, under the cover of darkness.

Mana Bising stood, but instead of walking, she picked up the young pig which was barely alive.

"Leave it," Man Caloy stopped and looked at her angrily. "Leave it so it will die there."

Mana Bising did not do as told. She trailed behind him slowly but carried the pig on her right side.

Since they did not know anyone in town who could put them up for the night, they headed to the town plaza. They planned to stay there until morning came. Luckily, they were able to stay inside a small playhouse, which, though it smelled of urine—they smelled just as bad anyway—gave them shelter against the endless battering from the rain. They remained silent, unspeaking to each other, while they sat on the ground. Both were in deep thought. They kept swatting away mosquitoes. They couldn't sleep. The only one who was fitfully sleeping was none other than the young pig. Though it seemed to be in a different kind of sleep too, as it barely breathed, was completely out of it all. All it did was shiver. Which wasn't a surprise, because even its masters almost froze to death, especially since their clothes were all wet. Apart from the heavy rain, it was dark and windy. Man Caloy could see the trees in the plaza, occasionally hit by the glare of lamplights, swaying with the wind, as though dancing in the quite spacious plaza. In the middle of the night, the lights went out and their surroundings and the entire town was blanketed in darkness.

Early the next day, the skies still dark, light rain falling and some wind blowing, they made their way to the jeep terminal. There they heard people talking to each other about some serious thing that had happened, fear written on their faces. The couple boarded the jeep that was at the head of the line. There were already three passengers inside also talking to each other with the same seriousness, one of the women wiping tears from her eyes as she spoke. They listened in on the conversation. Their eyes dilated at what they heard. They could hardly believe it. They looked at each other for a long time, both shaking their heads.

Man Caloy's hunger went away completely. The hairs on his arms stood. His face soured as though he had just drunk strong vinegar. He brought his mouth closer to Mana Bising to whisper: "How lucky are we that we did not make it to the boat if it indeed sunk."

"Until now, not a single survivor has been found," the woman in front of them continued talking.

Man Caloy slowly took the young pig from Mana Bising's arms. It was as though he were lifting delicate eggs. The sow woke up and struggled a bit. As soon as the young pig was safely in Man Caloy's arms, he stood and motioned for his wife to follow him to get down from the jeep.

They looked for a small store on the roadside. As soon as they found one, Man Caloy bought what he described to the store attendant as the tastiest biscuits the store had. He sat on the curbside, opened the packet of biscuits, and tried to feed the young pig covered with filth, his eyes full of pity.

"Here, baby, eat something," Man Caloy said to the pig while he tried to force open its still bloody mouth.

The pig wouldn't eat anything. It wouldn't open its mouth. It kept its eyes closed as though it preferred to sleep a very long sleep, even when huge drops of tears fell on it from Man Caloy's eyes, from his head which he brought closer to the pig in order to kiss it, the pig whose body was starting to grow cold, a body lovingly cared for and nurtured as though it were one of the man's own. ♦

WHEN HE WAKES UP, MUSHROOMS ARE SPROUTING FROM HIS NOSE

by Carlo Paulo Pacolor

Translated from Filipino by Erika M. Carreon

Since he knew how to cook, he mixed it in with egg. The next day, from his armpit, instead of hairs there grew a branch with lush leaves, birds nesting on it, and when he arrived at work his office-mates said, uy, what pretty colors. A week had passed, and he had turned into a jungle. One night he and his wife went out for dinner, and she asked him, mahal, don't you miss your old skin, like I do, because now you're all dirt, moss, worms, and your breath smells of rotting wood? Do you want me to go back to the way I was, asked the jungle. Of course. And so, ignoring the traffic, the jungle stepped out of their car, and while the people inside the jeeps, taxis, buses, and cars bore witness to his careful deterioration, a multitude of plants and animals wilting and turning into skeletons and then ash covering the streets, they cried in unison, weeping until all that was left of it was a single seed. But when the light turned green, all the onlookers started blasting their car horns, howling, "stop blocking the road!" The wife shed not a tear as she picked up the seed, drove away, and went on to dinner like they had planned. She went home with the seed still in her pocket. The moment she stepped into their bedroom, she placed the seed in the middle of the bed and unpeeled herself completely. They made love. Days passed. Nobody saw or spoke with them. Their friends and relatives then decided to visit them. When they arrived, the car and other belongings were still there but not the couple. Suddenly they heard shuffling coming from the bedroom. Hearts beating fast, they approached the bedroom, but upon throwing the door open, they were all dumbstruck at what they saw. Instead of the bed, there was a gaping hole in the middle of the room. Carefully, they crept closer until they could peer into its dark depths, and someone even tried calling their names, but they didn't hear a reply, not even an echo. They stayed awhile, waiting, in case all of a sudden the couple would crawl out of the hole, but this didn't come to pass. As the days passed, they left one by one, utterly dismayed, having thought, why, if something like that was possible, something even more spectacular should follow! But nothing happened. The last of them remained until sundown, deciding that this day would be the last he was to wait. He knew the couple through an acquaintance who had known somebody who had been textmates with their dentist. He prayed that he'd see even just a tiny insect appear so he had something to brag about to his friends, saying a bug came out of the hole, what I tell you, but when the sun had finally set, he realized that there was nothing else to wait for. And at the exact moment he had stepped outside, he heard a rumbling and the ground shook, and the house was swallowed whole by the abyss. The experts had agreed that a sinkhole had caused the cave-in, noted as "a fairly common geological phenomenon" in their records. As talk went on around the neighborhood, nobody mentioned the couple or the jungle anymore, and eventually everyone believed these to be details sprinkled over the story for flavor. Not even heart-wrenching or real. ♦

GEL

by Zosimo Quibilan, Jr.
Translated from Filipino by Sunantha Mendoza-Quibilan

D indo regretted rushing over. It was taking a while for someone to open the gate for him. In the beginning, the raindrops tickled his scalp. It wasn't funny anymore. He rang the doorbell again and again when the rain started to run down his face. The styling gel on his hair had mixed with it and stung his eyes.

A maid finally came to the gate. She asked him to stand there first and wait. She said her mistress might get angry if she let visitors in right away.

Dindo ran a hand through his now limp hair. He pulled the soaked shirt away from his body. He could feel his legs starting to shiver. His new pair of jeans had turned a deeper shade of blue. His Chuck Taylors, which had waded through inches of muddy rainwater, dripped with each step.

He was shaking the rain from his hair when Helen came out to meet him. She didn't mind that some of it spattered on her. Her eyes were filled with tears. She couldn't return Dindo's embrace.

It wasn't clear to Dindo why he had come, in the height of the typhoon, no less. Helen had paged earlier for him to call her. It was urgent, she'd said. He couldn't say no. She rarely ever paged him.

"I hate talking to message handlers. They're just so stupid," Helen had explained to him once.

Dindo didn't have a telephone, so he had braved the angry storm and headed to the corner store just to make that call. Helen had burst into tears the moment she heard his voice. She had gone on and on about how she and her boyfriend had had a fight. Could Dindo come over. She was all alone.

"Sure. On the condition that there'll be chicken pen-din," Dindo had jokingly mimicked Helen's colegiala accent to lighten up the conversation.

Dindo had gulped the moment he hung up the phone. He had almost been hit by the store window awning when a fierce wind suddenly blew.

He had wanted to hurry back home but the floodwater in the streets had risen. While wading home, he had thought about the tone of Helen's voice. Dindo had feared what it meant but he had also wanted to know what had really happened.

He now felt the opposite as he held Helen in his arms. She continued to sniffle.

"Your nose is getting bigger. Don't cry anymore."

Helen smiled, but then quickly frowned again.

"What happened anyway?"

"I don't want to talk about it."

"So what will we do? Wait a minute. Where's my chicken pen-din?"

Helen jokingly punched him. "Shmuck! Let's go sa lanai."

Her disposition changed the moment they sat down. She appeared to have forgotten why she was crying just moments ago. She asked Dindo how he was. "Sorry sa hassle. You're the first person that came to mind when. . . . Oh yeah I don't want to talk about it. What's keeping you busy these days? Are you and your girlfriend still together?"

"No, we've already broken up. Imagine if you had just waited." Dindo was surprised by the words that came out of his mouth.

Helen paused. "Do you think you can wait?"

"The question is, why am I here?"

Silence.

Helen reached for his face, cupping her hands as if to catch water. She caressed Dindo's cheek. She touched his sticky hair.

Dindo didn't have the chance to feel ashamed of his hair, even though he knew it reeked. He looked outside instead. He watched the heavy, sporadic raindrops slam against the marble floor. He was soothed by the lightness of Helen's hand.

The ring of the telephone startled Dindo like an electric shock. Helen's maid arrived at once to hand her mistress the receiver.

The bickering between Helen and her boyfriend resumed. Dindo was taken aback by his friend's reaction. She carried on like a child deprived of a toy. She hurled whatever she got her hands on. She threw a fit. She forgot that Dindo was there.

Dindo slipped quietly out the door. He no longer said goodbye. He couldn't help but scratch his head. The weather had grown crueler now. He figured it was better to get drenched again. It would be easier to fix his hair the way he wanted it. ♦

IN THE SOFTNESS OF YOUR BREASTS

by Early Sol A. Gadong

Translated from Hiligaynon by John Bengan

This is what you said:

Yana, I miss your adobo.

And so before the sun could shine, while you were still deep in sleep, I got up from lying on your chest—in the softness of your breasts—and prepared to go to the market in Bangga Aganan, along the highway of Pavia. You pointed this out to me the night before when we passed by the place after I picked you up at the airport.

This is what we talked about:

—Ched, Iloilo has changed so much, no?

—Yes, so many things have changed here.

—Ti, are you still "shabulized" even if the mayor's new?

—Sus, don't listen to those stories. Since before, until now, the Ilonggos have only been high on love.

You followed this with a laugh. But laughter that came from the throat, not from the chest.

ULIRÁT

—The traffic jams in Cebu are really bad now. It has doubled compared to five years ago. Almost like the traffic situation in Manila.

—Is that so? Well, actually, even Iloilo traffic's slowly getting worse, too. I feel that this is really what's happening in the big cities here in our country. When I went to Davao last month, traffic's also complicated. Even in your place in Kalibo, the roads are starting to get crammed.

—Oh? What were you doing in Davao?

—Ah, nothing. Just a short vacation.

—Aw, okay. Have you also visited Kalibo?

—Haha. Who will I visit there? We just passed by the place going to Boracay.

—We?

—I went with one of my friends.

I bought the ingredients that I had many times bought in the seven years that we were together:

- one-fourth kilo of chicken (a combination of thigh, which was your favorite part, and wing, which was mine; none of us liked chicken breast);
- two big cloves of garlic;
- a pack of pepper;
- two sachets of rekado;
- a small bottle of vinegar; and
- two small sachets of special seasoning.

I also bought a kilo of rice, even though during our conversation, you told me that you didn't eat that much rice anymore. No wonder you lost some weight. Lastly, I bought half a dozen eggs.

This is what you told me when I asked you what you ate in place of rice:

Sandwich and salad. Sometimes, pasta. I'm staying away from pork and beef. But I miss adobo.

Darkness and half-light was still breaking when I got back to your house in Deca Homes. I still caught sight of the planet Venus when I looked up before entering your fence. You had moved out of your parents' house in Sinikway near Lapuz. I had only been to your new place twice. Three years had passed since I first and last came here to visit.

This is what you told me when you brought me here for the first time:

I know this isn't the dream house you want, 'Ga. But this is only temporary. Just so we have something we can call our own.

I moved about quietly, careful not to wake you up. We slept in the living room even though there were two rooms on the second floor of your house. The air-conditioning unit was downstairs, you said, and you hadn't tidied up the bedrooms yet.

This is what I told you:

This is why I'm here. To help you clean up, like before.

You only laughed and then went upstairs. The laughter still came from the throat. You brought a mattress when you came back. You went upstairs again, and when you returned, you brought a comforter, a sheet, pillows, a towel, and night clothes for me.

This is what you said:

You want to clean up, right? As you wish.

I went to the kitchen and located what I needed. You had a complete set of cooking utensils even though I knew you could only cook instant noodles. I couldn't stop myself from smiling. How many times had you actually used these things?

I started chopping the garlic. Then, I sliced the chicken into small cuts. I placed the garlic and chicken into the pan, and then the other ingredients. I covered the pan with a plate and put it inside the fridge.

On your fridge, there was a magnet shaped into a durian fruit above the name "Davao." I remembered the fridge at my condo in Cebu. It was also filled with refrigerator magnets from places we had been to: Boracay, Bangkok, Cagayan de Oro, General Santos, Singapore, Baguio, Hong Kong, Kota Kinabalu.

I didn't pluck them off even though they made Andrea jealous, and we often fought over them. She broke up with me a year ago.

This is what she told me:

I don't even stand a chance against magnets, what more with your history with Merced.

I scooped a small tin of rice and began to cook.

I saw you turning sideways and wrapping your legs and arms around the pillow beside you.

At the time when we were still starting out on our jobs, we only owned two pillows at the boardinghouse that I was renting. Because of your plumpness, you got used to keeping a long pillow that you curled up to at night. So I usually gave you my pillow and I would rest my head on your chest—in the softness of your breasts—while your fleshy arms would hug me tight.

There was a year when I gave you only pillows as gifts on every occasion: during Valentine's, your birthday, and our anniversary. On Christmas, I gave you another pillow.

This is what you said:

You're tired of lying on my chest, aren't you?

You knew that it wasn't true. Your insecurity was what we often fought over. I couldn't understand why you'd rather believe the things that would upset you. I kept telling you, each time I placed my cheek on your soft breasts, embraced you, wrapped my feet around you:

This is the best place in the world to sleep.

I poured the chicken, the vinegar, and other ingredients into the pan. I covered the pan and turned on the burner of the gas range. Then, I took out another pan and fried four eggs. Half-cooked, as you preferred.

When the chicken was boiling, I set the fire to low. The first time you had a taste of my adobo, you said that it was different from what you'd had growing up since the dish didn't have fish sauce or annatto.

This is what I said:

This one's Adobo de Yana, that's why.

I set our food on the table, along with plates and utensils. I cleaned up what I used in preparing what I cooked when I saw your cellphone glowing near the pillow where I'd lain. I absently walked over to it.

This is the message I read:

Isabelle Ty

Good morning, my gugma. *kiss emoji*

I'm no lo . . .

I couldn't read the rest of the message.

The lights of your phone's screen dimmed.

You turned until your whole body was facing in my direction. Your plump chest rose as you breathed deeply. This part of your body was paler compared to your mostly brown complexion. A mole was peeking out on the upper part of your left breast. Also, a nipple

153

jutted out under your thin T-shit. I had read so many poems about love. But you, now, here—you were my poem.

Behind your unruly hair, a smile formed across your cheeks.

This is what you said:

Hmmm. Adobo de Yana.

Until now, the aroma of my adobo excited you. I searched for this excitement when we saw each other outside the Arrivals Area, when we embraced each other, when you said that I looked good with my short hair, and when you told me stories inside your car on the way to your house.

If this morning only began four years ago, this is what's going to happen next:

I will come to you while you lift your hands to welcome me.

You'll hug me.

I'll whisper into your ear, "Good morning, my palangga."

You'll answer, "Good morning, I love you more."

You'll hold my neck.

I'll try to get you up.

I'm lighter around the gut by about fifteen inches, and so I'll tease you:

I can't do it, 'Ga. You're too heavy.

We'll repeat this.

I'll try to get you up, but I can't carry you.

On my third attempt, you'll get up.

I'll again kiss and embrace you.

Then you'll tease me:

Hmmm. Just the armpits and already tasty.

I'll pinch you on the waist and tell you:

I'm not food. Let's have breakfast.

Your eyes will widen at the sight of the food on the table: rice steaming, half-cooked sunny-side-up, and the adobo you're craving for.

You'll make coffee.

You'll add sugar until the coffee is the same color as my skin.

You'll stir the coffee sweetened with muscovado and you'll let me lick the teaspoon you used for stirring.

You'll tell me this:

Yummy.

Then, you'll stir the coffee you were making.

In half an hour, the two of us will have breakfast while I rest my thighs on your legs. We'll talk about anything that comes to mind.

You were telling me before about parallel universes.

This is how our conversation went:

—I read something, 'Ga. There is what they call infinite universes, and we are just in one. And because of the concept of infinity, somewhere in a parallel universe, there is another Merced and another Dayanara.

—Is this Ched still Yana's soul mate in the parallel universe?

—Of course. Not just soul mates. An infinite number of parallel universes guarantees that, at least, there is one universe where Ched and Yana will live happily ever after.

—You mean other than this universe?

You laughed so hard at that. Laughter that I'd heard thousands of times before. Laughter that came out of the release of joy from the chest, without trying to stifle it. I want to remember when I'd heard again laughter like that from you.

When your laughter subsided, this is what you said:

This is what I'm sure of, 'Ga. Let's call this universe we're in Universe A. I'm sure whatever happens, Merced of Universe A will always, always be in love with Dayanara of Universe O.

(Why Universe O? I asked. // O as in "ours," you replied while gesturing air quotes. // It was me who laughed so loud this time.)

Sometimes, our talk became political. You were a member of the League of Filipino Students back when we were in college, and so our pillow talk included commentaries about sociopolitical issues.

This is what we talked about when martial law was declared in Maguindanao:

—People think that the declaration of martial law is only a peace and order issue.

—Oh? Isn't it so? There are many rebels there. Is there another dimension to it?

—Economic, 'Ga. It's also an easier means for the government to pocket money.

—Really? How?

—Remember that during martial law, a province has no need for the procurement process. One signature of the "martial" (you made air quotes), the documents for contractors for whatever infrastructure projects get instantly approved. Who do you think gets a huge kickback when this happens?

You had many such stories and I listened and shared my own views. But whatever we talked about, this would always be there:

You'd keep praising the adobo I prepared, while I praised again and again the coffee you made.

Then, I'd clear the table after us.

You'd take a wash and change.

I'd walk you to the gate, and wait for you to get on a jeep going to work.

I read something back then that I'd also shared with you, about the planet Alpha Centauri B. This planet is located at about more than four light-years from the solar system. In other words, if there is light coming from our planet, it takes four years for this light to be seen on Alpha Centauri B. If there's a being on that planet with eyes powerful enough to see what's happening on our planet, they would see every single day we spent in the last four years. And so if this morning began before those four years, this being would be pleased with our tenderness to each other.

But the memory of events that didn't take place could not satisfy the eyes, not even the stomach.

Three years had passed since I ended things with you and chose to be with Andrea instead. She was one of the top management at the supermarket where I worked in Cebu. We fell for each other. She understood what I wanted to achieve in life: a house of my own, a nice car, savings at the bank. You didn't share the same aspirations. You were content with what you earned working as accounting staff at the University of the Philippines. I had taken you to task about this when you visited me in Cebu for our seventh anniversary.

Afterward, you flew to Cebu many times to beg me to come back to you, but my decision remained. I didn't answer your messages and calls; I unfriended you on Facebook.

A year after I'd broken up with you, you disappeared from my life. You stopped sending text messages or calling.

It had been two years since we last talked to each other. So when I sent a message a month ago to let you know that I was dropping by Iloilo before going to Bacolod, I was surprised to receive a response.

I told you that I had a meeting with a prospective supplier for the supermarket I was managing. I asked if it was possible for me to stay the night at your place since there wouldn't be boats going to Bacolod by the time I arrived in the evening. I didn't expect you'd say yes.

It had been six months since Andrea and I broke up. I wanted to get back with you. I wanted to remind you that you are my soul mate. If I could only bring you to Alpha Centauri B to show you our memories before they all disappeared. I wanted to remind you about what you'd told me:

No matter what happens, the Merced of Our Universe will not stop loving the Dayanara of Our Universe.

The other night, you wanted to sleep on the floor while I sleep on the sofa. I asked you that we sleep next to each other on the floor. You said yes.

The breeze coming from the air-conditioning unit was cool. When I put my arms around you, you didn't protest. You even adjusted the sheet so the two of us could fit underneath.

I didn't dare kiss you. Perhaps, out of exhaustion from the trip, I quickly fell asleep.

In the middle of the night, I felt the warmth of your breath on my neck. Your face looked peaceful as you slept. And when I got up in the morning, you were embracing me while I rested on your chest—in your supple breasts. Like the way we had slept for hundreds of nights in the seven years that we were with each other.

That was why I couldn't help but remember our old habits every morning when we'd lived together back then. And if there truly was an infinite number of universes, in one universe, what I thought would happen will mark the first day of our reunion.

But in truth, this is what happened:

You groped around for your cellphone.

You opened it and read the message.

You smiled at what you read.

"Good morning," you said to me.

Then, you got up and turned the TV on. You tuned in to a news channel.

"I'll just go to the bathroom. Then, we'll have breakfast."

I locked the bathroom door.

I could hear you whisper and giggle as you spoke.

You spoke in English.

I sat in front of the table where the dish of pale adobo was set. You used to polish the sauce off the dish clean. You ate rice with your hands and dipped it in sauce, which was a mix of vinegar, oil, and spices.

This is what you'd say after:

Adobo with a secret ingredient does taste different.

You'd raise my arm and sniff my armpit.

How many hundreds of our days began like this, and ended with us sleeping, where I lay my head on your chest, you held me tight, and I slowly wrapped my legs around your thighs. And before the two of us fell asleep, we'd kiss—three times—until I'd lay my head again on your soft breasts, and would whisper, "This is the best place in the world to sleep." I'd kiss your forehead again and again and hold you tightly, even though we had five soft pillows around us.

The news anchor on TV was reading the teleprompter the details about the declaration of martial law in Mindanao the other night. Shocked by the news, I covered my mouth with my hand. I smelled the lingering scent of garlic on my fingers.

The news anchor continued to narrate the reason for the declaration of martial law but my eyes drifted to the Starbucks mug inside the shelf next to your TV. "Davao" was written on it. Behind the mug was a tumbled picture frame. I took a look at the photo in it.

It was a photo of you and another woman. Her skin was fair as coconut milk. Her midnight-black hair tied in a ponytail. She had small eyes and had a dimple on her right cheek. You were in a coffee shop. You sat next to each other on the couch. Her arm was around your shoulder and your cheeks touched. On the table in front of you, there were green salad, pizza, and cream pasta.

Before long, this is what I heard:

"I love you, too."

The toilet flushing.

The rush of water from the tap.

Then, the bathroom door clicking. ♦

CAN'T GO OUT

by Elizabeth Joy Serrano-Quijano
Translated from Cebuano by John Bengan

Darkness falls in the afternoon. It's going to rain again. The carabao and the goats have been herded off to shelter. The newly
harvested corn has been covered. The house smells of fuel because
our tiny lamp has been lit. Smoke rises from the hearth, a signal that
Mama is cooking something. The five of us can't go out. I want to go
out so I can wait for Papa. I want to look out for what he brings, but
I can't go out.

The other week, Papa brought meat from hunting. Mama prepared it in a delicious broth. Rod and I fought over a large piece of
wild boar meat. Mama got upset because we shouldn't fight at the
table.

But last night, she and Papa were arguing. The five of us slept on
empty stomachs. I couldn't find my malong cloth. I fell asleep in our
cold corner of the forest in Datal Fitak, a mountain in Matanao.

My teacher asks if we have ever seen a TV. I've seen one in a
picture but I don't know what it's for. I haven't been to Digos or to
Davao, but I've heard about those places. So many people, they say,

so many vehicles. Sometimes I don't feel so bad because so many people and so many vehicles might run me over.

Ma'am Edna, my grade three teacher, says that others wish on a foling estar. I'll also wish on a star that I might visit Digos even just for once. But the stars only come out at night, and I can't go out.

I've only ever ridden Uncle Basud's motorcycle the time we delivered our harvested corn. I haven't been in a jeep, or what Ma'am calls bus and van, airplane, ship. Sometimes my mind reaches the heavens. Are there also cars in heaven? Is there electricity, lights in the night that don't need fuel?

I've only seen and listened to a radio but our radio ran out of batteries, and our house is now more quiet. When the wind blows, our cogon roof dances and our bamboo walls snap.

Mama didn't go to Bangkal to buy batteries for the radio because there are soldiers. Anyway, I've seen a selfon. Because Ma'am Edna has a selfon. You can take a picture, listen to a song, you can read. I asked Mama if she knew how to use a selfon. She said to me, she doesn't even know how to write her name. She only reached grade one, and then she was married off to Papa when she was only twelve. How could she have gone to school if she couldn't go out.

Mama didn't agree to me being married off to our neighbor Randy. Mama wants me to finish at least high school. Will I finish? I've repeated grade three twice. In a week, I'll skip classes to help at the cornfield. My playmates are better off, they get to go with their mamas when the 4Ps are released. We didn't join the 4Ps because Papa wouldn't let us. We don't know our birthdays and Ma'am Edna kept asking for my birth setikyet. Mama said to me, you don't have that because you can't go out!

Can't Go Out

Papa didn't come home. And I can't find my malong. The wind outside seems to whisper something. The trees outside seem to speak and the footsteps of light feet lull me to sleep. When it's dark, even when you want to take a piss, you can't go out because there are raiders doing pangayaw. Wild creatures lurk outside. Rod's malong smells like piss after he wet himself on our bed because we can't go out.

———

I stir to the rustling of birds. Perok-perok, maya, agila, and banog, the loud ones early in the morning. I'm wide awake hearing Mama's scream. I rush downstairs and see two men.

"Your Papa's gone," says Mama, holding my malong soaked in blood. The men leave. I understand that my Papa is dead. I want to cry and look for Papa, but I can't go out.

I told Ma'am Edna when she asked me what Papa's work was, I told her Papa was a soldier. He had a yuniform and a gun. There was a red crest on the side of his yuniform. I bragged to my klasmit that Papa was a soldier. That was why he hunted deer and wild boar, because he was always in the forest. Every Friday I would wait for Papa because I knew he would bring something for me. Sometimes flowers from the jungle, and honey.

Rayzan said to me that Papa wasn't a soldier. That was why we had a fight and I didn't want us to be friends. Sometimes there were people who came to the house with Papa. They called Papa Ka Oding. I saw that they had papers, and letters, money, guns, and they were also with women who were pretty and had light skin. I didn't know where they were from. But Papa told us to play behind our

163

cogon hut. Whenever his companions were around, Mama would go to the cornfield.

I told Papa, "Women can be soldiers too? I want to be like you, Pa. I want to be a soldier!"

Papa stood up, went outside, and struck our dog. Papa said I shouldn't become a soldier, because soldiers have no mercy, they are abusive and they kill.

"Aren't you a soldier, Pa? Why can't I be a soldier too? You even have a companion who's a girl soldier."

Mama interrupted, "Greshel, your food, finish up, you'll be leyt for the bayang flag ceremony."

I didn't know it would be our last breakfast with Papa. Only my bloody malong is what I have left. Papa brought my malong that day he left after he and Mama had a fight.

"Rebelde, rebelde, but your children will die of hunger?!" Mama's voice was loud.

"This is for them, this is for you!" Papa left with his bag.

I lay back down and thought of the heaven that Ma'am Edna told us about. In heaven there is plenty of food, in heaven there is God. Papa said God is not real. Mama said there is a God. I want to believe there's a God so I could pray to Him about what I want. I want to go to Digos, eat hatdog, ays krim, and pitsa. Ma'am Edna told us these taste good and she showed us pictures. Ma'am even wanted to bring us to Matanao but Papa wouldn't let us, because we can't go out.

Gunshots! Gunshots! Gunshots! At first I could count the gun-fire. But there are too many gunshots and I can't anymore count because I can only count up to twenty. People are running, others yelling, "The soldiers are here!"

Soldiers?! Maybe Papa's with them! I'll go out! I see at the door Mama and my siblings covered in blood. Our walls and roof riddled with bullets.

"Mama! Mama! Mama!"

Mama stirs. And she says, "Don't go out, you can't go out!" ♦

RELATIONSHIP

by John E. Barrios

Translated from Akeanon by Merlie M. Alunan

1. AIDA

She skipped from the house just to come here. It's a good thing Richard her phone pal had agreed to this meeting. It would really make a difference to personally meet the person you've known for a long time. Three months is a long time as far as she is concerned. She was not so keen about it at first, fearing it might turn off Richard and he'd stop talking to her on the phone. But why would she be scared. Her mother said she's pretty. Her nanay had allowed her to work as a helper in Iloilo. You've finished the elementary, she said, they might send you to school. But three months is gone and there's been no mention yet of her going to high school. Probably because there's no one to take care of the house, the younger sibling of her employer had left for Cebu. The siblings quarreled over a used napkin left on the toilet bowl. They almost killed each other. The younger one was about to stab the older one. It was a good thing the live-in partner of her boss was quick to intervene. He grabbed the knife and pushed the younger one toward the orchid pots. She herself went crazy, rushing out to ask their cross-eyed neighbor for help. The neighbor was quite willing to lend a hand but she herself bumped against the gate. She stumbled. Now when they remember that event they find themselves laughing about it. They thanked her a lot for asking the cross-eyed neighbor for help. Until now her boss has not recovered from her encounter with her sister who fled to Cebu afterward. But that has also made her very happy because now the house is all hers the whole day. No obstructions to her long conversations with Richard on the phone. Yes, Richard is her *nobyo*. Phone calls have a unique power all on their own. The feelings are more explosive when they are transmitted by voice, more than when one is really seeing the person one is talking to. In truth it might be said that Richard had already taken all of her. That's the strange thing about her story. This is how it happened. One night she was left absolutely alone at home, her employers were out to attend a wedding, and Richard called. They talked for a long time on the phone. They set the phone smoking, then suddenly the line went silent. To her surprise, Richard's voice suddenly changed, he was asking her what she was wearing. She'd just finished bathing. It's very warm in their place at night. The house has a low roof. Without hesitation she told him she was wearing only a white towel. Are you wearing panties? Richard asked her. She was wondering why her nobyo would ask that. She just told him the truth. She heard Richard say, "I lab yu, Aida." She felt at a loss for an answer. She did not have any idea what was going on. She waited for him to speak again. Richard said he himself had just finished taking a bath and he asked her if she would allow him to touch her big breasts. She was amused because that was not possible. But she agreed. He did not stop at her breasts. His hands went down to the grassy triangle which lies between her plump thighs. Richard kissed her lips. Her first kiss from a man in her entire sixteen years of life. Not even her own father had experienced such a kiss, her own mother had once told Aida. She did not really know much about her father. She liked the kiss very much. She clung to Richard. Tight. Very soon she felt the whole house shaking. The weight of Richard's body. The lift and fall of Richard's hips. She also heard the creaking of the bamboo bench on which they were lying. She felt pain. Pleasurable pain. Until she felt the silent explosion in her very depths. She did not know where that came from. The phone fell from her hand. She was chasing her breath. In a little while she picked up the phone again. Richard asked her if she enjoyed it. She told him the truth. At that moment, she saw blood flowing from between her plump thighs. That was when she told him he had taken her honor. She knew then that she had found the man she would introduce to her nanay. Last night when they talked, they agreed to meet at the Es Em Pud Kurt. She told her nobyo the color of the blouse she'd be wearing. Yellow. And a flowery knee-length pair of pants. She'd wear the new sandals she bought from a midnight sale at Gaisano City. Richard would wear a red polo. Faded maong pants. So as not to be embarrassed, she stole a hundred-peso bill from her master's wallet so Richard would not say she has no money of her own. She hadn't been paid for two months now. She has been waiting for half an hour but no one wearing a red polo has shown up. It is past twelve and the diners at the pud kurt are arriving. Most of those she sees are students in their uniforms, and families. She notices a family who are not using serving spoons. That amuses her. Her mistress often said it is not good for people's spit to mix in one dish. This was the first thing she learned on her first day in Iloilo. The sound of forks and spoons deafens her. She does not like the sound of people slurping soup. She realizes now that her masters are made of different stuff. The man is a teacher. The woman works in the Capitol. She envies her masters. They also admit that they are not like the others. She is roused from her reverie when a man wearing a blue polo asks to sit in front of her. She looks around and notices that almost all the seats in the lowest portion of the mall are filled up. Some are eating and others are waiting to eat. She says yes. The man puts down his tray and moves the plate, the saucer, and the bottle of coke to the table. The man asks her if she is waiting for anybody. She just tells him the truth. The man smiles and starts sipping his soup. He is like everybody else. It's not a difficult thing not to make a noise when sipping one's soup. She learned that on her first day in the house of her masters. The man looks at his watch. Maybe he's not coming, says the man. She is surprised that the man would say that to her. Have you been waiting long too? he asks her. She just tells him the truth. The man smiles again. Are you new here in Iloilo? the man asks again. She tells him the truth too. The man smiles again. She is uneasy at this turn of events. As far as she's concerned the guy in front of her has no business talking to her like that. She doesn't know him, and though he's sort of good-looking and well-built, she isn't interested in him at all. She thinks of the shape of the mouth and the face of her phone pal. In the three months in which the two of them have been talking on the phone, she can almost draw his looks—the shape of the mouth, the fine cut of the nose, the color of his eyes, even his smell. She's been waiting for an hour but no one wearing a red polo has shown up. Smiling, the man wearing the blue shirt stands up and asks to be excused. When the man leaves she feels a little sad. Or ashamed of herself. Richard could have been here already. Richard might have seen her and did not like her looks. Everything that happened could have only been a joke. Richard is playing a trick on her. Who could ever be a man like Richard? Who is Aida anyway? She is only a servant girl after all. She hardly notices her tears falling slowly. She stands up quickly and finds the way out of the first story. It is past one already. She feels hungry. She also feels dizzy. She walks fast. In her hurry she bumps against a student who is also rushing. The books scatter all over. When the books drop on the mall floor she faints. But before she totally loses consciousness she catches a glimpse of the man in the blue polo looking at her from far away.

2. LORNA

She's 18. As soon as she gets off the txi she almost leaps up the 5 steps of the stairs so she would be inside the open square door at the side of the shoebox-shaped mall. Shoebox-shaped to remind the owner that he started as a shoe vendor. An example of how art is influenced by memory. She is meeting her bf Rick in the first level. 12 am. But she's 1 hr 18t already. Their Mth 101 prof delayed giving the exam. Fnls and can't be taken fast or ignored. The prof is a known terror. One might be good but one must also make sure. She's got to have good grades so she can still enjoy free education. 1 year more to go and she'll finish her Acntncy. The 1 sem when she lost her schlr-shp, she was forced to leave her ID with their sekyu 3 times. The first 2 cstmrs who hit on her were ok because they were also stdnts. But the 3rd was sort of not ok. Aside from his age, he also had bad breath. Though she did not allow kissing and refused to have her breasts touched, she did not like the breathing and the rough hands of the old one. But he was loaded and he was recommended by the gay-pimp from Jaro who also supplied the women for the mayor's guests. Easy money but she saved it all until she passed all her sbj.

Back to being a schlr again. 2x already she has turned down the txt from the gay-pimp from Jaro. What she has with Rick is different. They've been on for 6 months already. They knew each other from texting. They've been txtm8 for three months and then Rick suggested that they would EB at sm ct. The nights and days when they sent and received txt msgs to each other fired her feelings. Once she told a girlfriend how to reach heaven while reading the grn jkes that Rick had sent her. The times when Rick does not show up, she uses the cp in his place. She makes it vibrate, she said. That's enough to get her over. She's 18 now and she has to hasten her steps lest she fails to catch up with Rick. In her haste she fails to notice a girl who suddenly shows up from the gf of the mall with her head down and acting as if she's dizzy. The girl is also walking fast. When they bump against each other, her books which she is carrying in her left hand fly in all directions. Only the cp in her right hand did not fall to the floor of the mall. The only thing she could say is Sht! Sht! That's because you're not paying attention. She does not even look at the girl who seems to have fainted. The sekyu helps her and when she recovers her senses, she cries and runs out of the mall. She throws a curse at the fleeing girl. After picking up her things she almost runs to where she and Rick had agreed to meet, at Pnshpe. They are meeting there because she wants her bf to buy her something. It's her birthday and she knows he won't say no. As far as she knows, Rick has a big salary. He is the right-hand man of an SP mmbr of the province of Ilo2. Then she will ask for them to dine at Kny Rgrs. She peeps inside the store but not even a shadow of Rick is there. She'd like to think that her bf is also 18. She decides to get in. She goes in str8 until she is in front of a beautiful red blouse that she'd been wanting to have since 2 days ago. Lucky for her no one has taken an interest in it yet. She will ask Rick to buy this for her. She gets it from the hanger. She tries it on. She feels it. The fabric is soft. She'd like to own this blouse. She tucks it under her skirt. She does not even bother to check if someone is looking at her. When she turns toward the door the guard is looking at her shaking his head. She gets the blouse from under her skirt, returns it to the hanger and puts it back. She leaves the store with a bowed head. As she walks away she still does not understand why she does what she does. She's done this 2x already. The first was more controversial because she was caught and the manager called the principal. She was in her 1st year then and it had been difficult for her to put that incident away. It was only Big Bang and she could have paid for it easily, but there seemed to be a voice telling her to do it. The voice was so strong it easily overpowered her. The gdnce cnslor told her that such behavior has very deep roots in her being. This could be caused by repressed anguish, a traumatic experience when she was still a child. She should allow it to come out. But that was 4 yrs ago. Until now she still carries that fear in her heart. But she's afraid that something bigger would be lost to her if she talks about it. 1 more thing, she does not even know what she must reveal. She looks at her watch. 1 hour and 10 min has passed. She dcdes to wait. She goes near the banister that encircles the well that allows a view of the lower floor. She holds on to the steel bars and looks down. She sees a lot of people busily preparing the temporary stage. The famous David Pomeranz is going to have a concert at 4 pm. She remembers that she shouldn't be standing in this area. Her philosophy professor said the people standing around here are the ones without money, or most of them are poor. That made her sad, but at the same time she felt enlightened. She herself cannot say which of the 2 she belongs.

The mall isn't built just as a marketplace, it is built to be like a world. An illusion of a world. That's why the poor have a place in the mall. 1 of the many places that her professor mentions is the exact area where she is standing now. They might be penniless but there they are standing around with great conviction, making as their sbj whatever they see below them. They think they own the artists and singers performing in the temporary stage below. But of course it's because certain things like a cncrt is only an "idea." There's nothing more important to the viewer than the "idea" that one indeed is a Viewer. An extension of the arena built by the Romans for people's entertainment so they will forget their own state of being. The thick circle of glass at the top through which admits sunlight is like a church altar through which mystical light enters with its mythical significance. This light is not much different from the light one finds in the drawings of Christ in the Bible. In short the things that happen in a cncrt in the central part of a mall carries with it a sacred blessing. Her professor might be right because most of those around that circle of steel are the penniless ones. And most of them are looking down at what is happening below. Her thoughts are interrupted by her cp. She'd been txting him since a while back, even using the vc, but Rick's phone does not answer. She quickly opens her inbx. She reads Rick's txt: i cnt mke it we hav mtng. He sends 1 more msg: Gst frm mla wl ariv dis pm. Il mke up 2mrow. Frowning, she steps away from the steel banisters. She does not know where to go. It seems as if the cold metal has sucked up all her energy. The lively heartbeat is gone. She can't stop her tears from falling. Today is important to her. Important for her and Rick. She sees the CR sign. She goes in. As she enters the small passage to the CR, the man in the blue polo who had been watching her is sipping coffee inside

Shakey's Pizza. He puts his cp down carefully on the table and pulls out his wallet. He looks at the contents and returns it to his pocket.

3. FE

She's absent this afternoon. So what, she tells herself. She'd been working three years in the bank and she'd never given herself a break all this time. Even at home her mind won't stop thinking of the money she counts every day. She even brings home the thick wrappers for the bundles of money. While staring at her reflection in the CR mirror at the mall, she feels some satisfaction. Rare pleasure that had occurred only now in her life. Her smile reaches her ears. This is her second date with Dick in the movie house. Dick is her second nobyo after she had sworn off relationships with men for a very long time. Herman was her nobyo when she was in her first year of college, the cause of why she cut off men from her life. She poured all her love on Herman. But after one year she began to feel that something was amiss in their relationship. That was when she realized that Herman was the type of fellow whose satisfaction came only from words. In their one-year relationship they were always involved in politics, philosophy, and history. Her nobyo would sometimes quote Plato even while he was kissing her. So their classmates called their relationship a "platonic love affair." Dick is different. He is the total opposite of Herman. Dick is very sensual while Herman was an intellectual. Love, as she herself believes, should be able to move one to act spontaneously without thinking too much. That's what happened to her and Dick in the movie house last week, one day after she accepted him. Dick started with just massaging her fingers. Then he asked permission to put his arms around her shoulders. She allowed him. She even laid her head on her nobyo's shoulders. Then

Dick whispered, would she allow him to kiss her on the cheek? She laughed a little. What kind of a man is this nobyo of hers. Did he have to ask permission for everything he wanted to do? On the other hand, this is okay, he seems very gentlemanly. So when Dick kissed her on the mouth she was no longer shocked. She flowed into the delicious current that seized her whole being. It came to the point when she no longer knew what her nobyo was doing or where his hands were straying. All she knew was the delicious sensations he awakened. Her recollections are interrupted by the entrance of a student wiping the tears from her face. She wonders why her niece is here when she knows she's having an exam. She calls her niece's name. The student is shocked to discover whose voice it is. The student gives her a forced grin. She asks her niece what her problem is. She says she failed in one exam because her prof is angry at her. She's afraid she might lose her scholarship again. She understands what this means because last year her sister borrowed money from her. She asks her niece if she has eaten. The girl tells her the truth. She pulls out a hundred bucks and gives it to her. Her niece says thank you and hurries out of the CR. She goes back to study her appearance in the mirror. She notices her lipstick. She thinks of taking it off or else it will stain other parts of her face if she and Dick kiss. She's meeting Dick at 1:30 at Shakey's Pizza. Pepperoni pizza is Dick's favorite dish which he eats before watching the movies. It arouses his sexual powers. Must be the onions. Supposed to be an aphrodisiac. It doesn't do much for your breath though. She enters Shakey's at exactly one o'clock. Dick had already ordered. Her nobyo knows she's never late. They make short work of the pizza and go straight to the movie house. From the escalator she could see the night stars smiling from the ceiling of the mall. Beautiful, she tells herself. After buying the ticket they enter the corridor into the dark night. She doesn't know why the word *night* resonates with her. Perhaps because when she's alone she talks to it. She's told many of her secrets to it. The night is the only witness to the fact that she sleeps naked. Dick holds her hand as he climbs up to the darkest part of the balcony. There are few viewers of this movie. The title is *Women Cannibals.* This may not be its real title. Seems like a made-up movie, including the poster. Once seated, they see all at once on the screen a beautiful naked woman biting a man's penis. She asks Dick what kind of a movie it is. Dick only smiles. A night scene appears. The darkness inside the movie house is thoroughly overwhelming. Dick puts his arms around her. Kisses her on the lips. She kisses him back. Soft warm kiss. Dick's hand slips under her green blouse. Her eyes close as she feels his fingers on her breasts. Another hand creeps and finds its way between her thighs. Frantic fingers. She clings tight to her nobyo. He suddenly draws away from her, removes his belt and opens his pants zipper, and smiling, asks her to take him in her mouth. The request shocks her a little but she feels herself a slave that must obey. She cannot explain the sensations besieging her body. Dick takes hold of her hair. She closes her eyes tight. She does not want to see herself doing what she's doing. But her feelings tell her something else. She stops when light hits her on the head. Don't do that here, a voice says from a man carrying a flashlight. The light is blinding as it falls on her face when she raises her head. She tries to take refuge by Dick's side. Slowly she wipes off the saliva from her lips. In the big screen she sees the beautiful women cannibal quietly creeping toward the sleeping men. At a signal from the leader, they rise to their feet and together point their spears at the sleeping men. They hogtie the men to bring to their fort. She cries. She doesn't know whether to be embarrassed at the man who caught her, or embarrassed at herself. Don't do that here, the man with the flashlight admonishes them again. From her seat she sees the light from the flashlight being lowered. The women cannibals tie the men to bamboo poles. They are stripped naked. The eyes of the women cannibals widen. They are wondering at the strange bit of flesh hanging between the thighs of the men. They laugh at it. Dick, sitting beside her, is also laughing. He has just finished zipping up his pants. He puts an arm around her. She pays him no attention. This time she feels like deadwood. The two do not speak for some time. Dick begins massaging her hand. His fingers creep under her blouse. She closes her eyes. When they come upon one of her nipples she rises suddenly and tells him she wants to pee. She is thinking Dick would follow her. But he remains in his seat. She looks at herself in the mirror inside the CR. She can't even look at her own self. Her reflection is still but its eyes are staring sharply at her. She turns her back on her reflection. Then she decides to get her lipstick from her handbag and face her own image. Despite the sharp look on those eyes, she stares back at the image as she puts on her lipstick. The image moves and it is herself again. She wonders how this could happen. Is it a trick of sight? She studies her reflection again. Her lips are reddened with the freshly applied lipstick. The image smiles back at her. Thank you, she says to it. When she gets out of the CR, the cannibal women are eating the captive men. She feels nauseous at the scene. She sits down and tells her boyfriend she wants to go home. Dick does not say anything. Out of the movie house, she sees the stars shining up in the mall's ceiling. She smiles. She knows they're just mocking her. She knows the darkness inside a movie house is not real night. In her mind, tonight she'll sleep naked again with her windows open. She'll be happy even without a man again in her life. ♦

SOME NOTES AND FOOTNOTES ON LONELINESS

by Jay Jomar F. Quintos

Translated from Filipino by John Bengan

5 OCTOBER 2014[1]

You asked me to go on laag[2] one midday after we had some law-oy.[3]
We located the signs and landmarks in Tugbok District. You showed

---

1 It was the third month since I decided to move to Mintal, Davao City, to teach at
a university. In my first two months living there, all sorts of fear and apprehension,
loneliness, and pagkamingaw for family and friends in Manila stirred and clashed
in my mind. But, you arrived one day in August, walking through the apartment
door bringing durian and marang. So you were the housemate that Beng had
mentioned before. Your smile and offer of fruits brightened me up. And, like the
dripping crack of the ripened marang, between the sniffing and savoring of durian,
that day, every mystery began.

2 Laag (Cebuano): It means to journey to or visit different places. For example, "J
and I went on laag in Bago Oshiro to study the geography of Tugbok District."
Another example, "24th of August 2015 when J went on laag without inviting J."

3 Law-oy: A dish in the Visayas and Mindanao. Different vegetables and greens
such as okra, nightshade, water spinach, squash, sweet potato, and corn are mixed
and cooked. Sometimes, singugbang bangus (grilled milkfish) is added, or even bulad
(dried salted fish). Be careful not to burn the grilled milkfish in law-oy so it will not

me where Bago Oshiro began, how vast the seemingly endless expanse of Mintal was, and the narrow road along Sitio Basak. You said that Tugbok begins at a five-kilometer-square garden the Japanese had built in the 1950s and ends with an abandoned church near the market where, they said, you'd find an unkempt, mangy madwoman carrying a human skull. The woman always waited at the labyrinth and prayed as though to spare the entire Tugbok from a swarm of locusts.[4]

Our laag ended at Father Emman's[5] house. He asked why I'd chosen to leave Manila to teach at a university in Mindanao. I don't know how to answer such questions. I give a different response each time someone asks. I want to get away from the stringent and repressive rules that my family imposed, and sometimes I'd say that I want to find my kilometer zero, the sacred beginning of my laag toward the edge of the world where, perhaps, the dying meteor of love waited. Sometimes I also say that I want to forget and so I went to a place where no one knew me. In truth, even *I* am not sure anymore why I moved from Manila to Davao.[6]

---

taste bitter, and better to allow the fish to cook when mixed in the vegetable broth. Eating food that's bitter is an intense experience.

4 Before October of 2014 ended, the unkempt, mangy madwoman ran out of the church. She went to the five-kilometer-square garden and pounded into bits the human skull she carried. The world stopped in Tugbok District, everyone felt a strong quaking and heard a loud pounding that seemed to come from the sky. Soon they heard the woman's cry that she won't ever love again. The following day, the unkempt, mangy madwoman was not seen again.

5 Father Emman was a professor at the university where J and I taught. He was a former priest during martial law who went on missions in the mountains of Mindanao to spread the holy gospel of the Catholic Church. He left the Church when he decided to have a wife and children. It was only one of the million stars of the paragraph of the world: beginning and end, country folk and city folk, a tree and a saint made of wood, and sorrow and madness.

6 One lesson that Father Emman taught us is a truth about the amazing narratives

1 NOVEMBER 2014[7]

While I was cooking Spanish sardines pasta[8] for our lunch, you mentioned that an acquaintance asked you to watch a movie at the Gaisano Mall.[9] You asked me whether you should go or not.

"It's up to you," I said.

The sautéed garlic burned in olive oil and so the pasta I was making tasted bitter.

2 NOVEMBER 2014[10]

I didn't notice what time you got back to the balay.[11] The next morning, you invited me to go with you to Agusan del Sur to visit your

---

we have of the world, all beings, back in the olden times, have a history of journey. People left one place for another part of the world to look for new places to live, to get food, and a site to fulfill the bare necessities of their physical bodies. This, perhaps, is the right response whenever someone asks me about moving from Luzon to Mindanao.

7 Day of the Dead. Can we also commemorate on this day the death of the *kasingkasing* (Cebuano word for "heart")?

8 I'd often watched Mother whenever she cooked Spanish sardines pasta. It was one of my favorite dishes and so I often made it since I moved to Mindanao. I never liked Filipino-style spaghetti, and preferred Spanish sardines pasta. But, sometimes, I also ask myself about the politics and irony of forgetting: we forget personal experiences of memories that we no longer want to revisit, but along with this is the paradox of forgetting the long and complex history of the nation.

9 Gaisano Mall in Davao would often figure in the news because of not just one, or two, or three, but many persons who died after leaping from the fourth floor of the shopping mall. The suicides have one reason in common: love.

10 All Souls' Day. According to a Cebuano scholar of literature and cultural studies, a person's "soul" sometimes separates from the "body." If the "body" becomes a product of the different shapes of colonialism, the "soul" departs from the body to sail away in a sea of contradiction. But the "body" must find the "soul" because it gives meaning and sense to different beliefs and desires. If that is so, what happens if the "soul" itself cannot return to the "body"? Will the body overcome its senses and desires that pierce the depth of the soul? Or will the senses and desires merely remain in the body? No more, no less.

11 Balay (Cebuano): It has the same meaning as the Filipino word bahay (house). For example, "J and J live together in the balay."

field site in Bunawan[12] since you'd been planning a field trip for your Political and Legal Anthropology class. As we traversed the road to Agusan, we got to know each other better. You told me about your favorite films, music, books, as I told you mine. We discussed what annoyed us about the academe to which we belonged, and how you loathed the song "Imagine" by John Lennon.[13]

In the middle of our trip, you lay your head on my shoulder. Between the mango I was eating and the poem I was reading, "I love you like the way the nose kisses a ripe / mango / I am sated / every mystery is solved."[14]

3 DECEMBER 2014

We shared the champorado you made with tablea[15] from Tagum.[16] You told me that Tagum had the most delicious tablea you'd ever tasted in your life, and I believed you.

---

12 This is the place where you did your field work for almost two months to write your thesis on "sago," a palm from which people there, particularly the Agusanon Manobo, get their sustenance.

13 You almost condemned this John Lennon song, especially the lyric: "Imagine there's no countries / It isn't hard to do / Nothing to kill or die for / And no religion too ..." For you, if we follow what Lennon says in the song about the elimination of countries and religions, it would mean the eradication of different cultures in the world. What then would be the point of studying cultures if everything is homogenized? What then would be the point of anthropology?

14 Excerpt from the poem "Katuparan" (Fulfillment) by Rebecca Añonuevo which I'm reading.

15 Once while we were jogging and passed by a garden where cacaos grew, our shadows were trespassers plucking the cacao. You cut the cacao in half and handed me the other half. I've kept the seeds of that cacao until now. Tablea is made from cacao.

16 Tagum is a city in Davao del Norte. This is the place where you grew up and came of age. Once we went to a coffee shop in Tagum and stayed until dawn, we walked the stretch of the población while waiting for a bus going to Mintal. I remember that you were so amused when we recalled that movie we'd seen starring Sharon Cuneta and Ai-Ai de las Alas.

One of my favorites was champorado, especially with a serving of bulad.[17] At first, you laughed because I put "powdered milk" in the champorado instead of skimmed milk.

"Powdered is better because it's crushed and broken, just like this world," I said.

Since then you'd use powdered milk whenever we had champorado.

1 JANUARY 2015

At 12:30 in the morning of the New Year, I sent a text message mostly in Filipino: "Happy New Year, J. I wish you all the happiness in the world. *The moment is constant so the moment seizes us!* [18]"

After two minutes, I received a reply from you in Cebuano and Filipino: "Happy New Year to you too, J. You already know how to speak Binisaya. Almost, a little bit more, you'll be a Bisdak soon. Here's to a meaningful pagkakaibigan.[19]"

I slept poorly that night.

---

17 Bulad (Cebuano): it has the same meaning as the Filipino word daing (dried salted fish). For example, "J and J's favorite breakfast is fried rice, eggs, and bulad."
18 This is from our favorite Richard Linklater movie *Boyhood*. We watched the movie together and both loved the theme song "Hero" by Family of the Year. Perhaps, we were on the verge of passing "boyhood" and therefore could both relate to the protagonist.
19 Kaibigan (Filipino): Not an intimate companion, not a mate, not a significant other. But what if the word's form is changed to "ka-ibigan"? Take the prefix "ka" and connect it with the root word "ibig" and also add the suffix "an" to form the term which means "a partner in love." But these are merely grammar and punctuation. This is all I hold dear.

8 FEBRUARY 2015

We went to the Philippine Eagle Center in Calinan. We observed the different types of eagles, macaques, deer, and other caged animals there. There was sadness in our talk about the idea of "caging" animals for display as "spectacle," just there, and merely being looked at. In fact, each of us in this world is imprisoned. Different prisons—parenthesis, stanza, quotation mark, box, and even the prison of the mind and body and feelings that cannot be expressed.

We rode the same habal-habal[20] on the way home. I felt your body on my back.

I slept soundly that night.

15 MARCH 2015

We ran around Mintal again, one Saturday morning, the expanse of Bago Oshiro and Mintal. We thought of paths that others had not always taken. I ran ahead and waited for you at the end of Sitio Basak, I waited so that we could both wander far into the road that would harbor and conceal us.

I waited for a long time but it turned out you'd taken a different route.[21]

---

20 Habal-habal (Cebuano): Habal refers to a type of sexual position among animals, particularly dogs (mating dogs). This is also a word used to describe a utility motorcycle in the Visayas and Mindanao wherein one, two, or more passengers ride as though mimicking the image of animals mating. For example, "J and J rode the same habal-habal."
21 July of this year, we don't talk anymore. I went to Siargao on my own to try to break the waves using my brittle body. At the harbor in Siargao, I found myself standing in the middle of the port, not yet leaving, not yet returning, but only waiting for the boat to go on sea.

26 APRIL 2015

I gave you the book *Not All that Drops Falls*, a collection of poems by
Adonis Durado who writes in Cebuano. You liked the poems in the
collection and made a promise that someday, you too would write
poems about love.[22] In return, you treated me to a coffee shop in
Jack's Ridge, a place where the rhythm and stretch of Samal Island,
the Davao Gulf, and the city of Davao converge in one's eyes.[23]

While we were walking back to Mintal, we found a guyabano
ripening on a tree at Ma'am Eve's, a colleague at the university. We
both picked the guyabano and happily we ran laughing back to the
apartment.

7 MAY 2015[24]

The guyabano we plucked rotted. I threw it away without any of us
having had a taste.

16 MAY 2015

You had told me that you'd take me along on your field trip to Mati,
Davao Oriental, but you left without me. That day, I woke up alone
in the apartment to the sound of brown shrikes perching on the
window, and then the decaying roses bought the other week greeted

---

22 Months after this oath was made, you kept your promise by writing a poem
about love, but it wasn't for me but for M.
23 One can also glimpse from Jack's Ridge the private and public cemeteries in
Davao. This is the discombobulating dialectics of life and death, hardship and relief,
light and dark, love and grief, loss and forgetting.
24 We had not spoken to each other in days. You made breakfast without inviting
me and left the house without taking me with you, unlike before when you always
had me around in coffee shops, restaurants, zoos, and museums you visited. Around
this time your sister posted a photo on Facebook of you and your siblings together
with M.

me. Outside, there was the few-meter-squared garden where the rhetoric and hermeneutic of the different shapes and forms of doubt begin and end.[25]

31 MAY 2015

I woke up at three in the morning, raining in Mintal, cried and hugged myself like a fetus inside its mother's womb.[26] In the morning, I drank eight cups of coffee, would have to make do with every gulp while laden with pagkamingaw for my mother and sister.

In the evening, I walked the stretch of Ulas to Mintal, like walking from North EDSA until EDSA Taft. While walking, I go on with my devotion, like taking a road that seemed to lead nowhere, wishing that I was in a different world, in a different time, on a different occasion, and a different I.[27]

10 JUNE 2015

Now is the evening of forgiveness. I forgive myself and I also forgive you. Tonight, warm and humid, I set you free.[28]

---

25 In truth, sometimes faith and conviction escape me like how the brown shrike forgets its ritual of perching on the window every morning.

26 According to Freud, there are sections and moments in a person's life when he mimics the position he assumed as a fetus in his mother's womb. This is supposedly the saddest, most painful, and direst moment in a person's life when he feels broken instead of whole.

27 It's official: J and M are in a relationship.

28 But you said I should set this journal on fire, beside the birds dipping in the well of dry leaves and grass, the lamp whose other eye was blind, and a photo of three old women who were not smiling. I left it behind and continued to weave a curtain using the thread and needle of desire and faith. This is all that remains.

FUNGI

by Rogelio Braga
Translated from Filipino by Kristine Ong Muslim

Biring's first contact with its slippery surface brought only momentary surprise: she stepped on it and slipped. It was sheer white, all too radiant under the plastic sachet of Tide Ultra. Her surprise turned to bewilderment when she picked it up. It was scintillating, even through the hair strands and clumps of pubic hair adhering to it. Biring quickly pocketed it, rushed to the dilapidated hut she called home. She secretly slipped it behind the altar. *There, right, nobody would see it there*, she whispered to herself.

The next day, Buni invited Biring to play with her at the itaas. She told her there was another truck carrying old fabric that they could scavenge to resell to the tailor at the corner outside of the Promised Land.

"Let's go, Biring," said Buni. "Let's play jump at the itaas."

She ended up being called Buni because, according to the people of the Promised Land, when she came out of her mother, the first thing that the midwife assisting in her delivery noticed was the ringworm infestation that almost covered her left arm. She was said to

189

be the only child in the Promised Land who developed ringworm rashes where the said fungal infection occurred in dense circular clusters.

Biring refused Buni's invitation, having lost her interest in playing. It was as if there was something that beckoned for her to return to the hut, to the altar, to the white thing behind it. "Buni, come," she told her friend. "There's something I need to show you."

"Why, how come you no longer want to play at the itaas. Let's go. We're better off spending our time there, where there are lots of discarded fabric for us to take."

"No, stay here," Biring exhorted. "I told you, there's something I need to show you."

"What is it?"

"Magic," mumbled Biring.

Buni's eyes widened. "Really? Don't mess with me, or I'll beat you up."

Arriving at Biring's hut, the two decided to wait around until Biring's parents left to collect *pagpag*—or leftovers from restaurants, including half-eaten meat cuts from restaurant patrons—to be re-cooked for dinner.

Biring extricated the thing she hid behind the altar. "See here. It's magic, right?"

"Wow, Biring, where did you get this?" Buni asked.

"At the itaas, when I was scavenging for scrap metal."

Buni inspected it, carefully removing the hair strands and clumps of pubic hair on its surface. It shone even more brilliantly without all the hair stuck to it.

"It smells funny, Biring," Buni said.

"Stupid, you should not have sniffed it!"

The thing, indeed, gave off a strangely pleasant smell. And the smell wouldn't come off their palms. Their hands were even tainted with whitish streaks.

"Hide this, Biring. Your father might take it. Can we sell it?"

"I don't know. I don't want to sell it. This is mine." She quickly secured it inside her pocket.

That night, Biring had a hard time sleeping. Her forehead was once again throbbing. And just like before, a rash was forming on that sore part of her body. It was always this way. There were days when rashes suddenly appeared on her body. The first time it happened, it was on her cheek, and her mother told her that it wasn't rashes but scales, like those of a fish. And, it itched. It itched like hell. Her father said that her itchy scales were more than just scales. The next morning, while waiting for a truck from the countryside, Buni noticed the pus suppurating from the scaly lesions on Biring's cheek. Buni wiped the pus away.

"Nanay said they were scales," Biring said.

"I had the same thing, too," Buni said, showing an infected part of her rump.

"Oh, you also have scales."

"They tend to bleed when it's hot. Tatay said the yellow thing that's coming out of them is mucus," Buni explained.

"Will this go away?"

"Yes, I think so. All of us at home have it."

It did not surprise Biring to learn that her mother ultimately developed scales between her breasts, that her sibling had the same at the side of her mouth, that her father had his at the back of his ear. There were always nights when every single one of them was forced into wakefulness by the maddening itch of the scales.

Biring sat up, went to the altar. And because there was no rain last night, there was none of that sickly sweet stench inside the house. Her father likened the cloying smell to that of fermenting pineapple.

The Promised Land stank when it rained. The heady odor was produced by a combination of rotting food, rusting tin cans, vegetables, plastic, fabric scraps, all the broken castaways that were the sources of livelihood for Biring and Buni.

"What are you doing, you godforsaken kid?" Biring's father called out to her when he saw her going to the altar. "Why are you still up?"

"Nothing. I just have to get something."

Biring could not help but bring the thing close to her nose so she could inhale that familiar odor again. The strong odor persisted long after she had moved it away from her nose. At one point, she noticed how the sweat from her palms made the thing more slippery to the touch and intensified its already overwhelming smell. She toyed with it some more, in awe of how its contact with her sweaty palms made it near impossible to hold. It had grown slick to the point where it was like liquid slipping away from her grasp. The smell of magic was stronger now.

At first light the very next morning, Biring rushed to the itaas to tell Buni what she discovered about the thing.

"Really? Can we try it in water?" Buni suggested.

They headed to the lower part of the Promised Land, where the Spring was located. The Spring was in no way an actual spring where pristine groundwater flowed. The supposed "spring" was the stagnant, coffee-colored water that collected around the base of a mountainous garbage dump. The Promised Land's touted Spring was the rainy season's runoff around the colossal pile of cloth fabric bundles, filth, rotting vegetables, empty tin cans, plastic bags, and plastic implements, cast-offs that outlived their usefulness.

"Go ahead," Biring told Buni. "Do it."

Buni plunked her hand in the Spring. Their eyes widened in surprise when they saw the dirty water around Buni's hand instantly turn white—not clear but white. Buni swished the thing in her hand, just like what Biring did the night before.

Whatever it was that the two children started when they made the thing interact with water—it spread. It spread farther like the invisible magic of an invisible god, drowning out the suffocating stench of the Promised Land with its scent.

"Buni, there are bubbles! There are bubbles!" Biring jumped up and down with glee as the fetid water of the Spring began to bubble.

"Shhh," Buni was quick to remind her friend. "Don't shout, stupid, someone might see us and take this away from us." Then she held out her hand, offering it to Biring. "Here, your turn."

Biring went through the same motions as Buni, and the effects were the same. The two frolicked in their newfound fascination, slathered the water from the bubbling Spring across their cheeks, shoulder, forehead, thighs—and anywhere the water touched appeared to glow radiant. Its scent also clung to their bodies. In the days that followed, Biring and Buni continued to secretly bask in what they believed was the thing's magical powers.

"Buni, what's wrong with you?" Biring asked her friend when she once noticed her curled up with stomach pain.

"It really hurts. I can't take it anymore."

"When did that start? Did you eat the discarded food again from fast-food containers dumped at the Spring?"

"No. This all started when we used that thing."

"Stupid girl, did you put it in your mouth?" Biring began her victim-blaming.

"Of course not. Why should I when it was bitter."

"See, so you tasted it? How else would you know it was bitter."

"But Biring, have you felt anything different since we started using the magic?"

"No, why do you say so?" Biring lied. Her skin felt oddly smooth and fresh the day they played with the bubbles made by the thing when it interacted with the dirty water of the Spring. Along with the refreshing feel of her smooth skin was the stomach-churning stench of the Promised Land. But, it was as if her smooth skin resisted the greasy touch of the Promised Land's sickening air. What changed, though, was her heightened sensitivity to odors. And then her sense of taste. Latundan bananas, her family's usual dinner fare, made her nauseous. Her sibling also mentioned how she smelled different. And each night when Biring and her sibling had no choice but to fit themselves in their small sleeping area, she noticed how her sibling kept covering his nose.

One day, the two friends surprised all the people at the itaas, who were scavenging and hawking their scavenged wares. Biring and Buni were covered up from head to toe, even their nose areas. Their fellow scavengers smirked. Some nodded with amusement and hurled profanities at the two.

"Don't mind them," Buni told her friend. "Them putang ina are just envious."

That night, Biring excitedly accosted Buni.

"What's up? You have other news?"

"See this," Biring said, showing her forehead. "My scales are gone!"

Buni stared in amazement. From that time on, they rubbed the thing any chance they got against their scaly skin.

At some point, they noticed something about the magical thing: it was shrinking.

"No, it's going to grow back to its normal size," Buni said with conviction, fervently believing what she said was true.

"I don't think so. Can't you see how it is becoming smaller and smaller."

The thing eventually shrunk to the size of an average thumb, which worried Biring.

"You said it would grow back to its normal size again. Why did you lie to me?" Biring sobbed as she confronted Buni, who did not know what to do or what to say as she was in a panic, too.

"What if we try to bury it in the soil, just like a seed growing into a tree," Buni said. "What do you say?"

And so, they *planted* the thing, watered the ground where it was buried with water from the Spring. Days passed, and of course, nothing sprouted from the spot of ground they chose as the perfect place for growing the thing. And the longer they stayed at the Promised Land, the more unbearable the sour reek of the place became, the more nauseous they felt. The cloth covering their nose to ward off the nauseating smell became thicker and thicker. Their bodies ached for the thing's scent, how it had made their skin smooth, how it felt especially invigorating when they rubbed it against various parts of their body.

"Something's wrong, Buni, how come the magic thing hasn't grown yet?"

"Putang ina, I don't know. Should we dig it up?"

They did dig it up. Biring broke down, unable to find the thing in the spot of ground where they buried it.

"Where is it!"

"I don't know. Maybe it decided to leave us. Or maybe God took it. 'Tang ina, Biring. Our magic is gone."

"Do something, Buni, please do something . . ." Biring cried.

In the nights that followed, despair proved to be overwhelming for the two. They still could not get over the memory of the thing's slick surface, scent, and radiance. For each day that they pined for the thing, the more intense their hatred of their situation became— the festering greasy feel of their skin, the nauseating fermented-pineapple odor of the Promised Land, the flies that were attracted to their skin. There were even days that they closeted themselves in their respective huts. They also could no longer tolerate going to the itaas to scavenge for sellable items in the garbage dump.

"Buni, I have an idea," she told her friend one morning.

"What?"

"Let's hitch a ride in the garbage truck. We look for the magic outside. Someone might have taken it, or it found itself another Promised Land. . . . I don't know. Bahala na! What happens will happen."

"You're so stupid. You know there's no way I'll be allowed to do that."

"Why not? It's your fault we lost the magic. You were the one who said we should plant it . . . because you have shit for brains!" Biring taunted her friend.

Buni remembered how it was, indeed, her suggestion to plant the thing in the ground.

"Now what? Come with me."

"All right," Buni finally relented.

The two chose the last garbage truck taking the route to the Promised Land. Garbage trucks were scheduled to arrive at night in the Promised Land. Departure was at dawn. And because it was still dark then, nobody noticed Buni and Biring surreptitiously hiding themselves under the bundles of sacks and cartons.

"Pay attention to where we're going, Buni, we might not be able to find our way back," Biring whispered to her friend.

"Why are you always so stupid? Didn't your nanay and tatay tell you that all garbage trucks in this world end up in the Promised Land? If ever I get lost, doesn't matter where I am in the world, all I need to do is to hitch a ride in a garbage truck and surely, I would find my way back to the Promised Land."

"How come I can still smell the pineapple smell of the Promised Land?"

"Because we're in a garbage truck!"

Alighting from the garbage truck, they were immediately struck by the familiar scent of the magical thing they thought they had lost and had to go out of their way to find outside the Promised Land. Their knees trembled with anticipation. They knew they were close to finding it. They, however, had to settle for the subtle whiff of the thing's distinctive scent, which was often overpowered by the thick black exhaust fumes of motor vehicles. Interestingly, Biring and Buni could smell the thing off every person they encountered on the streets.

Slowly, they could no longer feel their gorge rising; they were no longer nauseous. The stink of the Promised Land was like a distant memory. The syrupy air? It dissipated with the dizzying view of sky-scrapers. Biring thought the impossibly tall buildings looked like the thighs of derelict giants that lived in the clouds.

"Buni, look, a big Spring!"

"That's not the Spring . . . that's Pasig River!" Buni said with barely concealed pride.

"I didn't know Pasig was this beautiful. What do you say we take a bath there later?"

"Tatay said it's deep. You know, he also told me that was where his mother and her three siblings went under when they were still kids," Buni recounted as she and Biring watched the grieving waters of Pasig.

"Went under? Why?"

"Tatay said if your hunger pangs won't stop and when there's so much pain in every part of your body that it feels as if you and your body are two separate things, then that's when you should go under the Pasig River."

"But why? What did he say was in Pasig?"

"The Mutya. Tatay said you should thoroughly wash yourself with clean water. The Mutya won't let dirty people in her domain. Tatay also said that the Mutya's dinner table is heaped with lots and lots of food. She's said to be rich and generous . . . as long as you've cleaned yourself well."

Biring contemplated Buni's recollections about the Mutya. "Do you want us to visit the Mutya?"

"How?"

"We just have to find the magic, and rub it all over our body. Remember its smell? I'm sure the Mutya will also like the smell," Biring said and then paused, realizing the fact that they had yet to find the thing. "We have to find it first."

"I tell you, Biring, just like in my father's story, let me go under the Pasig if I can no longer take the pain of my empty stomach. Let me be the one to use the magic first."

"No problem. But what really happened to your father's mother and her siblings?"

"The Mutya did not allow them to return to the surface. They were given care and fed delicious foods. Tatay said that whether or not he had stomach pains, he would still choose to go under the Pasig."

The two continued walking. They tried hard to track down the thing. They asked around, but people shooed them away. At night, they slept at the Pasig riverbank or lulled themselves to sleep by counting passing cars along Lawton Avenue. Whenever they were hungry, they ate food scraps in dump sites.

The city was unbelievably vast. The thing, on the other hand, remained diminutive and out of reach. This did not discourage the two, who barely remembered how far away they were from the Promised Land. As for the city, it kept changing what it wore daily: its outfits were always new and never boring.

Biring and Buni did not tire from observing the tall buildings, the vehicles that hurtled past them, the schoolbag-toting children on their way to school, the cars, the people inside the cars. All this seemed like an entirely different world for them. This was the world of enchantment. This was the one true source of the magical thing they were looking for.

One day, they passed by the foyer of a towering building. From the foyer came a gust of chilly air that seemed to beckon out to them. Entering the building's foyer gave one the sense that the entire world was reduced into a gigantic shoebox that could hold all the people in the world. The building's exterior was festooned with flags of various colors and designs. The chilly air welcomed them as they joined the throng of people entering the building. Biring nearly cried when she saw the high ceilings and its sparkling fixtures, the mirrors that glinted with the truth—if only they could show her the truth—and the floor that appeared to her to be shifting in its shallow intake of breath. She saw her reflection in the mirrors. Her hair taking on the color of subsoil, her darkening eye bags, the in-and-out motion of stringy, dirt-encrusted tangles of nose hair. But, it was the scent of the thing that the two found deeply enchanting.

"The magic is here," Biring said with certainty.

They followed the thing's scent trail. It took them almost the whole day searching. When they finally found the place where the scent was most pronounced, they stealthily snuck themselves in by timing the movement of the security guards stationed near the building's entrances.

"The smell's really strong here," Biring said.

"Yes, it's here. I can feel it."

They inspected every glass display stand. There were glass display stands for noodles, tinned goods, milk, and many others. They were amazed by the excessive displays, which to them represented the incarnation of another Promised Land. The wrapper design on every commodity was surprisingly familiar to them, too. Back in the Promised Land, instant noodle wrappers were strung into flaglets for Christmastime, the biscuit cans were either sold or used as dippers, buckets, or rice cookers, and the tin cans that could no longer be reused were flattened, weighed, and sold.

"Biring!" Buni called out when she found shelves filled with many different sizes and colored variations of the *thing*.

It shocked the two to be faced with way too many pieces of the thing, the thing they called magic, gathered in one place. There's the thing in a box, in a plastic wrapper, in its bare form but decked with a red or pink ribbon. They wanted to stop the people from taking more and more of the thing to place in their grocery carts. Some were taking tens, dozens of the thing. One old woman was even pushing a grocery cart filled to the brim with boxes of the thing.

They could not even bring themselves to touch it. They were not the only ones who owned bits and pieces of that magic. Some people were even hoarding more of the magic than they deserved in this lifetime or the next. Biring could not help but cry at the unfairness of it all. She faced Buni, who was still stunned by the sight of people after people taking what used to be their magic.

"Buni, let's go. Let's get out of this place."

They sat, heartsick and sulking, among the beggars living near Pasig.

"What do we do now?" asked Buni.

"We have to be able to take home at least one piece of the thing."

"But how? We don't have—we don't have any money."

"We do what we do best. We scavenge the dump for items to sell."

"How do we sell them? Where? We can't just go back to the Promised Land."

"It's settled. We sell scavenged items."

"I have an idea," Buni said, making a dramatic gesture. She extended her open palm and made a forlorn expression. "I'm sure this will ensure we get one piece of the thing to take home with us."

Biring did not feel quite so sure of the idea. "I don't know. I haven't tried doing that before."

"Don't worry. We're simply going to try, see if we can get away with it. Besides, why wouldn't you want to not get at least one of the magic?"

"I want."

"All right, let's go by the roadside and beg for money."

Their plan of begging for alms commenced the very next morning. They did it in front of Andrés Bonifacio's statue, the one that depicted the leader of the Philippine Revolutionary Movement with his hands on his hips, at the plaza right in front of the Philippine Post Office. The two extended their open palms, avoiding direct eye contact with the people passing by. With their necks and arms getting tired and numb from keeping the same posture, they said over and over, "One peso please, one peso please."

"Buni, are you okay," Biring said, worried about her friend who was lying curled up with persistent stomach pain.

"Pain's too much. I can't take this anymore."

"Squeeze down, squeeze it down tightly. That's what we do at home. We squeeze as hard as we can until the pain goes away."

"It hurts all over. I think the Mutya is calling me."

"Wow, Buni," Biring said, rising to her feet. "Lucky you. I think I must buy the magic as soon as possible."

She quickly slipped her hand inside her pocket. She searched Buni's pocket, too, and gathered all the coins they managed to amass after hours of begging by the roadside. She crossed Lawton, walked the rear of the Metropolitan Theatre to reach the building—still pulsing with its chilly air—that held the thing they wanted the most.

But it was different this time. A security guard spotted Biring before she even stepped into the marble floor of the building.

"I'm only here to buy something," she pleaded to the guard.

"Get out of here," the guard said.

Biring showed him the pocketful of coins. She had faith in the money's ability to buy her the privilege of entry into the building. But the security guard harshly whisked Biring's proffered hand away, and the coins clattered across the floor. Biring bent down fast to retrieve the scattered coins, fearful of people snatching them. She did not notice that nobody was paying attention to her and her coins.

It was only when she was at a safe distance from the guard that she had the courage to hurl profanities. "Putang ina mo! Putang ina mo! I hope your eldest child dies!"

She walked, her shoulders slumping with the weight of her hopeless situation, back to the Pasig riverbank where she and Buni were encamped. *Buni needs to be clean to face the Mutya . . . she has to be clean.*

Walking the stretch of plaza in front of the Philippine Post Office, Biring bought a bottle of mineral water from a street vendor.

She came upon Buni wailing and clutching her stomach in pain. Buni's mouth was open in a garbled scream, shedding bits of her cracked dry lips. Her eyes were rolled back, her legs shaking. Biring was used to this sight. Five of her siblings went through the same eye-rolling and convulsions, the same agonized groaning finality of mouths impossibly stretched so open that the flailing soul inside the body was already visible through the deep dark well of the throat.

Biring twisted the cap of the mineral water bottle, placed a few drops on her palm. And using her finger pads, she cleaned Buni, the dirty spaces between her fingers, her elbows, her knees, her toes. Using the hem of her clothes, Biring carefully rubbed the parts of Buni's body that were supposed to be clean so she could enter the Mutya's realm in Pasig.

Buni's convulsion was still not letting up. Biring asked for Buni's forgiveness for her failure to buy the magic, which Buni so desperately wanted to rub against her body before presenting herself to the Mutya of Pasig.

"They didn't let me inside the building, Buni. I was stopped at the doorway. Forgive me."

Because Buni could no longer stand up, Biring had to carry her. Biring was surprised at her friend's grossly lightweight body. It was like hauling a sack filled with plastic. Carrying her friend, Biring lingered in an area close to one side of Pasig. She decided that by the next scheduled passing of an LRT train, she would release Buni to the Mutya. Biring, anticipating the train's arrival, pressed her chest hard against her friend's stomach in the hope that it would alleviate Buni's pain.

When Biring had the chance to glimpse her friend's face, she was struck by something she hadn't really noticed before: she and Buni resembled each other. Biring saw Buni's tears, and she could not help but weep as well.

"I will also visit the Mutya, Buni. Set aside some foods in the feast for me." Biring took the LRT train advancing ahead as signal to drop Buni in Pasig River and turned away so she would not see the black water engulf her friend's body.

That night, she hitched a ride in another garbage truck, realized that Buni was right after all. Every single garbage truck in the world was headed to the Promised Land.

By dawn, she reached the Promised Land. Saw the crowd waiting for the truck's arrival. Saw the same garbage mountain with its myriad colors, textures, sizes, aromas. Aromas that, when taken together, smelled sour, like rotting pineapples. Swarms of flies greeted her return to the Promised Land. She never forgot that this was the exact same place where she first found the thing of magic.

"Relief! Relief!" Shouts rang out. People ran in the direction of parked trucks. Biring also joined the rush of people.

An old woman handed to Biring a plastic bag full of relief goods. Biring immediately untied the knot and opened the plastic bag. She saw repacked bags of rice, canned goods, instant noodles, and a box of the thing that she and Buni were looking for. Once again, she now held the magic. She took a whiff, inhaled the pleasant smell. She started walking in the direction of the hut she and her family called home, lugging the plastic bag containing the relief goods and her magic. ♦

SNAKE

by Perry C. Mangilaya

Translated from Filipino by Kristine Ong Muslim

Your wife gave birth to a snake, Rodel, according to his mother-in-law. This was how the news first reached Rodel. His immediate reaction was to regard it as a joke. *Ridiculous,* he thought. What had gotten into his mother-in-law to have come up with such a bizarre joke when she was not the type to be pulling pranks. The grave tone she used while talking to him over the phone, however, told a different story.

The news forced him to make an unexpected trip to his hometown in the Visayas, to that place that had seen modern progress, and to that one barangay that was not too far behind in terms of access to technological advancements. He decided not to tell the engineer, even his foreman, both of whom were his peers at the construction site, about the real reason for his sudden trip home. He simply told them there was an emergency and that he had to go home as soon as possible.

What baffled Rodel, however, was that if his wife had, indeed, given birth to a snake, then that meant she had been pregnant. And how could she have ended up pregnant when he was in Manila working for the past ten months as a construction worker. They were nearing the end of their construction project, which meant he could go home in the intervening period before the start of their new project. He was supposed to make the most out of his off-work period spent with his wife. After all, he had been clocking up on overtime and saved up a portion of his earnings aside from the amount sent monthly to his wife. And here he was, forced to go home out of schedule.

His mother-in-law told him that once he arrived home, she would tell him the whole story, as well as the reason for his wife's giving birth to a snake. He might even have doubts. But she assured him that the albularyo, the town's herbalist and witch doctor, could prove a snake had emerged from his wife's womb. His mother-in-law offered proof: a snapshot of the snake. It was purported to be a black snake, the size of a child's arm, and was stillborn.

What truly bothered Rodel was the albularyo's presence during his wife's delivery. There was a midwife in their village.

Rumors traveled fast, which Rodel expected. It was how it was in a small town, with news quickly reaching even neighboring villages. And with social media's help, the spread was like wildfire. Some people would be eager to believe, while some wouldn't, and speculations would abound.

But, for Rodel, he would believe only what his wife would tell him. Because she was his wife, he was convinced there was no way she would lie to him.

Rodel, lugging his knapsack and alighting from a tricycle, could already see people by the roadside staring at him. Their actions, as well as the way they looked at him, unsettled him. Some of them grinned knowingly. One muttered a cursory greeting because it was awkward not to say anything. As he turned his back, he could sense them reconvening to continue gossiping about him.

Concern and compassion were what he felt when he saw his despondent wife sitting on the long bamboo bench next to the open window. She merely looked at him, said nothing. No kiss, no hug, nothing. Her coldness was new to him; she used to enthusiastically greet him whenever he returned home. She would even wait for him by the roadside. But he understood her reticence. She might not have recovered yet from this recent ordeal.

"How are you feeling?" he asked.

At last, she made eye contact. "I'm already okay." Her faltering voice he attributed to trauma.

Rodel had been looking forward to his return trip home. For him, ten months away from his wife felt like several years. If his wife had her way, she would not let him work in faraway Manila. She long wanted to have a child. It might be because she had three siblings, and all of them already had three kids each. Rodel figured that their five years together without a child was behind his wife's unease. She mentioned they were getting older.

He remembered his wife telling him, "Why not just look for a job here? It's too hard to be alone."

"But Inay is always there," he said, referring to his mother-in-law. His father-in-law had been dead for a long time.

His wife said nothing.

He continued, "I can't afford to pass on this opportunity. Engineer's project is a major one. The work is consistent. We can save up and build our own house. We no longer have to live with your mother. If I stay here, work would be irregular. And most of the time, there aren't any jobs."

Like before, no response was forthcoming from her.

"By the time we have kids, we already have our own house."

"But how can we have kids if you're not always here?"

"I can't waste this chance," he insisted. "We can still have kids. Some couples in their forties are still able to have kids. And this is good for you, because we can save some money before then."

Again, she said nothing.

Even on the day of his trip to Manila, he remembered how hard she took it.

Another thing that Rodel found disquieting was the strange behavior of their neighbors. Their taciturn expressions were all out of character.

The same was true of his close friend Tony. He had passed by the front yard of Tony's house, and although Tony approached him to extend a perfunctory greeting, it had none of its usual warmth.

He still chalked it up to his wife's giving birth to a snake. He thought everyone was like him, having a hard time getting over the aftermath of a freakish event. How a snake could thrive inside the womb of a human. How it was formed. How they viewed him and his seeming acceptance. If it was difficult to believe that his wife had conceived a snake, then it was doubly difficult to make room for the possibility of a snake having sex with his wife.

These questions had answers, all according to his wife's explanation.

"You were cursed?" he pressed on. "What was Lolo Onyong's take?" He was referring to the famous old albularyo, who was also his wife's relative. Lolo Onyong was renowned for his healing powers not only in their barrio but also in the whole town. He was the go-to healer for illnesses that were beyond the reach of a traditional doctor.

"He said that the snake I killed was an engkanto's familiar."

"What happened exactly?"

"I was sweeping the overgrown area under the sampaloc tree at the back, when a black snake fell out."

"What did you do?"

"I smacked it over and over with a piece of wood until it died."

"And?"

"That night, I had the worst stomach pain. So I asked Inay to come and get Lolo Onyong, who said I had been cursed."

"Your stomach pain stopped?"

"Yes, but as weeks passed and turned into a whole month, I felt changes happening in my body. I suspected I was pregnant. Because I also did not have my monthly period."

"Did you see a doctor?"

"I did," she said, giving him a fleeting glance. "I had an ultrasound. And it confirmed my pregnancy. The ultrasound showed a heartbeat."

He looked at her for a considerably long time.

How can you possibly be pregnant when I'm in Manila, he wanted to accuse his wife but restrained himself. He felt it was wrong to blame her, especially in a situation as sensitive as this. What his wife needed the most nowadays was sympathy.

"Of course, I did not believe the result," she said to break the silence. "Even Inay was wondering how all this could happen. So she told me to let Lolo Onyong use his divining powers to figure out what's happening to me."

It frightened Rodel to hear the whole story from his wife. Lolo Onyong had confirmed his wife's pregnancy, as well as the snake inside her womb. Lolo Onyong also said that the snake must be prevented from growing further as that would kill his wife. This was how the engkanto had cursed his wife. As replacement for the eng-kanto's familiar, the snake was supposed to emerge alive from his wife's womb—which meant her death.

Through the albularyo's mysterious and magical spell, an incantation only known to the albularyo, coupled with a ritual that involved slapping around a leafy branch and lighting frankincense-infused coals to have the fragrant smoke blanket Adela's body, the engkanto's curse and the snake inside the womb were warded off. Fortunately, the snake was dead when it came out of Adela.

Lolo Onyong, too, had been shaken by the ordeal, even if he had already seen strange things in the past. Rodel's mother-in-law also had a hard time coming to terms with what happened, especially when she saw the evidence. Both Lolo Onyong and his mother-in-law purportedly saw the snake come out of his wife.

He finally understood why the midwife hadn't been called and why she had given birth prematurely.

As for the stillborn snake, it was said to have been buried under the sampaloc tree to appease the engkanto. Lolo Onyong also uttered his chant and performed a ritual, asking the engkanto to cease from bothering Adela again—a gesture that turned Lolo Onyong into a target for the engkanto. The following night, Lolo Onyong was delirious with high fever. Eventually, he was able to overcome the engkanto's wrath.

"So where's the photo?" he persisted.

She retrieved her cellphone from the pocket of her smock.

Looking at the image of the black snake rattled Rodel even fur-ther. It had blood all over it, no longer moving at the feet of his wife who was still lying down with her legs parted. It just came out of her, and according to the albularyo, had died in her womb as a result of his incantation and ritual.

"Isn't this a bad premonition?" he said, offering a clue to what was making him anxious. "What if this brings bad luck to our family, or to our barrio or town? In the past, I've heard older people talk about this exact same thing happening."

"Those were just tall tales," she said, shrugging off the matter.

He did not react, continuing to inspect the photo of the snake.

"Is this really a snake?" he asked.

"Of course."

"But it looks more like an eel."

"That's what they said, too. But Lolo Onyong said that's how engkanto's snakes look like. And that one was supposed to be the strongest of its kind, truly venomous."

He nodded, still looking at the photo.

"You said there was an ultrasound. Where is it?"

"I already threw it out."

"Why?"

"It's useless."

"I will talk to the doctor who did your ultrasound."

"There's no need for that," she said loudly and in a brash tone that stunned her husband.

"Why? Is there a problem?"

"I told you, the result of the ultrasound was all wrong," she said, trying to suppress the panicky lilt from her voice after noticing her husband's reaction to her initial outburst. "See, there's the evidence. I was really cursed by the engkanto."

He continued his scrutiny of the cellphone image. He was holding proof of his wife being at the receiving end of an engkanto's curse. It also affirmed his long-held belief in the existence of the engkanto. He had experiences involving the engkanto. There were times when he came home late and an engkanto would mess with him so badly that no matter how long he walked, he could never seem to reach home. He would end up in circles. He only managed to go home because he remembered Lolo Onyong's advice: to consume a small bit of mud and wear his shirt in reverse.

And that was not the only thing he experienced. One night, he slept in his house but woke up the next morning under the shade of the old sampaloc tree in their backyard. The albularyo speculated that while Rodel was deep in sleep, the engkanto opened the window, carried him out of the house, and placed him right next to the sampaloc tree. An engkanto was said to have favorites, mischievously playing with those favorites but not hurting them.

But that was a long time ago, way before modern technology. Now, in the age of social media, is an engkanto haunting still likely? Maybe, he thought. His wife, the famed albularyo, his mother-in-law—they could attest to it.

That afternoon, Rodel decided to visit Lolo Onyong. He had a lot of questions. He figured Lolo Onyong, being an albularyo, was better equipped to provide him with the clarity he so desperately needed.

"Wait," his wife said, holding his hand when he motioned toward the stairs.

"Why?"

"You'd probably hear neighborhood gossip. Don't listen to those."

He looked at his wife for a considerably long time. "Gossip? What about them?"

"Never mind," she said. "Let's just stick to what Lolo Onyong says. He's the albularyo and knows the supernatural better than anyone."

He agreed. As he walked, however, he still could not take his mind off what his wife said. *What about the gossip?* As a matter of fact, there was no need for his wife to tell him not to take neighborhood gossip seriously, as it was unlike him to pay heed to rumormongering, which he saw as nothing but concocted stories whose sole purpose was to damage the reputation of other people. Besides, those who listened to neighborhood gossip did not trust themselves.

And he took pride in his ability to distinguish truth from lies.

Then how come his wife would not ease off from haranguing him about the neighbors' version of events.

He saw some of their neighbors staring at him. They were eyeing him strangely, as if they had something in mind they could not tell him. But he stopped himself from following this train of thought. Their reaction was natural, considering he was married to the woman who gave birth to a snake. They probably had as many questions as him. They were probably wondering how he was able to take things in his stride, too.

Rodel found Lolo Onyong alone in his hut. Lolo Onyong rose to meet him, as if he expected this visit. Rodel did a mano, where he placed Lolo Onyong's hand against his forehead to signify respect. Then they both settled down in their seats.

"Adela already told me everything. But I still don't know what to believe."

"You don't believe your wife?"

"I believe her. I mean I still have a hard time taking in everything."

"You know, there's nothing new about it. I've already brought around others who had run-ins with an engkanto. I performed tawas on several women impregnated by the engkanto. Remember what happened to Minda, the one who gave birth to a boy who is what we call a child of the sun?

"Yes."

"Think about it. How did she get herself pregnant when she wasn't even married? She did not even have anyone courting her. And, as you can see, the child was not of this world. He was abnormally white, and his skin turned red fast when pressed. Most of all, he found the sun to be incredibly blinding. That's the nature of an engkanto."

Rodel kept staring at Lolo Onyong.

"And I couldn't be wrong when I did my tawas on her," Lolo Onyong went on. "When the boy reached the age of twenty-one, he would die. His engkanto father would claim him."

He nodded.

"And don't be fooled by the body in the casket. That's no longer Minda's boy. It was just a banana stump. The engkanto can make us see a dead body instead of a banana stump. Minda's boy is still alive in the realm of his engkanto father."

Rodel did remember the story about Minda and her boy, as it spread throughout the town and became gossip fodder—much like what was happening these days to his wife. He imagined how every crowd in town whispered about her.

The visit with Lolo Onyong did a lot to reassure him that his wife had, indeed, suffered an engkanto's curse.

It was getting dark when he arrived home. Since his route home was along Tony's house, he met his friend, who seemed to have waited for a chance to talk to him.

"I saw you earlier," Tony said. "I figured I would wait for you to pass by here on your way home."

"Is this about my wife?"

Tony nodded.

"I have just been to Lolo Onyong. He confirmed that it was an engkanto that made Adela give birth to a snake."

"So you really believe that your wife delivered a snake?"

"Yes," he said, feeling sure of himself. "There's evidence and a witness."

"You believe an engkanto caused Adela's pregnancy?"

"Lolo Onyong had proof. He is an albularyo. And I believe there is an engkanto because I experienced one before."

"You think a snake can grow inside a person?"

"It's an engkanto. That's why. It can make the impossible possible."

"Were you able to talk to the doctor who did Adela's ultrasound?"

"No. What for? I am good with everything."

"A friendly advice. Why not talk to the doctor and learn the truth?"

"Adela was cursed by an engkanto, and that's what happened."

"Just talk to the doctor. It might change your mind."

He looked Tony straight in the eye, trying to see what he was getting at. He did not promise Tony that he would talk to the doctor, but as he walked home, he could not take his mind off his friend's suggestion. Eventually, he chalked up to the age of modern technology Tony's lack of faith in the existence of the engkanto. *What technology does*, he thought.

"What happened to your wife was all over Facebook," his mother-in-law told him as he entered the house.

"Did someone upload the picture?" He asked her after going through the motions of a mano.

"My friend probably did it," Adela chimed in.

He was stunned. Because that meant his wife was already the subject of online buzz and that speculations were rife.

That night, he had a hard time sleeping. He imagined how hard his wife must have suffered, and he wanted to blame himself for it. If only he had listened to her and did not proceed to go to Manila.

In truth, what kept sleep at bay for Rodel was the odd demeanor of his neighbors. He felt they all wanted to tell him something, although he was still convinced that what his neighbors held back from him had something to do with the snake and his wife giving birth to it. His wife's strange behavior was also not helping. He could see fear in her eyes.

A few days passed, and the chairman of their barrio cut his nap short. With the chairman were people who worked for a TV station.

"Is Adela home?" the chairman asked. "There are TV people here who want to interview her."

"About what?" he asked even though he already knew the answer.

"The news about your wife giving birth to a snake has already spread," someone, a woman, answered. "We'd like to feature the story in our program next week."

"I don't want to be interviewed," Adela interrupted, her face not denying the contempt she felt for this intrusion by the media.

"Why not?" Rodel asked her.

"I just don't want to. They will just poke fun at me."

"There's no use hiding at this point. The photo has spread widely through Facebook."

"If that's the case, then there's no need to interview me."

"There's a human interest angle in your story, ma'am," the woman from the TV station answered. "This way we can show to the viewers that even in the information age, something like this can still happen."

"What do I get in return?"

"Many people said that you simply made it up. This is your opportunity to set things straight."

"No!" Adela said. "If they don't want to believe that I gave birth to a snake, then I can't do anything about it. Isn't a photo enough? No, I am not giving an interview."

"We don't have to show your face," the woman from the TV station persisted. "We can hide your identity."

"It doesn't matter," Adela said.

"I'm sorry," Rodel said.

"We'll just interview the albularyo who assisted in the delivery," the woman said. "May I know where we can find the albularyo's house?"

"If you can help it, please don't interview my Lolo Onyong," Adela said, trying not to lash out. "He won't like it. And all we want is to be left alone."

The TV crew members looked at each other, made another round of attempts to persuade his wife, with the chairman doing the mediating. He even tried to convince his wife to do an interview, and she still wouldn't budge.

The incident further troubled Rodel. For days at a time, he could not shake off his suspicions. He considered Tony's suggestion. There was no harm in talking to the doctor— even if the doctor would not confirm Lolo Onyong's version of events. Surely, the doctor's findings would likely contradict an albularyo's perspective.

So, one day, he sought out the doctor who did his wife's ultrasound. He decided not to tell Adela, because he knew how she would react.

"I am the husband of the woman who gave birth to a snake, doc," he introduced himself to the doctor, who had just finished conferring with another patient.

The doctor looked at Rodel for an inordinate amount of time before she offered him a seat.

"Was my wife really pregnant with a snake, doc?"

"There's no way a snake would form or grow inside a person's womb," she said, and then asked her female secretary to get her something.

"Is it possible that it just wriggled inside her, doc?"

"That's impossible. One other thing, she would have known if a snake happened to do that, because that would cause a lot of pain."

She handed him what her secretary had brought her. "This is a copy of your wife's ultrasound."

Rodel scrutinized it even if he could not make sense of it.

"Do you see that small round thing there?" She used the tip of her ballpen to point it out to him.

"Yes."

"That's blood, which proves your wife is pregnant. That ultrasound result indicates she's eight weeks pregnant."

He was silent, still eyeing the ultrasound image.

"I'm sure that's not a snake," she insisted. "Just like what's being propagated through social media. In the first place, the ultrasound won't lie."

The doctor's mention of lying—or his being lied to—really hit a nerve. Rodel just did not have it in him to entertain even the remotest possibility that his wife, the albularyo, and his mother-in-law would all lie to him. Adela was his wife. There was no way on earth she would lie to him. And who was this doctor, anyway, to imply the one thing that his wife would not do?

He did not tell her about Lolo Onyong's statement: even a doctor is no match for the powers of an engkanto. *Poor doctor*, he thought. *She does not know she has been fooled by the engkanto.*

He bid her goodbye, promised to himself never to return nor heed the opinion of this doctor who blatantly accused his wife of lying.

Getting off the tricycle, and because their house faced tracts of farmland affected by the summer drought, he noticed three boys ganging up on another boy. The fatter one of the three boys scooped dried-up carabao dung and dumped it over the head of a lanky boy whose back was turned against the three. The boy turned his head in surprise, scattering the powdery carabao dung all over himself.

"'Tang ina," he said, though he did not appear to be angry.

The three boys laughed; the lanky boy laughed along with them, but his laughter seemed forced. Lifeless.

"Hey, did you see the doctor?" Tony called out to Rodel, who was passing by Tony's house.

"I did."

"What did she say?"

"The ultrasound said Adela was eight weeks pregnant."

Tony stared at him, trying to read his expression.

"Poor doctor," Rodel continued. "She did not know the engkanto was making her see things."

"What do you mean?"

"When Lolo Onyong performed a tawas on Adela, a snake was seen in her womb. It wasn't human. The doctor was blinded by the engkanto."

"I can't understand you, Rodel."

"Come on. In short, Adela was victimized by an engkanto. And it was true, she had been pregnant, just like what the doctor said but couldn't see. The engkanto won't let the doctor see the snake through the ultrasound."

"What did the doctor say?"

"I did not tell her about the engkanto. I know she won't believe me."

"Pare, I don't want to be rude, but you might want to be observant, to see things as they are and not what they seem to be," Tony said, containing his annoyance. "A doctor already told you that your wife was pregnant. You don't really mean that an ultrasound machine would lie but not a person, right? Think about it."

He stared directly at Tony. *Even you*, he wanted to rage at his friend. *How could you accuse my own wife, Lolo Onyong, as well as my mother-in-law of lying?*

"Pare, don't you know that the entire barrio has been whispering about your wife's pregnancy?" Tony wasn't backing down.

"That's only natural," Rodel said, forcing a smile. "If you give birth to a snake, you'd be the talk of the town, too."

He could sense Tony's annoyance when their conversation ended. But Rodel could understand his friend's reaction, and once again, blamed Tony's skepticism on modern technology.

Rodel, however, was very much aware of the barrio people's persistent small talk about his wife. It followed him every day. Some of his friends, especially when they were drinking together, would say it to his face.

"You are probably the stupidest person I know," one of his friends ragged one time when they were drinking along with Tony. "What really gets to me is that the stupidest person happens to be my friend."

"You must be drunk, p're," Rodel said. "You're not making any sense."

"You have no idea. Tony and I are rooting for you. At the same time, we want to beat some sense into you."

"Why is it too hard to understand that an engkanto cursed my wife. There was evidence and an albularyo as a witness, plus my mother-in-law." Rodel was losing his patience.

"The hell with you," his friend, whom he grew up with, told him. His friend quickly downed a shot and then slammed the shot glass down. "If you don't want to listen to us, that's your call."

Their drinking session did not end well.

The passing days failed to take the edge off Rodel's restlessness. The ongoing neighborhood gossip about his wife took its toll on him. There were times when he was pointedly derided—not only when he was drinking with his friends; he was also accosted on the street. Had his trust for his wife wavered, he would have ended up picking fights with so many people. He put up with the hurtful things people said. Maybe, they spread rumors because they had nothing better to do with their lives. Or, maybe, they envied his strong relationship with his wife.

Nevertheless, he had sleepless nights. Mostly, he felt bad for his wife, who had no idea she was fodder for the town's malicious gabfest.

"I can no longer take how people keep dishing dirt about your pregnancy," he told her one night while they were lying next to each other in bed. They were both staring at the ceiling.

"I already told you not to mind the rumors," she said, her voice laced with anger. "They probably had nothing to do but to smear other people."

"You're right. But we can't live like this."

"What are you planning to do?"

"Let's move away."

She looked at him.

"I am planning to take you with me to Manila," he said, his gaze still directed at the ceiling. "We'll be okay there, where we're far away from the rumors."

"Where will we stay?"

"We can stay at the barracks in the meantime, until I can find a room we can rent."

Silence.

Then she faced him, weighing his sincerity. When at last she saw his determination to go through with the move, she embraced him, pressed her face against his chest. Her shoulders trembled as she sobbed. ♦

THE FISHMONGER'S LOVE STORY

by Timothy Montes

Translated from Waray by Merlie M. Alunan

Yes, I punched him. So what? He stole my dance. It was a dance for the reds, his ticket was white. And when Irma was about to come with me, he pulled her to him.

Well, who wouldn't lose his head then? Shameless! He could be the world's toughest guy, still he's not immune to bruises. He lost two teeth, and I got two painful scratches on my hand from his knife.

Oh yes, I was sort of drunk, a little bit. We dropped by at Mana Nena's for a glass of tuba each, the whole gang.

"Padi," said Padi Otik, "you'll soon be holding hands with Irma. Your dream come true."

"Just be careful," Tagata added, "you could get electrocuted."

Well, I'm just a humble fishmonger, but I've got money saved up so I can dance with the most beautiful girls this vacation season. I bought technicolor tickets so I'd be sure of my chances.

"The heck with it, Padi," Otik continued, "when Irma left for Manila, I didn't pay her any attention at all. She looked as plain as any woman fishmonger. Now, by Satan, she's as fair as any actress."

"Padi," Tagata added wood to the fire, "let's have a bet. If you get Irma, I'll have myself circumcised again immediately."

They were making fun of me then because they knew how taken I was by the vacationing Irma. Anyway, why should I be ashamed of this? The first time I saw her in the marketplace, I quickly lowered the price of my fish to make sure her Tita Coring would buy from me. Long-haired, wearing shorts, how white her legs were! She was a Manila girl now, that's why she didn't think anything about going out in shorts. When she came near, the fishy smell disappeared. When she left, the smell of her shampoo lingered in the air.

But I couldn't bring myself to express my interest in her. I sent fish to her Tita Coring every morning. So I could pay her a visit, I put myself on the good side of her spinster aunt first.

"Mana Coring," I asked permission at the end of that first week, "may I pay a visit to your niece?"

Well, how could she say no? I'd been sending them fish every day all of that week. I might lose some money on the fish I was selling, that's okay as long as I could catch a hairy one. When her Tita Coring gave me a nod, I got ready for the visit. I bought my gifts, I looked for the most beautiful flowers to give to the beautiful girl. I depended on my friends to help me. We practised the songs we would sing on the guitar.

Otik was about to start strumming on his guitar strings when a motorbike roared in. It was the braggart Barod, wearing a denim jacket, going up straight into the house of Mana Coring without a by-your-leave. Was that a good way to visit a girl? And she entertained him! And so, us serenaders had to sit around under the coconut grove and wait for him to leave so we could begin singing. We were like chickens with the plague.

"Come on, let's go home," said Padi Otik after a while. "My throat is itchy, maybe a cold is coming."

He was embracing his old guitar, he began shaking from the chill of the dew. The flowers in my hands were wilting, so I threw them into the bushes.

"Let's go home, I say," Padi Otik said again.

"In a while," said Padi Tagata. "After preparing so hard for this event, just so Padi Migoy would have a girlfriend from Manila? We can't just give up now. We got to take something back for our trouble." He threw away his cigarette butt and ran to the back of Mana Coring's house.

As for me, I raised my eyes to the lamp lighting up the sala where I could hear occasionally the rumble of the boastful Barod's voice, and the occasional response from the high-pitched voice of the girl I had come to visit. Just wait a while, I vowed to myself, I'll have my revenge against that good-for-nothing man. I wanted to tell my friends to deflate the tires of that devil's motorcycle. But it was then that Tagata returned, panting hard.

"Let's go. I got some panties off the line." He ran straight toward the road, and we followed him, trying to walk on tiptoe for the dogs had started to bark at us. We ran as fast as we could, as though we had stolen some gold.

"For sure, we're not on the loser's end anymore. Here, this one's for you, Padi," he said with a leer, giving me the panties. "Remember the fish with a beard."

But the garment was too large, its garters much stretched, and the embroidery was badly frayed.

"That's not Irma's," Padi Otik said laughing. "That belongs to Mana Coring for sure, and it's been turned into a rag."

"It was too dark there," Padi Tagata said, throwing away the useless garment he had taken such pains to steal. My two friends were laughing so hard, I had to join them, despite the ache in my heart.

That's why when we were all there at Mana Nena's store just before the dancing started, my barkada were making fun of me.

"Padi, make sure it's not an old pair of panties you would take off in the banana grove." They were teasing me hard, and I was still smarting from Barod's insult—Barod who had made at least three women pregnant, Barod who was feared in all of Balud.

When the dancing started, we went in and began looking around. The girls were all lined up on a long bench in a space separated from the floor by young coconut leaves. Irma was among them, wearing a pink dress, her long hair held together by a pink piece of cloth. She looked like a beautiful flower and my desire to dance with her rose even higher. I only had eyes for her while a special kuratsa number was being performed and when the announcer said that the next dance was for everybody, I was the first to approach her fair form. I struggled, I fought my way to her, and if I were a carabao, I would have horned my way to reach her side. For this is the law of the dance, we men who stood outside the enclosure of young coconut leaves would rush inside, like wild carabaos.

And Irma was near, smiling, waiting for me to pick her up. Maybe I was just drunk, it felt as if I was swimming in air in slow motion, getting nearer and nearer the form of this lovely girl of whom I had dreamed, maybe ten times or more. One more inch, I'd be holding her hand, I'd be waltzing with her. Her fragrance, the softness of her body would be all mine. She would come with me and the two of us would spin like a top and go to the moon. She would come with me to the banana grove. The moon would hide behind the mist, the boat would blow its whistle, and the world would explode.

But that devil Barod, I do not know where the hell he came from, but he showed up beside me. He pushed my shoulders away and pulled the hand of Irma and dragged her to the dance floor. He was fast, like a wind thief. I was left without a partner. From a beautiful dream I woke up to a grim reality. I felt like a serenader to whom had been thrown a pail of urine. I went near Barod. His hand was going down to Irma's waist. I tasted the sourness of tuba in my spit. All my irritation rushed to my head, I felt it whirling on my crown. I tapped him once on the shoulder and when he turned, I punched him without a word.

He fell to the ground and ate dirt. I jumped on him before he could come to his senses. We grappled and turned on the earthen floor of the dancing hall. I kept on hitting his face until even my hands felt sore.

When I stood up, I felt dizzy and could not see very well because dirt had gotten into my eyes. Barod was still slumped on the ground.

The people were shouting, loud and rowdy as in a cockpit. That devil of an announcer who hadn't dropped the mike kept on shouting, "To the red! To the white!"

When Barod stood up, the people stopped cheering. He had a knife in his hands! That was when I noticed that my hand was bleeding. It was starting to hurt.

"What the hell!" Barod shouted. "Why did you do that?"

That was when I realized I had nothing to say. Why was it shameful to admit the truth? If you were a man fighting for a girl, why was it so hard to say that you were in love? It was easier to punch the guy than to say the truth. People would just laugh at you, they'd say you've gone mad.

"What's wrong with you," Barod asked me. "You just up and punched me. Have you gone crazy?"

Irma was crying, she was standing beside him and holding on to his arm.

"All of you, you have witnessed," Barod was saying. "He punched me first. I've done nothing against him."

I remained speechless. My truth was different from his. Padi Otik and Tagata went near me.

"Padi," they said to me, "let's go home."

"You grabbed my partner from me," all I could say. "You have a white ticket . . ."

Like a sissy who had found a champion, I cried my frustration on the shoulders of my friends.

"A crazy deaf-mute, and a sissy too," Barod cried as my friends led me out.

"Hala, let us pass," said Otik to the gaping children. The gate was closed as they ran away from the dancing hall. The music was played again and the dancing resumed. Even the children were laughing at me as I cried.

"Please give us room. Let us pass. Hala, go back now, the drama is over. Forgive our friend, he was just drunk."

When I woke up a while ago, the pain in my heart was gone. My drunkenness had passed. I felt ashamed when Mana Coring passed by. I had no more fish to give away, I didn't want to lose more. Like the fish, I had salted my wounds so that they healed quickly. A while ago, Barod passed by in his motorbike, Irma was riding with him. I don't know where they were going.

Hala, Nading, let's put away everything. The dance is over. The sun is up. Sweep away all that trash they left behind, those empty bottles, torn-up tickets, peanut shells, and Chippy wrappers. The flaglets are drooping now, and the tables and chairs are dusty. The air is sour with the vomit of drunken men.

The morning was quiet. Any small sound exploded like something was crashing. The long wire was drooping and Mano Palab was driving the dogs away, they were dragging something with them. Don't regret that you haven't found the happiness you are aspiring for. Just keep looking around. The dance is over. Don't be sad. You must have fallen asleep, or maybe just tired. ♦

THE SAVANT

by Januar E. Yap

Translated from Cebuano by John Bengan

At the Chong Hua Hospital nursery, twenty bedwetters got wind of martial law. The fat, cranky midwife often listened to radio dramas on DYHP that now and then the news interrupted. The stage where the Liberal Party was holding a rally collapsed after a grenade exploded on impact. My grandfather, who crossed his legs next to influential leaders running against Makoy, tumbled over. He was pulled from under torn sheets of wood that had crashed on top of him.

The nation held its breath, cries and shrieks broke out. At the dawn of September 19, my mother was bearing down at the delivery room at Chong Hua. In the few months I was inside my mother's womb, I would hear the students in the streets shouting: Ninoy! Laban! Laban! The spirit of the age blew its way into my mother's belly, the reason why my head later grew so big. Since I was also a curious child, my neck grew long from stretching (the years and movies I would see until I saw the resemblance: E.T.—squat, long neck, huge eyes).

233

Still smarting from the name my grandmother had given him in haste (Jose, nicknamed Pepe), my father searched for one worthy of his son. If he would base it on the most popular names at the time in radio dramas, there were two choices: Puloy and Roco (the stone child). In comic books, there was Kenkoy, and then there was Zuma. My father liked Zuma because it was unique; names with the letter z are hard to come by. But when the nurse broke the news to him after hours of Cesarian procedure, "It's done, Noy. What a big head! What a long neck!" Pepe nearly passed out. Maybe he and Mama had been thinking too much about Zuma. Because I weighed only six pounds, five pounds probably went to my head.

They say I was born quiet. Perhaps it was the wind the strange times had carried that filled my head to bursting. But I also grew satellite dishes for ears. So pointy and wide they put Mickey Mouse's to shame. Spock from Star Trek would blush.

I was one of those twenty newborns at the nursery in Chong Hua while the firemen hosed down protesters in Mendiola. We were one class, Batch '72, our eyes shut as though we were asleep. (At least to the nurse who was duped!) Whenever the grumpy fatso turned and wasn't looking, we talked about our future. Baby Girl Asuy, who was right next to me, wanted to be a newscaster on TV, so whenever she delivered the news, she'd be able to reveal the truth in her face: "Meanwhile, the farmers' homes were sprayed with bullets . . ." and then her face would turn sour. Baby Boy Serafin wanted to become a priest. He would have quite a reaping during Sundays and he would know all the secrets of the women (and maybe also the men!) in his parish. Baby Girl Dolores's plan was simple, much like the way of life to which her relatives were accustomed. Her grandfather Lolo Andoy, an old Katipunero (who idolized Leon Kilat), had cracked

234

his voice from shouting in the streets along with folks whose soles had worn a century of drought. "The drought of freedom!" according to Lolo Andoy. Baby Girl Rodriguez's mother practically lived with the people of Panas in Cordova after endless demolitions done for the construction of a reclamation project. Baby Girl Dolores wished to put up a business swapping dollars in foreign currency exchange.

———————

"How did you know?" my friend Balbaks would often ask me. "Are you God? You're like a Jesuit, so swit, suwito!"

"I have a friend, a dawindi, an elf," I said. "We met at the top of Mama's cabinet. He's the one who told me. We used to live behind the Third Door, Duyan Compound . . ."

"But talking babies, man? Are you nuts?"

"Not really! Maybe we forget when we grow up. Good thing the elf told me . . ."

———————

When I was ten, I became friends with an elf. I first heard about him on the radio. His name was Puloy, husband of Petra, the libidinous wife who hooked up with a serpent.

But it was through Porting, our housekeeper, that Puloy and I met. Nang Porting had told me to look out for Puloy at four in the afternoon at the top of Mama's cabinet. The one with the mirror where I'd stuck a Spider-Man sticker. "You and Puloy are much alike. He also liked Spider-Man," said Nang Porting.

But Puloy was hard to catch since at four the school was just about to let us out. More so when Suwang would challenge me in a game of takyan, or when I would be one of the "cleaners" assigned that day. I would forget about Puloy whenever I caught a glimpse of Aurora (a classmate who got the nickname Au-au from the goons in our class who followed her around like puppies) who waited by herself for the ride home. I would stand by the post near the school gate, watching her while chewing on taffy. If only I'd been good at English, we would have been best friends.

It was during vacation for All Souls' Day that Puloy and I finally met. Here is what I remember:

He clung on the middle part of the crown carvings on top of Mama's cabinet. I thought elves grew beards. Turns out they don't.

"I'm not a famous dawindi," said Puloy. (P)

"So only those with beards get all the attention?" I asked. (E)

P: And those with bulging stomachs.

E: Really. Maybe that's only true for you.

P: No! It's true for all.

E: You're wearing something different.

P: This is what I'm supposed to wear.

E: You look like Andrés Bonifacio.

P: We only get to wear a barong during our child's wedding.

E: Where's your child?

P: Inside the belly of the serpent. With my wife.

E: Why?

P: Ah, they were his dinner.

E: So you won't get to wear a barong after all?

P: Oh, that's right.

That was our first meeting. Puloy couldn't remember his birthday. He was there when Lapu-lapu beat up Magellan and cut off his head. He was there on Dagohoy's last day in Bohol, when the champion's charmed amulet quickly hardened after a Castilian-looking dog had sunk its teeth on it inside a cave in Carmen. He was there when Rizal was shot on the grass by the bay. He was there when American soldiers arrived, and he witnessed the Japanese raping my grandmother's mother.

"The Japanese? Raped Lola Iyay? Nonsense!" I said as Puloy recalled to me events in our family.

P: (Got a nail clipper by the table and started to trim his fingernails) Hahaay, why are you arguing with me? You're just a kid.

E: Lola Iyay was the wife of a rich Chinese, a businessman, a landowner. They had many servants who would have helped them. What you said isn't true!

P: Don't know about you, shorty! It happened when her husband Ikong went back to China with three of their children. She was left with five, since your grandmother had eight siblings, right?

E: Why didn't they tell us then?

P: Really classy, shorty. You think it's something the old folks would be proud to talk about?

———

I learned from Puloy the stories of my family. I learned that after Ikong left for China with three of their children, he sent letters, and that he sent them through Pio, their Chinese neighbor. But the crafty Chinese, he never gave Iyay those letters. Instead, he rolled the paper with the lumboy leaves that every morning he smoked with this pipe.

Months, years came, the distance to China bewildered Iyay since her husband still had not returned home with three of their children. From then on she would look at the almanac and learn its maps. She would tell her five remaining children—Andres, Candido, Venancio,

Josefa, Soledad—that their father had settled in a yellowed spot on the map. That it was difficult to get there because they would go against the surge of a winding river. Though on the way back it is easier to ride the rapids . . . (It took some years before I found a piece of paper tucked between lists of debts. Among the scribbling were Iko's name written several times, a map of China, and on the back of which, a letter:

My beloved Iko,

If you get stranded at a bend in the river on the way to your homeland, bear in mind that I am here still, willing to receive you, my only love. True, it is hard to restore what we have grown accustomed to, difficult to recover the past, seeing time's formidable surge. The story of the river stirred me. If on your way home, you swim against the current, do not be afraid. Grab hold of the vines hanging along the river's edge. If you cannot hold on, let the waves carry you; I am at the end of the river, ready to catch you. This is not to say that I am strong enough not to be swept away, that I am not afraid. I am fearful that the river is truly powerful and per-haps we will be separated. All I can say, Iko, is that, as long as you return with our children, I will go with you to the farthest depths. How hard it is, Iko, to think of you every day. Each night, I burn a stick of incense to breathe in your scent. When loneliness becomes unbearable, I light up a bundle all at once. I could no longer describe you, what you look like, but I can still smell your Chinese balms, as though you have never left. What did you look like when you had not yet grown a beard? How difficult to imagine, Iko, since on the many occasions we were together, my love for you grew at the same time as your beard. What else can I do, Iko? The photographs you hid in the trunk have faded after famine, floods, and the ruthless Japanese who descended on our barrio! Nothing is left, Iko. The only photograph I have of you is this (map of China). You are only a mound of earth in the middle of our garden. But, Iko, this is a letter without a destination. This too shall drift into the emptiness between us.)

. . . but what made the passage tricky was that on the other end of Asia, they would have to wait for Muslim merchants sailing toward Jolo. There was the threat of pirates, the danger of sharks. Down the river a boat waited to take them to Zamboanga. From there they would travel to the city of Oroqueta.

Over the years, La Iyay saw each of her children, grandchildren, and great-grandchildren move to other parts of the world. One grandchild married a Japanese. A child who was a war veteran settled in America. Another grandchild worked in construction in Saudi Arabia. A grandchild managed a bikini bar in Manila. And another grandchild became a nurse in Vienna.

Until her last breath at the ICU in Chong Hua, La Iyay committed to memory every corner of the world. She knew a city from above and below, its capital. What sea surrounded a town, how vast the fading expanse between nations.

"Paper rolled with lumboy tastes sweet, Pio told me," said Puloy.

It was this sweetness that got Pio addicted to Ikong's letters. In the span of years, he slowly acquired land and wealth that belonged to Ikong. Iyay was left with a garden shaped like the map of the world, where each day, she stood on top of China.

The sweetness of Ikong's letters crystalized into sugar that gathered in the nethermost regions of Pio's body, spreading down to his feet. One night, ants began digging into his toes. Invisible ants that came only at night. While his wealth grew, his feet shrank. And because the sugar had fused with lumboy, it brought a malevolent stench that clung to every person who came near Pio.

It was only Pio's grandchildren who told Iko's grandchildren about their grandfather's sores. The affliction was brought on by a habit of smoking lumboy leaves rolled in paper from China. When La Iyay's clan knew about this, she was already weakening, bent from her many illnesses. From Ozamis, we brought her across the sea toward Sugbu.

As the eldest great-grandchild, I stayed by her side during our trip.

La Iyay: Have you eaten?

Ener: Yes, La.

La Iyay: What did you eat? I have some candy.

Ener: Thanks, La. I'm not into sweets.

L: Back when we were young, we loved sweets. Pio? He could munch on raw sugar.

E: Even today, La, the young ones love sweets. Unlike me.

L: And why is that?

E: I get fed up with sweetness, La.

L: (Looking out at the sea) They are coming.

E: Mao . . . what do you call that piece of land facing the sea, La?

L: Opon.

E: Right.

That was my last conversation with La Iyay. She didn't last two days in Chong Hua. The dextrose needle traced a swollen vein in her arm. I pressed the vein and saw a dark stone rise along the tube attached to my great-grandmother. The doctor said it was nicotine. I didn't say a word. It was the stone that kept La Iyay strong all these years. But the crumbling of such a stone had caught up with her.

———————

"Really?" said Balbaks, deep in thought.

"Yes, Baks, I feel bad for her," I said. "Of the three children that went with Lo Ikong, one son was left. Good thing we were able to reach him with the help of one of Pio's grandchildren in Hong Kong. We heard he's loaded, even owned a department store in Hong Kong."

"You're shitting me!" said Balbaks.

"Lagi. Problem is, the letters he sent are in Chinese. Nobody in the family knows Chinese."

"Didn't your uncle send your cousin Hermes to school to study Chinese?"

"Don't count on it. That bum's lazy," I said.

"So how would you understand Chinese?" he asked.

"Ask a friend who knows Chinese to translate!"

"What a hassle," said Balbaks.

"What do you want us to do? Smoke the letters with lumboy?"

"What?" Balbaks said. "Anyway, what happened to the elf?"

"You actually believed me?" I said.

"Damn, shorty!" Balbaks scratched his head. "You can raise the dead with stories, you know?"

"Slipped you right in my pocket," I laughed.

"But it sounded true, bay."

"Really now, I'm telling you," I said, "my grandmother, she kept a diary."

"Another diary? One of your tales again, shorty?"

"Listen to me . . ." I said.

When I was in high school and had grown up a bit, I opened the closet where Lolo kept his old police uniforms. I tried the uniforms for size. I marched inside Lola's room, pretending to be an officer. Sometimes, I would face the mirror and gave my reflection a salute. I even wanted a beard. I imagined growing a big tummy. It was cool, man.

But I was not satisfied. I searched through Lolo's cabinet, and there I found his medals, a holster for a gun, and different shaped hats. I wore them all, and at that moment, I swore to become a policeman until I die.

A policeman's uniform is beautiful to behold.

And, Baks, about Lola's diary: One day, I found dusty sheets of paper tied with string. I found these deep inside Lolo's cabinet, under belts that used to hold bullets.

On the middle side of the papers, I read:

Yusuf Abdul, Lopez Jaena, Misamis Occidental. Spent only a few months together. We could not marry because I had been arranged to be with the son of our Chinese neighbor Uy, who owns the town's pharmacy. I thought Yusuf was ready to take responsibility for my pregnancy, but he could not be found. Today, I begin to stand on my own, until I give birth to my fatherless beloved.

One day, Baks, while my father was reading about the ambush in Ipil in the papers, I dared to ask.

"Pa, who is Yusuf Abdul?"

His eyes widened in surprise. He removed his glasses, and said, "Why do you ask?"

"Just because," I said.

"Where did you find out about that name?"

"In Lola's diary."

"Don't ever say that name in front of your grandmother."

"Why?"

Papa told the story of Lola Soledad and Yusuf. Yusuf was a Muslim trader who stopped by Soledad's house every week to deliver imported soaps. He had bought the soaps from travelling merchants in Jolo, and then he would sell them in towns in Misamis.

Soledad was the youngest child, and so she was the one who came down from the house to receive the goods. Yusuf was thirty years old, and an expert when it came to the map of the world. Soledad was only seventeen, and she waited for Yusuf every week. On Fridays, she would go to her mother's garden that was shaped like the map of the world.

When Yusuf arrived, he would immediately say, "You're standing on Arabia, señorita Sol!" and Soledad would giggle.

"A few steps and you'll be in China," said Yusuf.

"But that's where I come from," Soledad said, which made Yusuf laugh.

"We'll meet over there, hmmm, the Pacific? The Pacific is vast, señorita Sol."

"I'll just follow the fragrance of the soap you brought."

"With the help of Allah, hopefully you'll find me."

True enough, they met at the Pacific. It was the beginning of Yusuf and Sol's journey. Each week, they would go to different countries in the garden shaped like the world. They would talk about anything to do with the country they visited.

One afternoon, while staying in the prosperous nation of America, an incident they did not foresee took place. Their eyes met suddenly and they saw the garden map that resembled the world. It was their world, and they were its only inhabitants. A world they wanted to know, understand, discover fully. And there, they began to chart its every nook, in the middle of the garden, as the scent of Yusuf's scattered bars of soap permeated the air. "In a few weeks, we will have explored the entire world," said Yusuf.

Indeed, they circled the whole world, but they could not do it again. After some months, Soledad's mother and siblings witnessed a world forming in her belly.

"Who is the father, Soledad?" her mother asked.

"It's Yusuf, Ma!" Soledad answered firmly.

"What in the world have you done?" said Iyay, furious.

But Soledad's firm response did not reach Yusuf, because after her kin learned of her situation, not once did they ever again see the Moro trader. Every morning, on the rooftop, Sol would contemplate; she would gaze at the world she and Yusuf had explored. But after some months, she began to see that the garden map was nothing but a pile of dirt choked with clusters of weeds. Wild grass growing above a grave, as though there were life underneath.

"Good thing, a few years later, your Lolo and Lola met," said Papa. "And because your Lola was older, her decisions were respected."

"Are you Yusuf's child, Pa?"

"I saw him only once. When I was twenty-four and about to marry your mother. He sent someone to see me. By then his health was poor, he couldn't talk. So he left me a letter."

"Where's the letter now?" I asked.

"Your grandmother burned it after she found the letter in my drawer."

That was what Papa thought, Baks. But I found the letter along with Lola's diary. She didn't burn it. It was one of the short messages that, perhaps to her mind, brought the words that would forgive her for living in another world.

Here is the letter:

Pepe, my son,

No soap could wash away the emptiness that I lived through after leaving the little world your mother and I had built. I lived a coward, my son. I lived always spinning around my own fear. I am alone, my son, until the last hour of my days. I saw the entire world only once, my son, there in the eyes of your mother, and every corner I had taken in my travels, I longed always for what had been. There was not a day that I did not dream of coming home to your mother's world.

If on your journey you will meet another being whose eyes reveal the same world as yours, do not let the moment pass. Let her know what you see, without hesitation. Do not go elsewhere. The chance will come only once in your life, my son. This I know. I am witness to my own lack of will.

Forgive me, my son. Your mother is the only world I have known.

—Your father, Yusuf

Ten years came to pass, Baks, and if I hadn't found myself working in media, I wouldn't have known where fate had shoved you. During our last conversation, we talked about my grandmother's story. But it's all right, good thing we met again so we could continue the story when we had the chance. Wait a second, you're a doctor now, you bastard.

"Sus, I worked really hard, Ner, uy!"

"You're a specialist now, Baks?"

"Only in surgery," said Balbaks, "I fix bones. Repair the broken, treat fractures."

"What a blowhard this Balbaks!"

"If you break anything, just let me know."

"Break my mind?"

We were at La Estaminet, the new French restaurant at the top-most floor of the Twin Summits Hotel. I brought him there after we had stumbled upon each other in the lobby of a different hotel.

"I've always read about you, Baks. Is it true that you went to Yogyakarta? But of course. It would be silly if you'd just imagined it," I said to myself aloud.

"I was also in France last month."

"What were you doing there?"

"Having a vacation, with my wife."

"Good for you," I said. "I get to travel a lot, but only on my own."

"I got married very recently, Ner."

"Where did you meet your wife?"

"Hahaa! You'll be surprised. You know her."

"Huh? D-don't tell me . . ."

"Hahaa! I searched for her everywhere, bro."

"Damn!"

"Really! What can I say, I found her."

"How is she?"

"She has a big belly now, bro. Due this December."

"That's wonderful."

"It's your fault." He grinned.

"Let's not talk about it, Baks."

"How about you, when are you getting married?"

"Ha?"

Balbaks's phone rang, and he picked up the call. "Hello, Love. Good thing you called. Ener is here with me . . . Ener, remember? You don't know him? Impossible! Ener, the one . . . hey, how could you?! Ener, Ener! Yesss . . . shhh, he's right here, I'll tell on you. Sige ka! I'll be home after an hour, okay? Bye, bye, love you. . . . Ner, really sorry, bro, but I've gotta go," said Balbaks. "See you after you're done with your projects in—where is it again?"

"National Museum, but I ordered a lot of food, Baks. Wait for the food, then bring it home."

"Nah, you can have it."

"Who will eat all that food at my place, a gecko?"

"Haha, true, sorry, bro, gotta go."

"Okay."

"Take care, bro."

When Balbaks had left, I called Bogart, a photographer friend whom I could easily drag out of his cave as long as there was food. Bogart was a film connoisseur, and tonight I wanted to know what he had to say about the film *Bayaning Third World*. As expected, the bastard's timing was excellent because he showed up just when the food arrived.

"What type of dish is this, Ner?" asked Bogart.

"Let's start with billi bi, soup with mussels and shallots," I said.

"What is bilibid?!"

"Now this is our pièce de résistance, chateaubriand with champignon sidings, chou-fleur, and feve di marasi."

"Bi bi bi, if you're such an expert, what's the French for 'sheep,'" asked Bogart.

"Agneau," I said.

"Beef?"

"Boeuf!

"Beefsteak?"

"Bifteck!"

"Duck?"

"Canard!"

"Shellfish?"

"Coquillage!"

"Carpa?"

"Truite!"

"German for cookie?"

"Zweiback!"

"Italian for restaurant?"

"Ristorante!"

"Lunch in Italy?"

"Colazione!"

"Lunch in France?"

"Déjeneur!"

"Breakfast in Germany?"

"Frühstück!"

"Breakfast in the Philippines?"

"Buwad!"

"It can be pan de sal, too!"

"Haha, that's true, man. How did you find *Bayaning Third World*?"

"Sus, just don't, man. Go see it yourself. Rizal from different angles, man. They were short of stripping Rizal bare! Man, it was brilliant. I was in awe. When you leave the theater, you'll want to be like Rizal, too!"

"Really?"

"Whew! Should we go on? My turn?"

"Shoot!"

"Ask me, ask me, baby!" Bogart started to sing, doing a little playful dance.

"Paul Newman and Robert Redford?"

"Haha, peanuts! *Butch Cassidy and the Sundance Kid*!"

"Ingrid Bergman and Paul Henreid?"

"*Casablanca*, baby!"

"Omar Sharif and Julie Christie?"

"*Doctor Zhivago*!"

"Spencer Tracie–Katharine Hepburn?"

"Haha, how many do you want? *Adam's Rib*, *Woman of the Year*, *Desk Set*, *Pat and Mike*, *The Sea of Grass*, *Keeper of the Flame*. Still wanna fight?"

"Humphrey Bogart–Lauren Bacall?"

"Pfft! *Key Largo*, *Dark Passage*, *To Have or Not to Have*."

"Don't make things up, *To Have and Have Not*!"

"Sorry, sir."

"Director?"

"Shoot!"

"*Annie Hall*?"

"Woody Allen!"

"*All That Jazz*?"

"Bob Fosse!"

"*Citizen Kane*?"

"Orson Welles!"

"*Gandhi*?"

"Richard Attenborough!"

"*Last Emperor*?"

"Bernardo Bertolucci!"

"*Z*?"

"*Z*?"

"Haha! Constantin Costa-Gavras! Aaa, *Being There*?"

"Hal Ashby!"

"*Gone with the Wind*?"

"David Selznick!"

"I'll go ahead!"

"Hey, where are you going?"

"Have the food wrapped, bring it home! It's paid for, Gart! I'll go ahead!"

"Hey! Dammit. Don't leave me, I'm not dead yet. Where are you going?"

"Going after Rizal!"

"You've lost your mind!"

"Adios patria adorada!"

"Hala, go right ahead, adios yourself! As long as I have takeout, I'm good!"

———

I drifted out of the hotel like I was floating. I sauntered to the parking lot as though my feet didn't touch the pavement. Tomorrow at dawn, I would go to the National Museum in Manila. But I was still not in the mood to go home and pack. I went to a bar I usually go to. I ordered five shots of vodka tonic, which I downed one after another. That was just the beginning, and afterward, my memory blurred, how I managed to get to the airplane, what was inside my bag, and where I found my ticket. At nine in the morning, I arrived at the National Museum in Manila. After speaking to the director, I went to the room where they kept one of Rizal's vestments. I was still drunk, a miracle that the old director didn't notice. Rizal's clothes looked small inside the case. I took off my clothes. I tried on Rizal's overcoat, which was too small, same with his trousers. In search of a mirror, I went to another room with an antique-looking glass. I faced the mirror and asked myself: "Who's taller, me or Rizal?"

But by then, three security guards were running toward me. I was sure it was me they were after. I ran to the stairs at the far end of the building and climbed. I went on until I got to the rooftop. I ran to the edge of the building. I threatened to jump, forcing the guards to step back. I stayed at the far end of the building for an hour, until a priest, a psychologist, a movie star, and others I didn't know came.

A crowd had gathered in the streets to watch Rizal. From where I stood they looked like ants, whispering among themselves. Suddenly, I needed to pee, so I undid the buttons of Rizal's pants. I sprinkled the people below. "Long live the Philippines!" I yelled. And when I was done the security guards grabbed and handcuffed me.

Months later, I wrote Balbaks:

Dr. Dante Balbuena
Head, Department of Orthopedics
Chong Hua Hospital
Cebu City, Philippines

My friend Baks,

Thank you for your letter. Perhaps you have heard about the news. I won't repeat it here. You know my story, the stories I have told you before. Maybe, when the news reached you, you did not find this surprising.

I have gone to every corner of knowledge, Baks. I tried searching each of its pockets, holes, dents, graves, gutters, the mud pools of water buffalos that had long been roasted. Knowledge, it turns out, is a void in loneliness. Because knowledge is found in loneliness. It is believed that loneliness is an empty space capable of holding anything, such as knowledge. It is lonely in the midst of knowledge, Baks.

Like the kite. Crafted from the knowledge of air and weight. If knowledge is applied, your kite can withstand the clouds. The farther it gets in the sky, the lonelier it becomes.

I remember one night a long time ago, Baks. We climbed the sambag tree facing Ces's window. Her family had been living in our neighborhood for months, but not even once had she spoken to any of us. And so one night we climbed up the sambag to look at what was inside their house. We saw Ces in her bedroom, removing clothes from her closet. To our surprise she folded the clothes again and put them back in the closet. Then her father walked into the room, gesturing to her not to make a sound. He brought Ces a dress that she quietly received. She wore it. The dress was too big that its sleeves hung loose on her shoulders. While she changed, a look of bliss spread across her father's face. He kissed Ces on the cheek. He walked toward the door and switched off the light. We couldn't see them anymore. We only heard a deep sobbing that unmistakably came from Ces. We came down from the sambag, Baks, and went home in silence. A different sort of silence, a void, in which we suffered a kind of loneliness that even at our age still throbs deep within us.

Now, Baks, you ask the limits of my knowledge, and I will answer you. There was no elf. Lola did not own a diary. But I am not saying that the stories I told you were only inventions of a restless imagination. Knowledge is not about the details you can extract from a list, a book, a map, a photograph. It is a feeling that returns every now and then, at moments when it is needed. And certainly, even at instances when it is not needed. It is a sensation that changes you once, the reason why you are what you are now. Why you have something to remember, to fear, to envy, and to run from. Why you choose to go on living or die.

I was put in a cell because I wore Rizal's clothes, Baks. The judge had a hard time deciding what sentence to impose on me. The cases they could file against me were trivial: petty theft, malicious mischief, estafa, and others. What is worse, Baks, is that the Rizalistas staged a massive protest to demand the court not to release me without first making an apology on television. So now, they are calling for a senate hearing. According to them, this should be done in aide of legislation, to determine how justice can be served should another person ridicule the honor and history of the nation.

But is it hard for me to ask for forgiveness, Baks. I may not arrive at the fundamental reason why I wore Rizal's clothes, even though I strongly believe that it is my right to do so. It is the right of each and every one of us, and therefore it is just.

However, Baks, I am alone here, and waiting. Such as the stories I had told you that are riddled with questions. Soon, we will understand all of this. The day will come.

Your friend, the savant,
Ener ♦

THE BREAKUP

by Firie Jill T. Ramos

Translated from Waray by Merlie M. Alunan

Paking and his Nanay Sayong were getting ready to pray the Holy Rosary as the dark was gently falling. It was the first Friday of the month, the day of each month when Nanay Sayong vowed to pray novenas for all of her remaining life. At twenty-nine years old, Paking had not once dodged his Nanay's bidding to say the Holy Rosary with her. He was only twelve years old when his Tatay died, and from that time, his Nanay Sayong never missed a novena on the promised day. Paking was just lighting the candles when he heard a loud commotion from the house next door. Something crashing. Voices yelling and screaming.

"Maria Santissima, go and help Taling," Nay Sayong whispered to him urgently. "I don't like the noises coming from that house next door."

The old woman had barely finished talking when they heard bare feet thudding on the ground, heading in their direction, and going up their porch. Their door slammed open. Taling burst in, wearing a torn blouse, hair in disarray, her face distorted with terror.

"Paking, please come to the house."

They raced each other back to Taling's house. When they got inside, Paking instantly saw Taling's husband, Cardo, sprawled by the hearth, just four steps from the door. Cardo had both hands on a fresh wound trying to stop the blood that was gushing out profusely. He glared at them, fear and anger in his face. The machete with its gleaming blood-stained blade was still lying on the floor beside him near his head.

Paking stopped, temporarily nailed on his feet, he felt the world spinning around him. His head was light and he felt ready to collapse.

Taling went straight left to the alcove, leaving the door leaf hanging open so that Paking saw his two godchildren inside. The three-year-old Sara and Junior who just turned two last March were soundly asleep. They were oblivious to the fact that just a few steps away, their father was lying in a pool of his own blood. Taling stared at the sleeping children for a little while. Then she picked up a T-shirt. She came out of the room and pressed the clothing on the gash on Cardo's neck.

"'King. Help please. Let's get him to a hospital."

Paking broke out of his momentary blankness. Blinking a few times, he heard Taling's words piercing his senses, and then he rushed out and ran to Apyong's house. Apyong was a driver of a passenger jeepney in their barangay, paying a boundary fee for his use of the vehicle.

In little time, Apyong's jeep rumbled into Taling's front yard. Paking got off, and after him, Apyong's teenage daughter. Paking put his arms around Cardo and walked him out of his shack, and helped him into the jeep. Apyong's young daughter stayed behind to mind the sleeping children.

Paking made the borrowed jeep fly on the road. The sarao's motor roared, choking occasionally when he in his panic made some untimely gear shifts. Grain-size blobs of sweat flowed down his body. His throat was dry and his heart was drumming in his chest. He kept praying there wouldn't be any counterflow, thinking of Apyong's warning that the brake was rather slow on the uptake. Luck, so far, had been on their side, people were at supper, and the road was clear, traffic was light, not too many vehicles were out. They needed to get to the hospital fast, Cardo was losing a lot of blood.

As he drove, Paking took quick glances in the rearview mirror at his passengers. Cardo was stretched out in the back part of the seat, almost falling out, his legs extended to the bench on the opposite side. His eyes, turned to Taling who was seated to his right, were venomous with hatred. Taling had one hand busy, pressing a piece of cloth against Cardo's wound trying to stop the bleeding, the other hand holding on for balance to the jeep's window side. Her head was turned away from Cardo, her eyes focused forward on the windshield. She would look at Cardo now and then, quickly removing her eyes with a look of disgust. Cardo was ranting, heaping threats and curses upon Taling.

"You! Si'a, si'a, how dare you. You wanted me dead so you could run around free with another man."

Taling pressed the cloth harder against Cardo's wound.

"Agi! Agi, nga yawa ka!" Cardo screamed, sitting up with a start and taking hold of Taling's hand that was pressing the cloth on his wound. She snapped back, "Shut up!"

Cardo stared outside of the jeep, turning his head away from Taling, grumbling.

"If I survive this—. Just wait. Nga yawa ka, expect more to come your way."

"Let's see," Taling shot back. Cardo glared at Taling. A scowl distorting his face, he spat outside the jeep.

Past the Alajas Machine Shop, Paking heard the bells of the Redemptorist Church. He glanced at his passengers.

"We're almost there."

Past El Reposo, Paking saw the crosses and the stone angels showing over the concrete walls of the city's graveyard. Casting a sideways look at them, he knocked on the jeepney seat beside him and mumbled a prayer,

"Tabi la, tabi la, we're just passing through. Please don't take any interest now on this other one here."

Taling returned her attention to Cardo. Moving closer to him, she put her hands under his armpits and pulled him up to sit straighter on the seat and keep him from sprawling.

They were now by the Redemptorist and as Paking maneuvered the vehicle into the Bethany Hospital compound, he still managed to make the sign of the cross with his other hand.

"King," Cardo commented mockingly, "you'll get beyond heaven, the way you're carrying on. Please whisper a word to San Pedro for me, will you?"

"Im' iroy, Cardo. Don't make that kind of joke now."

The jeep headed straight to the emergency. Paking jumped quickly out of the jeep and went to his passengers at the back. He helped Cardo down, supporting him as he walked him to the emergency room. Taling followed the two men, carrying the blood-steeped cloth. A tall thin nurse met them at the entrance and guided them to a vacant bed. The nurse made Cardo lie down. A doctor came and with him another nurse with yellow-dyed hair. They examined the wound which was beginning to bleed again.

"Deep laceration, severed artery. I can see his collar bone. Nurse, do the temp first, and then take him to X-ray. After the X-ray, take him to the OR."

"Yes, Doc," the thin lanky nurse said.

The doctor turned to Paking and asked, "How did he get this?" turning quickly back to look at Cardo's wound, putting on his gloves meanwhile.

"That's how he was, Doc. He came home with that wound," Taling spoke up. "I'm guessing he got into a fight when he was outside. He's drunk."

Cardo turned his head away when he heard Taling's words. He fixed his angry eyes on the curtains surrounding his bed. Tears were stinging his eyes, but before they could flow out, he quickly wiped them off with the back of his hands.

"What about you, Mrs.? What happened to you? Your face is all swollen."

"Oo, Doc," Taling replied, quickly running a hand to smoothen her hair and bringing it down to cover the left side of her face which was most battered. "Aw, inin, kuan Doc, it's nothing. I just happened to fall on my face."

"Sige, that's what you're saying," the doctor said with a wry smile on his face. "Ada, this husband of yours, his wound is big, reaching the bone. We have to operate on him."

The two nurses and the doctor were on either side of Cardo. Taling moved to the foot of the bed so the nurses and the doctor could position themselves properly around him. Taling touched her face gingerly, wincing a little at the pain she felt on the swollen part.

While the medical people were working on Cardo, Paking left the emergency room. His hurried steps took him to the hospital garden. He found a bench and sat down.

———————

Paking and Cardo were the closest of friends since they were children. Their folks were old residents of Manlurip, and the two of them also grew up in the same place. One late afternoon when they were both still unmarried, he found Cardo waiting for him to get out from his job at Washington Trading. He was sitting on the sidewalk.

"Oy, pare, what brings you here? Waiting long?"

"You took a long time, coming out. Aren't you supposed to be done at six?"

"Five o'clock, actually. But I'm in charge of the warehouse. I can't leave until the bodega is closed. It's my responsibility."

Cardo stood up and lighted a cigarette.

"Nga yawa, P're, Taling is pregnant," Cardo said.

Cardo had been after Taling for the longest time, the bedimpled morena, daughter of a snack food hawker in the market, the one near the meat section. Taling had long hair, a ready smile for everyone, and moved gracefully. Her eyes had long lashes, and when she turned them on you, you would feel as if she saw everything to the very depth of your soul. People also referred to Taling as Alias Coca-Cola Beauty, because her body, they said, had the symmetry of an eight-ounce Coke bottle—small waist and broad hips.

"The Alias Coca-Cola girl? Younger sister of Jun Brown, the butcher in the market?"

"Oo, p're."

"Hala ka, nim' iroy, you're not telling me you plan on running away from this one too, like you did with that other one in Ormoc. If you try to escape from this one, Padi, you won't ever be able to return to Tacloban forever."

"Exactly what I'm afraid of, nga yawa. So I suppose it's goodbye my happy days for me this time, that's what I think. Puta, pare, that brother of hers nga yawa, he might cut me up."

"Well, that's because you peck anywhere the pecking is good, nga yawa you don't take care to check who you're putting on the lurch. Now then, have you paid your respects to Jun?"

"How can I not do it? They went to my work place earlier today, in motorbikes, and there were three of them."

After a week, Cardo and Taling were married in civil rites. Taling's mother, a market vendor, cried for her youngest daughter all throughout the wedding ceremony which was presided over by a justice of the peace. Cardo built a little hut across the street from Paking's house. From his porch, Paking could look down on the yard of Cardo and Taling's domestic premises.

When their daughter Sara was learning to take her first steps on their porch, Taling started selling puto and iraid, snack food that she and her mother used to sell in the market. Then she added dried fish, rice, some canned goods, and tuba to her stocks. Listening from their own house, Paking overheard his Nanay Sayong once, talking to Taling while she was buying tuba.

"Day Taling, I'm buying tuba again. Half a gallon, make sure it's bahal, ha?"

"Of course, Nang Sayong. Here's your special."

"Mamay ano, this small store of yours is becoming bigger."

"Buyag, Nang. Well, I'm really working hard on this, 'cause if I depended on Cardo, we would all starve. You know about that fellow, when he receives his pay, it goes straight to the galonan. When he comes home, his pocket is drained, he's drunk, and he's also angry."

"Just keep on praying, Taling. Pray to San Antonio de Padua, that he will see the light."

"Haguy, Nang Sayong, the saints are probably deafened by my prayers already."

"Don't be discouraged, Iday."

"I don't mind his being jobless every now and then, as long as he doesn't do the things he does. He comes home drunk and angry, acting like lord and master. If he doesn't like the food I serve him, he would throw away everything in the yard, clay pot and all."

"Nothing we can do about it. It is what it is. You can't very well leave your husband, you know. It's no good to have your children grow up without a father. You'd be no better than any disgraced woman."

When he was a boy, Paking would often catch his Nanay Sayong standing by the hearth, wiping her tears. He would ask her, "What is it, Nay?" and she would tell him, "Got a mote in my eyes." He remembered seeing bruises, on her arms, her feet. Several times, Apoy Teban came to give her a massage because she had pulled a muscle, or dislodged a joint, which she would say she got when she stumbled in the river while washing clothes.

He was in grade six when a man came to their house, the fore-man of the jobsite where his father was working. When the man left, he went into the house and peeked into his Nanay's room. She had her back to the door, her hands were raised, she was hitting the air above her head with her fist. Paking saw his Nanay's face reflected in the mirror, tears streaming from her eyes but her face was beaming with joy, as though some pall has been removed from it. He heard his Nanay sobbing,

"Salamat, Diyos ko, salamat Senyor San Antonio, salamat for listening to my pleadings. I promise to pray the novena as long as the breath is on me."

The hair on his skin prickled, Paking hurriedly left the house and ran straight to the beach. When he returned in the afternoon, his father's corpse had been taken home. He had been electrocuted while he was painting the Jansen Building of DWU.

Earlier, as he puttered in the kitchen, preparing the evening meal, Paking heard the quarreling going on in the house across the street. It made him uneasy, sensing a palpable strain of violence in the voices of Cardo and Taling.

"What's wrong with you, nga birat ka, what devil has got into you!"

"Puta ka, whore, you've been crapping on my head all along these many days now. You're not just selling tuba, you're selling more. You're selling bites of pleasure. How long has this been going on?"

Cardo slung abuse after abuse on Taling, his voice raised, as though he wanted the whole barrio to know of their shame.

"Who is the gossip that brought you this story, ha? My little store is feeding you, diputa ka, don't ever say foul things against it. You don't even help me run it!"

"Watch out if I catch you. I will surely catch you. Don't deny it. Someone told me about it. Baa, you will really get it from me, I'll break that face of yours into many pieces."

"Just try it, nim'iroy, just try it. If you do, only one of us will come out alive."

Paking was about to go down, walk over to the other house and call Cardo to break up the quarrel between the couple. But it was the time for him and his Nanay to say the Rosary. Time did not wait for him, he was unable to help the couple, he was too late. If he only had known it would go this far . . .

From where he was sitting, Paking saw a woman enter the main door of the church, face the altar, and spread out her arms. Then she knelt and began moving toward the altar on her knees. He could not see her face, but he could imagine it, the eyes closed, the lips moving in whispered prayer. What could she be praying for? Was it for freedom such as his Nanay Sayong had prayed for? Or was she praying for forgiveness for a bitter wish perversely granted? This was what his Nanay's endless novenas were for. Paking shivered.

His Nanay never remarried. When any of their relatives would mention the idea of marriage—she was still young, it would be fine for her to remarry—his Nanay would reply, What for? My heart is finally light and easy. Or she would say, I won't have myself tricked again, I find no bitterness sleeping all by myself, no not at all.

———————

In a while, Paking saw Taling going out of the emergency room. She went to the sikyu who quickly pointed to her where he was sitting. She walked over to him. When Taling was near, he scooted over to one end of the bench. Taling sat down on the space he had vacated for her. She sat down and began crying. Paking did not know where to look, he shook his head and all he could utter was,

"Tsk tsk tsk."

Taling stood up, removed her wedding ring from her finger. She took hold of Paking's hand and laid the ring on his palm, closing his fingers around it. She looked at him intensely.

"I'm going home to get the children. You take care of him."

He took his gaze away from her. He looked away and heaved a deep breath. Paking nodded his head, twice, softly.

Taling stood up and walked away briskly toward the hospital gate, not once turning her head. He followed with his eyes the departing figure of Taling, until she crossed the street and boarded a jeep that was cruising for fares by the entrance of the Redemptorist Church.

Paking lighted a cigarette and looked at his watch. He was calculating the time it would take for Cardo to come out of the operating room. ♦

WHY BERTING AGÎ NEVER SMILES

by John Iremil Teodoro

Translated from Kinaray-a by Merlie M. Alunan

Berting Agî was still up when a scream ripped the silence of the drizzly night, heartrending and full of pain. He was just clipping the red mosquito net under the edge of his mat, muttering "Amay namon" and "Maghimaya ka Maria." He listened intently. Then he lay down, forgetting the rest of his interrupted prayers. In a little while he heard a tricycle starting somewhere up in the coconut grove, moving toward Berting Agî's store. An old woman was crying in pain. Her screaming rose above the sound of the motor. "Abaw, Basti! Basti! Bana ko!"

Berting Agî quickly recognized the voice. It was Nay Gloria, the wife of Basti Kalubay, Junior's mother.

Berting Agî got up. As soon as he had lighted the lamp, his cellphone rang. A text from Vilma, his manicurista friend, "Wra run c tay basti. Bago Ing bugto gnhawa na."

267

Tay Basti was admitted to the Antique Provincial Hospital a week ago. The old man felt a sudden tightness in his chest as he was chopping wood. A stroke, they said. Berting Agî paid him a visit just the other day. She went to the hospital first before going to Royalty to buy the necessaries for her store. He brought the old man a loaf of Pullman bread from the Tibiao Bakery. The hospital was full and overcrowded. The old man lay in a folding bed in the corridor. Looking at the old man, Berting Agî could tell he had not long to live. She was secretly glad. It would mean that Junior would have to come home to Maybato. He had been gone these seven long years since he married that Ilocana woman whom he met in Manila.

Berting Agî came out of his store and found his Tatay at the gate. "Who was that, 'To?"

"Nay Gloria. Tay Basti just died in the hospital. Vilma texted me. She was there."

"Ti, what can anyone do if fate dictates. Basti was a good man, a," his Tatay said and went back home to tell his wife.

Junior is coming home. He's coming home, Berting Agî said to himself. He tossed and turned on his bed before falling asleep.

Junior Kalubay, the eldest son of Tay Basti and Nay Gloria, was Berting Agî's boyfriend, if you could call him that. It was a secret relationship. These many years in which they hadn't seen each other, even Berting came to doubt whether she and Junior were ever on.

They were of the same age, she and Junior. Their birthdays followed one another in the month of May. They went to school together at the Maybato Elementary School. When they graduated from the elementary grades, Berting was valedictorian and the salutatorian was Junior.

Berting finished high school at the Antique National High School and Junior at St. Anthony's College. Junior was somewhat well off because Tay Basti worked at the DPWH. An ordinary employee but he was regular. Berting's family depended mainly on fishing which was her Tatay's livelihood. During the season of storms, they went hungry. That's why in the first year, Berting was in the special section, the bright section, but he was unable to keep up his good grades because he would be absent when his Tatay could not give his fare money to go to school in town.

After high school, Junior went to the John B. Lacson Maritime School in Iloilo City. He went to nautical school. Berting stopped schooling. He knew her parents were hard up. For poor families like theirs, it would be unbearable pride to insist on continuing his schooling. He threw his energies into catching bangus fry in the bay. He wanted enough money to buy a piglet. He raised the piglet and sold it nine months after so he could buy two or three more. He wanted to raise capital so he could start a tiyangge, a little store. It did not take two years for Berting to open a store just beside their house.

The friendship of Berting and Junior went on even though they did not go to high school and college together. When Junior came home from Iloilo, he would spend most of his time at Berting's tiyangge. When Junior took part in the Maybato basketball league, Berting was the team's water girl and cheering squad leader.

———

"Stupid Ilocano woman!" Nay Basyon, elder sister of Nay Gloria, fumed. "She could bear her husband taking the ro-ro by himself with three children in tow! The nerve! Said she could not leave her job in Makati. Fuck her!" The old woman's spit rained all over as she ranted.

"Leave it be. That's how they earn their living," Nay Gloria answered gently. "Junior's bringing a car. He won't have a hard time."

"I say that Ilocana woman is a miser and a snoot. Have we ever seen her shadow here in Maybato? Not even once, never. If Junior were only a janitor in Makati, would she pay any attention to him, do you think?"

They were in the kitchen. Berting Agî and Vilma were washing the glasses that would be used for coffee for the mourners.

"Vilma is better. Look at her. You don't pay her any attention because you're not sure her child really belongs to Jerome. But she's helping you out. You depended on her to keep watch in the hospital," Nay Basyon added.

Berting and Vilma exchanged glances.

"You'd have been better off if Junior had married Berting. He might be an agi but he is dependable, and certainly more generous." Nay Basyon threw these words before going to the sala to shout at the children who were noisily chasing each other around where the dead was lying in state.

Vilma could not control her laughter at the last words of the old woman. Berting grew red in the face.

"Forgive Basyon's big mouth. That one really has a loose tongue," Nay Gloria told the two.

———

A great tiredness seized Berting's whole body when she lay down that night, the first night of Tay Basti's wake. If anybody dies in Maybato, Berting Agî was summoned first. He was asked to decorate the house of the dead one. He would make cellophane roses, crepe paper, and ribbons. Everyone knew she owned a big white sheet to which the flowers would be attached. She gladly allowed his barrio mates to borrow it, considering it as her aid to them in their time of trouble.

This morning after breakfast, she brought her white curtain over without being asked. She took over the job of arranging the space for the wake, knowing that none of Junior's siblings had any knack for decoration. Nay Gloria was in town at the Dalisay Funeral Homes, not wanting anyone else to deal with her husband's cadaver. Vilma, however, the pseudo-in-law of Tay Basti, was generously lending her assistance. She and Berting Agî cleaned the sala. A good thing that Jerome, Vilma's sort-of husband, put up the curtains.

Berting Agî had been on her back an hour, but sleep would not come to her. At fifteen minutes after twelve, her eyelids refused to close. She tossed and turned on her bed. She was thinking of Junior. Nay Basyon said he'd be arriving tomorrow morning. He was bringing his car and his three children would be with him. It was a lucky thing that Junior had just disembarked. He was on a two-month furlough. That was why he could come home this soon.

Seven years since Berting Agî and Junior last saw each other. But there wasn't a day that she did not think of Junior. From the time she woke up in the morning, stretching her limbs, Junior was in his mind. Sweeping the yard, doing the laundry, tending the store, feeding the pigs, while cooking or eating, Junior would be in her mind. Praying before she slept, she would include Junior in her prayers. She prayed that God would give Junior grace and protection in his travels, and good health. She even included the Ilocana woman who was his wife even if she had never met her. She also prayed for the welfare of his children even if she hadn't seen any of them.

But Berting Agî's soul couldn't be pure all the time. Sometimes she also felt mad. Sometimes the flower of hate would sprout in her heart. Hatred for Junior. Junior who abandoned her and left her alone among the coconut trees of Maybato. There were times when she doubted whether Junior ever thought of her too.

On those times when Berting Agi felt as if he were drowning in his longing for Junior, he would recall over and over that one particular night when their bodies coupled and became one. That was on a February 14th, during a Mr. and Ms. Valentines contest organized by the Sangguniang Kabataan in their Barangay. Junior and Susan represented their purok. There was a tremendous contest among the participants to sell tickets at ninety-nine centavos so that they wouldn't have to pay taxes for the contest. Abaw, Berting really combed the town of Maybato to make sure that Junior and his partner would win. Because Susan's father was a carpenter for the governor, big politicians bought up their tickets, and that made them win. Susan and Junior were crowned Queen and King of Hearts that night.

But something happened inside Berting Agî while the coronation was going on. She felt like leaving the basketball court where the stage was. She marched out and went back to her store and hid there. She was mad. She was mad at Susan. She was mad at Junior. The event finished without her, she never went back.

The coronation was followed by dancing which lasted until one o'clock at dawn. Berting did not go out of her room at all. A little past two she heard someone calling at her door. She got up and went to the door, thinking it could be his Nanay or Tatay. He asked who it was. Another knock answered her. It could be a drunk who wanted more to drink and would like to buy a lapad or cuatro cantos. When she opened the door it was Junior. He had already changed out of his barong.

"So you've been here all along, hiding from us. We were looking for you for the photos. Why are you here?" the young man asked her.

"Nothing, just sleepy. So I went home."

Junior grinned. He got in and sat at the table. "You might have one bottle. Give me a drink. I'm really thirsty," he said.

"Maan, you're already drunk. Go home and go to bed. I'm very sleepy," Berting said and entered his room and lay down.

"I'll sleep here," Junior answered, following Berting inside.

Berting was pleased but before she could say a word, Junior was with her in bed. She turned her back to the young man. But Junior held him from the back. A sudden fever seized Berting when her skin got in contact with Junior's warm body and felt his hot breath on his ears.

"You left because you were jealous of Susan," Junior whispered to her teasingly.

"Why would I be jealous?" Berting pretended to be angry.

"Just own it, bala. There's just the two of us here anyway." Junior caressed Berting's chest.

Berting said nothing. But she did not stop Junior's fingers playing with her nipples. She was melting in the delight and warmth wrapping her body.

"Don't be jealous about Susan, a. Not my type. I'm always yours," the young man whispered, his tongue licking Berting's ears. Berting writhed in ecstasy. Junior smiled to himself. He lifted Berting's T-shirt and forced her to turn around so he could suck his nipples.

Berting was twisting and moaning in rapture. In a while Junior got up. He secured the door.

He went back inside and stood by the bed to take off his T-shirt and pants. Before lying down beside Berting, he also removed his T-shirt, shorts, and briefs. Berting tried to cover his body with his hands. Junior smiled as he bent to take off his own underwear. He sat at the edge of the bed beside Berting. He took Berting's hands and guided them to explore his body—from the neck down to his navel, farther down to his erection.

Berting was suspended in bliss. She had some idea that Junior was well-endowed, but not as well-endowed as this. She came to understand why *Kalubay* is Junior's alias, a name he inherited from his Tatay, Basti, the subject of many a tuba session, because he had a penis as huge as a kalubay.

"Eat me," Junior begged.

Berting rose and bent down, taking Junior into his mouth. She gave him head and heard Junior's moan of pleasure. He wanted to shove it all down his throat but the man was so huge. Berting found herself choking, her throat felt like ripping apart.

It wasn't Berting's first experience of a man. She was still in high school when she had nighttime scenes like this in the beach with Gerry Bugaong. But Junior was different. Aside from the considerable size of his member, his touch was loving and gentle. Gerry was rough. Only interested in getting himself off quick.

On that historic February 14th, Junior stayed in Berting's tiyangge until morning. Only the tall coconut trees around Berting's store were the silent witnesses to the love that passed between the two young men.

When Junior was staying more in Manila waiting to board his ship, he would meet up with Berting when he was in Maybato. Junior and his friends would hang out in Berting's store. Gerry Bugaong was also Junior's friend. Like Berting, Gerry missed college too, on account of poverty. His father took ill when he was still a child, and Gerry took over the responsibility of feeding the family.

Gerry was also a good person, but Berting preferred Junior. Gerry understood this. Once in a drunken state, Gerry Bugaong forced himself on Berting, insisting to sleep over. Berting assented, wanting to avoid trouble. She did not want a scandal. Her parents lived next door.

Despite Berting's refusal, Gerry forced her to have sex.

"'Yut! Inarti imo dyan. I know you want Junior. Does he make you eat him too?" he said in an angry tone.

So Gerry would calm down, he took him in his mouth. Before he could come, the fellow was already snoring. Berting rose and switched on the bulb in the altar by her head. The room lighted up. He looked down at the snoring Gerry. He was not bad-looking. But his skin was burned by the sun. His hair was yellowish from being constantly soaked in seawater and the burning sun. That's how he earned the name *Bugaong*, after this fish with yellow and black stripes. He was as tall as Junior and had about the same physique. But Junior's skin was smooth. Berting took Gerry in his arms. The man moved a little and made a small moan.

When Junior embarked on his ship at last, he seldom came home to Maybato. All Berting had were the memories that he kept carefully in his heart's treasure box. There was Gerry after all, ready all the time to cover up for the emptiness that Junior had left in the life of Berting Agî.

———————

Berting Agî and Vilma were in the kitchen of the bereaved, cooking pansit molo, when they heard a commotion outside.

"Abaw, Junior! Your Tatay is no more!" Nay Gloria's voice in lamentation.

"Ay, it's Junior, he's here!" Vilma cried and stood up. She let go of the onions that she was chopping.

Berting was left alone in the kitchen. He sat down and took over slicing the onions. He resisted the urge to run outside to see Junior. His feet felt like they had weights. So what if he saw him? Was he ready to see Junior again?

In a little while the noise outside lessened. Nay Gloria had stopped weeping. The grieving family were all in the sala. Berting felt as if her heart was being pierced when she heard Junior's voice.

"Ayan, tingnan n'yo ang Lolo Basti ninyo. Mabait 'yan," Junior said to his children in a soft and loving voice. His Tagalog bore a heavy Kinaray-a accent.

That voice was so dearly familiar to Berting. The voice of the man whom she loved more than anything in this world. This is the voice she sounded in her mind every morning when she woke and at night as she went to bed.

Vilma returned to the kitchen after a while. "Hoy, agî, why did you not go out?" A naughty smile played on her face as she queried him. "Di kaya ng powers?" she said teasingly.

"Maan, you left the onions. It'd be lunch soon but this snack food is not even cooked yet." Berting pretended to be mad.

"Supalada!" Vilma retorted, peeping into the big pot to check if the water was already boiling. "Nong Junior seemed to have grown fairer," Vilma added. Berting kept quiet.

"Hoy, Berting! You're here all the time!" Junior exclaimed when he entered the kitchen. He went near and put an arm around Berting's shoulder.

"Where are the children now . . ." Junior said and went back to the sala. He came back with the two children in tow, two boys. "Kids, this is your Tito Berting. He is my best friend here in Maybato." Junior introduced him to the children. "O, you ask for his blessing."

The children drew near to kiss his hand. "Maan, Junior, my hands smell of onions."

"Sige lang. That's all right," Junior told him.

After the children had kissed his hand, they asked permission to go to the beach with their Lola Gloria. The children were attracted to the beach. "Okey. Basta don't go swimming yet. Not allowed. After your Lolo's burial, we'll go swimming," Junior admonished his children.

"Ti, how are you, Bert? Do you have a wife now?" Junior spoke in a bantering voice. He sat across from Berting and helped him peel the garlic.

A derisive sound came from Vilma. Berting felt her face redden. Junior was embarrassed. To ease the awkward silence that fell between the two of them, Junior smiled and asked again, "I'd like to know if you've found a new boyfriend in Maybato."

Vilma could not stop her laughter. Junior and Berting also laughed awkwardly.

When the pansit molo was cooked, Berting asked Vilma's permission to go home. She said she wanted to check what his Nanay and Tatay were having for lunch, he offered as an alibi. When Berting left the house in mourning, the iron gate was open and Junior's blue car was parked inside. A new car. Gleaming in the noonday sun.

When she got to her store, someone was frying fish in the small kitchen at the back. Gerry Bugaong. He had just come up, he'd been fishing for aloy.

"Ting, I brought you some aloy. Very fresh. So lucky today. I caught a lot." He was grinning as he spoke.

"Salamat," Berting answered softly. She went straight to her room and lay down. Junior was just as handsome now to her eyes. His arms around her shoulders and his sweet voice still had the power to charge her body with an electric current. Electricity that pierced through her skin to the very bones, reaching deep into her soul. Berting hugged her pillow. Her whole being was swathed in pure and thick sadness.

"What's wrong? Are you not feeling well?" Gerry asked her. He was peeping through the curtain that set Berting's room apart.

"Nothing. I'm fine."

"Ti, should I cook rice now?"

"Sige. Salamat."

Berting listened to Gerry cleaning the pot as his tears flowed copiously. "Gaga nga Vilma. Why did she have to tease me? That's why I'm crying," he whispered to his pillow.

Shortly after, Berting's cellphone rang. When she looked at it, she saw a message from Vilma, "Agî! Your nobyo is looking for you. Have lunch here kuno." Berting messaged back, "GAGA!" Vilma answered back, "HAHAHA! Apekted ang agitot!"

The bereaved family went swimming. Vilma persuaded Berting to go swimming too. Berting was very reluctant. Her family lived beside the sea. She did not find the sea attractive. But Nay Gloria also asked Berting to join them, so she could not refuse.

At the beach she witnessed what kind of a father Junior was. He was also like a child. He joined his children and Vilma's chasing each other on the beach. The youngest child looked very much like Junior, he had almond-eyes that always held a gleam of mischief, was red-lipped, long-legged, and had glowing skin.

Berting felt glad that Vilma seemed to have earned her place in the family of her child's father. Vilma looked like a coarse woman, loud-mouthed—the whole Maybato could hear her bellowing laughter when she let go—but she was a good woman and she loved her child. She also earned enough to take care of herself, doing home service pedicure, manicure, and haircut.

Everyone had gotten out of the water, but still Junior and Berting never found the chance to talk to each other. Junior was too busy taking care of his kids. Nay Gloria invited Berting to have lunch at their place. Berting said yes but did not go with them. She went to her Nanay and Tatay's house for her Tatay's linabog nga bagis. Her Tatay's recipe was famous all over the barrio. Berting had a lot to eat. After the meal she felt very sleepy. She fell asleep and her mother tended the store.

Berting woke up late afternoon. She heard voices from the bench outside his tiyangge. He peeped out and saw a bunch of drinkers. Gerry and his Cebuano barkada. Junior was also there.

"At last the lady of Maybato is awake," Gerry cried. "Come out here. Junior's here."

Berting came out and sat with drinking party. He and Junior were facing each other. Berting took careful watch of Junior. He'd changed a lot, Berting noticed. He already had a small paunch. He kept a small smile on his face as he listened to the stories of Gerry Bugaong.

Berting's and Junior's eyes met a few times. Berting read a sadness and shame in the eyes of Junior.

The drinking ended late at night. Everyone was drunk except Junior. Gerry was the drunkest. He couldn't even walk straight. Berting put an arm around him and guided him to his bedroom. When they were lying down, Gerry, his eyes closed, said to Berting, "Junior said I should take care of you."

Once more Berting felt anger flowering inside her heart.

––––––

The morning when Junior was to leave, Berting went to town to buy the necessaries for his tiyangge. He left for town very early. He did not want to witness Junior leaving. When he came home, the blue car wasn't there anymore in front of their house.

"Hoy, Berting, you left for town very early. Why? Junior was looking for you before he left." Berting's Tatay told him when they met at the gate.

Berting said nothing. He went straight inside his tiyangge and set out the stuff he bought.

"There's kalo-kalo here, Berting. Have breakfast. I've boiled some eggs too," his Nanay said as she went out. She left the stuff on the table.

Berting did not feel any hunger. He did not feel like eating. He continued to put things in place. When he had finished arranging the things he had bought, he sat down and looked at the cookies and snack food he had hung out to display. The colors were varied and bright. But Berting did not feel glad about them. He felt the seeds of anger growing in her heart again. He was mad at Junior Kalubay. Junior abandoned him again. When will Junior return to Maybato again? he asked herself.

"When Nay Gloria dies, e." Berting Agî could not stop himself from shouting this. "Yudiputa!" He cried and stood up and pulled down the stuff he had taken so much time to display. He picked up the jars of candy one by one and threw them down. He did not notice his Tatay and her Nanay standing by the door of his tiyangge watching him quietly. Gerry Bugaong was also there with his parents.

"'Ting, enough already. What's wrong with you? What's the problem?" Gerry's voice was kind and gentle. He was wearing his shorts, as if he'd just woke up.

"Maan! I just feel terrible!"

Berting only stopped his violent actions when Gerry came over and held his hand. They squatted together on the sandy floor of the tiyangge among the scattered goods and jars of candy. From that day onward, Maybato never saw Berting Agî smile again. ♦

from

THE NEXT GREAT TAGALOG NOVEL

by Allan N. Derain

Translated from Filipino by Tilde Acuña and Allan N. Derain

I've been dubious, for quite some time now, about offending certain friends—friends in the department of immediate decline. Though I feel I'm just about to blow up, right here, right now, if I continue to carry this deadweight, this truth only yours truly for now is cognizant of, but shall later be revealed to all those willing to open their eyes—the truth that Philippine literature has gone down to the dogs, and has been beyond any redemption. Which began when Virgilio Almario declared Moises Gerona's *Mahiganting Langit* to be the fulfillment of our long wait for the next great Filipino novel.

About Moises Gerona, I know Almario was his former teacher, but I had no idea how tight his ties to the powers-that-be were. But I shouldn't be surprised. "To a promising young writer destined for greatness." That was how the great poet signed his book for him. He showed it to me, written in his copy of *Ang Hayup na Ito* after he approached his much idolized poet for an autograph. He told me this was the first book of poetry he bought, so the value of Almario's signature was not just sentimental but also monumental. "Ang hayup na 'to!" I muttered to myself. That's all I can say about Moises.

And as for Almario, maybe this is just how writers who reach the pinnacle of their glory end up being—always on the lookout for newbies who they can convert as acolytes to serve as their future extensions and clones, in the belief that they too can discover through this "a promising writer destined for greatness." This is the very same reason why blurbs are being dispensed like some endorsement from the Vatican. But what are blurbs but cheap giveaways these days. Should we take blurbs seriously? Does anyone still believe in blurbs? But the endorsement came from a National Artist, so people just gawked and grovelled. And here begins our journey to perdition. Again, with the blurb.

I have no ill will against Gerona or even against Almario. Actually, everybody knows that Moises Gerona is a very close friend. We were classmates back then in UP Diliman, batch '96, both enrolled under the BA Araling Pilipino program. We weren't just classmates, we were block mates. Our schedules looked like Xerox copies of each other's. His hangout places were also my hangout places. There was no actual BA Araling Pilipino block then, because only we two took the course. So every subject we took was like a newly discovered planet with only us two being its residents. So Moises was a companion in the profoundest sense of the word. Just like how my own shadow is a companion to me. Or maybe I was the shadow to Moises. Until he decided to shift to the Malikhaing Pagsulat program ...

Who can say where the writings we start today will lead us tomorrow? The novel *Mahiganting Langit* called down by Lilia Quindoza Santiago (who teaches now in Hawaii, which is unfortunate because I think she is the only critic who actually understands Moises, what the guy's writing has really been all about), in addition to winning the grand prize for novel in Filipino category in the 2005 Palanca Awards, also bagged a National Book Award in 2007. Dean Alfar, prime mover of the Philippine speculative fiction scene, admitted that writing speculative fiction in Filipino (he used the word *Tagalog*) is possible, and the novel of Moises Gerona is a proof of that. Upon Anvil Publishing's first release of a thousand copies, the Department of Education highly recommended the book as "a novel that should be read by this new generation of young Filipinos who long to look back at the great history of their Nation." Teachers teaching Filipino in high school and college praised the novel as very Filipino and very patriotic. Like Rizal's *Noli Me Tangere* and *El Filibusterismo*, someone proposed that *Mahiganting Langit* or *ML* (as it is popularly known to students) be considered a required reading. According to critic Isagani R. Cruz, due to the novel's political and social awareness, it shall stand alongside the great Tagalog novel *Ibong Mandaragit* by Amado V. Hernandez. "The fiery rage that engulfs this novel is difficult to subdue even after one closes the book," Bienvenido Lumbera wrote in his review. Though it is common knowledge within the literary circle that PEN Philippines led by F. Sionil Jose and UMPIL (Unyon ng mga Manunulat sa Pilipinas) led by Almario are dead to each other's existence, but for Moises Gerona's sake, the literary phenomenon who is said to have revitalized the curiosity of ordinary Filipinos in reading serious literature, the two groups came to unite as one voice. "It's the next great Tagalog novel," proclaimed

F. Sionil Jose who doesn't really read Tagalog novels but Bien (Lumbera) "nagged" him into it. And because it was F. Sionil Jose who gave the verdict, an international publisher stepped in to express its interest.

Mahiganting Langit was translated to English by Vintage, an imprint of Random House that is also the publisher of famous novelists such as Javier Marias, Ian McEwan, Jeanette Winterson, Philip Roth, Vladimir Nabokov, and Michael Ondaatje. The title of Moises's novel became *Vengeance from the Sky*. The translation was recently released in bookstores last year. The book launch and signing happened in New York, where Moises mentioned in his speech that when his local publisher sent him his copy, and that when he first came to read his novel in Filipino as an actual book, he himself while reading his work, immediately saw its shortcomings. Though he understood that it was too late to make up for these flaws because the book was already in the hands of his readers. And this, even after he had given this book his everything. Worst of all, he said, apparently, no one other than him had seen these shortcomings.

When he delivered his craft talk before a large crowd of students in Recto Hall of UP Faculty Center, he said that writing a novel had been a lifetime dream for him. He thought that it was not by accident that Kafka, Dostoevsky, and Nabokov—the Holy Trinity of his very own faith—were all novelists. He pointed out that a writer who has written a novel has also written a book. Those two outputs are co-equal, and here one can see the work ethic of a novelist. A range is always being measured while a target is being pursued because for the novelist, the horizons of the world he creates and the pathways traversed toward a certain ending is—and should be—clear. Despite these literary visions, nothing is certain about the novel. The novel form shall always be reinvented and in this act, novels become novel. "I am always being excited by the constant uncertainty of whether what I am writing is a novel," Moises added in Filipino. "No one really knows what a novel is, what it can or it cannot be, especially the last."

His conclusion was met by an earnest round of applause from the jam-packed auditorium, a rarity in the history of Recto Hall. The program proceeded immediately with an open forum. The queue before the mic signaled to the emcee that a lot of questions were about to be asked, so he made a recap of the day's event right away and apologized because they'd exceeded their allotted time. He added that the guest speaker hopefully might answer more questions right after the event. It was almost seven in the evening when the program ended. But Moises did not manage to leave right away because of the long line for his book signing. Dinner was prepared care of the dean's office. The entire affair was literally a hero's welcome for the long-lost son of the University, as if no one remembered that despite everyone's identification with the returning hero, embracing him as a home-grown talent, the celebrant was not even a graduate from his so-called home college.

I left the venue. Not minding to pass the chance to rub shoulders with our guest of honor.

Going upstairs, I went to my room, at the second floor of the same building. That was just beside Jun Cruz Reyes's former cubicle. I became a regular faculty of UP after Sir Jun left. During his last year here, he had a three-unit course per semester until he finally quit so he could spend time with his other passion—painting. It was a shame that we did not get to be neighbors.

I spent the night inside my cubicle going through my students' papers. It was about ten when I heard a knock. Rarely does anyone drop by my cubicle especially in late hours; that's why I myself got up and reached the door instead of telling the visitor to come in since the door was unlocked, just like I always do when I feel too lazy to get up and open the door. I saw Moises standing before my door. Have I mentioned that he was wearing barong, an embroidered formal attire, during his lecture? It was the same barong he donned in the last literary festival where we saw each other. I think it fits him well and he should therefore find more occasions to wear it.

Moises smiled. Then he showed me his copy of my book, *Mga Dapat Tandaan Kung Magpapatiwakal.* He told me he saw it in the lit fest he had just attended. He asked if I could write for him a dedication.

"Sus! You shouldn't have. I could've given you your free copy."

"The lit fest advocates buying Filipino books."

"Well, I'm embarrassed. Come in, come in. Have a seat. This is my castle keep, supposedly, because there are really three of us crammed up in here. Three faculty members, all untenured. Excuse the mess. I also have a copy of your novel. I would've asked also for an autograph but it's such a shame that it isn't here right now. It's in my house. That's where I keep it. Together with other books I've done reading. It used to lie at my bedside all the time. Which I read after prayer, before going to sleep. A sleeping pill. No, I'm just joking."

Moises took a seat on the lone chair, one meant for student consultation. He handed over the book I must sign.

"Make the dedication nice, okay? Something I can show off to others, so they will know that a friend wrote the message."

I really thought of what to write. I asked myself what to tell this person, this person right before me whom I thought I knew very well but it's possible that it has never really been the case. And I realized there was nothing to tell. Actually, we didn't have anything to tell each other. Which was probably true because I would never see his face again right after that night.

Moises lit up a cigarette.

"Oh, so you now smoke." As if I never knew. "How long have you been smoking?" Again, as if I never knew.

He did not respond right away. The silence remained for quite a while. As if he were indeed recalling where and when he first tried smoking; as if he had trouble remembering. Was he waiting for me to remind him? Seemed like he intended to finish smoking before responding.

"If your work is as stressful as mine and the people you speak with every day are as toxic, you cannot not smoke."

"You mean, the coteries of politicians and businessmen you have to talk to every day for your projects?"

"Yeah, them and the people behind the production. Scatterbrained producers and directors who see writers as their slaves. Do you smoke?" He offered a cigarette.

"No thanks. You know, I tried smoking once. But when somebody told me that I have to let the smoke run through my lungs, I said, no way! Nothing is going to touch my lungs even for a bit, I won't allow it. They're my lungs."

He searched for an ashtray. I don't have one here, I told him. So I opened the window, so he could dispose the cigarette butt outside. There in the windowsill, he quietly finished his cancer stick.

"There," I told him as I handed over the book I just signed for him.

For Moises, Who came and made true his promise. From a fellow traveler, Manolo.

The next day, the Faculty Center was burned to the ground. The speculation was, it all started from the second floor, where my cubicle was, because the blaze blackened that area in the worst possible manner. Though no one was hurt during the incident, most of us faltered after realizing the aftermath of the catastrophe. We could never look at FC the same way again, our home for the longest of time. It was daybreak, a few hours left until the firemen extinguished the flames but the smoke and embers still rose heavenward, toward the roof where it met the falling cloud-cottons from the kapok tree. Some of us broke down and cried like someone dear had passed away. The books, records, rare collections kept and treasured by some of us will be unrecoverable. Initial investigations blamed faulty wiring. The structure had been considered a condemned building since last year. Rats had already infested its roofing. There were many other speculations regarding what sparked the fire. Maybe, there was a faculty member who forgot to turn off his computer or perhaps left a charger unplugged. Which happens often, said the guard. Or, others suspect, maybe someone smoked in one of the rooms and left a live cigarette butt on the windowsill.

There was a time when I thought I could not have written *Mga Dapat Tandaan Kung Magpapatiwakal* as a book. If it had been written as a short story, it would have obviously been an easy task writing it. But a full-length book demands another level of stamina. Though as some plant forms can survive even beneath the ground, the same goes with my writing. Thriving despite the distance from the sun. Silently developing its form and substance.

Things began to take shape when I returned to my three old notebooks. From these, I remembered Rogelio Sicat's method of writing his memoir. In the process, I also saw how the suicide note I was writing should advance. It was while drinking alone at Sarah's that I came to finally realize to whom my protagonist is addressing his suicide note. I suddenly remembered what Rogelio Sicat wrote in his memoir. That the Irish people are better off for even drunken Irish fishermen know who James Joyce is. Sicat wrote this with a hint of envy, I think. This was how I was able to finally imagine my second character to be an old fisherman, an avid follower of Rogelio Sicat's stories in *Liwayway* magazine. This is going to be the same old fisherman to whom my suicidal protagonist would address, the protagonist I named Patricio Viray, taking after the name of my grandfather (may he rest in peace). This is also the reason why he will choose to end his life by drowning himself in a river. He wanted the old man to be the first to see his corpse and to read his suicide note, though this, as I also realized, is already beyond work-able logic. I can almost hear an adamant Jun Cruz Reyes demanding believable character motivation. It will solve things, I think, if I stick to the idea of having a writer for my main character. As writers are readily accepted as eccentrics, the eccentricity of my character's attempts toward metaphysical and literary meditations about plunging himself to his death would be somehow made understandable.

Jumping into the deepest part of the river without a witness. That is my favourite scene of death. Silent, determined, no bitterness whatsoever. There, it would be like coming back home into my mother's womb. There, different freshwater fish will watch over me. So it can be said that I am embracing my graveyard and it embraces me back. But only for a while. Because it will spew me back toward the surface. My corpse will float and will be found stranded along the shore.

Being thus soaked, the letter I kept inside my pocket was reduced to a pulp. Which is why it isn't really practical to keep it there in the first place. Another complication. Which is why I have to keep the letter in another hiding place, not on my corpse. So it will also become possible that the person who finds my corpse will be different from the person who finds my letter. Which begs the question: Will the old fisherman, the avid fan of Rogelio Sicat, be able still to read the letter that I actually wrote for him? Because if not, then for whom am I writing this?

A friend of mine too once wrote a suicide note which he addressed to his mom. He left it atop their dresser where the authorities would surely take notice. But he did not push through with the suicide proper. He just wanted to tell his mother all his resentments. If I am to do the same, my letter will contain nothing but personal gripes against relatives and acquaintances. But that should not be the point of my suicide. Not displeasure with life but a sharp reflection about it. And my letter as repository of all these reflections. On death as power.

The best reader of such reflections would be no other than that old fisherman who read, cried, and spent one sleepless night over the story "Tata Selo" by Rogelio Sicat, because he understood well the meaning of Tata Selo's final line that says: "Kinuha nilang lahat sa amin, ay kinuha nang lahat!" (They took everything from us, oh how they took everything!)

As an avid reader, this old man would send letters to the editor to extend his heartfelt gratitude and satisfaction. Oftentimes, he also sends entries for raffles and other contests sponsored by milk and soap products. He even once sent a poem he wrote in secret.

Here then is a simple solution to my problem. What's stopping me from coursing the suicide note via courier to ensure that it will reach my intended reader? But this will turn my suicide note into just another ordinary correspondence. A suicide note not paired right beside its author's corpse would never look nor sound urgent. Complications and even more complications.

When he read the first few parts of the early draft, Jun Cruz Reyes told me that he saw nothing new in what I wrote. Sartre in *Nausea* and a bunch of other existentialists in their respective works have already said what I said. But, if I'd be interested, he would like to invite me to a special informal lecture on the craft.

So there in his room, on the third floor of what was then the Faculty Center, a space he shared with his co-faculty Reuel Molina Aguila, gathered a number of students who wanted to learn the how-to of writing a story. Many of those who came were not enrolled in his class. They all had different reasons for meeting with Amang (as they fondly call Jun Cruz). Some wanted their stories, poems, novel manuscripts, and film scripts workshopped, some consulted for their theses and exhibits, some borrowed books and CDs, and some were just invited for drinks. No more than ten people could fit inside that room, so most of them waited outside, all of them generously accommodated by Jun Cruz Reyes. Students, artists, filmmakers, researchers, and even band members happened to visit at once, making that tiny office something like the National Commission for Culture and the Arts.

What an antihero is and how it can be utilized to create an unreliable first-person narrator was the special lecture that afternoon. Attendees took out their notebooks and pens, earnest to take down notes. The man's gentle voice was occasionally accompanied by the rasps coming from the aircon. "The first-person narrator is unreliable not because he is a liar who just wants to deceive the reader, but that may also be the case on some occasions. But, more importantly, he is unreliable because if a self tells a story, it is subjective and that self is automatically biased . . ." From time to time, I glanced not just at the pointillist pen-and-ink artwork on his wall, but also at the bulk of books on the floor that overflowed from his shelves. Some titles caught my attention. *This Earth of Mankind* by Pramoedya Ananta Toer, *Will to Power* by Friedrich Nietzsche, *Tin Drum* by Gunter Grass, *The Savage Mind* by Claude Levi-Strauss, *The Film Sense* by Sergei Eisenstein, and *Écrits* by Jacques Lacan. All mixed up, and had there been a system in that chaos, only Jun Cruz knew. "Once you let your narrator speak, find out what he is not telling you in his story . . ."

While listening, I thought of an interesting way to level up my character into becoming an antihero. And this was what I came up with: turn Patricio Viray into a plagiarist. He was caught plagiarizing an old story by Rogelio Sicat, from an old issue of *Liwayway*. But what he only initially wanted really was to learn Sicat's writing style. He studied everything the writer wrote. Even parts from the writer's memoir.

From the memoir he came to learn about Sicat's childhood friend in Nueva Ecija, who often accompanied the would-be *Agos* writer on fishing trips by the river. Most of the time, while on the boat, the two would just pass their time discussing the poems and stories that they both read from *Liwayway*. Could this childhood friend be the old fisherman he was looking for?

Patricio needed to check if the said childhood friend was still alive. He must leave for Nueva Ecija to find this out for himself. And once stepping inside the old man's house, Patricio would discover the bundle of *Liwayway* magazines the avid reader has kept, and with it, the clippings of Sicat's stories throughout the years. An archive lovingly curated and the pages graciously saved from becoming mere wrappers for tinapa and kindling for cooking stoves, as most old magazine issues were used back in the day. A treasure trove in Patricio's eyes.

It is here where Patricio will find his temptation: a story he thought hidden from the reading public as it is not collected in *Pagsalunga*, Sicat's book of short stories, nor included in any anthology. The type of story that even Sicat himself would want to forget. Because it is among those in the factory of instant stories. Did the great Rogelio Sicat keep his own factory of stories back then? But what if he did? It's not a rare occurrence among writers of *Liwayway*. Even Macario Pineda, Pedro Dandan, Brigido Batungbakal, Efren Abueg, and Edgardo Reyes had their own factory of instant stories.

But what if Patricio has seen through such state of seeming mediocrity? And the story he would still consider worthy of being imitated if imitation is indeed a form of recognition? And copying the story (to his credit) would save it from oblivion?

Sure, go ahead and convince yourself. Who are you trying to fool? says his conscience. And it is here where he starts to become an unreliable narrator, as Jun Cruz Reyes would have it in his lecture. Patricio will not admit even for a moment—even to himself—that he is tempted to become Sicat, much less to be like Sicat. Is it his mistake when he ignores, as most plagiarists would tend to do, the rich holdings good libraries keep, like very old issues of very old magazines? Is it a big mistake to dream of becoming a writer while alienating oneself from one's nearest library? Fine, it's in the library if it's in the library. But who would go out of one's way to confirm if such a story exists in any given dust-covered corner of the library? Scholars, obviously. If these scholars let him off the hook, the envious would not. How can a plagiarist think he can escape the hands of the law?

Jun Cruz taught us that we need to find personal demons for our characters for them to become flawed. In Patricio's case, Sicat becomes the demon who won't leave him in peace. A demon with a shadow that tightly binds his helpless captive. Just like the shadow of an old master. From here, I draw his motivation, of why he needs to send the old fisherman his own death note and why writing such a note following his own actual death will eventually bring him his redemption.

Listening to Jun Cruz Reyes helped me a lot. The progress of my story was off the charts!

His lunch, fried fish with rice wrapped in plastic, bought maybe from the Katag cafeteria, had long been waiting on his table. Barely touched though it was already almost four in the afternoon. I caught a waft of coffee aroma mixed with other smells—muscovado sugar, cigarette smoke, damp paper, and newly painted wood. The breeze from outside also carried with it the smell of freshly cut grass. From the window facing where I sat, branches of old acacia trees snakily twisted were in view. On one of those branches an oriole bird perched. Its call sounded like a lost kitten, crying. In my province, farmers would often say that this bird wouldn't let itself be caught alive for long because it would rather choke itself to death than spend its days locked in a birdcage.

I dreamt too of having my own space just like this, but one without a roommate. Piles of books that I intended to read, surrounding me like trees in the woods. And a window that welcomed into my room the mournful sound of the oriole along with the smell of freshly cut grass. A little consolation in the life of an academic. Though my salary wouldn't be as much, I was quite sure I would still be happy and content.

Toward the lecture's ending, we were left with a reading assignment: *Brothers Karamazov*. We were told to study the psychology of every Karamazov sibling so we could observe different examples of complex characterization. But the best antihero, according to the lecturer, was in another work, still by Dostoevksy, *Crime and Punishment*, in the person of Raskolnikov. So if possible, we should read that book as well.

"Sir, what are those? Short stories?" asked one of the students.

"Novels, all of them," answered Jun Cruz Reyes.

The student who dared ask looked as if he had had a taste of rotten meat. In silence, he was probably wondering why the lecturer assigned tomes of novels as readings—though the curious student simply wanted to write a short story.

Jun Cruz finally stood, signaling the end of the meeting. He said he had to claim some books he had photocopied at the Shopping Center. He asked me and Moises to come along since the stop where we waited for our jeepney ride home was also in that area. Other students left the room. Jun Cruz left us for a while and went to the restroom before packing up his things. Upon his exit, he chatted a bit with three or four students who had been waiting for him outside.

We were the only two left in the room when I noticed Moises suddenly becoming quite inquisitive with his surroundings. He left his seat to inspect the bookshelves. Moises had been going in and out of this cubicle for years. He had probably familiarized himself already with the whereabouts of things in this room.

After a few minutes, he snatched a book from one of the shelves. I had no idea which book, as his hand was swift. As if reading the question marked on my face, he showed me the cover. *Discipline and Punish* by Michel Foucault.

"We were assigned *Crime and Punishment*, not that one," I told him.

"Stupid, I know," he answered with a mysterious grin. That ceased being mysterious after he slipped the book inside his bag.

Aside from the fact that his family was well off, I had not known Moises as someone who pilfered things, especially books. It was my first time seeing him doing that and, of all places, in Jun Cruz's personal library.

I pouted toward the whiteboard where borrowers list their names and the items they borrowed. This served as some system of borrowing as Jun Cruz Reyes lent books to anyone who wanted them. His personal library was really a communal library, as long as one asked.

"Do you know that all Foucaults have already been stolen from the Main Lib?" said Moises as if his stealing was a direct consequence of all those previously stolen books. As if because someone went ahead and stole books there, he could rationalize stealing here.

"Foucaults are only found in the catalog but once you check the shelves you will find nothing," he continued. Was that his best justification? As if stealing books should be no different from panic-buying?

"You should take one too. Here's one. *Madness and Civilization.* This really is for you. I'm sure you need it." He handed me the book as if it contained all the answers to my life's questions. "I haven't read this one yet, so we can exchange loots after."

"Superb scholarship rendered with artistry," read the blurb from *The Nation* written on the book's front cover. "Foucault's books belong, both by reason of its content and profundity, in the class of such treatises—at once historical, scientific, and ethical—as Norman O. Brown's *Life Against Death*," declared *The New York Times Book Review* on the back cover.

Moises had issues with both book collectors and book collecting. He said books should never be confined within one single owner. Sources of wisdom should flow freely. A platitude he just heard from an activist friend also notorious for pilfering books, I think. It was said that this friend of his stole books from National Book Store to redress society's capitalist system. That is why the said activist would usually take Nora Roberts, Danielle Steel, and Robert Ludlum titles.

Why would it be so important, to a person such as Moises Gerona, to acquire an item of Jun Cruz Reyes's? Why a book owned by Jun Cruz Reyes in particular? I remember an anthropologist explaining about fanatics stealing holy objects from churches during Holy Week. An example cited was the cult of the Dead Christ from Capiz whose members come to church on Black Saturdays to steal home a tiny piece of the shroud that covers the Dead Christ. As they kiss on the feet of the resting icon, they covertly bite into the holy cloth to snip a small fragment or even just a tiny thread. They believe that if worn or taken along in their body, this small piece of loot can act as an amulet. Jun Cruz Reyes's books are not really sacred objects. But Moises's underhanded moves exhibit a certain kind of fetish. Especially for items supposedly owned by a greatly admired figure. I also remember the spear, bow and arrow, flute, jar owned by the village chief mentioned in Jun Cruz Reyes's lecture on the precolonial concept of power, and what effects these items have on anyone just by the mere act of touching them or even being near them.

Is this not also true as far as Moises's inner motivation was concerned? That through these books he was stealing, it was also like taking home like a trophy a part of Jun Cruz Reyes? And those books serving as an extension of Amang's essence would work like amulets for him, as long as they were in his holdings? And he was unaware of this primitive itch, working inside him, as it was repressed deeply in his unconscious.

I'm trying really hard to make this sound academic, but in reality, pondering on Moises's behavior this way could be a waste of time. For all we know, he is just a kleptomaniac, plain and simple.

That was the last time Moises would visit Jun Cruz's place. The professor himself would soon notice the depletion of select titles from his shelves. He would ask those who frequented his cubicle about these mysterious disappearances. He would ask the usual suspects and those with histories. Among them would be Moises. Jun Cruz Reyes's questioning would offend him and he would take it personally as an unjust accusation. It is true though that despite his grudge, Moises will still visit Jun Cruz from time to time. He will continue consulting his mentor about the novel he is in the process of writing. They will continue to talk about projects, though the meeting place would either be in the office of the Creative Writing Center, if not in Katag cafeteria. But never in the professor's room.

But Moises was not alone in this modus. There were multitudes of them and multiplying. Stealing books according to one's needs would be the trend among many of Sir Jun's students. It was Moises's fault because it all started with him. Though a better explanation here, I think, is called for. Because it seems to me that this is beyond simple book theft. Stealing books has posed a certain charm in the very act itself. Blame the novel *Savage Detectives* by Roberto Bolaño. Since the novel became popular among young writers and wannabes, many of them started to have the idea of wanting to become lumpen. And the most literary means available for them of becoming so would be to pilfer books with exemplary academic and literary value. This is true especially with those who have yet to prove themselves. To act like an antisocial while waiting for the greatly coveted readers' recognition to come. Or like someone greatly deprived by society. The Dispossessed. That's a good title for the next story I will write. With Moises Gerona as the main character. "How many times have you been dispossessed?" someone would ask Moises in the story. "Countless times," Moises's character would respond. He believes, even though he would not admit, the more intense the deprivation, the more badass you become though you haven't yet given or said anything except "I, too, am a victim!" And this is going to be the main point of my story: that this thing we call literature—and by literature, I mean what we have here right now, not the literature of Bolaño or of Mexico or Chile or of any place in South America—is like a theatrical presentation. Anything, even one's own wounds, can be displayed like a performance and may be used as a spectacle. And if I am to write this story, that is actually the story of us all who dared to write, I would never have it published. Posthumously, maybe. But never in my lifetime. It should wait for my demise. Or perhaps, once the Philippines have already moved on from the age of capital to a new dispensation. Because if I would make public such a story, it is like blasting away with own hands the very thing that has sheltered me and has kept me safe thus far. So venting out my vexations this way should be enough for now.

Meanwhile, Foucault's other book was already in my hand and I was not sure what to do with it. Should I return it to its place in the shelf so I can show Moises that I am not as degenerate as he is? But what if conversations in the near future bring up Foucault? What can I contribute to the would-be discussions of his radical ideas concerning history and philosophy? A blank stare, since there are no more copies of his books left in the library.

So I slipped the book inside my bag, thinking, I'll keep it here for now, and return it once I finish reading. Or, I can list it on the whiteboard, to avoid trouble. I stood up, intending to take the whiteboard marker. Should I include on the list the book Moises took? If Jun Cruz were to read the list, wouldn't he wonder why we didn't personally ask him for these books? That might complicate things. How long have I stood before that whiteboard while anxiously weighing what my next step would be? A minute? Several? An entire afternoon? Until today, I might still be standing in that very same spot, still thinking of the possible paths I should take.

Jun Cruz Reyes finally came back, and I hadn't even touched the marker I intended to pick up. I retreated back to my chair. So as not to seem caught in an awkward moment, I simply threw my glance out of the window. Where I noticed the oriole still silently perched on the branch. I realized, it was the only witness to what Moises and I did. Another oriole came to rest on the same branch, but it didn't stay long. It seemed like it just came to fetch its friend, so the two flew off together.

"Let's go," Jun Cruz Reyes told us, after arranging the contents of his backpack. In the same backpack, he placed the plastic-wrapped rice meal he didn't get to eat.

––––––––––

We walked the distance of A. Roces Sr. Street toward the Shopping Center. Jun Cruz Reyes partly stepped ahead of us, while we closely followed behind. Lining up the road were fire trees that seemed engulfed in flames made by the bright tangerine color of their flowers. Our pathway was covered with their fallen petals, so we could not avoid stepping on a blaze or two in each step.

Jun Cruz Reyes halted for a while and looked back at us. "What are you thinking right now?"

I and Moises uneasily looked at each other before responding. He was referring to the fallen flowers we were stepping on.

"It's like being in a scene from an Akira Kurosawa film," I answered. "Seen from an aerial shot, it will show us walking a path on fire or a blood-stained road, depending on the brightness or dull-ness of the cinematography's color treatment."

"How about you, Moises, what can you say?"

"It seems like we are in a surreal story. We are stepping, not on flowers, but eyes in tears. Although we see that each eye we stepped on would bleed out a milky sap, but we feel good walking over them because we can feel their crisp crushed under our feet."

Jun Cruz Reyes continued walking. "You two are my best stu-dents at the moment."

A brief silence. As if Sir Jun was waiting for the effect of his words. We on the other hand did not know whether we needed to say something as a response.

"Moises," he continued, "you are a convincing liar, so I know you will be a great fictionist someday. If you won't give up and just con-tinually do what you're doing, I'm guessing, years from now, you will win awards, and maybe even write a book or two."

Moises was speechless.

"You, Manolo, on the other hand, you too are somehow fine. But you need to be consistent."

"Sir Jun," I replied with a question, "is it possible to achieve per-fection in the form of a book?" I knew that consistency was what he was looking for, and not perfection. But why must one be consistent when perfection is not possible in the end?

"Is a perfect novel possible?" Moises butted in without waiting for Sir Jun to answer my question. "Maybe all we can do is dream about it, as if dreaming to the moon."

"We can also perhaps explore, even within our minds, the possi-ble contents of a perfect novel," suggested Sir Jun. "Delve into its possibilities until we are able to gradually write it. And if you

succeed in writing it and it is still not the perfect novel you are looking for, at least you have written a good novel."

Before having reached the Shopping Center, we had chatted on
plenty of things already, like the reasons why some oldies still join
Palanca, the million-peso yearly allowance and other such perks
enjoyed by our National Artists, the upcoming UP National Writers
Workshop, and the faculty rank promotion that discriminates teachers like Jun Cruz Reyes, who write and teach at the same time. After
arriving at the Shopping Center, we parted ways with Jun Cruz
Reyes. Moises and I also took separate ways. I to Philcoa. While he
on his way to Katipunan. ♦

ABOUT THE EDITORS

Tilde Acuña teaches courses on creative writing in Filipino, popular culture, Philippine literature, and interdisciplinary research at the Department of Filipino and Philippine Literature - University of the Philippines, where he earned his MA in Philippine Studies (Philippine Literature and Art Studies). *Humanities Diliman*, *Kritika Kultura*, *Likhaan*, *Jacket2*, *Banwa*, *Ani*, and other journals, anthologies, and zines have published his works. He is the author of *Oroboro at Iba Pang Abiso* [Oroboro and Other Notices] (forthcoming from University of the Philippines Press).

John Bengan is a writer and translator from the Philippines whose work has appeared in *Likhaan*, *Kritika Kultura*, BooksActually's *Gold Standard*, *Cha: An Asian Literary Journal*, *Words Without Borders*, *LIT*, *Shenandoah*, and *World Literature Today*. He lives in Davao City. He holds an MFA in creative writing from The New School. A recipient of a Ford Foundation International Fellowship, he has won prizes from the Philippines Free Press Literary Awards and the Carlos Palanca Memorial Award for his short fiction. He lives in Davao City.

Daryll Delgado is a writer from the Philippines. Her first book, *After the Body Displaces Water* (University of Santo Tomas Publishing House, 2012), was awarded the Manila Critics Circle/Philippine National Book Award for best book of short fiction in English, and shortlisted for the Madrigal-Gonzales First Book Award in 2013. Her novel, *Remains* (Ateneo de Naga University Press), came out in 2019. She is at work on a third book, excerpts from which have come out in *Cha: An Asian Literary Journal* and *The Near and the Far, Volume 2* (Scribe Publications, 2019). Other works can be found in *Words Without Borders*, *Perro Berde*, *Kritika Kultura*, *Tinalunay* (University of the Philippines Press, 2017), *Maximum Volume: Best New Philippine Fiction* (Anvil Publishing, 2014). She studied Journalism and Comparative Literature in the University of the Philippines (UP), and has taught in UP, Ateneo De Manila University, and Miriam College. She works for an international NGO, where she heads the research programs for Southeast Asia and writes global reports on labor rights issues. She was born and raised in Tacloban City, and maintains a Quezon City residence—in between regular fieldwork around Southeast Asia—with her husband, William.

Amado Anthony G. Mendoza III teaches courses on Southeast Asian literature and creative writing at the Department of Filipino and Philippine Literature, University of the Philippines Diliman. He obtained his Master's in Philippine literature from the same university in 2019. He is the author of the novel *Aklat ng mga Naiwan* [Book of the Damned] (Balangiga, 2018) and co-edited and co-translated an upcoming volume of Wiji Thukul's poems titled *Balada ng Bala* (The Ballad of a Bullet) (Sentro ng Wikang Filipino,

2020). His research and other creative works have been published in *Likhaan, JONUS, Southeast Asian Studies* (Center for Southeast Asian Studies, Kyoto University), *Talas,* and *Tomas.*

Kristine Ong Muslim is the author of nine books of fiction and poetry, including *The Drone Outside* (Eibonvale Press, 2017), *Black Arcadia* (University of the Philippines Press, 2017), *Meditations of a Beast* (Cornerstone Press, 2016), *Butterfly Dream* (Snuggly Books, 2016), *Age of Blight* (Unnamed Press, 2016), and *Lifeboat* (University of Santo Tomas Publishing House, 2015), and co-editor of two anthologies—the British Fantasy Award-winning *People of Colo(u)r Destroy Science Fiction* and *Sigwa: Climate Fiction Anthology from the Philippines* (forthcoming from the Polytechnic University of the Philippines Press). She is also the translator of several bilingual volumes: Marlon Hacla's *Melismas* (Oomph Press, 2020) and *There Are Angels Walking the Fields* (forthcoming from Broken Sleep Books), as well as Mesándel Virtusio Arguelles's *Three Books* (Broken Sleep Books, 2020), *Hollow* (forthcoming from Fernwood Press), *Twelve Clay Birds: Selected Poems* (forthcoming from University of the Philippines Press), and *Walang Halong Biro* (De La Salle University Publishing House, 2018). Widely anthologized, Muslim's short stories have appeared in *Conjunctions, Dazed Digital, Tin House,* and *World Literature Today.* She grew up and continues to live in a rural town in Maguindanao, southern Philippines.

ABOUT THE AUTHORS AND TRANSLATORS

Corazon Almerino is a lifelong learner of Cebuano poetry and fiction. She wrote two books of poetry in Cebuano; one of which she co-authored with Linda Alburo and Ester Tapia, the other one a chapbook sponsored by the National Commission for Culture and the Arts. Her story "Sugmat" won the Palanca Award in 2009. She was awarded residency fellowships in the US and Brazil. She currently lives in Los Angeles.

Merlie M. Alunan was awarded Professor Emeritus upon her retirement from the University of the Philippines Tacloban College in 2008. She lives in Tacloban City and continues to write books that support the work of writers in the Visayan mother tongues. Her poetry has been recognized by the Palanca Memorial Awards for Literature. Her life work has also been honored by UMPIL, the Sunthorn Phu Award by the Kingdom of Thailand, the Ananda Coomaraswamy Fellowship of the Republic of India. Four books, *Sa Atong Dila* (University of the Philippines Press, 2015) and *Susumaton: Oral Narratives of Leyte* (Ateneo de Manila University Press, 2016), *Tinalunay: Anthology of Waray Literature* (University of the Philippines Press, 2017) and *Running with Ghosts and other Poems* (Ateneo de Naga University Press, 2017) won the National Book Award in 2016 and 2017 and 2018, respectively. Alunan lives in and writes from Tacloban City.

Roy Vadil Aragon is a fictionist and poet who writes mostly in Ilocano language. Many of his poems, short stories, and essays have been published in *Bannawag*, the leading Ilocano magazine. He published his first printed book, *BAGI dandaniw*, a collection of selected Ilocano poetry, in 2015. In 2017, he published *PAKSUY dandaniw & poems*, a chapbook of poems in Ilocano and English. His selected Ilocano short stories, *BANNUAR ken Dadduma Pay a Fiksion*, was published in 2018. In 2000, he released a digital book of Ilocano poetry, *Napili ken Saan a Napili a Dandaniw ken Dadduma Pay a Riknakem*, the first Ilocano poetry ebook. In 2019, he published two more Ilocano poetry collections, *RABII 100 a #tweetniw* and *BARIBARI*. Besides writing, he edits and designs books, works as a freelance translator-editor, maintains a food blog *Pinakbet Republic* (pinakbetrepublic.blogspot.com), and administers a widely popular Ilocano Food page in Facebook (facebook.com/ilokanofoods).

Genevieve L. Asenjo teaches literature and creative writing and writes in three major Philippine languages as poet, fictionist, and novelist. She has authored five books. She writes about migrants from the farm to the big cities; water as stranger and why it remains a beloved; the memory of taste, and the melancholy of the tongue. Her works are described as sensual and sharp, edgy and evocative, and innovative in its use of language. She completes a review on the naming done by Filipino anthropologists on an indigenous people's community in her home-island Panay. Her forthcoming collection of short stories from the University of the Philippines Press is a historiographic metafiction on the indigenous peoples of the tourist-island Boracay.

John E. Barrios is the author of the book, *txtm8rs at iba pang kwexto* (txtm8rs and other stories) and *Engkantawo ag iba pang matag-ud nga Istorya* (Supernatural and other stories). His stories also appeared in anthologies such as *Kuwentong Siyudad, Kathang-Isip, Laglag-panty, laglag-brief, Transfiksyon*, and *Wagi/Sawi*. He teaches at the University of the Philippines Visayas in Iloilo.

Rogelio Braga is an exiled playwright, novelist, essayist, publisher, and political activist from the Philippines. He published two novels, a collection of short stories, and a book of plays before he left the archipelago in 2018. He was a fellow of the Asian Cultural Council for theatre in Southeast Asia in 2016. His first play written entirely in English, *Miss Philippines*, is currently under development commissioned by the Yellow Earth Theatre in the United Kingdom. He lives in London.

Bernard Capinpin is a poet and translator. He is currently working on a translation of Ramon Guillermo's *Ang Makina ni Mang Turing*. He resides in Quezon City.

Erika M. Carreon co-founded and co-edited *Plural Online Journal*. She has an MFA in Creative Writing from De La Salle University-Manila, where she taught with the Literature Department from 2010 to 2018. Her literary works have appeared in *High Chair, Kritika Kultura, Philippines Free Press*, and *Sigwa: Climate Fiction* *from the Philippines* (forthcoming from the Polytechnic University of the Philippines Press). She provided artwork for Adam David's zine, *The Nature of Beasts vol. 1* and Mesándel Virtusio Arguelles's *Three Books* (Broken Sleep Books, 2020). With Neobie Gonzalez, Carreon launched the indie art page *Occult's Razor*, and under *Occult's Razor*, they produced their first project, *A Descending Order of Mortal Significance*, one of the best Filipino books of 2017 according to *CNN Philippines*. She is currently studying for a PhD in Creative Writing at the University of Melbourne.

Shane Carreon is the author of poetry collections *travelbook* (2013) and *Then, Beast* (2017) and recipient of a Fulbright Fellowship, Academy of American Poets Prize, Allen Ginsberg Poetry Award, Nick Joaquin Literary Award, and Carlos Palanca Memorial Award for Literature. Ze teaches at the University of the Philippines.

Kristian Sendon Cordero is a poet, fictionist, translator, and film-maker based in Bikol. His books of poetry in three Philippine languages have won the Madrigal-Gonzales Best First Book Award, the Philippine National Book Awards, and the Gintong Aklat Awards (Golden Book Awards). In 2017, he represented the Philippines in the International Writing Program at the University of Iowa. He was also appointed artist-in-residence by the Center for Southeast Asian Studies at the University of Michigan, Ann Arbor. As a translator, he has translated the works of Rainer Maria Rilke, Jorge Luis Borges, Franz Kafka, and Oscar Wilde into Bikol and Filipino. His current projects include the Bikol translations of Jose Rizal's two novels. He is one of the recipients of the Southeast Asian Writers Award given by the Thai royalty in November 2020. He serves as deputy director of the Ateneo de Naga University Press and runs an independent bookshop and art space, The Savage Mind, in his home city.

Soleil Davíd moved from the Philippines to the United States at age 17. Her work has appeared in *Arkansas International, MARY, Cream City Review*, and *The Margins*, among others. She earned a BA from UC Berkeley and an MFA from Indiana University, where she served as Poetry Editor of *Indiana Review*. Davíd has received support from PEN America, VONA and Bread Loaf Translators' Conference. She lives in Washington, DC.

Allan N. Derain is a writer, visual artist, and teacher. Author of *Iskrapbuk*, his debut collection of stories that was shortlisted for the Madrigal First Book Award, and novel *Ang Banal na Aklat ng mga Kumag*, winner of the Carlos Palanca Memorial Award Grand Prize, Loyola Schools Outstanding Scholarly Award, National Book Award, and Reader's Choice Award. Translator of Guy de Maupassant's *The Necklace and Other Tales* and editor of the anthology *May Tiktik sa Bubong, May Sigbin sa Silong*, winner of the National Book Award, Gintong Aklat Award, and Loyola Schools Outstanding Creative Work distinction. Illustrator of his novel and Isabelo de los Reyes's *Ang Diablo sa Filipinas*. His latest book is the short story collection *The Next Great Tagalog Novel at Iba Pang Kuwento*. Derain teaches Literature and Creative Writing at the Ateneo de Manila University and is working on his second novel about the aswang.

Eliodora L. Dimzon teaches language and literature courses at the Division of Humanities, College of Arts and Sciences of the University of the Philippines Visayas. Prior to her teaching stint, she has served as research associate at the UP Visayas Center for West Visayan Studies and has done research and published papers on Hiligaynon literature and folklore. She has contributed to the Sagisag Project of the Sub-Commission for Cultural Education of the National Commission for Culture and the Arts and the latest edition of the *Encyclopedia of Philippine Art of the Cultural Center of the Philippines*. She obtained her bachelor's degree in Comparative Literature from UP Visayas and her master's degree also in Comparative Literature from UP Diliman. Her master's thesis explores the transfigurations of the babaylan in contemporary Hiligaynon short stories.

Early Sol A. Gadong writes poetry and short stories in between her teaching, research, and public service engagements at the University of the Philippines Visayas. She is the author of the short story collection *Nasa Sa Dulo ng Dila* and the children's books *Si Bulan, Si Adlaw, kag Si Estrelya* and *Ayoko Po Sana*, as well as a number of zines and chapbooks. Some of her works have earned recognition in the Carlos Palanca Memorial Awards for Literature. She is the founder of ZineZoned: Iloilo Zine Fest, a regular gathering of writers and artists who display and sell their DIY zines at various venues in Iloilo City. She currently serves as the Vice President of Hubon Manunulat, a writers' collective based in Western Visayas.

Omar Khalid was born and raised in the mountainous town of Tabango, Leyte in the 1970s. At present, he lives with his two dogs Poptpot ang Airrah. He collects records, old phonographs, old amplifiers, and books on literature, philosophy and physics. When not writing in the evening, he strums his guitar along with the loiterers and drunks, and when he falls asleep, he dreams colorful dreams of his homeland finding true freedom. He has won several awards for his fiction and poetry. In 2016, his book of stories *Kining Inalisngaw sa Akong Tutunlan* (*This Vapor from My Throat*) was published by Saniata Publications.

Perry C. Mangilaya, an award-winning writer, novelist, fictionist, editor, and artist from Bagacay, Ibajay, Aklan, is the editor of *Liwayway Magazine* under Manila Bulletin Publishing Corp. He received an award from the Palanca Awards, GAWAD Komisyon of KWF, UN-Millennium Development Goals (UN-MDGs) of NCCA and PBBY-Salanga Writer's Prize. He authored the book *BILIG*, a novel, and published over a hundred short stories, seven novels, numerous children's stories, poems, essays, articles, flash fictions, columns, comics and other literary works in various magazines, newspapers, journals, and anthologies. He is also a book editor and language reviewer of DepEd K–12 program for Filipino.

Sunantha Mendoza-Quibilan takes pictures, writes, and mothers. These days, she is mostly baking bread and growing houseplants.

Timothy Montes is an academic vagabond who currently teaches literature and art appreciation in De La Salle University Manila. He has a Proustian fixation on small-town life in the island of Samar, where he grew up facing the typhoon winds coming in from the Pacific. He believes that gossip-mongering is the authentic narrative voice of the Filipino storyteller.

Eric Gerard H. Nebran is an educator, translator, and illustrator from General Santos City. He is currently a PhD Comparative

Literature candidate at the University of the Philippines–Diliman. His dissertation is on the construction of his hometown's social history based on people's *kuyaw* (extraordinary) narratives. His research interests include orality, history, pop culture, and digital humanities. He has lent his support to various independent literary publications and cultural productions.

Carlo Paulo Pacolor is a gender non-conforming non-binary folk a.k.a. "bakla." They write fiction, drama, and essay; sometimes they also direct. In the last few years they have been producing independent shows and whatchamacallits under the very very loose collective TambayTimes Kids, such as *Standby April!* and *Kulitan Nights*. In 2019 they toured *Brujas* in nine museums and galleries in Metro Manila, and came out with an independently printed limited text *Handbook ng mga Bakla sa Napipintong Pagtatapos ng Daigdig*. Recently, their text *Queer Frequency 1* was read and recorded in Seoul, South Korea. They is currently writing a full-length drama play. They is based in Tandang Sora, Quezon City.

Dominador "Doms" Pagliawan is a Waray artist, journalist, educator, researcher, and book author. Born in Catbalogan City in 1966, he graduated valedictorian in elementary, cum laude in college, Regional Winner of the Ten Outstanding Graduate Award (TOGA '92), and National Finalist in the search for Ten Outstanding Students of the Philippines (TOSP '92). A teacher by profession, he holds a master's degree in Literature, and a doctorate in Literature and Communication. As a multi-awarded artist, he writes poetry, novels, short stories, songs, and essays. He is also a sculptor, painter, cartoonist, and recording artist, having had four music albums produced. A four-time writing fellow in UP creative writing workshops, he published in 2011 the book *Kuraramag,* his first collection of short stories in Waray, his native language whose poor body of literature he vowed to help. In 2015, he published *Tabsik hin Kagamhanan,* which became the first original novel in Waray. A former radio announcer and TV newscaster, he writes a regular newspaper column and does the paper's editorial cartoons. His nearly 30 years of teaching have been spent in various colleges and universities such as the Leyte Normal University and AMA University. He is a frequently invited speaker and lecturer. Many of his written works have been published in national and international publications, and include his academic papers that see print in international journals. To date, he has already published seven books ranging from textbooks to original works.

Zosimo Quibilan, Jr. won the 2006 Philippine National Book Award for Short Fiction and the 8th Madrigal-Gonzalez Best First Book Award in 2008 for *Pagluwas (Going to the City)* published by the University of the Philippines Press in 2006. He and Sunantha Mendoza-Quibilan live in South Pasadena, CA.

Jay Jomar F. Quintos is a faculty member at the University of the Philippines Mindanao. He has published his critical and creative works in *Humanities Diliman, Likhaan Journal, Plaridel, Daluyan,* and *SunStar Davao.* He is also an independent filmmaker.

Firie Jill T. Ramos writes poems (siday), fiction/susumaton, and children's stories in Waray. She won the 2019 National Commission for Culture and the Arts Writers Prize for the Novel in Waray. Her poems and stories have appeared in different anthologies and journals. She has a degree in Communication Arts and Education from the University of the Philippines and has worked as a teacher for two decades. Firie Jill T. Ramos, who lives in Tacloban City, is currently working on another novel.

Isabel D. Sebullen is a three-time Palanca awardee. Her short stories have also won the PAGCOR-Liwayway, Quin Baterna, and Gawad Ka Amado short story writing contests. She currently chairs the Board of Directors of the Screenwriters Guild of the Philippines (SGP) and served as SGP president from 2009 to 2015.

Elizabeth Joy Serrano-Quijano received a BA in Mass Communication from Holy Cross of Davao College, where she developed her dedication to journalism and passion for creative writing. She works as a college instructor, teaching Development Communication at Southern Philippines Agribusiness and Marine and Aquatic School of Technology (SPAMAST)–Malita, Davao Occidental. She is proud of her Igorot, Kapampangan, and Blaan roots. Her writing is also her advocacy for the indigenous people of Davao del Sur. Translations of her stories by John Bengan have been published in *Words Without Borders*, *World Literature Today*, *LIT*, and *Shenandoah*.

Ariel Sotelo Tabág (born August 16, 1978 in Santa Teresita, Cagayan) is an Ilocano fictionist, poet, editor, translator, and musician. He has received prizes and grants from the Palanca, National Commission for Culture and the Arts (NCCA), Komisyon sa Wikang Filipino (KWF), National Book Development Board

(NBDB) Trust Fund, and Gaudy Boy expenses several Ilocano literary contests for his Ilocano short stories, novels, and poems. He is the author of *Karapote* (*Curion*), short story collection; *Ay, Ni Reberen!* (*OMG, Reverend!*), novel; *Panangarakup iti Ipus ti Layap* (*Embracing the Tail of the Shooting Star*), poetry collection; *Kapessat ti Bagis* (*Sibling*), novel; *Panangsapul iti Puraw a Kabalio* (*White Horse Search*), and *Villa ken Dadduma Pay a Sarita* (*Villa And Other Stories*). He has also translated in Filipino: *Biag ni Lam-ang* of Pedro Bucaneg, two dramas of Mena Pecson Crisologo, fiction works of Juan S.P. Hidalgo, Jr. and Cles B. Rambaud and other Ilocano writers. Tabág is also a fellow of the 41st UP National Writers Workshop (2002) and a delegate to the Taboan (2010) and 6th Philippine International Literary Festival (2015). He has served as Secretary General of GUMIL Filipinas (Ilocano writers' association). He edits the Poetry Section of *Bannawag Magazine*.

John Iremil Teodoro is from San Jose de Buenavista, Antique. He is an Associate Professor and the Graduate Program Coordinator at the Literature Department in the College of Liberal Arts of De La Salle University. He is also the Associate for Regional Literature of La Salle's Bienvenido N. Santos Creative Writing Center. He holds a Bachelor of Science in Biology from the University of San Agustin in Iloilo City, and a Master of Fine Arts in Creative Writing and a Doctor of Philosophy in Literature from DLSU. He is a multi-awarded writer in Kinaray-a, Filipino, Hiligaynon, and English. He is the author of more than 12 books and his collection of short essays *Pagmumuni-muni at Pagtatalak ng Sirenang Nagpapanggap na Prinsesa* won the National Book Award from the Manila Critics Circle and the National Book Development Board. Teodoro, a scholar of Hiligaynon literature, contributes reviews, travel pieces, and cultural reportage to *AGUNG*, *The Daily Tribune*, and *Liwayway Magazine* where he is writing a regular column on books and the importance of reading. He is presently the Secretary General of Unyon ng mga Manunulat sa Pilipinas (UMPIL, or the Writers Union of the Philippines.)

Januar E. Yap was born in Cebu City, Philippines. He currently teaches at the University of the Philippines Cebu College of Communication, Art and Design. He is also Opinion Editor for *SunStar Cebu*. He was a fellow to the 67th UP National Writers' Workshop and the National Writers Workshop in Dumaguete City. His short stories in Cebuano have won the Don Carlos Palanca Memorial Awards for Literature. His works, which include short stories and poetry in English and Cebuano, have appeared in various anthologies. He is currently a recipient of the National Commission for Culture and the Arts Writer's Grant.

PERMISSIONS

ABOUT GAUDY BOY

From the Latin *gaudium*, meaning "joy," Gaudy Boy publishes books that delight readers with the various powers of art. The name is taken from the poem "Gaudy Turnout" by Singaporean poet Arthur Yap, about his time abroad in Leeds, the United Kingdom. Similarly inspired by such diasporic wanderings and migrations, Gaudy Boy brings literary works by authors of Asian heritage to the attention of an American audience and beyond. Established in 2018 as the imprint of the New York City–based literary nonprofit Singapore Unbound, we publish poetry, fiction, and literary nonfiction. Visit our website at www.singaporeunbound.org/gaudy-boy.

WINNERS OF THE GAUDY BOY POETRY BOOK PRIZE

Play for Time by Paula Mendoza
Autobiography of Horse by Jenifer Sang Eun Park
The Experiment of the Tropics by Lawrence Lacambra Ypil

FICTION

The Foley Artist by Ricco Villanueva Siasoco
Malay Sketches by Alfian Sa'at
And the Walls Come Crumbling Down by Tania De Rozario

CPSIA information can be obtained
at www.ICGtesting.com
Printed in the USA
FSHW011603270121
77998FS